'What are you hiding from me, Emma?'

'Nothing…' But it s

Larenzo took anothe
You're hiding somet
but—'

'What do you *think* I ⸻ off
scornfully. She nodded towards the stairs. 'A *baby*?'

The words hung there, seeming to echo through the sudden silence of the room. Larenzo stared at her, saw how bloodless her lips were as they parted soundlessly. The thought hadn't fully formed in his mind until she'd said the words. He'd sensed she was hiding something, had felt her panic and fear, had heard a baby cry… And yet it hadn't all come together for him.

But it did now, crystallising with shocking clarity, and without a word for her he turned from the room and bounded up the stairs.

'Larenzo—' She hurried after him, one arm flung towards him in desperate supplication. 'Larenzo, please, don't—'

He could hear the child crying, the voice pitiful and plaintive.

'Mama. Mama.'

He threw open the door and came to a complete and stunned halt as he saw the baby standing in her cot, chubby fists gripping the rail, cherubic face screwed up and wet with tears.

And Larenzo knew. He would have known just by looking at the child, with her ink-dark hair and large grey eyes, the cleft in her chin. He turned to Emma, who was gazing at him with undisguised panic.

'When,' he asked in a low, deadly voice, 'were you going to tell me about my child?'

One Night With Consequences

When one night...leads to pregnancy!

When succumbing to a night of unbridled desire
it's impossible to think past the morning after!

But, with the sheets barely settled, that little blue line
appears on the pregnancy test and it doesn't take long
to realise that one night of white-hot passion
has turned into a lifetime of consequences!

Only one question remains:

How do you tell a man you've just met
that you're about to share more than just his bed?

Find out in:

Nine Months to Redeem Him by Jennie Lucas
January 2015

Prince Nadir's Secret Heir by Michelle Conder
March 2015

Carrying the Greek's Heir by Sharon Kendrick
April 2015

Married for Amari's Heir by Maisey Yates
July 2015

Bound by the Billionaire's Baby by Cathy Williams
July 2015

From One Night to Wife by Rachael Thomas
September 2015

Her Nine Month Confession by Kim Lawrence
September 2015

Look for more *One Night With Consequences*
coming soon!

If you missed any of these fabulous stories,
they can be found at millsandboon.co.uk.

LARENZO'S CHRISTMAS BABY

BY
KATE HEWITT

MILLS & BOON

Published in Great Britain 2015
by Mills & Boon, an imprint of Harlequin (UK) Limited,
Eton House, 18-24 Paradise Road, Richmond, Surrey, TW9 1SR

© 2015 Kate Hewitt

ISBN: 978-0-263-25086-2

Harlequin (UK) Limited's policy is to use papers that are natural, renewable and recyclable products and made from wood grown in sustainable forests. The logging and manufacturing processes conform to the legal environmental regulations of the country of origin.

Printed and bound in Spain
by CPI, Barcelona

After spending three years as a die-hard New Yorker, **Kate Hewitt** now lives in a small village in the English Lake District with her husband, their five children and a golden retriever. In addition to writing intensely emotional stories she loves reading, baking, and playing chess with her son— she has yet to win against him, but she continues to try.

Learn more about Kate at www.kate-hewitt.com.

Visit the Author Profile page
at millsandboon.co.uk for more titles.

CHAPTER ONE

THE SOUND OF the car door slamming echoed through the still night. Emma Leighton looked up from the book she'd been reading in surprise; as housekeeper of Larenzo Cavelli's isolated retreat in the mountains of Sicily, she hadn't been expecting anyone. Larenzo was in Rome on business, and no one came to the villa perched high above Sicily's dusty hill towns and villages. Her employer liked his privacy.

She heard brisk footsteps on the stone path that led to the villa's front door, an enormous thing of solid oak banded with iron. She tensed, waiting for a knock; the villa had an elaborate security system with a numbered code that was only known by her and Larenzo, and the door was locked, as Larenzo always insisted.

She held her breath as she heard the creak of the door opening and then the beep of buttons being pressed, followed by a longer beeping indicating the security system had been deactivated. As her heart did a queasy little flip, Emma tossed her book aside and rose from her chair. Larenzo never came back early or unexpectedly. He always texted her, to make sure she had everything ready for his arrival: his bed made with freshly ironed sheets, the fridge stocked, the pool heated. But if it *wasn't* him…who was it?

She heard footsteps coming closer, a heavy, deliberate tread, and then a figure, tall and rangy, appeared in the doorway.

'*Larenzo*—' Emma pressed one hand to her chest as she let out a shaky laugh of relief. 'You scared me. I wasn't expecting you.'

'I wasn't expecting to come here.' He stepped into the spacious sitting room of the villa, and as the lamplight washed over his face Emma sucked in a shocked breath. Larenzo's skin looked grey, and there were deep shadows under his eyes. His hair was rumpled, as if he'd driven his hand through the ink-dark strands.

'Are you—are you all right?'

His mouth twisted in a grim smile. 'Why, do I not look all right?'

'No, not really.' She tried to lighten her words with a smile, but she really was alarmed. In the nine months she'd been Larenzo's housekeeper, she'd never seen him look like this, not just tired or haggard, but as if the life force that was so much a part of who he was, that restless, rangy energy and charisma, had drained away.

'Are you ill?' she asked. 'I can get you something...'

'No. Not ill.' He let out a hollow laugh. 'But clearly I must look terrible.'

'Well, as a matter of fact, yes, you do.'

'Thank you for your honesty.'

'Sorry—'

'Don't be. I can't bear lies.' A sudden, savage note had entered his voice, making Emma blink. Larenzo crossed the room to the liquor cabinet in the corner. 'I need a drink.'

She watched as he poured himself a large measure of whisky and then tossed it back in one burning swallow. His back was to her, the silk of his suit jacket straining against his shoulders and sinewy back. He was an attractive man, a beautiful man even, with his blue-black hair and piercing grey eyes, his tall, powerful body always encased in three-thousand-euro suits.

Emma had admired his form the way you admired Michelangelo's *David*, as a work of art. She had decided when she'd taken this job that she wasn't going to make the mistake of developing some schoolgirl crush on her boss. Larenzo Cavelli was out of her league. Way, way out of her league. And, if the tabloids were true, he had a different woman on his arm and in his bed every week.

'I wasn't expecting you until the end of the month,' she said.

'I had a change of plans.' He took out the stopper in the crystal decanter of whisky and poured himself another healthy measure. 'Obviously.'

She didn't press the point, because, while they'd developed a fairly amicable working relationship over the last nine months, he was still her boss. She couldn't actually say she *knew* Larenzo Cavelli. Since she'd taken the job as housekeeper he'd come to the villa only three times, never more than for a couple of days. He mostly lived in Rome, where he kept an apartment, or travelled for work as CEO of Cavelli Enterprises.

'Very well,' she finally said. 'Will you be staying long?'

He drained his glass for a second time. 'Probably not.'

'Well, the night at least,' she answered briskly. She didn't know what was going on with Larenzo, whether it was a business deal gone bust or a love affair gone bad, or something else entirely, but she could still do her job. 'The sheets on your bed are clean. I'll go switch the heating on for the pool.'

'Don't bother,' Larenzo answered. He put his empty glass on the table with a clink. 'There's no need.'

'It's no trouble,' Emma protested, and Larenzo shrugged, his back to her.

'Fine. Maybe I'll have one last swim.'

His words replayed through her mind as she left him and walked through the spacious, silent rooms of the villa to the back door that led to a brick terrace overlooking the mountains, a teardrop-shaped pool as its impressive centrepiece. *One last swim.* Was he planning on leaving, on selling the villa?

Emma gazed out at the Nebrodi mountains and shivered slightly, for the air still held a pine-scented chill.

All was quiet save for the rustling of the wind high up in the trees. Larenzo's villa was remote, miles from the nearest market town, Troina; in the daylight Emma could see its terracotta-tiled houses and shops nestled in the valley below. She went there several times a week to shop and socialise; she had a couple of friends amidst the Sicilian shopkeepers and matrons.

If Larenzo was planning on selling the villa, she'd miss living here. She never stayed anywhere long, and she would have probably started feeling restless in a few months anyway, but... She glanced once more at the night-cloaked hills and valleys, the mellow stone of the villa perched on its hill gleaming in the moonlight. She liked living here. It was peaceful, with plenty of subjects to photograph. She'd be sad to leave, if it came to that.

But maybe Larenzo just meant a swim before he left for Rome again. She switched on the heating and then turned to go inside; as she turned a shadowy form loomed up in front of her and her breath came out in a short gasp. She must have swayed or stumbled a little, for Larenzo put his hands on her shoulders to steady her.

They stood like that for a moment in the doorway, his strong hands curling around her shoulders so she could feel the warmth of his palms through the thin cotton of her T-shirt, and how her heart pounded beneath it. She didn't think he'd ever actually touched her before.

She moved one way, and he moved another, so it was almost as if they were engaged in a struggle or an awk-

ward dance. Then Larenzo dropped his hands from her
shoulders and stepped back.

'*Scusi.*'

'My fault,' she murmured, her heart still thudding, and
moved quickly through the kitchen to flick on the lights.
Bathed in a bright electric glow, things felt more normal,
even if she could still feel the imprint of his hands on her
shoulders, so warm and strong. 'So.' She turned to him
with a quick smile, a brisk look. 'Have you eaten? I can
make you something.'

He looked as if he was about to refuse, and then he
shrugged. 'Why not? I'll go change while you cook.'

'What would you like to eat?'

Another shrug as he turned away. 'Whatever you make
will be fine.'

She watched him disappear down the hallway, her lips
pursed in an uncertain frown. She'd never seen Larenzo
like this. Not that they'd actually had that much conversation, beyond discussing pool maintenance and house
repairs. But even when talking about such mundane matters, Larenzo Cavelli had exuded a compelling charisma
and energy, a life force. He was a man who, when entering a room, made everyone turn and take notice. Men
tried to suppress their envy, and women undressed him
with their eyes. Emma counted herself as wilfully immune to the man's magnetic vitality, but its absence now
made her uneasy.

Her frown deepening, Emma opened the fridge and
stared at the few items inside. She always did a big shop
right before Larenzo arrived; she bought all the ingredients for gourmet meals for one and made them for him
to eat alone, usually out on the terrace overlooking the
mountains.

Now she glanced askance at the half-dozen eggs, a few
slices of pancetta and the end of a wedge of cheese that

comprised the entire contents of the fridge. With a sigh she took it all out. A bacon and cheese omelette it was.

She was just sliding it onto a plate when Larenzo came downstairs, dressed now in faded jeans and a grey T-shirt, his hair damp and spiky from a shower. She'd seen him casually dressed before, many times, but for some reason now, perhaps because of how different Larenzo seemed, her heart gave a weird little flip and she felt awareness shiver over her skin. Clearly he still possessed some of that charisma and vitality, for she felt the force of it now.

'Sorry it's just an omelette,' she said. 'I'll do a big shop tomorrow.'

'That won't be necessary.'

'But—'

"Aren't you going to join me?' He arched an eyebrow, nodding towards the single plate she'd laid out, a challenge simmering in his eyes.

In the handful of times he'd been at the villa, Larenzo had never asked her to eat with him. The two of them alone on the terrace would have been awkward, intimate, and Emma happily ate leftovers in the kitchen, one of her photography books propped against the salt and pepper shakers.

'Um...I've already eaten,' she said after a second's pause. It had to be past ten o'clock at night.

'Come have a glass of wine. I don't feel like being alone.'

Was that a command? Emma shrugged her assent; she wouldn't mind a glass of wine, and perhaps Larenzo would tell her what was going on.

'Okay,' she said, and she fetched two glasses while Larenzo selected a bottle of red wine from the rack above the sink.

While Larenzo took his plate of eggs out to the terrace, Emma retrieved her sweater from the sitting room, slipping her arms through the sleeves as she stepped outside. The moon was high and full above the pine-blanketed hills, the Nebrodi range's highest peak, Mount Soro, piercing the night sky. Larenzo was already seated at a table overlooking the pool, the water glimmering in the moonlight, but he rose as Emma came forward with the two glasses and proffered the bottle of wine. She nodded her assent and sat down while he poured.

'This is very civilised,' she said as she accepted the glass.

'Yes, isn't it?' Larenzo answered. 'Well, let's enjoy it while we can.' He raised his glass in a toast and Emma lifted hers as well before taking a sip. The wine was rich and velvety-smooth, clearly expensive, but she put her glass down after one sip and gave her boss as direct a look as she could.

'You're sure everything is all right?'

'As right as it can be,' Larenzo answered, taking a sip of wine.

'What does that mean?'

He set his glass down and stretched his legs out in front of him. 'Exactly that. But I don't want to talk about myself, not tonight. For a few hours I'd just like to forget.'

Forget what? Emma wondered, but clearly Larenzo didn't want her to ask.

'You've been my housekeeper for nearly a year and I don't really know the first thing about you,' he continued, and Emma stared at him in surprise.

'You want to talk about *me*?'

'Why not?'

'Because…well, because you've never expressed an interest in knowing anything about me before. And actually, I'm quite a boring person.'

He smiled, his teeth gleaming in the darkness. 'Let me be the judge of that.'

Emma shook her head slowly. This evening was becoming almost surreal. 'What do you want to know?'

'Where did you grow up?'

An innocuous enough question, she supposed. 'Everywhere, really. I was a diplomat's kid.'

'I think I remember you mentioning that in your interview.' He'd interviewed her in Rome, where she'd been working as a chambermaid in a hotel, just one in a string of jobs she'd had as she moved from city to city, exploring the world and taking photographs.

'And you haven't minded being stuck up here in the hills of Sicily?' he asked, his wine glass raised to his lips. 'All by yourself?'

She shrugged. 'I'm used to being on my own.' And she preferred it that way. No ties, no obligations, no disappointments. The occasional bout of loneliness was not too high a price to pay for that kind of freedom.

'Even so.'

'You obviously like it,' she pointed out. 'Since you own this place.'

'Yes, but I travel and spend time in cities. I'm not up here all the time.'

'Well, as I said, I like it.' For now, anyway. She never remained anywhere for too long, always preferring to move on, to find new experiences, and from the sceptical look on Larenzo's face he seemed to guess a bit of her natural wanderlust.

'Have you met anyone up here?' he asked. 'Made friends?'

'A few people down in Troina.'

'That's something, I suppose. What do you do for fun up here?'

Emma shrugged. 'Walk. Swim. Read. I'm easily entertained, fortunately.'

'Yes.' He gazed out at the mountains and Emma had

the sense he was thinking about something else, something painful.

'But it's not the kind of job you'd stay in for ever,' he said at last.

'Are you trying to get rid of me?' she asked lightly. She'd meant it as a joke but Larenzo took the question seriously.

'No, definitely not. But if something were to happen…' He trailed off, his gaze still on the hills, and Emma set down her wine glass.

'Larenzo, are you thinking of selling this place?'

'Not selling it, no.'

'But something,' she pressed. 'What's going on, really? Do I need to start looking for another job?'

He let out a long, low breath and raked his hands through his hair. 'Whatever happens, I'll make sure to give you a good reference.'

'What are you talking about, whatever happens?' Emma shook her head. 'I don't understand you.'

'I know, and I don't want to explain it now. It will all become clear soon enough.' He nodded towards the pool. 'How about a swim?'

'A *swim*?' Emma glanced at the pool, the water glimmering in the moonlight. 'It's a bit cold for me.'

'Not for me,' he said, and she watched in amazement as he stripped off his shirt and jeans and, clad only in his boxer shorts, dived into the pool.

The splash echoed through the still air and Emma watched, shivering slightly, as Larenzo swam the length of the pool before surfacing and slicking back the wet hair from his face.

'Come in,' he called. 'The water's lovely.'

Emma shook her head. 'I only just turned the heating on. It's got to be freezing.'

'Even so.' He arched an eyebrow, his mouth curling in a smile that was pure temptation. Emma's gaze was inexorably drawn to his bare chest, all lean, rippling muscle, his bronzed skin beaded with water. 'Dare you.'

Emma hadn't thought this evening could get any more surreal. But swimming with her boss in a freezing pool?

'Come on, Emma.' He held out his hand. 'Just jump in.' Heat simmered in his eyes and she felt an answering stab of lust through her middle.

This was so foolish, so dangerous, and yet…the sight of Larenzo in the pool, nearly naked with moonlight streaming over his body and droplets of water twinkling like diamonds on his bronzed skin, was hard to resist. And already this evening felt separate from reality, a time apart.

'Chicken?' he taunted, his eyes and teeth glinting in the darkness, and Emma laughed.

'You really want to get me in that pool.'

'I want someone to swim with.'

Excitement licked through her veins. She didn't think Larenzo was coming on to her; he never had before. And yet…

'Fine,' she said, and, shrugging off her sweater, she dived fully clothed into the deep end.

She surfaced, sucking in a hard breath, because the water really was cold. 'And now I'm getting out,' she told him as she trod water. 'It's as freezing as I thought it would be.'

'I didn't think you'd do it,' he said, laughter threading his voice, and Emma was glad that she'd managed to distract him from whatever had been bothering him, even if she got hypothermia in the process.

'You thought wrong,' she said, and swam towards the edge of the pool. With her wet clothes weighing her down it was hard to haul herself up on the pool's edge.

And then she felt Larenzo behind her, his hands on her shoulders, the strength and heat of him just inches from her back. She sucked in a shocked breath as he slid his hands to her waist and helped her up.

She flopped inelegantly on the side of the pool and then scrambled to her knees, amazed at how much that one little touch had affected her. She shivered, for with her soaked clothes the night air now felt icy.

'Here.' Larenzo hauled himself up and went to the heated cupboard for several towels. 'Wrap yourself up.'

'I should really change,' she said. She glanced down at herself and saw that her T-shirt was sticking to her skin, revealing even the floral pattern on her bra, her nipples peaked from the cold. 'Thanks,' she muttered, and clutched the towel to her chest.

Larenzo's gaze hadn't dropped to her chest, but his mouth curved all the same and again Emma felt another kick of excitement. She retreated back to the table, the towel still clutched to her chest.

'I should go to bed.'

'Don't go quite yet,' Larenzo answered. He slung the towel over his shoulders and sat down across from her, pouring them both more wine. Emma eyed the full glass and Larenzo's bare chest, his perfectly formed pecs flexing as he moved, and felt as if she'd just jumped into the deep end of an entirely different kind of pool.

'I'm freezing—' she began and he nodded towards the cupboard.

'There are towelling robes in there. Change out of your wet things. I don't want you catching cold.'

'Larenzo…' Emma began, although she didn't know what she was going to say. Why was she protesting so much, anyway? Chatting in the moonlight with a devastatingly attractive man was no hardship. And it wasn't as if Larenzo was going to make a move. He might have dared her to jump in the pool, but she was pretty sure her boss didn't mix business with pleasure.

Even if she wanted him to…

'Fine,' she said, and retreated to the towelling cupboard.

With the door serving as a screen between her and Larenzo, she tugged off her wet clothes and wrapped herself in the heated dressing gown. The sleeves hung past her hands and the sash trailed the ground, but at least she was warm again. She doubted she'd provide any sort of temptation to Larenzo now.

'Tell me your favourite place you lived in as a child,' Larenzo commanded as she sat down across from him and picked up her wine glass—he'd filled it again, while she'd been changing.

Emma considered for a moment. Answering questions, at least, kept her from gawping at Larenzo's chest. Why on earth she was feeling this unwelcome attraction for him now, she had no idea. Perhaps it was simply the strangeness of the evening, his unexpected arrival, his demand for her company. 'Krakow, I suppose,' she said finally. 'I spent two years there when I was ten. It's a beautiful city.' And those years had been the last ones where she'd felt part of a family, before her mother had announced her decision to leave. But she didn't want to think, much less talk, about that. 'Where did you grow up?' she asked, and Larenzo swirled the wine in his glass, his expression hardening slightly as he gazed down into its ruby depths.

'Palermo.'

'Hence the villa in Sicily, I suppose.'

'It is my home.'

'But you live most of the time in Rome.'

'Cavelli Enterprises is headquartered there.' He paused, his shuttered gaze on the darkened mountains, the moon casting a lambent glow over the wooded hills. 'In any case, I never much liked Palermo.'

'Why not?'

He pressed his lips together. 'Too many hard memories.'

He didn't seem inclined to say anything more, and Emma eyed him curiously, wondering at this enigmatic man who clearly had secrets she'd never even guessed at before.

Larenzo gazed round the terrace, the patio furniture now no more than shadowy shapes in the darkness, and then turned to look once more at the mountains. 'I'll miss it here,' he said, so quietly Emma almost didn't hear him.

'So you are thinking of leaving,' she said, and Larenzo didn't answer for a long moment.

'Not thinking of it, no,' he said, and then seemed to shake off his weary mood, his gaze snapping back to her. 'Thank you, Emma, for the food and also for your company. You've done more for me than you could possibly know.'

Emma stared at him helplessly. 'If there's anything else I can do...'

To her shock he touched her cheek with his hand, his fingers cool against her flushed face. *'Bellissima,'* he whispered, and the endearment stole right through her. 'No,' he said, and dropped his hand from her face. 'You've done enough. Thank you.' And then, taking his plate and his glass, he rose from his chair and left her sitting on the terrace alone.

Emma sat there for a few moments, shivering a little in the chilly air despite the dressing gown. She wished she could have comforted Larenzo somehow, but she had no idea what was going on, and she wasn't sure he'd welcome her sympathy anyway. He was a proud, hard man, caught in a moment of weakness. He'd probably regret their whole conversation tomorrow.

Sighing, she took the wine bottle and glasses from the table and headed inside. Larenzo had already gone upstairs; the lights were off, the house locked up. After rinsing out the dishes and switching on the dishwasher Emma went upstairs as well.

She paused for a moment on the landing; Larenzo's

master bedroom was to the right, her own smaller room the last on the left. She heard nothing but the wind high up in the trees, and she couldn't see any light underneath Larenzo's doorway. Even so she had a mad urge to knock on his door, to say something. But what? They didn't have that kind of relationship, not remotely, and knocking on Larenzo's bedroom door, seeing him answer it with his hair rumpled and damp, his chest still bare…

No. That was taking this strange evening a step too far.

Still she hesitated, glancing towards his doorway, and then with a sigh she turned and went to her own bedroom, closing the door behind her.

CHAPTER TWO

HE COULDN'T SLEEP. Hardly a surprise, considering all that had happened in the last few days. Larenzo stared gritty-eyed at the ceiling before, with a sigh, he sat up and swung his legs over the side of his bed.

All around him the house was still and silent. It was nearly two in the morning, and he wondered how long he had left. Would they come for him at dawn, or would they wait for the more civilised hour of eight or nine o'clock in the morning? Either way, it wouldn't be long. Bertrano had made sure of that.

Letting out another sigh at the thought of the man he'd considered as good as a father, Larenzo slipped from the bedroom and walked downstairs. The rooms of the villa were silent, dark, and empty, and he was loath to turn on a light and disturb the peacefulness. He could have stayed in Rome, but he'd hated the thought of simply waiting for the end, and he'd wanted to have a final farewell for the only place he could call a home. Bertrano would tell them where to find him; the police in Palermo had most likely already been alerted. He had a few hours at most.

And for those few hours he wanted simply to savour what he had. What Bertrano Raguso had given him, although Larenzo had worked hard for it. Ironic, really, that the man who had saved him would also destroy him. Fitting, perhaps.

He ran his hand along the silky-smooth ebony of the

grand piano in the music room; he'd bought it because he loved music, but he'd never found the time to learn to play. Now he never would. He played a few discordant notes, the sound echoing through the silent villa, before he moved onto the sitting room, stopping in front of the chessboard on a table by the window, its marble pieces set up for a game he would never play.

He picked up the king, fingering the smooth marble before he laid it down again. Bertrano had taught him how to play chess, and Larenzo had savoured the evenings they'd spent together, heads bent over a chessboard. Why had the man who had treated him like a son turned on him so suddenly? Betrayed him? Had it been a moment's panicked weakness? But no, it had gone on longer than that, perhaps even months, for Bertrano to lay the paper trail. How had Larenzo not known? Not even guessed?

He glanced at the pawns neatly lined up. In the end he'd served no more purpose than they did. With a sudden burst of helpless rage he struck the pawns, scattering them across the board with a clatter.

The realisation of all he was about to lose hit him then, with sickening force, and he dropped his face in his hands, driving his fingers through his hair, as a single sob racked his body.

Bertrano, how could you do this to me? I loved you. I thought of you as my father.

'Larenzo?'

He stiffened at the sound of Emma's uncertain voice, and then he lifted his face from his hands, turning to see her standing in the doorway of the sitting room. She was in her pyjamas, nothing more than boy shorts and a very thin T-shirt; Larenzo could see the outline of her small breasts and he felt an entirely inappropriate stab of lust, just as he had when he'd seen her soaked and dripping in the pool.

He hadn't spared much thought for his housekeeper before tonight, but now he envied her freedom, her ease.

'Couldn't you sleep?' she asked as she came into the room. She glanced at the scattered chess pieces, a silent question in her eyes.

'No, I couldn't.' He turned to the fireplace, where the kindling and logs were already laid for a fire. 'It's cold in here,' he said, and reached for a match to start the blaze. From behind him he could hear Emma righting the chess pieces.

When the fire was cheerily crackling in the hearth he turned to face her; she was touching the pawns he'd knocked over, her head bent, her hair swinging down to hide her face.

'Fancy a game?'

She looked up in surprise. 'What?'

He nodded towards the chessboard. 'Do you play?'

'I know the rules.'

'Well, then. It appears neither of us can sleep. Shall we play?'

'All right,' she said after a pause, and she sat down in one of the chairs as Larenzo sat in the other.

'White goes first,' he told her and she bit her lip, studying the board with a concentration so intense he found it endearing. Again he felt the powerful thrust of attraction. These few hours of enjoyment would be the last pleasure he had for a long while.

Finally she moved her piece, her slender fingers curling around the figure. She glanced up at him, a smile lurking in her eyes, playing with her lips. 'Why do I have a feeling you're going to crush me?'

'You can always live in hope,' he answered lightly, and moved his pawn.

She laughed, shaking her head. 'That would be foolish in the extreme.'

'Perhaps.' He liked watching her, seeing the way the

firelight played over her golden skin, how humour lit her golden-green eyes. He stretched out his legs and his foot brushed her ankle, sending another throb of desire through him.

He thought she felt something too, for her eyes widened and her body tensed briefly before she moved another piece on the board.

They played in silence for a few minutes, the tension spooling out between them. Larenzo brushed her foot again with his own, enjoying the silky slide of her skin. She sucked in a quick breath, her fingers trembling as she moved her rook.

'I'm four moves away from checkmate,' he told her, and she let out a shaky laugh.

'I knew this was going to happen.' She glanced up at him wryly and he held her gaze, felt the force of the attraction between them. He'd never considered his housekeeper as an object of desire before; employees had always been off limits, and he'd seen her so rarely. But tonight he craved that human connection, the last one that might ever be offered to him. To touch a woman, to give and receive pleasure…

Setting his jaw, Larenzo turned back towards the board. Making love with Emma tonight would be an entirely selfish act. He couldn't drag her down with him. It was bad enough that he was here at all.

He moved his bishop, and then stilled as he felt Emma's hand on his own, her skin cool and soft.

'Larenzo, I wish you'd tell me what's wrong.' He didn't answer, simply stared at her fingers on his. He stroked her palm with his thumb and she shivered in response but did not remove her hand.

'It doesn't matter,' he said in a low voice, and stroked her palm again. 'There's nothing you can do about it, and it's my own fault anyway.' For trusting someone he'd loved.

For believing someone could have pure motives. For being so bloody naive. So damn *stupid*.

'Are you sure I can't help?' Emma asked softly. She squeezed his fingers and Larenzo closed his eyes. Her touch was the sweetest torture he'd ever known. He thought of telling her the one way she could help, the one way she could make him forget what dawn would bring. He resisted. He could not be that selfish, not even on the threshold of his own destruction.

'No, I'm afraid not. No one can.'

Her gaze searched his face and then she rose from her chair. 'Perhaps I should leave you alone, then.'

'Wait.' The single word was wrenched from him. 'Don't go.'

He felt her surprise as the silence stretched on. She didn't move, either backwards or forwards. He bowed his head.

'I don't want to be alone tonight,' he confessed, his voice low, and then she took a step forward, laid her hand on his shoulder once more.

'You aren't,' she said simply.

Emma didn't know whether it was Larenzo's obvious pain or the attraction that had snapped through the air that had compelled her to stay. Perhaps both. She wanted to comfort him, but she couldn't deny the yearning she had felt uncoil through her body when Larenzo had looked at her with such blatant desire in his eyes. No man had ever looked at her like that before, and it had thrilled her to her core.

The moment stretched on between them as she stood there with her hand still on his shoulder, his head bowed. His skin was warm and smooth underneath her palm, and slowly Larenzo reached up and covered her hand with his own, his fingers twining with hers. The intimacy of the gesture rocked her, sent heat and need and something even deeper and more important spiralling through her. They were simply holding hands, and yet it felt like a pure form of communication, the most intimate thing she'd ever done.

Finally Larenzo broke the moment. He took his hand from hers and turned. Emma could feel the heat rolling off him, inhaled the tangy scent of his aftershave, and desire crashed through her once more. This man was more than a work of art. He was a living, breathing, virile male, and he was close enough for her to touch him. To kiss him. Which she wanted to do, very much.

'Do you have family, Emma?' he asked, startling her out of her haze of desire.

'Y-y-y-yes.'

'Are you close to them?' He gazed at her, his silvery eyes searching her, looking for answers. 'You must not see them very often, living here.'

'I...' How to answer that seemingly innocent question? 'I see my father sometimes. He's currently posted in Budapest, and we've met up occasionally.'

'And your mother?'

Why was he asking her all these questions? She didn't want to talk about her family, and certainly not her mother, yet in the darkened intimacy of the room, of the moment, she knew she would answer. 'No, I'm not close to my mother. My parents divorced when I was twelve, and I didn't see her much after that.'

'That must have been hard.'

A small shrug was all she'd allow on that subject, but Larenzo nodded as if she'd said something important and revealing. 'And siblings? Do you have any sisters or brothers?'

'One sister, Meghan. She lives in New Jersey, does the whole stay-at-home-mom thing.' The kind of life she'd deliberately chosen not to pursue or want. 'We're close. We Skype.' She shook her head in confusion. 'Why are you asking me all this, Larenzo?'

'Because I never had a real family of my own, and I wondered.' He turned, his back to her as he gazed at the fire. 'I wondered how families are. How they're meant to be.'

'What happened to your family?'

'I don't know. My mother left me to fend for myself when I was young, maybe two or three. An orphanage took me in, run by a convent. Not the nicest place. I ran away when I was eleven. Spent the next few years on the street.'

He recited these facts dispassionately, without any self-pity at all, and somehow that made it all the more terrible. 'That's awful. I'm sorry.' Emma would never have guessed such a past for this man, with his wealth and power and magnetism. 'Was this in Palermo?'

'Yes.'

'Those are hard memories.'

'Yes.' He let out a long, low sigh. 'But let's not talk about that tonight.'

'What do you want to talk about?'

'Anything.' He sat down on the sheepskin rug in front of the fire, and patted the floor next to him. Emma came to sit across from him, folding her legs underneath her, conscious of the strangeness of this situation: both of them in their pyjamas, the firelight casting pools of light over their skin, and yet of the ease of it too. It felt weirdly natural to sit there with Larenzo, in the dark, with the fire. Surreal and yet somehow right.

'What do you want to do with your life, Emma?' he asked as he tossed another log on the fire. 'I assume you don't want to be a housekeeper for ever.'

'Would there be something wrong with that?'

He gave a faint, bemused smile. 'No, there's nothing wrong with that. But you are a beautiful, capable young woman, and I imagine you want to see more of the world than a remote Sicilian hilltop.'

'I like to travel,' she admitted. 'I've moved around a lot already.'

'As a diplomat's kid.'

'Yes, and since I finished school. Itchy feet, I suppose.'

'What did you study at school?'

'I did a photography course just for a year, and then I got a backpack and a rail pass and went to see the world.' Determined to enjoy everything life had to offer, never to be tied down, never to be hurt.

'Sounds fun.' He turned to her, an eyebrow arched. 'I think I've seen you with a camera round the place. Have you taken photos here?'

'Yes…'

'May I see them?'

She hesitated, because no one had ever seen her photographs. No one had ever asked. And showing them now to Larenzo felt even more intimate than when they'd held hands. She'd be showing him a part of her soul. 'Okay,' she finally said. 'I'll go get them.' She hurried up to her bedroom, and then leafed through several folders of photos before selecting a few of her favourites. She brought them back to Larenzo, handing them to him silently.

He studied each one carefully, a slight frown puckering his forehead as Emma waited, nibbling her lip. She realised she wanted him to like them, to understand them, and she held her breath as she waited for his verdict.

'They're not holiday snaps,' he said finally and she let out a little laugh.

'No.' She preferred to take candid shots of people, strangers and sometimes friends caught in an unexpected moment, held in thrall by an emotion, whether it was happiness or sorrow or something else.

'This one.' He gestured to a portrait of Rosaria, one of the shopkeepers in Troina. She was sitting on a stool in the back of her bakery, her hands on her thighs, her head thrown back, her face a mass of wrinkles as she let out a deep, belly laugh. 'That's joy,' Larenzo said quietly, and Emma's heart swelled with the knowledge that he did understand, that he'd seen what she'd been trying to capture.

'Yes.'

'I don't think I've ever felt that.' He turned to give her a swift, dark glance. 'Have you?'

Shock rippled through her at the question, and the answer that slipped from her lips without her even realising she was going to say it. 'No,' Emma whispered. 'I don't think I have.' She'd travelled the world, climbed mountains, scuba-dived, done a million and one adventurous and amazing things, had always considered herself a happy person...and yet joy? That kind of deep, abiding, *real* joy?

It had remained beguilingly elusive. And she hadn't realised it until Larenzo had asked her the question.

'You have a skill,' Larenzo said as he turned back to the photographs. 'A true talent. You shouldn't squander it.'

'I'm not—'

'I mean you should exhibit these.' He glanced at her, his eyebrows raised. 'Have you shown them to anyone, to a professional?'

'You're the first person who has seen them.'

He held her gaze, his own darkening. 'Thank you,' he said quietly, and wordlessly Emma nodded.

The moment spun out, stretching and shifting into something else as their gazes remained locked and Emma's breath shortened. A log popped in the fireplace and embers scattered across the hearth, but neither of them so much as twitched.

The desire Emma had felt before now crashed over her in an overpowering wave, obliterating rational thought, obscuring everything but this moment. She wanted this man more than she'd ever wanted anything or anyone before, and as she saw the heat blaze in his eyes she realised with a thrill he felt the same.

Slowly, deliberately, Larenzo reached one hand out towards her, his fingers first skimming her cheek and then his palm cradling her face. The warmth of his palm against her cheek felt electric, every nerve ending she had tingling and quivering with awareness. Larenzo's thumb brushed her mouth, and her lips parted in expectation as a tiny gasp escaped. If he kissed her, she'd be lost. And she knew she wanted to be lost.

His hand tensed briefly against her cheek, and for a terrible second she thought he was going to drop it and move away. This glorious moment would be over. Then he brought his other hand up to frame her face, cradling her between his palms before pulling her inexorably towards him, his lips coming down on hers, soft and hard, cold and hot, everything all at once as a thousand new sensations blazed through her and her mouth opened to his kiss.

Larenzo hauled her towards him, her legs sliding across his as she straddled him, felt the hard press of his arousal against the juncture of her thighs and excitement pulsed hard inside her.

He was kissing her deeply now, with a hungry urgency that Emma felt in herself as she drove her fingers through his hair and pressed even more closely against him, her body arching instinctively as Larenzo pressed back.

After an endless moment that still didn't seem long enough, Larenzo broke off the kiss, his breath coming out in a rush.

'I wasn't going to do that.'

'I wanted you to do it,' she whispered. She couldn't bear it if he stopped now.

He leaned his forehead against hers, their bodies still pressed together, both of their hearts thudding. 'I want you, Emma. I think I want you more than I've ever wanted anyone before.'

A thrill ran through her at this simply stated fact. 'I want you too.'

'But I can't offer you anything other than this night.' He closed his eyes briefly. 'A few hours at most. That's all. That's all it could ever be.'

'I know,' she said softly. When he'd kissed her, she hadn't thought of anything but the moment, yet she acknowledged now that she'd never have expected some kind of commitment from a man like Larenzo. 'I don't want more than this night,' she told him. 'I'm not looking for some kind of relationship, Larenzo, trust me. I just want you, tonight.'

He leaned back a little so he could look into her face. 'If you're sure…?'

She nodded, amazed at just how sure she was. Everything about this night had been surreal, even magical. This felt, bizarrely and yet completely, like the logical and necessary conclusion. 'I'm sure.'

'Then come with me.' He untangled himself from her and rose from the rug in one fluid movement, holding his hand down to help her up. With their fingers linked he led her silently upstairs to his bedroom.

Emma gazed at the king-sized bed with its navy silk sheets she'd changed herself and felt a tremor of—what? Not fear. Anticipation. And a little nervousness, because, while she *was* sure, this was still a new experience. An entirely new experience, and she didn't want to admit to Larenzo just how new it was, how unlike her this decision had been.

He glanced back at her, his fingers still twined with hers. 'Having second thoughts?' he asked quietly, his gaze sweeping over her. 'Cold feet? I wouldn't mind.' He let out a ragged laugh. 'Well, I'd mind, but I'd understand.'

'I'm not having second thoughts.' She swallowed, lifted her chin. She wouldn't tell him about her inexperience. It didn't matter to her, and she didn't want it to matter to him, or put him off. 'Are you?' she challenged, and he let out a soft huff of laughter.

'Definitely not.' He tugged her towards him. 'Come here, Emma.'

And she came willingly, her breasts pressing against his bare chest as his mouth came down on hers once more and for a few blissful, buzzing seconds she forgot everything but the hunger and need for this, for him.

Larenzo reached down and with one swift tug he had her T-shirt up and over her head; the feel of her breasts brushing the crisp hair on his chest was so intense it almost hurt. She'd never felt so much, felt so alive, not when she'd been on top of a mountain or deep in the ocean. All her adventures paled in light of this.

She let out a gasp that he muffled with his mouth, his hands sliding down her back and then cupping her bottom as he settled her against his arousal.

He moved his mouth from her lips to the curve of her neck, the touch of his tongue against her sensitive skin making her shiver.

Then he drew her to the bed, laying her down on top of the silken sheets and covering her body with his own.

She twined her arms around his neck and arched up towards him, craving the connection of their bodies fused in every place. Of being that close to another person… even if it was just for a single night. A few hours. And she knew Larenzo needed it too, craved it as much as she did. She was giving him herself, the only comfort she could offer him now.

Larenzo slid a hand between her thighs, slipping her pyjama shorts down her legs and then tossing them on the floor. The feel of his fingers against her most sensitive flesh had Emma arching upwards again, her head thrown back as sensations fizzed and popped inside her.

And then they exploded and her breath rushed out on a ragged cry as Larenzo worked magic with his fingers and left her boneless in his arms.

'Oh...'

'That's just to start,' he promised with a soft laugh, and then he tossed his own pyjama bottoms aside before he slid seamlessly inside her—and then stopped. 'Emma...'

She saw the confusion on his face, the uncertainty, and knew he'd guessed her inexperience. 'You haven't...' he began slowly and she answered by tilting her hips up.

'It doesn't matter,' she said fiercely, and as her body found its instinctive rhythm Larenzo matched it, burying his head in the curve of her shoulder as his body surged into hers.

If she'd felt any pain or discomfort, it was long gone as the exquisite friction of Larenzo's body created a plea-sure deeper and fiercer than what she'd already felt at his experienced hands.

She let out another long, ragged cry as the sensations exploded inside her again and with a shudder Larenzo emptied himself into her and then was still.

They lay like that for a few seconds before he wrapped his arms around her and rolled onto his back.

'Why didn't you tell me you were a virgin?' he asked quietly.

Emma could still feel him inside her, still feel the bone-melting ripples of pleasure that had utterly rocked her mo-ments before. 'Because like I said, it didn't matter.'

'I might have done things differently...'

'I liked the way you did things.'

He laughed softly then, his arms tightening around her. 'Thank you, Emma,' he said quietly, and she wasn't quite sure what he was thanking her for. She propped herself on her elbows to gaze down at him, and saw the ravages of both grief and pleasure on his face. She had no regrets, and yet she still wished she could smooth the furrows of worry from his forehead. She brushed his hair from his eyes instead, savouring the feel of him.

'I should be thanking you,' she said, and Larenzo smiled faintly before glancing out at the night sky; the moon was on the wane, dawn only an hour or two away. 'You should sleep.'

Did he want her to leave? Uncertainly Emma started to roll off him, but Larenzo clasped her to him once more.

'Stay,' he said, his voice rough with emotion. 'Stay until morning.'

And so she did.

CHAPTER THREE

THEY CAME AT DAWN. Larenzo heard the first car drive up, the crunch of gravel, the sound of a car door shutting quietly, as if they were trying to hide their presence. As if they could.

He stilled, every muscle tensing, Emma still in his arms. *Emma.* He would spare her an ugly scene. She deserved so much more than that, but that was all he could give her now.

Slowly he slipped from the bed, doing his best not to disturb her. She sighed in her sleep and turned, her tousled hair falling across one cheek, a tendril lying across her breast.

He gazed at her for a moment, drinking her in: the golden, freckled skin, the wavy golden-brown hair, her lashes fanned out on her cheeks, although he knew if she opened her eyes, they would be golden-green. His golden girl for a night, gone in the morning.

At least he would be gone.

Quickly Larenzo turned, reaching for his jeans. He pulled on a rugby shirt and ran his hands through his hair, took a deep breath. And looked one last time at Emma, at freedom and happiness, pleasure and peace. He'd known them all with her last night, and now they were nothing but memories. Resolutely he turned from her and left the room.

Emma awoke to the thud of boots on the stairs, the sound of stomping down the hall. She was still blinking the sleep from her eyes, one hand reaching for the sheet to cover herself, her mind barely processing what she'd heard, when the door was thrown open and three men crowded there, all of them glaring at her. Her heart seemed to still in her chest, everything in her going numb with horror as she stared at these strange men.

'What—?'

They spoke in rapid Italian, too fast for her to understand, although during her two years in Sicily she'd become fairly conversant in the language. Still, she understood their tone. Their derision and contempt.

She clutched the sheet to her breasts, her whole body trembling with indignation and fear. *'Chi sei? Cosa stai facendo?'* Who are you, and what are you doing? They didn't answer.

One man, clearly the leader of the pack, ripped the sheet away from her naked body. Emma gasped in shock. *'Puttana.'* He spat the single word. Whore.

Emma shook her head, her mouth dry, her body still trembling. She felt as if she'd awakened to an alternate reality, a horrible nightmare, and she had no idea how to make it stop. *Where was Larenzo?*

One of the men grabbed her by the arm and yanked her upwards. She came, stumbling, trying futilely to cover herself. He reached for her T-shirt and shorts discarded on the floor and threw them at her.

'You are English?' he asked, his voice clipped, and she nodded.

'American. And my consulate will hear—'

He cut her off with a hard laugh. 'Get dressed. You're coming with us.'

Quickly, clumsily, Emma yanked on her clothes. Dressed, even if only in flimsy pyjamas, she felt a little braver. 'Where is Signor Cavelli?' she asked in Italian.

The man eyed her scornfully. 'Downstairs, at the moment. But he'll spend the rest of his life in prison.'

Emma's mouth dropped open. *Prison?* What on earth was he talking about? Were these awful men police?

'Come on,' the man commanded her tersely, and with her mind spinning she followed the men downstairs.

Larenzo stood in the centre of the sitting room, his eyes blazing silver fire as he caught sight of her.

'You are all right? They didn't hurt you?'

'Shut up!' The words were like the crack of a gunshot as one of the men slapped Larenzo across the face. He didn't even blink, although Emma could see the red imprint of the man's hand on Larenzo's cheek.

'They didn't hurt me,' she said quietly and the man turned on her.

'Enough. Neither of you are to speak to one another. Who knows what you might try to communicate?'

'She has nothing to do with any of it,' Larenzo said, and he sounded scornful, as if he were actually in control of the situation. With an icy ripple of shock Emma saw that he was handcuffed. 'Do you actually think I'd tell a woman, my housekeeper no less, anything of value?'

The words, spoken so derisively, shouldn't have hurt. She knew, intellectually at least, that he was trying to protect her, although from what she had no idea. Even so they did hurt, just as the look Larenzo gave her, a look as derisive as those of the *carabinieri*, did.

'She's nothing to me.'

'Even so, she'll be taken in for questioning,' the man replied shortly and Larenzo's eyes blazed once more.

'She knows nothing. She's American. Do you want the consulate all over this?'

'This,' the man snapped, poking a finger into Larenzo's chest, 'is the biggest sting we've had in Sicily for twenty years. I don't give a damn about the consulate.'

They'd been speaking Italian, and, while Emma had caught the gist of it, she still didn't understand what was going on.

'Please, let me get dressed properly,' she said, her voice coming out croaky as she stumbled over the Italian. 'And then I'll go with you and answer any questions you might have.'

The man turned to glare at her with narrowed eyes. Then he gave a brief nod, and, with another policeman accompanying her, Emma went upstairs to her bedroom. The man waited outside the room while she pulled on underwear, jeans, a long-sleeved T-shirt, and a fleece. She brushed her teeth and hair, grabbed her purse and her passport, and then, just in case, she took her backpack and put a change of clothes, her camera, and her folder of photographs in it. Who knew when she'd be able to return? Just the realisation sent another icy wave of terror crashing through her.

Taking a deep, steadying breath, she left the room. The man accompanied her downstairs; the front door was open and she saw several cars outside. Larenzo was being shoved into one. She turned to the man.

'Where are we going?'

'Palermo.'

'Palermo? But that's nearly three hours away—'

The man smiled coldly. 'So it is. I'm afraid you'll have to be so inconvenienced.'

Three hours later Emma sat in an interrogation room at the anti-Mafia headquarters of Palermo's police department. She'd been given a paper cup of cold coffee and made to wait until finally the man who had made the arrest back at Larenzo's villa came and sat down across from her, putting his elbows on the chipped tabletop.

'You know your boyfriend is in a lot of trouble.'

Emma closed her eyes briefly. She was aching with exhaustion, numb with confusion and fear, and she missed Larenzo desperately even as she forced herself to remember she hadn't actually known him all that well. *Until last night. Until he held me in his arms and made me feel cherished and important.* 'He's not my boyfriend.'

'Whoever he is. He's going to prison, probably for the rest of his life.'

Emma licked her dry lips. 'What…what has he done?'

'You don't know?'

'I have no idea. All I know is he was—is—CEO of Cavelli Enterprises.' And that when he kissed her her mind emptied of thoughts. He made her body both buzz and sing. But then words began to ricochet through her, words Larenzo had spoken to her last night. *It's my own fault.* What had he done?

The man must have seen something of this in her face for he leaned forward. 'You know something.'

'No.'

'I've been doing this for a long time.' He sounded almost kind. 'I can tell, *signorina*. I can tell when someone is lying.'

'I'm not lying. I don't know anything. I don't even know what Cavelli Enterprises did.'

'And if I told you Larenzo Cavelli was involved with the Mafia? You wouldn't know anything about that?'

Bile rose in her throat and she swallowed hard. 'No, I certainly wouldn't.'

'It didn't concern you, the amount of security he had for that villa?'

She thought of his insistence on locking the doors, the elaborate security system. 'No.'

'Don't play dumb with me, *signorina*.'

'Look, maybe I was dumb, but I really didn't know.' Emma's voice rose in agitation. 'Plenty of people have detailed security systems.'

'Cavelli never said anything to you?'

Again his words raced through her mind. The grief on his face, the resignation she'd heard in his voice, the sense that everything was over, that this was his last night. He must have known they were coming to arrest him. He must have realised his activities had been discovered. Even so she couldn't reconcile the man she'd known, however briefly, with the Mafia. And yet as tender a lover as Larenzo had been, he was still virtually a stranger. She had no idea what he'd got up to when he'd been away from the villa. No idea at all.

'Signorina?'

'Please,' Emma said wearily. 'I was his housekeeper. I barely saw him. I don't know anything.'

Eight endless hours later she was finally released from the police. When she asked about returning to the villa, the man at the desk shook his head.

'The villa is being searched by the police. Everything there is potential evidence. You won't be able to go back for some time.'

And so Emma headed out into the busy streets of Palermo, mopeds and sports cars speeding by, her mind spinning as she tried to think what to do now. She had no real reason to go all the way back to the villa. She had nothing of value there but a few clothes and photography books.

But where could she go?

She ended up at a cheap hotel near the train station; she sat on the single bed, her backpack at her feet, her whole life in tatters.

She told herself she was used to moving on, and it would be easy enough to look for a new job. She could spend some time with her father in Budapest while she decided where she wanted to go, what she wanted to do.

And yet that prospect seemed bleak rather than hopeful; she might be used to moving on, but she hadn't been ready this time. She'd liked her life in Sicily. The villa had been the closest thing she'd ever known to a home.

And as for Larenzo...

She'd known, of course she'd known, that their one night together wasn't going anywhere. But it had still *meant* something. She'd felt a deep connection to him last night, an understanding and a tenderness... Had it all been false? According to the police, he was a Mafioso. The inspector had told her they had incontrovertible evidence, had said there were photos, witnesses, files. Everything to convict Larenzo Cavelli of too many horrible crimes. Extortion, the police had said. Theft. Assault. Organised delinquency, which was the legal term for involvement in the Mafia.

Faced with all of it, Emma knew she had no choice but to believe. Larenzo Cavelli was a criminal.

The next morning, after a sleepless night, Emma went to an Internet café to arrange her passage to Budapest. Yet as she clicked on a website for cheap airfares, she realised she didn't want to go there. She didn't want to traipse around Europe, taking odd jobs, at least not yet. She wanted to go somewhere safe, somewhere far away from all this, to recover and heal. She wanted to see her sister. Quickly Emma took out her mobile and scrolled through for Meghan's number.

'Emma?' Concern sharpened her sister's voice as she answered the call. 'You sound...'

'I'm tired. And a bit overwhelmed.' She didn't want to go into the details of what had happened on the phone; they were too recent, too raw, and she was afraid she might burst into tears right in the middle of the Internet café. 'My job in Sicily has ended suddenly, and I thought I'd come for a visit, if you don't mind having me.'

'Of course I don't mind having you,' Meghan exclaimed. 'Ryan will be delighted to see you.'

Emma pictured her tousle-haired three-year-old nephew with a tired smile. It had been too long since she'd seen him or her sister. 'Great. I'm going to book a flight for tomorrow if I can.'

'Let me know the time and we'll pick you up from the airport.'

Twenty-four hours later Emma touched down in New York and, after clearing immigration, she walked straight into her sister's arms.

'Is everything okay?' Meghan asked as she hugged her tightly. Emma nodded wordlessly. Nothing felt right at that moment, but she hoped it would soon. All she needed was a little time to get over this, and then she'd be back on the road, taking photographs, looking for adventure, as footloose as ever. The prospect didn't fill her with anything except a weary desolation.

She spent the next week mainly sleeping and spending time with Ryan and Meghan; she wanted to shut the world out, but she couldn't quite do it, and especially not when her sister looked up from *The New York Times* one morning, her eyes narrowed.

'I'm just reading an article about how business CEO Larenzo Cavelli was arrested for being involved in the Mafia.' Emma felt the colour drain from her face but said nothing. 'Wasn't that your boss, Emma?'

'Yes.'

'That's why your job ended?'

Emma nodded jerkily as she poured some orange juice. 'Yes.'

'You were working for someone in the *Mafia*?'

'I didn't know, Meghan!'

Meghan sat back in her chair, her eyes wide. 'Of course you didn't know. But good gracious, Emma. I'm so glad you're here, and you're safe.'

Emma closed her eyes briefly. She could picture Larenzo as he braced himself above her, his face suffused with tenderness as he gave her more pleasure than she'd ever known or thought possible. And then just hours later, when she'd heard the thud of the boots in the hall, the men glaring at her as they ripped the sheet away from her body...

'So am I,' she said quietly. 'So am I.'

After that she couldn't shut out the world any more. She read in the newspaper that Larenzo had confessed to everything, and there would be no trial. Within a month of her arrival he'd been sentenced to life in prison.

Two days after that, Emma realised she hadn't got her period that month. One three-minute test later, she discovered the truth. She was pregnant with Larenzo Cavelli's child.

CHAPTER FOUR

Eighteen months later

'LOOK AT ME, Aunt Emma!'

Emma waved to her nephew as he clambered to the top of the climbing frame at the playground near her sister's house. It was late October, and the leaves of the maple trees in the little park were scarlet, the sky above a cloudless blue. It was a beautiful, crisp day, and yet even so she couldn't keep herself from picturing the mountains of Sicily, and remembering how clear and pure the air was up there at this time of year.

Shivering slightly in the chill wind, Emma told herself to stop thinking about Sicily. She would never go back there. Never see the Nebrodi mountains again. *Never see Larenzo Cavelli again.*

Which was just as well, considering the man was a criminal.

Instinctively her gaze moved to the stroller a few feet away, where her daughter Ava was sleeping peacefully. She was ten months old, born on Christmas Eve, and Emma still marvelled at her. Still marvelled at the way her own life had changed so drastically.

When she'd discovered she was pregnant, she'd been shocked and numb for days, as well as embarrassed that she hadn't even *thought* about birth control when she'd been with Larenzo. That was how much he'd affected her. How much she'd wanted him in that moment.

Meghan, as eagle-eyed as ever, had guessed she was pregnant within a matter of days, and Emma had ended up telling her sister everything.

'What do you want to do?' Meghan had asked in her direct way as they'd sat at her kitchen table, Emma shredding tissues while Meghan got up to make tea. 'I love babies,' she continued as she switched on the kettle, 'and I think each one is a blessing, but I'll support you no matter what.'

'Thank you,' Emma had answered, sniffing. 'Truthfully, I don't know what to do. I never planned on marrying or having a family...not that marriage is a possibility in this case.'

'Why haven't you?' Meghan asked, one hip braced against the counter as she fixed Emma with a thoughtful stare. 'Most people think about being with someone, at least.'

'I don't know.' Emma shredded another tissue, avoiding her sister's perceptive gaze. 'You know me. I like to be on the move. See new things. I don't want to be held down.'

'And a baby is the ultimate in being held down,' Meghan answered with a sigh.

'Yes...' Which made it seem simple, but Emma felt as if nothing was.

'I know Mom leaving affected you badly, Em,' Meghan said quietly. 'More than it did me. I was at college. I was already out of the way.'

'She was your mother too,' Emma answered, still not looking at her sister. By silent agreement she and Meghan had never really talked about their mother. Emma hadn't even seen her in at least five years. Louise Leighton had moved to Arizona with her second husband when Emma was still in high school; Emma had spent a wretched few months out in Arizona with her, but it had been awkward and stilted and just generally awful, and she'd left pretty quickly, after one blazing argument. Her mother hadn't protested.

Since then, beyond a few pithy emails, her mother had never made any attempt to contact her. She didn't know if Meghan was in touch with her or not; she'd never asked, told herself she didn't care.

'Anyway,' Meghan resumed, 'what I'm trying to say is, I understand if motherhood scares you. You didn't have the best example.'

'I'm not scared,' Emma answered. She pressed a hand against her middle, almost as if she could feel the tiny life moving inside her. 'I just feel like my whole life has been upended. Everything that happened in Sicily…' She trailed off, fighting against the memories that continued to swamp her, and Meghan came over to give her a hug.

'It's hard,' she said. 'And you have some time.'

As the days slipped by Emma had come to accept this new life inside her, and realise that, to her amazement, she actually welcomed it. She watched her sister with Ryan and knew she wanted that same kind of bond, that closeness with another person. Already she felt a surprising and unshakeable love for this person who was a part of her.

Once she had pictured her life unspooling like a rainbow-coloured thread as she traipsed about the world, having adventure after adventure. But perhaps motherhood would be the greatest adventure of all.

It had been that, she thought now as she gazed at her sleeping daughter. From the moment she'd been born, dark-haired and grey-eyed, Ava had possessed the Cavelli charisma. Whether she was screaming to be fed or simply demanding to be heard, the force of her personality could not be denied. She was her father's daughter.

And her father was serving life in prison.

Emma had had a year and a half to become accustomed to the fact that Larenzo was a Mafioso, and yet the knowledge still had the power to stun her. She couldn't look back on their one night together without experiencing a shaft of bittersweet longing, as well as a sense of bewilderment that the man she'd thought she'd known, at least a little, was someone else entirely.

'Are you almost ready to go?' Meghan asked as she walked up to her in the park. Her cheeks were red with cold and she cradled a thermos of coffee. 'Ryan will want his lunch before playgroup, and, if I'm not mistaken, your little madam is going to wake up soon and want hers.'

'Undoubtedly.' With a wry look for her sleeping daughter, Emma reached for the handles of the pram.

'Emma...' Meghan began, and Emma tensed instinctively. She'd known a conversation was coming; she'd been living with Meghan and her husband, Pete, for over eighteen months now. They'd been happy to support her through her pregnancy and she'd taken a few odd cleaning jobs until she'd been too ungainly to manage it, in order to contribute to the household expenses.

Then Ava had been born, and her life had become a sleepless whirlwind; she'd stood in its centre, dazed and helpless to do much other than care for this baby that still managed to startle her with her existence.

But her daughter would be a year soon and Emma knew she needed to find her own way. Make her own life, for her own sake as well as her sister's.

'I know,' she said quietly, her gaze on Ava sleeping in the pram, the pink blanket pulled up to her chin, which had a cleft the same as Larenzo's. 'I need to get a move on.'

'No.' Meghan put a hand on Emma's arm. 'I wasn't going to say that. I'd never say that, Emma. You're welcome to stay with us as long as you like. Always.'

Emma shook her head. She knew her sister meant well,

but she also knew that she couldn't stay. She hadn't contributed anything to the household finances since Ava's birth, and she and Ava had taken up the spare bedroom for far too long. Meghan and Pete wanted more children, and they needed the space.

'I've been meaning to get my act together for months now,' she told her sister. 'I've just—' she let out a long, low breath '—felt frozen, I suppose. And keeping Ava fed and changed has taken more energy than I care to admit.' She let out a shaky laugh. 'I don't know how you do it.'

'Motherhood is never easy, and Ava is a demanding baby,' Meghan answered. 'But this isn't about me or Pete, Emma. It's about you. What's best for you. I want you to have your own life. Maybe meet someone…'

Emma shook her head. She couldn't even *think* about meeting someone. She might not have loved Larenzo Cavelli or had her heart broken, but even so something in her felt a little dented. A bit bruised. And she'd never been interested in a serious relationship anyway. She was even less so now, with a bad experience and a baby in tow.

'I know I need to get a job.'

'It's not about money—'

'But it is, Meghan, at least in part. As wonderful as you are, you can't support me for ever. I'm twenty-seven years old, and I chose to have a child. I need to step up.' She took a deep breath. 'I know I seem like a sleep-deprived zombie most of the time, but I have been thinking about possibilities. Maybe moving to New York and getting a job there, something to do with photography.'

As far as a plan went, it wasn't very sensible, and Emma could tell her sister thought so from the look on her face. 'New York? But it's so expensive. And I'm not sure there are too many jobs in photography going…'

'I know, but…' The other option was staying in New Jersey, finding some poky apartment she could afford on the salary she'd get as a waitress or cleaner, the only kind of job for which she was qualified. 'I like to dream,' she admitted with a wry sigh, and Meghan nodded in understanding.

'What about another job as a housekeeper? A live-in position, so you could have Ava with you?'

'I'm not sure there are many of those going around.'

'You only need one.'

'True.' Emma glanced down at her daughter, who was starting to stir, her little face turning red as she screwed her features up in preparation for one of her ear-splitting howls. 'We'd better get going,' she told Meghan. 'Princess Ava needs her lunch.'

Back at the house she and Meghan fed Ava and Ryan, and then ate their own lunch while the two children played nearby.

'All right, let's do this,' Meghan said, ever practical, and resolutely Emma nodded as her sister pulled her laptop towards her and brought up the webpage for an agency that supplied jobs in the cleaning and hospitality industries.

Emma suppressed a groan as some of the available jobs scrolled by: night-time cleaning at a business park in Newark, janitorial work in a local elementary school.

'I don't…' she began, but Meghan cut her off with a quick shake of her head.

'We'll find something. Something perfect. There's no rush.'

But there *was* a rush, Emma thought glumly, even if she didn't want to say as much to her sister. Meghan might be happy to have her stay indefinitely, but she wasn't always so sure about Pete; as the breadwinner he surely felt the strain on the family finances more than anyone.

And she also knew she wanted more for her life than living in a spare bedroom, changing diapers and dreaming of sleep.

Maybe a poky apartment and a job cleaning school toilets would be it, at least for the interim. If she was careful she could save enough money to go somewhere, maybe travel again, this time with Ava. She pictured herself working her way through Europe, her baby in a backpack, and, while it held a certain quirky charm, she was also realistic enough to acknowledge how difficult that would be.

She could, she supposed, go to stay with her father, but he had been decidedly nonplussed about his unmarried daughter having a baby by a man who was serving a life sentence in prison, and in any case her father was immersed in his work, as he had been since his wife had left him fifteen years ago. He hadn't even seen Ava yet.

No, she needed to do something on her own. Stand on her own two feet, however wobbly she was.

'Let me have a look,' she said, and pulled the laptop towards her. She browsed the jobs for a few more minutes, taking down details, until Ava started crying, ready for her afternoon nap.

'I'll take her upstairs,' Emma said, scooping her protesting daughter into her arms. Ava wrapped her chubby arms around Emma's neck and snuffled against her chest. Her daughter was demanding, even difficult, but she still managed to make Emma's heart melt with love. She'd never regret her decision, even if she ended up cleaning toilets for the rest of her life.

Life could still be an adventure, she told herself as she settled Ava in her crib. It was all about attitude. No matter where she was or what she did, she could still enjoy her daughter, maybe even try photography again. She hadn't picked up her camera since Ava's birth, except to take a few photos of her daughter. The spontaneous, candid moments she'd captured on film all over the world had been hard to find here, and Emma had been too exhausted and overwhelmed to look for them.

She was just coming downstairs, Ava asleep hopefully for at least an hour and Meghan at playgroup with Ryan, when the doorbell sounded. Hoping the noise wouldn't wake Ava, ever a light sleeper, Emma went to answer it.

And stared straight into the face of Larenzo Cavelli. Shock blazed through her as she looked at him; he was thinner, the angles of his cheekbones a little sharper, everything about him a bit harder. A faint scar ran down one cheek, starting by his eyebrow and ending at his jaw. She noticed these changes distantly, her mind dazed and spinning; she could not actually believe it was him. He was here. How? And *why*?

'Larenzo...' she finally managed, her voice a rasp, and his face didn't show so much as a flicker of emotion as he answered.

'Hello, Emma.'

Larenzo gazed at Emma dispassionately; she was clearly shocked to see him, but he felt nothing when he looked at her, except perhaps a twinge of remorse, a flicker of bittersweet memory. That night they'd shared so long ago felt as if it had happened to someone else. It *had* happened to someone else. Eighteen months in prison changed you. For ever.

'May I come in?' He took a step towards her and she drew her breath in sharply, one hand fluttering to her throat.

'Don't—' she began, and he stilled. She almost looked afraid. Afraid of him.

'Do you think I'm going to hurt you?' he asked, wondering why he was surprised. Everyone else had believed the worst of him. Why shouldn't she?

Emma's eyes widened, her hand still at her throat. 'I don't—I don't know. Why are you here, Larenzo?'

Her voice wavered; she really was afraid. She thought

he was *dangerous*. It should have occurred to him before, of course. He'd thought all of his naive delusions about humanity had been stripped away, but clearly he'd clung to this last one. The memory of his one night with Emma had sustained him through prison. He didn't like having it tarnished now.

'I'm here,' he finally said, his voice cool, 'because I felt I owed you something.'

'You don't.'

'Considering your employment with me ended so abruptly, I thought you deserved some recompense,' he continued as if she hadn't spoken.

'Recompense...'

He stepped past her and dropped the envelope with the bank draft onto the hall table. 'Six months' pay. I thought you should have it.'

She stared at the envelope with something like revulsion. 'I don't want your money,' she said in a low voice. 'I don't want anything from you.'

'This money was honestly earned,' Larenzo informed her coldly. 'I can promise you that.'

'Why should I believe anything you say?' she shot back. 'How are you even *here*? The judge gave you life in prison—'

'I was released last week. Clearly you don't read the papers.'

'No, I...' She licked her lips, her gaze still wide. 'I haven't had time.'

'Well, if you'd read them,' Larenzo said, his voice coming out in a cold drawl, 'you would have known that all the charges against me were dropped.'

'They were?' She looked bewildered, her gaze darting between him and the stairs. Was she thinking of making a run for it, barricading herself in a bedroom? Did she really think he was going to *hurt* her? He was caught between fury and despair at the thought, and then he blanked out both emotions. He might have held onto the memory of Emma through prison, and their night together might have compelled him to find her now, but he didn't actually feel anything for her. He couldn't feel anything at all.

'Yes, they were. Otherwise I wouldn't be here. Obviously. Unless you thought I'd escaped?' He arched an eyebrow, smiled as if this were all so very amusing. 'Stage-managed some sort of breakout?'

'I…I don't know what I think.' She walked slowly past him, to the small sitting room at the front of the house. Larenzo followed her, watched as she sank onto the sofa, her head in her hands.

'How did you find me here?' she asked after a long, silent moment, her head still bowed.

'This was the address you gave on your employment application.'

She glanced up at him, her eyes widening once more. 'And you came all the way to America to give me six months' pay? If you really possessed such a conscience to see me adequately *recompensed*, you could have just deposited it in my bank account. You should have my details from when I was in your employment.'

Larenzo's mouth tightened. 'I was in America anyway.' She shook her head slowly, still dazed. Larenzo let his gaze rove over her, remembering her golden skin, her laughing eyes that looked so serious and dark now. She looked different, he realised. More womanly. She must have gained a little weight, and yet it suited her. Her breasts were fuller under the soft pink sweater she wore, and her face was a bit rounder. Her skin was as golden as he'd remembered, her golden-brown hair wavy and tousled about her face. His golden girl. What a joke.

'Why are you in America?' she asked and Larenzo snapped his gaze away from her.

'I'm relocating to New York.'

'New York—'

'Is that a problem?' he enquired coolly. 'I only came here to give you your pay.'

'I know, but…' She glanced up towards the stairs once more, and Larenzo's gaze narrowed. That was the second time she'd done that. What was upstairs? Was Emma hiding something from him? God knew he'd learned to become suspicious of everyone and everything. Trust was a concept he no longer even remotely considered.

'It doesn't matter,' she said quickly, as if coming to a decision. She rose from the sofa. 'Thank you for the six months' pay. That was…kind of you, considering.'

'Considering?' he repeated, his gaze narrowing. 'Considering what?'

Colour washed Emma's cheeks. 'Just the situation…'

'You mean considering I'm a criminal? Is that what you mean, Emma?' He didn't know why he was pushing her, only that he was. That he wanted her to say it, admit what she thought of him. Perhaps it would be like lancing a wound.

Emma lifted her chin, her eyes flashing in challenge. 'And what if it was?'

'I thought you knew me better than that.'

'I didn't know you at all, Larenzo. You were my employer, and I saw you a few times. We never even had a proper conversation before—' She stopped abruptly, the colour deepening in her cheeks as she looked away.

'Before what?' he demanded, his voice low and insistent. He was punishing himself as much as her by raking this all up, bringing the memories he'd tormented himself with to the fore. 'Before I made love to you? Before you wrapped your legs around my waist and—'

'Don't.' The single word came out in a suffocated whisper. 'Don't remind me.'

Larenzo's lip curled. 'You don't want to remember?'

'Of course I don't.' She glared at him, her golden-green eyes full of misery. 'I don't know why you were released from prison, Larenzo, or why the charges against you were dropped, but I just want you out of my life.' She pressed her lips together as she held his stare. 'I trust that won't be an issue.'

'An issue?' he repeated. Fury beat through his veins, fired his blood. 'I came here as a matter of courtesy. Clearly the effort was wasted.'

'I think it's best if you go now.'

'Fine.' He nodded curtly and curled his hands into fists at his sides, not trusting himself not to grab her by the shoulders and demand to know what he'd ever done to make her think he was a mobster. A Mafioso. *Mio Dio*, how could everyone he'd ever known have judged him so harshly and completely?

Because the evidence had been there, thanks to Bertrano. Because he'd confessed, even if he'd felt he had no choice.

She held his gaze, her chin still lifted, her shoulders thrown back, standing proud and defiant even though he knew she was afraid. Of him.

He opened his mouth to say something of his innocence, but then he closed it. Why claim something she would never believe? 'Goodbye,' he said instead, and turned towards the hallway.

A child's cry suddenly echoed from upstairs. From the corner of his eye he saw Emma freeze, her face drain of colour. He wouldn't have thought anything of the cry, considering he knew Emma was living with her sister and her family. And yet...

The child cried again, the plaintive wail of a baby. Emma didn't move. Neither did Larenzo. Every sense he had was on alert, although for what he could not say.

'Aren't you going to go to the child?' he asked, his voice deliberately mild as the baby continued to cry, the sobs becoming louder and more urgent.

Emma swallowed, and he watched the workings of her slender throat. 'I will. When you leave.'

He gazed at her for a taut moment, saw how her eyes had become huge golden pools in a face drained of colour. 'Is it your sister's child? Why is she not going to fetch the *bambino*?'

'She's not here.' Emma licked her lips, and Larenzo thought he saw panic in that wide gaze. 'Please, Larenzo. Just go.'

'I will.' He cocked his head towards the stairs. 'But maybe you should get the *bambino* first.'

'No.' The word came out like a gunshot, fast and loud. Larenzo raised his eyebrows. Emma stared him down. 'I told you, I don't want you here. Now go.' Her voice rose in a raggedy edge of terror, and Larenzo took a step towards her.

'What are you hiding from me, Emma?'

'Nothing—' But it sounded feeble. He took another step towards her.

'Tell me the truth. You're hiding something. I don't know what it could be, but—'

'What do you think I'm hiding from you?' she cut him off scornfully. She nodded towards the stairs. 'A *baby*?'

The words hung there, seeming to echo through the sudden silence of the room. Larenzo stared at her, saw how bloodless her lips were as they parted soundlessly.

The thought hadn't fully formed in his mind until she'd said the words. He'd sensed she was hiding something, had felt her panic and fear, had heard the baby cry...

And yet it hadn't all come together for him. But it did now, crystallising with shocking clarity, and without a word for her he turned from the room and bounded up the stairs.

'Larenzo—' She hurried after him, one arm flung towards him in desperate supplication. 'Larenzo, please, don't—'

He could hear the child crying, the voice pitiful and plaintive. 'Mama. Mama.'

'Please,' she said again, choking on the word, and Larenzo ignored her.

Mama. Mama.

He threw open the door and came to a complete and stunned halt as he saw the baby standing in her crib, chubby fists gripping the rail, cherubic face screwed up and wet with tears.

Emma came into the room behind him, breathing hard, and the baby flung her arms out towards her. 'Mama.'

And Larenzo knew. He would have known just by looking at the child, with her ink-dark hair and large grey eyes, the cleft in her chin. He turned to Emma, who was gazing at him with undisguised panic.

'When,' he asked in a low, deadly voice, 'were you going to tell me about my child?'

CHAPTER FIVE

EMMA STARED AT Larenzo and saw the fury blazing in his gaze. Why, oh, why had she said that about hiding a baby? She'd meant to be bold, to pour scorn on the presumption, but she'd seen how she'd given him the idea instead. She'd told him about Ava.

Now she sagged against the doorway, completely at a loss as to what to do or say. Larenzo took a step towards her, his hands balled into fists.

'So this is why you were so desperate for me to leave—'

'Mama,' Ava called, her arms still outstretched, and Emma straightened and walked swiftly towards her daughter, scooping her up in her arms, and pressed her cheek against Ava's downy hair.

'Please,' she murmured to Larenzo. 'Let me settle her and then we'll talk.' Although what she could tell him, she had no idea. She'd never imagined this happening, ever. She'd never expected even to see Larenzo again.

Ava continued to snuffle against her chest and Emma soothed her mindlessly, her mind spinning in futile circles. She settled her back in the cot as Larenzo waited in the hall and hoped her daughter might drift off to sleep once more. She'd slept for only twenty minutes, which unfortunately wasn't that uncommon, but on a good day Emma could count on an hour.

Quietly she slipped out of the room and closed the door. Larenzo stood there, arms folded, eyebrows raised. He opened his mouth to speak but Emma shook her head and pressed a finger to her lips, cocking her head to indicate he should follow her downstairs.

In the kitchen she wiped the counters and tidied up the last of the lunch dishes, needing to keep busy, to keep from thinking how on earth she was going to handle this. Handle *him*. Larenzo watched her, one powerful shoulder propped against the doorway, everything about him arrogant, assured and definitely intimidating. She couldn't *handle* this man at all.

'You do not deny she's mine,' he said finally, and Emma shook her head.

'How can I? She looks just like you.'

'Yes.' He raked a hand through his hair, his gaze shuttered and distant as he shook his head slowly. 'We didn't use birth control.'

'No.'

'I never even thought…'

'Nor did I. Obviously.'

'She must have put a dent in your plans,' he said after a moment, his voice turning sharp, and Emma narrowed her eyes.

'What do you mean?'

'All your travel plans. You told me you liked to move around. Itchy feet, you said.'

She was surprised and weirdly gratified that he'd remembered what she'd said, but also piqued that he was throwing it back in her face now. 'That changed when I became pregnant.'

'You never considered a termination?'

Her mouth dropped open. 'Is that what you would have preferred? Because—'

'No.' He shook his head, one swift, violent movement. '*No*. But I could understand if—'

She let out a rush of breath. 'I thought of it at first, I

suppose, but never seriously. I never thought I wanted a husband or children, but I couldn't…she was a part of me.' A lump formed in her throat and resolutely she swallowed past it. 'I loved her even before she was born.'

'And you've been living here since her birth?' His gaze moved around the small kitchen, and Emma prickled.

'My sister has been very kind—'

'Yes, of course. But what about your father? Is he still in Budapest?'

So he remembered that too. 'Yes, he is, but I wanted to be here. And frankly he wasn't thrilled about me being pregnant, unmarried, and the father—'

'In prison,' he finished flatly, and Emma nodded.

'In any case, we're fine here.'

'But you can't stay here for ever.'

'Meghan is happy for us to stay,' Emma shot back. She wasn't about to admit to Larenzo that she might need to move out. 'Anyway, I don't see how this concerns you, Larenzo—'

'Are you serious?' He cut her off, his voice harsh. 'She's my daughter.' He paused, struggling to control his emotions while Emma watched in apprehension. 'What's her name?' he finally asked.

She hesitated, reluctant to part with even that much information. What if Larenzo wanted to be a part of Ava's life, of their lives? How on earth could she cope with that?

'Emma, I deserve to know her name!' His voice came out raggedly, and with a shaft of guilt Emma remembered how he'd told her about his childhood in Palermo, how he'd never had a real family. And with that came other memories of their night together, tender ones that she'd tried to keep herself from remembering. They tumbled through her mind in a bittersweet rush of poignant longing and she was helpless against it. No matter what Larenzo had done, she'd loved this man. For a night.

'Ava,' she said quietly.

'Ava,' he repeated, and she closed her eyes against the wonder she heard in his voice. 'How old is she?'

'Ten months. She was born on Christmas Eve.'

'Would you have ever told me about her?' he asked after a moment.

She opened her eyes and stared at him helplessly. 'Larenzo, you were in *prison*. You were convicted of about a thousand charges all related to being in the Mafia. How could I tell you?'

He gazed back steadily, unmoved by her argument. 'The charges were dropped.'

'I didn't know that. And I still don't know why they were dropped—'

'You still think I'm guilty?' he cut her off, his voice hard.

'I don't *know*,' she cried. 'Larenzo, you have to understand how it was for me. The day you were arrested... those men...'

Even now, a year and a half later, the memory of that night made shame and fear roil through her. 'It was horrible. And then I spent the whole day in the anti-Mafia headquarters in Palermo while they told me you were involved in the Mafia, how they had all this evidence...what was I supposed to believe?'

'Me. You could have believed me.'

'You confessed,' she shot back. 'I read it in the papers. So I did believe you.'

He pressed his lips together, his gaze narrowed and hard. 'Of course you did.'

'And yet you still seem to think I should have believed in your innocence.'

He didn't answer, and Emma bit her lip. She felt cold inside, so terribly cold. For a year and a half she'd been so certain of Larenzo's guilt, and yet now, having seen him only for a few minutes, she felt doubt creep in along with the bittersweet memories. Who was the real man—the Mafia monster or the one she'd made love to?

'But just now,' he finally said. 'You wanted me to leave. Even now, when you knew the charges had been dropped, that I was free, you were trying to keep me from my child.'

'Because as far as I know, you're still a dangerous man,' Emma retorted. Larenzo's eyes narrowed and she almost took a step back. Yet even now she realised she wasn't actually afraid of him. She didn't think he'd hurt her, but...

What was she afraid of, then? Because she certainly felt the cold claws of terror digging into her soul, icing over her mind. 'Even if you are innocent of the charges they laid against you,' she continued more calmly, 'you must have Mafia connections, something that made the police—'

'Not in the way you think,' he bit out, and Emma just shook her head, overwhelmed with too many terrible emotions to respond. 'I am a free man,' Larenzo said in a low voice. 'And you can't keep me from my daughter.'

Emma pressed her hand to her forehead. 'We can't talk about this now,' she said. 'My sister will be home in a few minutes, and Ava is going to wake up soon. I never even expected to see you again, Larenzo. Having you turn up out of the blue...' She shook her head. 'It's a lot to take in.'

'I understand,' he answered levelly. 'But know this. I *will* be back, and I will see Ava again. Don't think for a moment you can keep me from her.'

His mouth compressed and his eyes flashed silver and Emma's stomach did a sickening little flip. She had no idea what to think, to believe.

'We'll talk,' she managed. 'Soon.'

Larenzo held her gaze for an endless, agonising moment, and then with one swift nod he turned and left the room. Emma heard the click of the front door closing and she sagged against the kitchen counter, utterly emotionally spent.

'Emma?' A minute later her sister's voice, lilting with curiosity, floated down the hall. 'Who was that leaving the house?'

Emma straightened as her sister came into the kitchen with Ryan in tow, her eyebrows raised, a smile playing about her mouth. 'Do you have a secret admirer?'

'Hardly.' Emma took a deep breath. 'That was Larenzo Cavelli.'

'What?' The smile slid clear off Meghan's face and numbly Emma explained the events of the last hour. Ava woke up just as she was finishing and she hurried upstairs, grateful for a moment to collect her thoughts, few as she had.

'Mama.' Ava wound her arms around her neck as Emma closed her eyes and breathed in her daughter's scent, baby powder with a hint of the banana she'd eaten for lunch. Ava pressed her cheek against Emma's chest, letting out a snuggly sigh, and Emma's heart gave a painful squeeze. She would do anything for Ava. Anything to keep her safe... even if it meant keeping her from her father.

Yet how could she do that? And should she, if Larenzo were really innocent?

'Ava, sweetheart,' she whispered against the baby's silky hair. 'What are we going to do?'

She stayed upstairs for a few moments, cuddling Ava and then changing her diaper, wanting to put off the conversation she'd have to have with Meghan. Wanting to put off thinking about Larenzo Cavelli and what she was going to do.

Yet even in the dim quiet of her and Ava's bedroom, memories invaded. Memories not of Larenzo as he'd been only moments ago, coldly angry, clearly ruthless, but as he'd been the night their daughter had been conceived. The tenderness he'd shown, as well as the despair. That sorrow and resignation she'd felt in him, had yearned to take away, and the aching, reverent gentleness of his touch…

Remembering that man made all the certainties she'd cultivated over the last eighteen months scatter like ash.

What if he wasn't guilty?

But what if he is?

'Emma?' Meghan's voice was sharp with concern as she called up the stairs. 'Are you coming down?'

'Yes, I'll be there in a moment.' Taking a deep breath, Emma settled Ava on her hip and headed downstairs. Ryan was playing in the playroom adjoining the kitchen and she put Ava on the floor with him, scattering a few blocks and soft toys around. Knowing her daughter as she did, Ava would throw all the toys across the room and then try to grab the trains Ryan was playing with. Her daughter knew what she wanted…just like her father.

'I can't believe Larenzo Cavelli came here,' Meghan said, her voice hollow with shock. She filled up the kettle, shaking her head slowly. 'How did he even know…?'

'The address was on my employment application.'

'And he wants to see Ava?'

'I don't know what he wants exactly, but he told me I couldn't keep him from his daughter.'

Meghan was silent for a moment, her face pale with strain. 'So do you think he is innocent, if the charges were dropped?' she asked and Emma bit her lip.

'I don't know anything any more, Meghan. For a year and a half I thought I knew the truth. I didn't like it, of course, and at times I couldn't believe it, but I thought I *knew.*'

'And now you think you didn't?' Meghan sounded sceptical, and rightly so. How could Emma take anything Larenzo said at face value?

'I don't know. But I suppose I should find out why the

charges against him were dropped.' She reached for the laptop they'd left lying out on the kitchen counter, the browser still on the employment agency's listings. Had it only been a couple of hours ago she'd been worried about what sort of menial job she'd take? It almost seemed laughable.

Quickly Emma typed in the browser's search engine *Larenzo Cavelli charges dropped*. Hundreds of results came up within seconds. She clicked on the first one, and began to read the news article.

All charges have been dropped against convicted felon Larenzo Cavelli when new evidence came to light that business partner Bertrano Raguso was in fact behind the illegal activities...

Meghan peered at the article over her shoulder. 'Do you think it's true?' she asked in a low voice.

'I have no idea.' Emma scanned the rest of the article, skimming over the terrible list of Larenzo's alleged crimes that she'd read in the paper once already. Once had definitely been enough.

'If his business partner really was guilty, why would Larenzo confess?' Meghan asked as she nibbled her lip.

'I don't know.' Emma gazed at the photograph of Bertrano Raguso, a silver-haired man in his sixties, his face set into haggard lines. 'But if they let Larenzo go...'

'But they'd have to, if they have another confession.'

'I don't know if it's that simple.' Emma rubbed her forehead, felt the beginnings of a headache. From the playroom she heard the clatter of blocks being flung across the room, and then Ryan's yowl as one connected with his head. 'I need to see to Ava,' she said. 'I'll have to think about this later. About what I'm going to do.'

'You should consult a lawyer—'

Emma flinched at the thought. She didn't want to get involved in some messy, drawn-out custody battle that would no doubt be splashed across the newspapers, due to Larenzo's notoriety. But what if the alternative was granting him access to Ava? Exposing her to God only knew what kind of danger?

Unless he really was innocent…but how could he not have known about his partner's activities? And why would he have confessed?

Emma let out a tired sigh. Her mind was racing in circles and she knew she had no answers now. 'He might not actually want to be involved with Ava,' she said, trying to convince herself as much as her sister. 'He might just want to see her once…'

'You need to be prepared,' Meghan answered swiftly. 'Emma, the man is—'

'We don't know what he is.'

'Can you really doubt—?'

'I told you, I don't *know*.' And yet if there was any chance Larenzo was guilty, any chance of putting Ava in danger…

'I'll talk to a lawyer,' Emma said. 'I should do that much, at least. Just…just in case.'

Ava and Ryan had both started crying and so Emma scooped her daughter up and distracted her with a few board books before rejoining Meghan at the laptop. Her sister had typed custody lawyers into the search box, and, with her heart thudding sickly and her head still spinning from all that had happened in such a short span of time, Emma watched the results come up, and then she reached for her phone.

CHAPTER SIX

Nervously Emma smoothed her hair, straightened her skirt, and then opened the door to the restaurant where she was meeting Larenzo. It had been three endless days since he'd shown up at her sister's house, and Emma had almost started hoping that Larenzo had decided to leave them alone. Yet tangled up in that hope had been an absurd disappointment that he might have given up so easily.

She'd spoken to a lawyer two days ago, and he'd told her that since the charges against Larenzo had been dropped, he would most certainly have a legal right to see Ava. Access could be limited or denied if a court decided there was any danger to her daughter, but it was by no means clear cut or simple.

The next day Larenzo had called and Emma's heart had actually lifted at the sound of his voice. They'd set up a meeting over dinner at a local restaurant, and Emma knew she had no idea what she wanted from this meeting. Her emotions and thoughts were all over the place, and no matter how she tried to order them they raced off in all directions as soon as she thought of Larenzo, remembered how he'd once been with her.

The atmosphere, she saw as she came into the restaurant, was elegant and understated, candlelight flickering over snowy white tablecloths. It almost seemed romantic, which didn't help her disordered thoughts, her clamouring emotions. No matter what she and Larenzo decided about Ava, romance had no place in their lives any more.

She gave her name to the *maître d'* and he showed her to a table in the back, set in a private alcove. Larenzo was already seated, and he rose as she approached. He wore a white button-down shirt and plain grey trousers, and yet he still seemed bigger and darker and more magnetic than any other person in the room.

Once, only once, she'd allowed herself to be drawn by that magnetic force. Now she knew she needed to be immune. To stay strong.

Emma sat down across from him, busying herself with putting her napkin in her lap as Larenzo settled back into his seat, seeming to take up too much space, too much air. Why had it become hard to breathe?

'Thank you for coming,' he said.

Emma took a deep breath, letting the air fill her lungs. 'I didn't really have much choice, did I?'

He pressed his lips together and Emma could almost feel the tension crackle between them. 'This doesn't have to be unpleasant, Emma.'

'And how do you figure that?' she shot back. She'd wanted to stay calm for this meeting but already her composure was cracking, revealing the fear and uncertainty underneath. 'I'm here to discuss a man with Mafia connections being involved with my daughter—'

'*My* daughter,' Larenzo cut across her, his voice low and intense. 'She's my daughter too. Never forget that.'

'Unfortunately, I won't.'

He sat back in his chair, his fingers laced together as he gazed at her. 'Do you hate me?' he asked, as if it was a matter of academic interest, and Emma could only stare at him, flummoxed. *Where had that come from?* 'Because,' he continued, 'you seem as if you hate me.'

'I...' She searched for words, disconcerted by how

much his question had unsettled her. 'I don't hate you,' she said finally. 'I don't feel anything for you.' Which was a bold-faced lie. She didn't know what she felt for Larenzo Cavelli, but it was definitely something. 'But I love my daughter,' she continued shakily, 'and I want to protect her—'

'And you think I don't want that?'

'I don't know what to think about you, Larenzo. I have no idea what to believe.'

'How about the truth?'

'Which is?' she demanded, her voice rising. 'Eighteen months ago you confessed to a long, sordid list of crimes. A week ago, your business partner was convicted of those same crimes, thanks to new evidence, but what am I meant to believe? How on earth do you expect me to trust you?'

Larenzo expelled a long, low breath. 'I don't,' he said flatly. 'You can't trust anyone in this world. That's one thing I've come to realise.'

'Why did you confess if you weren't guilty?'

He pressed his lips together as he flicked his gaze away. 'Because there was overwhelming evidence to convict me.'

'How?'

'Look, I don't want to get into all that now. I left that life behind—'

'And I'm supposed to just *accept* that?'

Larenzo leaned forward, his gaze glittering. 'Emma, do you honestly think I'd put my own child in danger? Do you think I'd be here if I thought I'd be hurting Ava?'

Emma bit her lip. She didn't think that, but she was still afraid. Still reluctant to relinquish control, to let Larenzo into Ava's life. Into her life, in any way at all, and with a jolt she realised it wasn't just because of his possible criminal connections. It was because this man affected her. And she was afraid to let him do that again.

Larenzo leaned back in his chair. 'I left Italy for good

and severed all ties to Cavelli Enterprises. Bertrano Raguso is in prison for the crimes he committed. That is all
you need to know.'

'Why New York?' Emma asked. The waiter came forward to take their order, and she gazed blindly at the menu.
She had no appetite at all. Finally she picked a relatively
plain chicken dish, and Larenzo ordered for himself, before
they were left alone again and he answered her question.

'I wanted a new start. Cavelli Enterprises had no hold-
ings in America.'

'What's happened to Cavelli Enterprises?'

'Its assets were seized by the government. Everything's
frozen while the investigation continues.'

'So even though there was evidence…?'

Larenzo's mouth hardened into a flat line. 'Bertrano is
claiming he is innocent, but the evidence is incontrovertible.' His mouth twisted. 'In the meantime the company
will most likely be liquidated, and its remaining assets
distributed to shareholders.' He spoke dispassionately, as
if it was a matter of indifference to him. Emma searched
his face, saw a hardness underneath his bland expression
that she didn't think had been there before.

'Were you close to him? This Raguso?'

Larenzo hesitated, one hand resting flat on the tabletop.
'A bit,' he finally said.

'And do you think he did it?'

'I know he did.' He shifted in his chair, his gaze arrow-
ing in on her. 'While I was in prison, my staff investigated
and found proof of his guilt. But enough talk of what is
past. It's the future that concerns me.'

'The past is important, Larenzo—'

'I've told you all you need to know,' he cut across her.
'I want to talk about Ava.'

She knew it was coming, and yet she still resisted.
'What about her?'

For a second his face softened, his mouth curving into something almost like a smile and just that little look made Emma start to melt. 'What is she like? From the little I saw of her already, it seems like she knows her own mind.'

'She does. She's a force to be reckoned with, that's for sure.'

'Her strength will serve her well later in life.'

'So I keep telling myself.' To her shock Emma realised she was smiling, and Larenzo was actually smiling back.

'I want to see her,' Larenzo said firmly, and Emma took a deep breath.

'There's a playground near the house—'

Larenzo's expression darkened, his eyes flashing silver fire. 'A playground? Do you think you can fob me off with an hour or two at a local park?'

'It's a start, Larenzo—'

'I've missed the first ten months of my daughter's life. I want to spend time with her, Emma. Real time. Not be introduced to her as if I'm some stranger in a park playground.'

Emma stared down at the table, conscious of how quickly Larenzo had torn apart her suggestion. She'd wanted to stage-manage his entrance into Ava's life, to exert some control over the proceedings, and hopefully to limit them. She should have known Larenzo wouldn't let her do that. He was a man who was in control. Always.

'Very well.' She took a deep, even breath and let it out slowly. 'What do you suggest?'

'I've taken an apartment in New York, and it has plenty of room. I suggest you and Ava move there with me.'

Emma gaped at him, stunned into silence for a few seconds. 'You want me to move in with you?' she finally managed, her voice ending in something close to a squeak.

'I'm not suggesting we have some sort of relationship,' Larenzo clarified coolly. 'I have no interest in that. But I want to see my daughter as much as possible, and be a real presence in her life. Your current living arrangements are neither sustainable nor suitable.' He lifted one powerful shoulder in a shrug. 'The answer seems obvious.'

'To you, maybe.' Emma nearly choked. She shook her head and reached for her glass of water. She'd never expected Larenzo to suggest something like this. To live with him...*to be that near to temptation*...

'I don't see an alternative,' Larenzo answered. 'I want unlimited access to my daughter—'

'Unlimited? Larenzo, be reasonable—' At the very most she'd thought she'd have to have some kind of joint custody arrangement with Larenzo. But this?

This was dangerous. Impossible. *Tempting*...

'I don't really see what the problem is,' Larenzo replied calmly. 'Surely you agree it's better for Ava to have two interested and loving parents in her life?'

Emma swallowed. 'Yes, but that doesn't mean we have to live together—'

'What, precisely, do you object to?' Larenzo asked. His voice had gone quiet, dangerously so. 'You'll have your own room, your own bathroom, and your quarters will be far more comfortable than they are currently.'

Emma stared at him helplessly. He made it all sound so simple, and yet it wasn't. It couldn't be. 'Everything's changed so quickly,' she finally said. 'I can't process it all—'

'Then take your time,' Larenzo answered. 'You have until tomorrow.'

'*Tomorrow*—'

'I want to see my daughter, Emma.'

'I know you do.' Except she hadn't expected Larenzo to feel this strongly, this *fiercely*, about his role as a father. That he did surprised her, but she realised she couldn't resent it. She knew what it was like to have a parent who chose a life without you. Who walked away from her child.

Despite all the obstacles, all the unknowns, she realised she was, amazingly, glad Larenzo wanted to be involved... even if she was scared about what it meant.

'I can't just *live* with you,' she finally burst out.

Larenzo arched an eyebrow, all arrogant assurance. 'Why not?'

'Because...because...' Because she was afraid of this man, and it had nothing to do with any criminal connections. She was afraid of his power over her, her need for him. 'I need to have my own life, Larenzo. I was planning on moving out of my sister's house for that reason. I'm twenty-seven years old and I'm not going to freeload off people for ever.'

'So this is a question of money?'

'Not just money,' she returned. 'It's about independence and autonomy. I need to be my own person—'

'And you can't do that living in my apartment?' He made her feel ridiculous, and yet she *couldn't* just fall in with his plans, fit into his life without having one of her own.

'I can't believe I'm even thinking of moving in with you,' she said, shaking her head slowly.

'It makes sense.'

Emma didn't answer. It *did* make a certain kind of bizarre sense, which both aggravated and alarmed her. Three days ago she'd thought Larenzo Cavelli would spend his life in prison. Two days ago she would have fought tooth and nail to keep him out of her daughter's life.

And now she was thinking of living with him? She pressed her fingers to her temples and closed her eyes. 'This is so crazy.'

'Maybe so,' Larenzo agreed with a shrug, 'but it's our reality. I won't take no for an answer, Emma.'

She opened her eyes and stared at him, saw that coldness in his eyes, the hint of how hard he could be. 'What would you do if I did say no, Larenzo?'

'It won't come to that.'

'But if it did?'

He hesitated, then stated flatly, 'I'd sue for custody.'

Emma jerked back, appalled. 'So this is basically blackmail.'

'No.'

'Then what would you call it? "Live with me or I'll take your child." That's what you're saying, Larenzo.'

'And what are you saying?' he answered, a hint of anger in his voice. '"You're my child's father and I don't want you involved in her life," even though you know I am innocent.'

'I didn't say that—'

'You've been saying that for ten months, Emma.'

She took a deep breath. Arguing would get them nowhere. 'Things have changed, Larenzo. I recognise that. But you can't expect me to fall in with your plans without a second's thought—'

'I haven't. I told you, you have until tomorrow.'

'Well, thanks for that,' she answered sarcastically. There was no reasoning with this man. No swaying him. So what was she going to do?

The waiter came with their meals, giving Emma a few minutes' respite from the intensity of their conversation.

She picked at her chicken, her gaze lowered; she didn't think she could swallow a single mouthful. Then, to her shock, she felt Larenzo's hand on her own, his palm warm and strong just as it had been a year and a half ago, when he'd covered her hand with his own and she'd felt, for a moment, closer to this man than anyone else on earth.

'Why are you fighting this, Emma?' he asked quietly, and his voice was as sorrowful as it had been back on that night. His touch and his words catapulted her to that time when she'd felt so much for this man, had longed to comfort him. Had seen tenderness and understanding in his eyes, had felt it in his arms.

A lump rose in her throat and she blinked rapidly, swallowed past it. 'I don't know,' she whispered, and it sounded like a confession.

'I want to be with Ava. I never had a family of my own, except...' He stopped, his voice choking, and shook his head. 'I don't want this to be acrimonious, God knows. I want to get to know my daughter and love her. Please let me do that.'

She gazed up at him, saw the sincerity and emotion in his eyes, and felt her last reservations melt away. She believed Larenzo. She believed he was innocent, but, more importantly, she believed he wanted what was best for Ava.

She only hoped it was best for her too.

CHAPTER SEVEN

'I CAN'T BELIEVE you're doing this.'

Meghan stood behind Emma as she finished packing her suitcases—just one for her and one for Ava, really not much at all to bring to her new home. Her new life.

'It makes sense, Meghan,' she said, which was what Larenzo had said to her last night. Last night she'd lain in bed, staring at the ceiling, unable to sleep as she'd thought about her future, when she'd heard Meghan's and Pete's raised voices downstairs, and had known they were talking about her. She'd crept to the top of the stairs, everything in her stilling as Pete had declared,

'She can't stay here any longer, Meghan. I've been patient, God knows, but two more mouths to feed is expensive, and if this Cavelli character has connections to—'

'He was cleared of all charges,' Meghan had cut across her husband.

'Even so—'

'She doesn't have anywhere else to go, Pete.'

'Then she needs to find somewhere,' Pete had answered grimly, and Emma had crept back to her bed.

Pete was right. She couldn't stay here any longer, for too many reasons. And she no longer wanted to deny Larenzo access to his daughter, even if she was afraid of what that might mean. Not for Ava, but for her.

'You could stay here,' Meghan persisted, and Emma met her sister's eye in the mirror hanging over the bureau.

'You know I couldn't,' she said quietly, and Meghan flushed and looked away.

'I was afraid you might have heard that conversation—'

'Pete's right, Meghan.'

Meghan bit her lip. 'I like having you here, Emma. You've been away for so long—'

'New York City isn't that far. I'll visit lots, I promise.'

'I'll worry. I still don't trust Cavelli. Even if he was cleared of charges...'

'What happened to innocent until proven guilty?' Emma asked lightly. 'I trust him, Meghan, and I know he wouldn't hurt his daughter.' She paused, her gaze on the clothes she was folding. 'He was good to me when I worked for him.' She bit her lip as a pang of bittersweet longing assailed her. 'He was very good to me.'

'But can you really trust him?' Meghan persisted, and Emma thought of what he'd said last night at dinner. *You can't trust anyone in this world. That's one thing I've come to realise.* When had he realised that? When he was a child at the orphanage, or when he'd been sent to a prison for crimes he might not have committed? A lifetime of betrayal, perhaps, and yet there was still so much she didn't understand.

'Yes, I can,' she answered Meghan. 'At least when it comes to Ava.'

Twenty minutes later Larenzo pulled up in front of Meghan's house in a luxury sedan, a car seat already installed in the centre of the back seat. He loaded the two suitcases in the boot, glancing at Emma.

'That's all you have?'

'I travel light.'

'But Ava—'

'The crib and changing table and things belonged to Meghan. They're hoping for another baby someday, so...'

'You don't need to worry about any of that,' Larenzo said. 'I've taken care of it.'

'Okay,' she murmured, and Larenzo held out his arms for Ava.

'May I?'

Wordlessly she nodded and handed him their daughter. He held her awkwardly, clearly not used to the chubby bundle of arms and legs that was an almost toddler. 'Hello, sweetheart,' he murmured, smiling into Ava's inquisitive face. She gurgled and grabbed his chin in her chubby fists and Larenzo laughed, the sound rusty and surprising and also achingly wonderful. Emma realised she hadn't heard Larenzo laugh before. It reminded her of the photo she'd shown him, back in Sicily; it was a sound of joy. Suddenly she felt almost near tears. She swallowed hard and watched as Larenzo buckled Ava into her car seat; he fiddled with the straps and with a laugh that managed to clear the tears away Emma helped him.

'These things are impossible,' she said. 'Especially when Ava is resisting.' She buckled the straps over Ava's tummy, conscious of Larenzo standing so close to her, his head bent near hears. She closed her eyes, willed herself to develop a little strength. A lot of resistance. Otherwise she was going to have way too many difficult moments with Larenzo. 'There.' She patted the buckled straps and straightened, her breast brushing against Larenzo's arm as she did so. Desire shot through her veins and she quickly turned away and got in the car, deeply unsettled by her own reaction to this man who had catapulted so suddenly back into her life.

Larenzo started the car; Emma was in the passenger seat, her face turned towards the window. He had no idea what she was thinking, if she still resented his presence in Ava's life.

He'd told Emma he didn't trust anyone, and, while that

was true, he was conscious of how he was asking her to trust him with the most precious thing of all: their child. But he also knew he couldn't change who he was, who he'd become. Trust was now an alien concept, and always would be. Even so, he could appreciate what Emma was doing.

'Thank you,' he said abruptly, and she turned to him warily.

'For what?' she asked and he cleared his throat.

'For agreeing to live with me.'

'When the alternative is having you sue me for custody,' she answered after a moment, 'there wasn't really any question, was there?'

Guilt needled him at the realisation of how effectively he'd blackmailed her. Was he really any better than Bertrano, when he resorted to such tactics? And yet Emma would have denied him his own flesh and blood, the child he'd never expected to have, the family he'd longed for since he was a child himself.

'Well,' he said after a moment, 'I'm still grateful.' Emma did not reply.

They drove in silence for the entire hour's journey into the city; Ava babbled and gurgled in the back seat, and by the time they approached the Lincoln Tunnel she was tired of the car and began to protest, straining against the straps of her car seat.

Emma tried to distract her with a few toys and then a rice cake, all of which entertained Ava for about three seconds before she hurled each item to the floor.

'Sorry,' Emma said as she glanced down at the floor of the back seat. 'You have a sea of rice cake crumbs down there.'

'It doesn't matter.'

'Are you sure you're prepared for this?' she asked as Ava drummed her heels against the seat. 'Ava is a force to be reckoned with.'

'So I can see—and hear,' Larenzo answered dryly. 'I don't know if I'm prepared. But I'm willing to take it on.' She need never doubt him in that.

'Did you ever want children?' Emma asked. 'I mean, before...'

'Before I went to prison?' Larenzo filled in flatly. 'I don't know if I really thought of it. I didn't have time for a relationship.'

'Yet you've certainly had your share of women.'

His mouth tightened as he slid her a sideways glance. She'd spoken without expression, and he had no idea what she thought of that aspect of his past. Not that it actually mattered, since there would never be anything like that between them. He had nothing to offer Emma, or anyone. Not in that way. 'I don't deny it,' he said after a moment.

'Having a baby in your apartment, as well as her mother, might cramp your style a bit.'

Larenzo shook his head. 'I've no interest in anything like that any more.'

Emma raised her eyebrows, clearly sceptical. 'Larenzo, you're what? In your mid-thirties? Surely you're going to want a woman again.'

Want a woman. The last woman he'd been with had been Emma, and he'd wanted her almost unbearably. Just remembering the sweetness of her touch, the innocent and utter yielding of her body when he'd needed her so badly, made lust shaft through him with a sudden, painful intensity.

He shifted as discreetly as he could in his seat and kept his eyes on the road. He might have told Emma he wasn't interested in relationships or sex any more, and in truth his libido had disappeared while he'd been in prison, along with all of his other feelings and desires. But he could feel it returning in force now.

'What about you?' he asked. 'You might meet someone.' A thought that he disliked instinctively, although he knew he had no right to.

'I can't even imagine meeting someone,' Emma said with a small sigh. 'Ava takes up all my energy.'

'She won't be a baby for ever.'

'No,' Emma said slowly. 'But, Larenzo, this…situation can't last for ever.'

He turned to her sharply, his eyes narrowed. 'What do you mean?'

'I can't live with you for ever. I accept that it's expedient for now, and of course it gives you time to get to know her, but eventually…I need my own life. You'll need yours. When Ava is a little older, we can come to a custody arrangement we can both live with.'

Larenzo didn't answer for a moment. He knew she was talking sense but everything in him rebelled against it. Ava was the only family he'd ever had. He wasn't going to give her up, not even in part, as easily as that.

'We'll discuss the future when it is relevant,' he said, making his tone final. They'd driven through the Lincoln Tunnel and now came out into midtown Manhattan, all of them blinking in the bright sunlight. Even Ava had stopped protesting against the hated car seat as she gazed curiously at the gleaming skyscrapers and the streets teeming with people.

Emma turned to stare out of the window, and Larenzo saw she looked almost as wide-eyed as her daughter. 'Have you spent much time in New York before?'

'Not really. As a kid I always lived abroad. My apartment is on the Central Park West, right near the Natural History Museum. It's a good area for children.'

'You've only been in America for a week, haven't you?' Emma asked. 'How did you manage to secure an apartment so quickly?'

'Money talks.'

'And even though the assets of Cavelli Enterprises are frozen, you have money?'

'I had my own savings, which were released to me when the charges were cleared.'

She turned to give him a direct look. 'Are you ever going to tell me the whole story, Larenzo?'

His hands tensed on the steering wheel and he stared straight ahead as he navigated the roundabout at Columbus Circle. 'I've told you what you need to know, Emma.' Perhaps it was foolish to keep the truth from her about Bertrano; it was shaming that he still felt a loyalty to a man who, despite years of shared history, of happy memories, had completely and utterly betrayed him. And he knew that telling Emma his part of the story, how he'd been duped and deceived, wouldn't make much difference. Yet it would make a difference to him. He didn't want to admit how naive he'd been, how *hurt* he'd been. Not to Emma. Not to anyone.

And maybe Emma sensed some of what he felt, for to Larenzo's surprise she laid a hand on his arm, the touch of her fingers as light as a butterfly's. 'I hope you will be able to tell me someday, Larenzo. For your sake as much as mine.'

They didn't talk after that until Larenzo had pulled up to the elegant brick building that faced Central Park. A valet came out to deal with the car, and a doorman went for their bags.

Larenzo turned to get Ava out of her car seat; she practically flung herself into his arms and Larenzo held his daughter to him, breathing in her clean baby scent as her dark hair tickled his face. *His daughter.* Even now he nearly reeled from the shock and force of that knowledge. He had a family.

'Do you want me to take her?' Emma asked, reaching for Ava, and Larenzo shook his head.

'She's okay with me.' Although he wasn't so sure about that when Ava began to flail, scrambling to get down.

Emma laughed and reached for her, and reluctantly Larenzo gave Ava over to her. 'I guess she wants her mother.'

'Actually, I think she just wants to crawl all over this marble floor and get really dirty,' Emma answered lightly. She smiled at him, and he thought he saw sympathy in her eyes. 'She'll get used to you.'

He nodded, his throat too tight for words. He'd thought he had nothing left inside him; he'd been sure he was broken and empty inside. But knowing he had a daughter, knowing he could have someone to love and be loved by, filled him up to overflowing.

Emma followed Larenzo into the sumptuous foyer of the apartment building, all marble floors and glittering chandeliers. A doorman nodded respectfully to Larenzo as they passed, and then they stepped into a large wood-panelled lift, complete with a sofa and gilt mirror.

'Fancy,' Emma murmured as they soared upwards to the penthouse and then stepped into the huge foyer of Larenzo's apartment.

'This marble is a bit hard for a baby,' she said, tapping the black and white chequered marble with one foot. 'I wouldn't want Ava to fall and hurt herself.'

'I'll arrange to have it carpeted immediately,' Larenzo answered without missing a beat, and Emma wondered if she'd been challenging him. How far would Larenzo go to accommodate his daughter? Did she even want to answer that question?

She felt a churning mix of emotions as she stepped into the living room, its large windows overlooking Central Park, now ablaze in autumn colours. On one hand, she was grateful that Larenzo was interested in his daugh-

ter. How could she not be? And yet she was also afraid.
Afraid of the darkness of his past, the secrets he wasn't
telling her. But more than that: she was afraid of feeling
too much for him, of getting too used to this. To him. Of
caring for a man who had no intention of reciprocating her
feelings. Surely she wouldn't be so weak. She wouldn't let
herself.

'Would you like to come see the nursery?' Larenzo
asked, coming to stand behind her at the window, Ava in
his arms.

Emma turned. 'There's a nursery?'

'I had it all delivered yesterday.'

Wordlessly she nodded and followed Larenzo down the
luxuriously carpeted hall to the bedrooms.

'My bedroom is here,' he said, indicating a door on the
left. 'And your bedroom is here.' He pointed to a door directly across from his. 'The nursery is adjoining yours. I
thought you'd prefer that.'

'I do,' Emma said, although the thought of having her
own bedroom after ten months of sharing cramped quarters with her daughter was a luxury she intended to enjoy.
'Thank you,' she added belatedly, and Larenzo just nodded as he opened the door to the nursery.

She'd been expecting something basic and expedient,
ordered and set up in a hurry, but the room she stepped
into looked as if it had taken months of planning. The walls
were painted a pale lilac, and matching curtains framed
the deep window that overlooked the park. Deeper purple
accents were scattered around the room: a throw pillow on
the rocking chair, a silk-patterned lampshade, a close-up
photograph of a violet on the wall. It was a lovely, creative
room that was perfect for a baby without being cloyingly
sweet or infantile.

'I thought you might like something other than the stan-
dard pink,' Larenzo said, and Emma heard a surprising

note of uncertainty, even vulnerability, in his voice. 'But of course if you don't like it, you must change it. You can redecorate anything in the apartment as you like.'

'I don't want to redecorate,' Emma answered honestly. 'I love it. It's perfect, Larenzo. Thank you.'

'Good.'

Emma set Ava down on the plush carpet and she crawled towards a purple rocking horse—actually, Emma saw, a unicorn with a glittery horn—set in the corner, reaching up to grasp the handles as she pulled herself to standing.

'She's clever, isn't she?' Larenzo said with pride. 'She'll be walking soon.'

'And then there will really be no stopping her.' Emma gazed round the room again, noting all the unique touches. 'So did you hire an interior decorator?' she asked, and Larenzo shook his head.

'No, I did it myself. I enjoyed picking out all the things.'

'It must have taken an age—'

'No, just an afternoon. I hired painters to come and do the walls, and I put the furniture together myself.' He paused and then added, 'I told you I wanted to be involved, Emma.'

'I know, but...' She shook her head, overwhelmed by the thought and consideration Larenzo had clearly put into the nursery. She pictured him with an instruction leaflet and a set of tools, laboriously putting the crib and changing table together, and felt as if a fist had clenched around her heart. 'I suppose I didn't really think you'd be a hands-on dad,' she confessed, and Larenzo raised his eyebrows.

'Why not?'

'I don't know. You were so busy with work when I was your housekeeper. You hardly had time to come to the villa. And your lifestyle...'

'Things are different now.'

'Yes.' Emma swallowed, trying to banish the images

that had sprung into her mind, memories of the last night Larenzo had come to the villa, had come to her. She had to put that behind her. Heaven knew Larenzo had. 'Yes,' she repeated more firmly. 'Things are different now.'

CHAPTER EIGHT

AFTER SETTLING AVA in her new crib for an afternoon nap, Emma went to her bedroom and began to unpack her few possessions. She could hear Larenzo moving around in his bedroom across the hall, and the closeness of the quarters made her feel...aware.

She was still overwhelmingly attracted to Larenzo. It was a fact she had to acknowledge, and perhaps acknowledging it would help her to deal with it. Larenzo had made it abundantly clear that he had no interest in her that way any more, and she didn't even want him to. At least, she *shouldn't* want him to. Emma let out a rueful sigh as she acknowledged the truth—and strength—of her feelings. But she also knew their relationship, if they even had one, was way too complicated already.

And yet the tenderness he'd shown with Ava, the consideration he'd shown her...they chipped away at her defences. Made her remember. Made her want things she had absolutely no business wanting.

She might believe in Larenzo's innocence, but that didn't mean he was *safe*.

Ava was still sleeping after she'd unpacked, and so Emma headed out to the living room. The room was spacious and luxuriously appointed, if a little bland. No personal photographs or mementoes, but then Larenzo had bought the place only a week ago. It had probably come furnished.

She prowled around the room, glancing at the antique vases, the gilt mirrors, feeling restless and not quite knowing why.

She gazed out of the window at the leafy enclave of Central Park and as she imagined taking Ava to one of the playgrounds there, exploring the city with her daughter, her spirits lifted a little. She could make this work. She had to make this work, at least for a little while.

'Was your room adequate?'

Emma spun around to see Larenzo standing in the doorway of the sitting room. He'd changed from his more casual clothes of this morning to a well-tailored suit in navy-blue silk, and he looked, as he always did, devastatingly attractive. Even from across the room Emma felt the force of his magnetism, and it nearly propelled her forward, towards him. She held onto the window sill for balance as she answered him.

'Yes, thank you. More than adequate. This is a beautiful apartment, Larenzo.'

'You must change anything you don't like.'

She thought of telling him she wouldn't be staying long enough to warrant such changes, but somehow she couldn't make herself say the words. She just nodded instead, and Larenzo turned towards the door.

'I have to go out now, for some business meetings, but I should be back this evening.'

'Okay.' Emma wasn't sure why this surprised her, but it did. What had she expected—she and Larenzo would spend the day together? Larenzo had made it clear they would be living separate lives, brought together only by Ava, which was how she wanted it. How she had to want it. 'Do you—do you want me to make something for dinner?' She saw surprise flash across Larenzo's face and she wondered if she'd pushed some undiscussed boundary, crossed some invisible line. Maybe Larenzo had no intention of eating with her or Ava. She had no idea how this was meant to work, how it was going to work.

'If it's no trouble, that would be fine,' he finally said.

'It's no trouble.'

With a nod of farewell, Larenzo left the apartment and Emma stood there for a moment, feeling the emptiness all around her, not able to decide if she was relieved he had gone...or disappointed.

She made her way to the kitchen, which was huge, a hymn to granite and stainless steel, with every possible kitchen gadget and appliance. There was, however, no food. She stared into the empty depths of the enormous sub-zero fridge and wondered what Larenzo had been eating for the last few days.

When Ava woke a little while later Emma buckled her daughter into the top-of-the-line stroller that she found in the foyer.

Outside on Central Park West, a brisk autumn breeze blowing and Ava thankfully distracted by all the sights and sounds around them, Emma headed towards Columbus Avenue and the local shops. She felt better with every step she took, the city's vibrant life seeming to infuse her with energy and purpose.

At a local grocery she bought all the ingredients for lasagne, a simple but warming meal on this cold autumn day. She paused in front of a wine shop and then recklessly bought a bottle of Chianti to go with it. She'd already pushed the boundaries of their arrangement by suggesting she cook for Larenzo. Why not own it?

This was her life, at least for now, and she wanted to enjoy it. Ava started getting restless in the stroller, so Emma headed back. Once she was up in the apartment she brought the groceries into the kitchen and settled Ava onto the floor with a few wooden spoons and copper pans. While her daughter made as much noise as she possibly could, Emma bustled around, assembling the lasagne and tossing a salad.

She started to relax as she worked; she'd always enjoyed cooking, and it actually felt good to be mistress of her own kitchen, instead of an interloper in Meghan's. As much as her sister had made her feel welcome, Emma had been conscious of how much of an imposition she really was. Here, at least, she had a job to do, a potential role. Perhaps she could act as Larenzo's housekeeper. It would be a way of earning her keep and making herself useful.

She was just sliding the lasagne out of the oven when Larenzo appeared in the doorway of the kitchen. He'd taken off his suit jacket and loosened his tie, and his jaw was darkened with five o'clock shadow, all of it making him look deliciously rumpled and sexy.

He paused, taking in the sight of the kitchen, and Emma realised what a mess it was, with pots and spoons all over the floor for Ava's entertainment, and the detritus from her cooking all over the counters.

'Sorry, I'm not very good at cleaning up as I cook,' she said.

'No, it's fine.' Larenzo glanced around the room again, and Emma couldn't tell anything from his expression. 'I like it,' he said at last. 'Shall I set the table?'

He was already getting the forks and knives from the drawer, and Emma watched him, a strange pressure building in her chest. This was all so…normal. So cosy.

Ava had noticed her father and abandoned her pots and spoons to crawl over to him and pull herself up, clutching his legs. Larenzo glanced down at her, his whole face softening into a smile that made that pressure in Emma's chest turn painful.

'I'm afraid she's dented a few of your pots and pans,' she said stiltedly, turning her gaze to the salad she was needlessly tossing. 'She doesn't know her own strength.'

'I don't mind.' Larenzo scooped Ava up with one hand, settling her on his hip as he took the cutlery to the table in the dining nook of the kitchen. 'This is a bit more manageable than the dining room,' he said as he laid the table. 'I think the table in there seats twenty.'

'Planning on having any dinner parties?'

'No. I don't think I know twenty people who would come to a dinner party I hosted, unless it was to gawp and gossip.' He spoke tonelessly, without self-pity, and Emma eyed him curiously as she brought the lasagne to the table.

'You don't have many friends in America?'

'I don't have many friends, full stop,' Larenzo answered. 'A stint in prison shows you who your true friends are, and mine turned out to be rather few.'

He tried to put Ava in the high chair he'd brought to the table, but the toddler shrieked and arched her back, sticking her legs straight out. Emma watched, amused, as Larenzo tried his best before looking up with a wry smile.

'She's really quite strong.'

'Yes, and she doesn't like being strapped in.' Emma plucked Ava from the chair and put her back down on the floor. 'She'll want to join us when we sit down.'

'I suppose I have a lot to learn.'

'Fortunately Ava provides a steep learning curve,' Emma answered with a smile.

Emma brought the meal to the table and they both sat down. Just as she'd predicted, Ava crawled over to them, wanting to be part of things.

Larenzo glanced down at his daughter, smiling when she lifted her arms for him to pick her up. He settled her in her high chair this time without Ava making any protest. 'Tell me about the last ten months,' he said to Emma when he'd sat down again. 'Or even before that. How was your pregnancy?'

'Mostly uneventful, thankfully,' Emma answered. 'I

was pretty nauseous for the first three months,' she continued. 'But then it settled down. She was quite the kicker, though. I couldn't sleep most nights because it felt like she was playing football inside of me.'

Larenzo smiled at that, his whole face lightening, and Emma quickly looked down at her plate. Larenzo's smile was dangerous.

'And the birth? It went well?'

'As well as these things go,' Emma answered frankly. 'It hurt. A lot.'

'Why didn't you get pain relief?'

'No time. She came a week early; she wasn't due until New Year's Eve. And I didn't think I could actually be in labour, because the contractions were irregular and they didn't hurt all that much.' She let out a sudden, embarrassed laugh. 'I can't believe I'm telling you all this.'

'Why not? I want to hear it.'

'Really?' She heard the scepticism in her voice, and Larenzo must have too, because he nodded firmly.

'Absolutely. I missed this, Emma. I want to know now.'

But would he have wanted to know then? If Larenzo hadn't gone to prison, would he have been an involved father? Would they be dating or even *married* now? Emma's cheeks heated at the thought. She was glad Larenzo had no idea the turn her thoughts had taken. She cleared her throat and continued. 'Well, Meghan had been telling me how first babies take for ever, and as it was Christmas Eve I was hoping the contractions might die down. I didn't want to be in the hospital over Christmas.'

'Understandable.'

'But they didn't, and by the time I realised we needed to go to the hospital, Ava was almost ready to make her arrival.' She smiled at the memory. 'Meghan was pushing me in a wheelchair into the delivery ward, and I was bellowing at the top of my lungs. I'm not so good with pain.'

'I wish I could have been there,' Larenzo said quietly, and Emma knew he meant it.

Before she could think better of it, she asked the question that had been dancing through her mind. 'What do you suppose would have happened, if you hadn't gone to prison?'

Larenzo frowned. 'What do you mean?'

'I would have stayed on as your housekeeper. I would have told you I was pregnant right away.' She held her breath, waiting for him to say something, although she didn't know what.

Larenzo sighed and leaned back in his chair. 'The truth is, Emma, if I hadn't gone to prison, if I hadn't known I was going to go to prison, there wouldn't have been a baby. That night happened because I knew I was going to be arrested in the morning.'

'Oh.' Emma blinked, stupidly feeling hurt by this, and not quite sure what to do with that emotion. 'I see.'

'You gave me something precious that night.'

'My virginity?' she filled in, trying to joke, but it came out flat.

'No, I didn't mean that, although that of course is precious too.'

She really didn't want to be having this conversation. She kept looking at her plate, focusing on the food she no longer felt like eating.

'I meant comfort,' Larenzo said quietly. 'Human connection. Pleasure, not just physical pleasure, although there certainly was that. But pleasure in talking to you, and being in your company. Playing chess, seeing your photographs… that night made a memory that sustained me through many dark days in prison.'

'Oh.' And now she didn't feel so hurt. She felt…*honoured* that she'd been that important to him, and deeply thankful that their one night together had meant something to him, as it had to her. 'Well, I'm glad about that, I suppose.'

'And look at the result.' He glanced at Ava, who now had tomato sauce in her hair, before turning back to Emma with a smile. 'I don't have any regrets, since she came out of it. But I think she needs a bath.'

'Do you want me to—?' Emma half rose from her chair as Larenzo unbuckled Ava from her high chair.

'I can do it,' he said.

'She can be pretty tricky in the tub—'

As if to prove her point, Ava started wriggling out of Larenzo's grasp, and soon his shirt was splattered with tomato sauce.

Larenzo looked rather endearingly amazed by his daughter's gymnastics and Emma rescued him. 'I've found this is the best way sometimes,' she said, and, tucking Ava under her arm as if she were a parcel, she took her to the bathroom.

Larenzo followed, standing in the doorway while Emma put Ava down and turned the taps on. 'Fortunately she likes her bath,' she said, and turned to look over her shoulder. Her breath dried in her throat as she saw he was unbuttoning his shirt. What, she wondered distantly, was so mesmerising about his long brown fingers sliding buttons out of their holes? Something was, because she couldn't tear her gaze away from the sight.

'I'd rather not get my shirt wet,' Larenzo explained. 'I have a feeling Ava is a splasher.' He shrugged out of his dress shirt, revealing a plain white T-shirt underneath that clung to the defined muscles of his chest and abdomen.

'She is,' Emma answered, and finally managed to drag her gaze to Larenzo's face. She couldn't read the emotion in his eyes, and she hoped that he hadn't noticed how she'd been staring. *Wanting*.

She knew she should go back to the kitchen and clean

up their dishes, but she felt as if her feet were rooted to the floor, and all she could do was watch as Larenzo battled Ava out of her clothes and then plopped her in the tub, one strong hand resting on her back to keep her steady.

'Is this right?' he asked, and the uncertainty in his voice made Emma's heart ache.

'Yes…yes, that's perfect.' She felt as if her feelings were a kaleidoscope that Larenzo twirled every time he spoke. In these unguarded moments of honesty everything in her swelled with feeling, ached with loss.

What if things could have been different? What if that night *had* still happened, without the arrest, and she and Larenzo had built a relationship? What if they'd become a proper family, rather than this awkwardly constructed temporary one?

Emma knew she shouldn't torment herself with such thoughts. She'd never been looking for that kind of relationship, and, in any case, there was no going back. And yet as she gazed helplessly at Larenzo bathing their daughter, she almost wished there were.

Half an hour later Emma had cleaned up the kitchen when Larenzo emerged from the nursery with Ava in her pyjamas.

'You've buttoned up her pyjamas wrong,' she remarked in amusement as Larenzo raked a hand through his hair.

'Those things are worse than a straitjacket. There are a million buttons.'

'It's a learned skill.'

'Clearly.' He pulled his damp T-shirt away from his chest, and Emma tried not to stare at his perfect musculature, or remember how warm and satiny his skin had felt, how she'd once put her lips to his taut abdomen…

'She's ready for bed, I think,' Emma said. 'I'll get her bottle ready.' She'd brought a can of infant formula from Meghan's, and now she poured cooled boiled water into a bottle and added a few scoops of the white powder. 'You were a little low on groceries, by the way,' she said. 'I don't think there's anything for breakfast.'

'I can arrange for food to be delivered, unless you'd prefer to do it yourself.'

'Actually, I was thinking about that,' Emma said. She'd finished making the bottle and Ava was reaching for it with both hands. 'I'm not comfortable just living off your generosity, and one thing I know how to do is be a house-keeper.'

Larenzo stilled. 'What are you suggesting?'

'I could be your housekeeper. You don't have to pay me, but at least it will make up for mine and Ava's room and board.'

Larenzo's face had darkened as she spoke. 'Ava is my daughter, Emma, and you are her mother. This isn't a question of *room and board.*'

Emma took a deep breath, knowing she needed to say this even if part of her didn't want to. 'It is for me, Larenzo.' He didn't answer and she continued, keeping her voice steady with effort, 'Look, you said yourself you aren't interested in a relationship. You want to get to know Ava, and I respect that. But the only reason I'm here is because Ava is. So it makes sense for me to have a role. A job.'

Still Larenzo didn't speak, and Emma could see the emotions battling on his face. She just didn't know what they were. Did he want there to be more between them? Or was that just her foolish, wishful thinking? Sighing, she hoisted Ava more firmly on her hip. 'I'm going to put her to bed. Think about it, at least.'

She was at the door when Larenzo finally bit out, 'Fine, you can act as housekeeper. But I don't want any respon-sibilities you needlessly put on yourself to take away from Ava's care.'

'Many women manage a home and a baby,' Emma answered, doing her best to keep her voice mild. 'I think I can too.' Larenzo said nothing and as she headed to the nursery with Ava, Emma wondered why this didn't feel more like a victory.

CHAPTER NINE

ANOTHER SLEEPLESS NIGHT. By now Larenzo was well used to insomnia. He'd slept badly in prison, on a thin mattress in a tiny cell with a thousand other prisoners shifting, coughing, and groaning around him. Ironic that he slept just as badly now that he was free, lying on a king-sized bed with the apartment quiet and still.

And Emma sleeping across the hall.

Although he knew he shouldn't, he imagined rising from his bed, opening his door, and going into Emma's room. Watching her sleep, her golden-brown hair spread across the pillow, her lithe body clad in those scanty pyjamas he remembered from their night in Sicily.

Then he imagined sliding into that bed with her, taking her in his arms, burying his face in her sweet-smelling hair, burying himself inside her body…

With a groan Larenzo rose from the bed and went to the en-suite bathroom to splash some cold water on his face. He had no business thinking of Emma that way. His libido might have leapt to life since he'd seen her again, but he had nothing left in his heart to give her. No ability to have a relationship, to trust or to love someone.

He loved Ava, because she was sweet and innocent, and she was his. His love for his daughter was rock solid, utterly unshakeable. But loving a woman? Trusting someone with the heart that had shattered into tiny fragments of nothingness?

Impossible.

And the alternative, some kind of fling or affair, would only further complicate what was already a tenuous arrangement. His face settled into a scowl as he thought of Emma's suggestion. *Housekeeper.* He didn't want her here as a housekeeper. She wasn't his damned employee. She was here because she was the mother of his child, because she *belonged*—

Larenzo let out his breath in a hiss as he bowed his head. Emma belonged with Ava, but not with him. Not like that. Never like that.

So perhaps, much as he had instinctively disliked the idea, it was better that she act as housekeeper. Perhaps having a clearly defined role would help them navigate this arrangement with a minimum of awkwardness.

A soft cry interrupted the wrangling of his own thoughts and Larenzo realised that Ava had woken up. Quickly he left his room and went to the nursery. His daughter was standing up in her crib, her face streaked with tears. Larenzo's heart twisted with a powerful mixture of love, protectiveness, and sorrow. Sleeping in a strange place had to be a frightening experience for the child.

He picked her up, and again his heart twisted as Ava settled against his bare chest, her cheek resting over his heart. Larenzo stroked her back and without even realising what he was doing, he began to croon a lullaby in Italian. '*E dormi, dormi, dormi, bambin de cuna. To mama no la gh'è la a-sé andà via.*'

The words came to him unbidden, from a deep well of memory. He stroked Ava's hair and watched as his daughter's eyelids eventually drooped.

After several minutes when he was sure she was deeply asleep, he laid her back in the crib and watched her for a moment, her thick, dark lashes fanning her plump baby cheeks.

'That's a beautiful lullaby.'

Larenzo stiffened, his gaze moving from his sleeping daughter to the woman standing in the doorway of the nursery. Emma's hair was tousled about her shoulders, her golden-green eyes wide and luminous. Larenzo dropped his gaze and saw with a hard kick of desire that she was wearing just what he'd imagined: a thin T-shirt that moulded to the shape of her breasts and a pair of boy shorts. He felt his body respond, and in only a pair of drawstring pyjama bottoms he knew Emma would be able to tell if she lowered her gaze just as he'd lowered his.

'She's asleep,' he whispered, and moved quietly out of the nursery, brushing past Emma as he did so. He sucked in a hard breath as her breasts nudged against his chest, and her hair whispered against his cheek. He inhaled the scent of her, sweetness and sleep, and he averted his face from the temptation of hers.

Emma closed the door behind him and they stood in the hallway, only a few inches separating them, the only light coming from a lamp Larenzo had left on in the living room, its warm glow spilling onto the floor.

It was so reminiscent of that night in the villa, the way things had shifted between them in the quiet and dark. Barriers had disappeared, defences had dropped. In that bubble of solitude and intimacy there had only been the two of them, seeking and finding both solace and pleasure.

And there were just the two of them now, standing so close together, the only sound the sigh and draw of their breathing.

'What did it mean?' Emma asked in a whisper, and Larenzo forced himself to meet her gaze, to hold himself still, when all he wanted to do was drag her into his arms, forget everything but this, *them*, for a little while.

'What did what mean?'

'The lullaby. I couldn't make out the Italian. I'm rusty, I suppose.'

'Oh... Sleep, sleep, sleep, cradle baby. Your mother is not here, she has gone away.' Belatedly he realised how it sounded. 'It's the only lullaby I know. I didn't even realise I knew it until I started singing.'

'Is it from your childhood?' Emma asked, and Larenzo blinked.

'I suppose it has to be. But I don't remember anyone singing me any lullabies.' He heard the note of bitterness that had crept into his voice and he tried to shrug it off. No point in dwelling on the past, just as he'd told Emma. 'Anyway, Ava seemed to like it.'

'Thank you,' Emma said softly, and she reached out and laid a hand on his arm. The touch of her fingers on his skin was electric, jolting his senses as if he'd stuck his finger into a socket. He held himself still, staring down at her hand, her slender fingers curled around his biceps.

She'd touched him like this back in Sicily. And he'd put his hand on hers, and for a moment he hadn't felt alone. He'd felt as if someone was on his side, someone actually cared...

But that was a lifetime ago, and it hadn't been true anyway. Their night together had been a moment out of time, out of reality. An aberration.

Larenzo forced himself to shake off her hand. 'It was nothing,' he said and without saying anything else he turned and went back to his bedroom.

Emma woke to sunlight pouring through the windows of her bedroom, and the sound of Ava gurgling with laughter from the adjoining nursery. She stretched, savouring the moment's relaxation before the day with all of its demands began.

Then she heard Larenzo's answering laughter and realised he was in the nursery with Ava. Just the rumbling sound of his voice as he talked to their daughter brought the memory of last night back with slamming force. Emma didn't think she'd seen or heard anything as beautiful, as *desirable*, as Larenzo cradling their baby to his bare chest as he sang her a lullaby in lilting Italian.

Watching him in the darkened nursery, she'd wanted him almost as much as she'd wanted him that night back at the villa. Wanted to feel his hot, hard skin against hers, his lips on hers as he treasured and cherished her with his body...

For a few seconds, when she'd touched his arm, simply because she had no longer been able to keep herself from it, she'd thought he was battling the same kind of temptation. Thought, and even hoped, that he might give in to it. In that moment she'd known if he'd kissed her she'd be lost, just as she had been before. Nothing would have kept her from him.

But he'd walked away instead, and Emma had spent a restless night trying to banish the ache of longing inside her. Now she got out of bed and hurriedly dressed in jeans and a sweater before going into the nursery.

Larenzo was dressed in an elegant and crisp suit, and he'd already changed Ava's diaper and was now wrestling her into a bodysuit. Ava was resisting him, her whole body rigid as she stared up at him in stubborn determination.

'I think she's winning,' Emma said, and Larenzo glanced up, his mouth curving wryly.

'There's no thinking about it. It's definite.'

'Do you want me to—?'

'Please.' He stepped aside and with a smile Emma finished dressing Ava, who saw that the jig was up and relaxed her body as she blew a raspberry.

'Clearly you have the touch,' Larenzo observed.

'Years, or rather, months of practice.' She turned to face

him, her heart bumping against her ribs as she realised how close he was. The woodsy scent of his aftershave tickled her nostrils and made heat lick low in her belly. 'You look smart. Are you going somewhere?'

'I have a few meetings at the office. But...' He hesitated, a note of uncertainty creeping into his voice. 'We can have breakfast first, if you'd like. I went out early this morning and bought some bagels and coffee.'

'Okay.' Emma followed him into the kitchen, Ava balanced on one hip. The smell of freshly brewed coffee and toasted bagels made her mouth water. 'So if you're not CEO of Cavelli Enterprises,' she asked, 'what are you doing exactly?'

'I'm starting a new company,' Larenzo answered as he poured them both coffees. Emma settled Ava into her high chair with a few torn-off pieces of bagel. 'LC Investments.'

'And what are you going to do?'

'I hope to invest in start-up businesses, the kind of places that might have trouble getting loans from one of the big banks.'

'That sounds rather noble.'

He shrugged and handed her a mug of steaming coffee. 'I have some sympathy for the underdog.'

Because he could relate? And yet Larenzo Cavelli was so powerful, so charismatic, so arrogant. He'd even seemed so back in Sicily when he'd been handcuffed and at the police's mercy. Standing there now, one hip braced against the counter, his large hands cradling a mug of coffee, he managed to look like the lord of all he surveyed, his confidence careless and yet utterly assured. And yet this man had come from the street.

'Did you feel like the underdog as a child?' she asked after a moment.

Larenzo pursed his lips as he considered. 'I suppose

I would have, if I'd thought about it. I was just trying to survive.'

'I'm amazed at how far you've come. You should be incredibly proud of yourself, Larenzo, going from street orphan to CEO.'

His mouth tightened and he shook his head. 'I had some help.'

Who from? she wanted to ask but decided not to. 'Even so.'

Larenzo put his empty coffee mug on the dish drainer. 'I should go,' he said shortly, and Emma felt his emotional withdrawal like a palpable thing. 'I don't know when I'll be home,' he added. 'Don't wait for me.'

Emma nodded, feeling the rejection even though she knew she shouldn't, and Larenzo left. He kissed the top of Ava's head before he went, and Emma sat down at the table to finish her coffee, caught between missing Larenzo and enjoying the prospect of a day spent in the city. She was looking forward to going out and exploring New York, and yet, even though he'd just gone, she already missed Larenzo. She was so curious about him—this man who was hardened and suspicious, who could be so ruthless and cold, and yet also showed such gentleness and kindness.

Her cell phone rang and Emma slipped it out of the pocket of her jeans, and saw that it was Meghan.

'Hey,' she said as she answered the call and Meghan drew her breath in sharply.

'Are you okay?'

'Am I okay? Yes.' Emma gazed out of the window at the view of Central Park, and then glanced at the remains of her perfectly toasted bagel. 'I'm fine. Just finishing breakfast.'

'Cavelli isn't…he's being decent to you?' Meghan asked cautiously.

'More than decent. He already has a bond with Ava. He

even got up with her in the night.' Emma pictured Larenzo wearing nothing but his pyjama bottoms, the lamplight washing over his bronzed skin, and she suppressed a shiver of desire.

'Really,' Meghan answered, the disbelief audible in her voice.

'Yes, really. I told you before, Meghan, Larenzo wants to be a part of his daughter's life.'

'I didn't realise you'd become his champion,' Meghan retorted, and Emma sucked in a breath.

'Meghan…'

'Seriously, Emma, you've changed your tune since yesterday.'

'I haven't—'

'How do you know Cavelli isn't just pretending he's interested in Ava—?'

Emma recoiled at the suggestion. 'He's not. Anyway, why would he?'

'I don't know, maybe he's trying to polish his image for the public? Whatever it is, I don't trust him, Emma, and you shouldn't either. I know the charges against him were dropped, but you know the saying, where there's smoke, there's fire.'

'And sometimes there's just smoke.' The fierceness of her response surprised them both. 'In any case,' Emma continued, 'you know as well as I do that I can't keep Larenzo from seeing his daughter.' And she didn't even want to any more. Not when she'd seen how tender he was with her.

'You still don't have to live with him. I talked to that lawyer again and mentioned that Cavelli had practically blackmailed you into living with him. It could provide evidence that he's unfit—'

'Meghan.' Shock as well as anger blazed through her. 'You have no right to talk about my business with a lawyer.'

'I'm looking out for you,' Meghan cried. 'Emma, obviously you still have some feelings for this man. That's understandable, considering your shared history. But I think you're in over your head. You don't know Cavelli, or what he's capable of. And someone has to be responsible and think about Ava—'

'I am thinking about Ava,' Emma shot back. Her voice shook with the force of her feelings. 'Trust me, I am. And Larenzo is very good with her. I don't want to keep him from Ava's life, no matter what happened in his past.'

'And what if it turns out he really is dangerous?'

'It won't. I trust Larenzo in that.'

'How can you trust—?'

'I just do, Meghan,' Emma cut her off, knowing she meant it. 'And I need to go now. Ava's starting to fuss.'

Ava, who was happily chewing on a bagel, looked at her curiously. Emma disconnected the call and flung the phone onto the kitchen counter. Her whole body was trembling.

She wanted to deny everything her sister had said; she wanted to scrub her brain and pretend she'd never heard it. And yet beneath Meghan's older-sister I-know-best attitude, Emma knew there was concern and perhaps even truth.

She still didn't know Larenzo at all. It just felt as if she did.

Ava threw the bagel onto the floor, and Emma decided it was time to go out for the day. All of New York was waiting for her to explore, and she could certainly use the distraction.

She fetched Ava's coat and hat and then buckled her into the stroller, armed with an arsenal of snacks and toys to keep her daughter entertained. Then she hit the streets.

Central Park on a crisp autumn day was one of the loveliest places on earth, Emma decided as she wheeled Ava along the twisting, tree-shaded pathways. She could hear the distant laughter of children on a playground, and some tourists were posing for photographs in front of the statue of Christopher Columbus. Every colour seemed sharp and bright, as if the whole world had been brought into crystalline focus.

As Emma strolled along Ava watched everything avidly; they made it all the way to the Central Park Zoo where they both watched the animal statues dance around the iconic clock. Emma bought a hot dog from a cart and shared it with Ava, enjoying people watching from a park bench, and then when her daughter fell asleep in her stroller she walked back uptown, stopping in front of the gorgeous esplanade with Bethesda Fountain as its magnificent centrepiece.

Every step she took felt as if she were breathing life back into her soul. She hadn't realised until then just how much of a rut she'd been in, living with her sister and staggering through her days. It had taken Larenzo's suggestion to get her out of it, and for that she was grateful.

Ava was starting to stir, and so Emma walked back towards the apartment on Central Park West. She stopped at the playground directly opposite the park's entrance and unbuckled Ava from her stroller before putting her into one of the baby swings. Ava chortled with glee as Emma pushed her, enjoying the autumn sunshine on her face.

She didn't know how long she spent in the playground with Ava, savouring the day, but it must have been more time than she'd thought for the sun was starting to sink behind the buildings on Central Park West when a hand suddenly clamped down hard on her shoulder.

Emma whirled around, her heart seeming to leap right into her throat, and saw Larenzo glaring at her ferociously.

'*Where* have you been?'

CHAPTER TEN

'YOU SCARED ME, LARENZO.' Emma shrugged off his hand and pressed her palm to her thudding heart. 'Good grief. Why did you sneak up on me like that?'

'Answer the question, Emma.'

She blinked up at him, amazed at how different he seemed now, scowling down at her, everything about him hard and fierce and utterly unyielding. Right now she could almost believe he really was a Mafioso.

'Where have I been?' she retorted, her voice rising in both anger and fear. 'Here, in the park, with Ava. It's a beautiful day and I wanted to get out and see the city.'

'You didn't tell me you were going to the park.'

'I wasn't aware I had to inform you of all of my movements.' She glared at him, conscious that the parents and caregivers around them were obviously pretending not to listen while eating up every word. 'What's with the third degree?' she demanded as she lifted Ava from the baby swing.

Larenzo was silent for a moment, the ravages of his anger still visible on his face. 'I don't like not knowing where you are.'

Emma stared at him, exasperated. 'So what are you going to do? Implant a chip in my shoulder, or how about an ankle tag? Seriously, Larenzo, I need my freedom.'

Larenzo didn't answer and with a sigh she buckled a

protesting Ava into her stroller. 'Let's go back to the apartment. We're causing a scene.'

Larenzo glanced around the playground, his scowl deepening as he saw several mothers whispering and shooting them speculative looks.

'Fine,' he said, and reached for the handles of the stroller. Emma walked beside him while he pushed Ava back towards the park entrance.

They had just reached the park gates when Larenzo stiffened, and then, shoving the stroller towards her, strode across the pathway.

Emma watched in stunned disbelief as Larenzo approached a man and without so much as a qualm took the expensive digital camera he was holding and began to push its buttons.

'Hey, you can't do that—' the man exclaimed.

'Do not,' Larenzo said, biting off each word and spitting it out, 'take pictures of my family.'

'So the rumours are true, you do have a child?'

Larenzo's face was thunderous as he handed the camera back to the man. 'I repeat, do not take photographs of my family.'

Without another word he turned back to Emma, standing there with her jaw hanging open slackly.

'Cavelli,' the man called, 'is it true that you planted the evidence on Raguso? People are saying—'

'Come on,' Larenzo said, and took the stroller from her. 'Let's go.' He began resolutely walking towards the park entrance, and mutely Emma followed.

She waited until they were back up in the penthouse apartment and Ava was settled with some toys on the floor of the living room before she started asking for answers.

'Larenzo, what on earth was that all about?'

'The photographer?' He shrugged out of his suit jacket,

not even looking at her as he answered. 'He was a member of the paparazzi. I should have known they would realise I was here. Until the press dies down, you shouldn't take Ava out in public.'

'So I'm a prisoner here?' she demanded, and Larenzo turned to look at her, his mouth twisting grimly.

'It doesn't look like a prison to me.'

She flushed, realising her poor choice of words. 'You know what I mean, Larenzo. I'll go crazy if I have to stay in here twenty-four seven.'

'For a few days only. These things never last long.'

Emma took a deep breath. 'Why does he think you planted the evidence on your business partner?'

Larenzo's nostrils flared and Emma could see how the skin around his mouth had turned white. He was angry, very angry, and yet when he spoke his voice was measured and controlled.

'Because he is trying to sell newspapers, and to do that he needs a story. Surely you know how these things work, Emma.'

She thought of her sister's phone call this morning. *Where there's smoke, there's fire.* 'Is there any truth to that claim, Larenzo?' she asked quietly.

He stared at her for a long, taut moment, and beneath the icy anger Emma thought she saw a flash of hurt in his eyes, quickly veiled.

'What exactly are you accusing me of, Emma?' he asked.

'I don't know.' Belatedly she realised what she'd been implying. She didn't really think Larenzo was guilty, but she still didn't understand him. 'I just wish I knew more, Larenzo. I feel like there are things you aren't telling me—'

'I told you, Raguso is guilty. There is no doubt. The evidence was there.'

'You said there was evidence against you—'

'Because it was planted!' Larenzo's voice rose in a sudden, anguished roar. 'It was planted, all right? I was framed, and I was too stupid and naive to realise it.' He let out a shuddering breath as he raked his hands through his hair. 'Satisfied?'

Emma didn't answer, and Ava looked up, her lip wobbling at the shouting and the tension she sensed crackling between the two adults. 'If you were framed,' Emma asked slowly, 'why didn't you tell me that from the beginning? There is no shame in it—'

'I feel shame,' Larenzo answered. He dropped his hands and looked away from her, his expression shuttered even as his voice thickened with emotion. 'I feel great shame.'

She blinked back tears at the raw pain she heard in his voice. 'Oh, Larenzo—'

'We will not discuss this any more.'

Emma could sense when a door was being slammed in her face. And yet she'd finally received some insight into Larenzo's experience, even if it left her with more questions than ever. 'All right, fine, we don't need to talk about that. But why were you so angry when you found me in the park? I don't need you to keep tabs on me—'

'I phoned the apartment several times and there was no answer. With Ava's nap schedule, I thought you would have been in the apartment at least for the afternoon. I was worried.'

'But you said there was no danger—'

'I was worried you'd left,' Larenzo said starkly. He stared at her, his face filled with bleak honesty. 'I thought you had taken Ava and left me.'

Emma gaped at him, amazed and humbled by the vulnerability she saw in Larenzo's eyes. 'If I was going to leave, Larenzo,' she said quietly, 'I'd have the decency to tell you first. And anyway, I just got here. I'm not going anywhere.'

He shrugged, his face hard and impassive once more. 'I know your sister doesn't want you here. You are close to her. She is probably like a mother figure to you since you are not close to your own mother. I was afraid she'd spoken to you, and you had changed your mind.'

Emma swallowed, stunned by his perception. 'She did speak to me. She called me this morning.'

Larenzo nodded. 'And did she tell you to go back?'

'No, but you're right, she's not happy I'm here.' She thought of mentioning the lawyer, and then decided against it. She didn't want to make Larenzo angry, or worse, to hurt him, with such information, and she had a feeling it would. This man who seemed so proud and arrogant and untouchable hid a surprising vulnerability.

'I can understand your sister's point of view,' he said, and Emma raised her eyebrows.

'Can you?'

'Of course. If I were your sister, I would be wary too. But I hope she will realise in time that you are in no danger. I hope you realise that too.'

'I do realise it, Larenzo.' Guilt lashed her that he would believe she still doubted him. 'I'm sorry I keep questioning you.'

'It's understandable,' Larenzo answered wearily. 'This is a difficult situation for all of us, but for you in particular.'

'Thank you for acknowledging that.'

He nodded, and Emma felt they'd come to a truce, and even an understanding. She took a deep breath and then bent to scoop up Ava, who had started to grizzle.

'I should start making dinner. I didn't realise how late it had become, when I was in the park.' Which was, she supposed, a sort of apology.

'I'll watch this one while you do it,' Larenzo said and, in a gesture that felt both bizarre and natural, Emma handed over Ava, who went willingly to her father.

* * *

Over the next few weeks Emma settled into a new routine that felt both comfortable and strange. Larenzo worked most days, and, after seeing to her housekeeping duties, Emma spent the days with Ava exploring the city. The autumn days continued crisp and clear and she enjoyed getting out and walking through the park, going to the Children's Museum, which Ava loved, and visiting the local shops. She'd even signed Ava up for a toddler gymnastics class, and she'd met a few other mothers at the local library's story hour. It might not have seemed much to most people, but she was more active and involved here than she'd been in her months at Meghan's.

She also developed a routine with Larenzo. An early riser, he usually got up with Ava while Emma had the unimagined luxury of a lie-in, and then they all had breakfast together in the sun-filled kitchen before Larenzo went to work. He came home no later than six or six-thirty each weekday night, and they had dinner together before bathing Ava and reading her stories, a precious hour spent as a family. Because they were a family, even if it was unexpected and unconventional. Sitting on the sofa, their daughter between them, trying to race through reading a board book before Ava tossed it to the floor, comprised some of the happiest moments Emma had ever known, and yet they also felt tenuous. Fragile. She wondered how long this 'sort of' family could really last.

At first, when Ava was asleep, they went their separate ways in the apartment. Larenzo would work in his study and Emma would read or watch TV in her room. Then one night, a week or so after she'd arrived, restlessness drove her out of her bedroom to the living room, where she scanned the shelves of expensive leather-bound books.

Larenzo came out of the kitchen, stopping when he saw her. 'Is everything all right?'

'Yes, basically.' Emma glanced over her shoulder, her mouth drying at the sight of Larenzo in faded jeans and a T-shirt, his feet bare, his hair rumpled. He looked jaw-droppingly gorgeous and just the sight of him made her belly swoop. She'd thought in the weeks since she'd been here she'd get used to seeing him, but nothing ever prepared her for the devastating sight of him, or her body's unstoppable reaction.

He cocked an eyebrow, waiting for more, and Emma let out a little laugh. 'I'm just kind of bored.'

'Why don't you go out, see a film?'

'By myself?'

'You once told me you liked your own company,' Larenzo reminded her.

'I know,' Emma admitted. 'I just don't feel like it tonight.' She was tired of being alone. Spending time with Larenzo had made her realise how wonderful and invigorating and fun company could be. *His* company.

'Well, then.' Larenzo shoved his hands in the pockets of his jeans and rocked on his heels. 'How about a game of chess?'

Remembrance rippled through her as she thought of the last game they'd played, that night in Sicily. The expectation and awareness that had tautened between them...

'Okay,' she said, and followed him into the sumptuous wood-panelled room. Two deep leather club chairs flanked a large window that overlooked Amsterdam Avenue, a low table with a chessboard between them.

Emma sat down and studied the board with its ornately carved pieces. 'I think I'm about to get my butt kicked,' she said wryly. 'Again.'

'Don't give up before you've even started,' Larenzo answered with a faint smile as he sat down opposite her. 'White moves first, remember.'

'I remember.' Those two words seemed to fall into the

stillness of the room like pebbles tossed into a well, creating ripples of awareness. Larenzo's gaze was heavy-lidded and intent as he looked at her, and Emma's heart started to thud.

'I remember too,' he said softly, and she knew he wasn't talking about chess.

She stared down at the board, the pieces blurring before her eyes as she swallowed hard. 'Do you think about it?' she asked softly. 'That night?'

Larenzo didn't answer for a long moment and she didn't dare look at him. 'All the time,' he finally said, and Emma jerked her gaze up towards his, startled and yet suddenly, blazingly hopeful. 'You should move,' he said gruffly, and, barely aware of what she was doing, she moved her knight.

They played in silence, expectation and memory uncoiling inside her, seeming to fill the room with a palpable force. It would be so easy for Larenzo to reach across the board, frame her face in his hands as he had on that night. Slide his lips across hers as she opened and yielded beneath him…

Her hand trembled and she knocked a few pieces over, scattering them across the board. 'Oh, I'm sorry,' she said, biting her lips, and Larenzo righted them easily.

'It's all right. I was going to checkmate you in three moves anyway.'

'Oh, dear.'

'Good game.' He held out his hand, his eyes glinting with both challenge and desire, and Emma took it, her fingers sliding along his as a tingle spread from her fingers all the way up her arm. His hand was so warm and dry and strong. She pulled away reluctantly.

'Another?' Larenzo suggested, and she nodded, not wanting this evening to end.

'Okay.' She moved a pawn and Larenzo countered by moving one of his. Just a few moves later Emma was down a bishop. 'I'm hopeless at this,' she said as she studied the board. Even though she was losing, she was savouring this time with Larenzo. His study was cosy and warm, the lamplight spilling across the board, the heavy damask drapes now drawn across the window.

And as for the man himself... She didn't think she'd been imagining the heat in his eyes. She certainly felt an answering desire in herself. Every so often she sneaked a glance at Larenzo's face; his eyes were narrowed as he studied the board, his mobile mouth pursed. He rested his chin in one hand and Emma longed to reach out and touch him. *Kiss him.*

She forced her gaze back to the board. 'So how did you learn chess, anyway?' she asked. 'I don't imagine they taught that at the orphanage.'

There was a slight pause and then Larenzo answered, 'My business partner taught me.'

Emma looked at him in surprise. 'Your business partner? You mean Bertrano Raguso?' Larenzo gave a short nod.

'So you really were close to him,' she said slowly.

'We were friends,' Larenzo allowed. 'Good friends.'

'Was he the one who planted the evidence against you?'

Larenzo nodded again, and realisation swooped through her. No wonder Larenzo didn't trust anyone. 'I'm sorry,' she said quietly. 'That must have been very hard, to be betrayed by someone you cared about.'

'I wondered how he could do it,' Larenzo said after a moment, his gaze on the board. 'If he was just desperate... I wish he'd told me how things were. I would have helped him.' And then, as if he felt he'd said too much, he moved his queen and put Emma into check.

The weeks slipped by and the leaves fell from the trees, creating a carpet of red and gold on the lawns and pathways of Central Park. Ava had begun to cruise, clinging to coffee tables and chair legs as she made her way around the apartment. Each Saturday Emma took her to New Jersey to visit Meghan and her family; her sister had thankfully stopped warning her about Larenzo. Meghan didn't mention him at all, which Emma supposed was better than her running him down, but she wished Meghan could see, as she now did, how different Larenzo was from what they'd both once thought.

The more time she spent with him, the more she liked him. He could be dryly amusing or gently intent, and his tenderness with Ava had brought the sting of tears to her eyes more than once. And she was having more and more trouble ignoring the chemistry between them. Just brushing past him in the elevator or touching his hand when he handed her something made Emma's insides go liquid with longing. And knowing that he remembered their night, that he might feel even just a little of what she felt…

It was the sweetest form of torture. Emma knew she had to resolve it one way or another. Either she had to stop dreaming about Larenzo, or she needed to ask him if he wanted their friendship—because she did believe they were now friends—to turn into something more. But *something* had to give, because the truth was, she acknowledged one night as she stared up at the ceiling, that she was falling in love with the father of her child.

CHAPTER ELEVEN

'WHAT'S WRONG?' LARENZO glanced up from his tablet where he'd been scanning news headlines, and Emma jumped guiltily.

'Nothing's wrong,' she said quickly, and swiped at a few crumbs on the kitchen table with a damp cloth. Ava banged her spoon on the table and then happily flung it to the floor.

Larenzo picked it up and handed it back to his daughter. 'I can tell something's bothering you,' he said mildly. 'Why don't you tell me what it is?' He tried to ignore the tightening of suspicion and fear in his gut. These last few weeks with Emma and Ava had been nearly perfect. Perhaps too perfect, because perfection wasn't real, couldn't last.

And yet he'd enjoyed this time with Emma and Ava so much...the mornings alone with Ava, and then breakfast, the three of them around the table, a *family*. He, a street rat from the slums of Palermo, finally had his own family. It felt like a miracle. It *was* a miracle. And just seeing Emma frown, sensing her disquiet, made him fear the worst now.

This family, after all, still was more façade than anything else. It wasn't as if they actually cared about each other.

Although he knew in his gut—and his heart—that that wasn't true. He cared about Ava...and he cared about Emma.

'It's nothing,' Emma said as she swiped some more

toast crumbs into her hand and deposited them into the bin. 'Really, it's nothing.'

Larenzo let it go, because he wanted to keep things the way they were, and he was worried, judging from Emma's frown, that they were already changing.

'What are you up to today?' he asked instead and she rose from the table, moving around the kitchen a bit too briskly, not meeting his eye.

'Tumbling class for Ava and then a few errands.' She gave him a brief, distracted smile. 'Nothing too exciting.'

Did he detect a note of restlessness in her voice? Was she unhappy with her life here? He knew she hadn't wanted to come here originally, but he thought in the last few weeks she'd come around. He'd believed they'd enjoyed each other's company.

But maybe he was wrong.

'Sounds fun to me,' he said lightly, and Emma just shrugged. The fear and suspicion inside him felt like acid corroding his gut. She was hiding something from him, he was sure. He knew the signs. He'd lived them.

He rose from the table and pressed a kiss to Ava's head. It took all his self-control to smile at Emma as if nothing were wrong before heading to the office.

He had rented an office in midtown to serve as the head-quarters of his new operation, LC Investments. It was, Larenzo realised with every day he spent trying to set things up, going to be a long, hard slog. Even though the charges against him had been cleared, mud stuck. People assumed he had some connection to or knowledge of the criminal activity Bertrano had been neck-deep in, and he could hardly blame them. He'd been so blind. Wilfully, stupidly blind, and he would pay the price for that for the rest of his life.

All he could do now was conduct himself honourably and prove to everyone, eventually, that he was indeed an honest man.

Prove it to Emma.

Did she believe in his innocence? Sometimes, when they spent time together, when she'd gazed at him so hungrily from across the chessboard and he'd imagined hauling her into his arms…then he thought she did. But other times he remembered how she'd flung so many accusations at him, how she'd tried to hide Ava from him, and he doubted. He feared. And fear, he'd learned, was a cripplingly powerful force.

Now he pushed those churning emotions aside and focused on work. He had a meeting that afternoon with a brilliant scientist who needed funding for a new voice-recognition technology he'd patented. Larenzo was looking forward to it; it was exactly the kind of thing he'd wanted to support when he set up his new business. It was the kind of thing he'd tried to support as CEO of Cavelli Enterprises, and he'd left the running of the company's other interests to Bertrano. He wouldn't make that kind of mistake again. He knew better now than to trust anyone, not even the people you loved.

As soon as Larenzo left the apartment, Emma breathed out a discontented sigh. He was amazingly attuned to her moods, but the last thing she wanted to do was tell him what was bothering her.

Last Saturday she'd taken Ava to New Jersey to see Meghan, and the conversation she'd had with her sister had kept her up for most of the night. It had started innocuously enough, with Meghan asking her to come for Thanksgiving, which was next week.

'I'm sure we'd love to,' Emma had said. 'I'll ask Larenzo.'

'Do you need his permission to come here now?' Meghan had asked frostily, and Emma had stared at her in dismay. Over the last few weeks they'd mutually, silently agreed on a ceasefire when it came to Larenzo, but her sister had looked as if she was about to come out with guns blazing.

'No, I don't need permission,' she'd answered, although that wasn't quite true. She always asked Larenzo if she could visit her sister on the weekends, since she knew she was taking away precious time he had with Ava. Larenzo had always said yes. But she hadn't been asking for permission. Not exactly. 'I just want to make sure he's free,' she'd told Meghan, who had stared at her as if she'd sprouted a second head.

'Who cares if he's free?' Emma had stared at her in confusion and Meghan had shaken her head slowly. 'Emma, you don't actually think I'm inviting him, do you?'

'I...' She'd stopped, because of course she had thought that. It was Thanksgiving, the holiday that was meant, more than any other, to spend time with your family. And Larenzo was part of her family, whether Meghan liked it or not. 'I suppose I did,' she'd said slowly, and Meghan had shaken her head again, the movement definitive.

'Emma, let me make this clear. I will never invite that man to my house, to my family, or into my life. The fact that you even thought for a second that I would shows me just how much he has brainwashed you—'

'Give me some credit, Meghan,' Emma had snapped. 'I can judge a person for myself.'

Meghan had pressed her lips together. 'I don't think you're seeing this particular person clearly.'

'And I don't think you are,' Emma had countered. 'Meghan, everything you know about Larenzo has come from newspapers trying to sensationalise a story in order to sell more papers.'

'Do you really think he can be entirely innocent?' Meghan had asked disbelievingly. 'There was so much evidence—'

'He was framed,' Emma had answered. 'He told me so himself.'

Meghan had rolled her eyes. 'Of course he would say that.'

'I believe him.'

'Of course you do. Emma, this man could be manipulating you—'

'And if he isn't? If he's completely innocent, and you're judging him without even bothering to get to know him?' Meghan hadn't answered and Emma had pressed her point. 'Meghan, Larenzo is part of my life now. He's Ava's father, and he's a *good* father. If you continue to blackball him like this, it will only end up driving us apart.'

Meghan had paled. 'So it's him or me?' she had asked, her voice choking.

'*No*. I don't want it to be that at all.' Emma had felt near tears as she'd stared at her sister, horrified at how quickly things had escalated. 'Please, Meghan.'

'You have to make your choice,' Meghan had insisted, and Emma had stared at her helplessly.

Now, as Emma buckled Ava into her stroller to take her to her gymnastics class, she wondered just how she could make such a terrible choice. With her father in Budapest and her mother out of her life, Meghan was the only family she had, the person she'd been closest to for her entire life. The thought of losing her made everything in her cry out in despairing protest.

And yet what was Meghan really asking her? To walk away from Larenzo? Her sister knew she couldn't, not even if she wanted to, and she *didn't* want to.

Which led her to the sinking realisation that whatever she had with Larenzo was neither real nor lasting. He'd made it abundantly clear that he wasn't interested in a relationship, had no time for either trust or love. Never mind that this attraction snapped between them, or that they'd actually enjoyed each other's company. Fundamentally

Larenzo couldn't change. He'd acknowledged that himself. He'd never changed his position on looking for a relationship, and she didn't think he ever would.

If Emma was smart, she'd do what her sister suggested and keep at least an emotional distance from Larenzo. She'd even start thinking about moving out, finding her own place, her own life. She and Larenzo could come to a custody arrangement as she'd originally suggested. That was the sensible thing to do, the only thing to do, and yet everything in Emma resisted.

Which was incredibly stupid, because she knew what it was like to care about someone more than they cared about you. To have someone walk away. Better to walk away first, to be that strong.

'So are you going to tell me what's bothering you now?' Larenzo asked that evening at dinner. His voice was mild, but she felt the steel underneath his words. He didn't like her having secrets.

Emma pushed the pasta around on her plate. 'How do you know anything's bothering me?'

'Because you're a naturally cheerful person. You have this...' Larenzo gestured with his hand '...glow about you.'

Emma looked up, her heart lightening ridiculously at his words. 'Glow?'

'You light up a room.' As if realising he'd said too much, Larenzo turned back to his meal. 'So I can tell when you're not yourself.' He paused, taking a sip of wine. 'You weren't yourself when I first came to your sister's house, but I think in the weeks since then you've gained some of your glow back. For lack of a better word.' He looked up with a faint smile, although his eyes were still shadowed.

'Moving to New York was good for me,' Emma admitted.

'Despite your initial reserve,' Larenzo stated dryly.

'Don't rub it in.' She toyed with her pasta some more, choosing her words with care. 'I do want to thank you, Larenzo, for giving me this opportunity. I was stuck in a rut living at Meghan's, and I didn't even realise how deep it had become until I left.'

He nodded, and Emma knew now would be the perfect time to tell him she was ready to move on to the next phase of her life, and find her own place. A real job. The words didn't come.

'Emma?' he prompted, because he could clearly see there was more she wanted to say. *Needed* to say.

'I spoke with my sister when I visited her,' she finally said. 'She's…not pleased about me being here.'

'I knew that.'

'I mean, really not pleased. She feels I'm becoming…' She hesitated, not wanting to reveal what she was starting to feel for Larenzo yet needing to tell him something of what was going on both with Meghan and in her own heart. 'Too friendly with you,' she finally said.

'A certain amount of friendliness between us is surely beneficial to Ava,' Larenzo answered coolly. Emma could already see how he was shutting down, his silvery eyes turning to blank screens, his mouth compressing. Even the temperature in the room seemed to have dropped.

'I think so,' she answered, 'but my sister doesn't.'

'So what does she want you to do?'

'Maintain a little distance, I guess,' Emma answered after a pause. 'Keep things…businesslike.' Meghan hadn't said as much, but Emma knew her sister would be pleased if she kept her arrangement with Larenzo as simply that: an arrangement.

'If that's what you prefer,' he said in a clipped voice. 'I suppose it's reasonable.'

'You do?' She struggled to keep the hurt from her voice.

Just like that, he was going to abandon their evenings playing chess, their precious time together with Ava?

'The most important thing is that we both have a strong and loving relationship to Ava,' Larenzo answered with a shrug. 'I don't suppose it matters what we do or don't feel for each other.'

'Right,' Emma answered numbly. 'Of course.'

'I have some work to do,' Larenzo said as he rose from the table. 'I'll give Ava a bath and put her to bed, and then I'll go to my study.'

Emma nodded, accepting the rebuff, and watched as Larenzo took Ava from her high chair. She felt as if she'd just ruined whatever they'd been building together, which showed, she supposed, just how fragile it really was.

She didn't see Larenzo again that night, and the next morning he left for the office as soon as she'd come into the kitchen for breakfast. As soon as he'd gone Emma sank into a chair, Ava on her lap, and indulged in a few minutes of wretched self-pity. Larenzo had completely withdrawn from her, and she knew now she'd told him about Meghan's concerns because she'd wanted him to dispel them. She'd wanted him to tell her how glad he was that they were friendly with one another, and even more than that. That he was starting to care.

But her gamble hadn't worked, because obviously Larenzo didn't feel the way she did. At all.

She straightened, forcing the sadness back, and reached for her phone to call Meghan and tell her she'd be happy to come for Thanksgiving.

That night she told Larenzo, keeping her voice as cool as his had been, that she'd be going to see her sister for the holiday weekend, leaving Wednesday and coming back on Saturday. She didn't ask if it would be all right.

His eyes narrowed as he gazed at her. 'Four days? That seems excessive.'

'Thanksgiving is an important holiday,' she answered. 'For family,' she emphasised, wanting in that moment to hurt him, but Larenzo's face remained expressionless.

'I see,' he said as he took a sip of his after-dinner coffee. 'I wouldn't know. Very well,' he finally said. 'I suppose you can go.'

Stung, Emma flung back at him, 'I wasn't asking your permission.'

'Even so, I am giving it,' Larenzo answered evenly. 'We are equal in Ava's guardianship and care, Emma.'

'Not legally—'

His eyes flashed and he put one hand flat on the table in a gesture that was controlled and yet somehow communicated a sense of great anger, only barely leashed. 'Are you threatening me?'

'No, of course not,' she backtracked, colour rising into her face. 'I only meant that we don't actually have a formal arrangement—'

'Then I will put one in place immediately. We can consult my lawyer on Monday.'

'I already consulted a lawyer,' Emma retorted before she could think better of it, and Larenzo went even more still.

'Did you? How...interesting.'

She searched his face, empty of expression as it was, for some flicker of emotion, some sense that he cared at all, and found nothing. Had Meghan been right? Had he been manipulating her with those forays into friendliness? Considering how completely he'd cut her off now, it seemed all too possible.

'We leave tomorrow morning,' Emma said, and without waiting for a reply she left the room.

Thanksgiving was miserable. She tried to enter into the spirit of the holiday, making handprint turkeys with Ryan and helping Meghan with the pumpkin pie, but everything in her felt weighed down, as if she could barely put one foot in front of the other. Meghan, of course, noticed.

'You really do care about him,' she said quietly, when it was just the two of them on the night of Thanksgiving. The turkey had been eaten, the dishes washed and dried, the children put to bed. Pete was upstairs reading stories to Ryan as Emma and Meghan enjoyed a glass of wine in the playroom, curled up on opposite ends of the sofa.

'It doesn't matter,' Emma answered listlessly.

'Why not?'

'Because I told him what you'd said, more or less, and he withdrew completely. We used to spend the evenings together, eat meals as a—well, together.' She swallowed past the lump that was steadily forming in her throat. 'Now I barely see him.'

'Now, that's interesting.'

Emma looked up from her moody contemplation of her glass of wine. 'Oh? How so?'

Meghan sighed. 'It shows he has a sense of honour,' she said. 'Maybe.'

'What do you mean?'

'That he would see the importance of family to you. That he would respect someone else's wishes.' She sighed again, shaking her head. 'I don't know. Ever since I spoke to you I've been regretting what I said. Maybe I was too harsh, but I'm just so afraid for you, Emma.'

'I know.'

'But if he really was framed like you told me, and he is a good father like you said...' Meghan trailed off while Emma waited, impatience brimming.

'Then?' she finally demanded. 'Then what?'

'I don't know,' Meghan admitted. 'Only that maybe we're doing him a disservice. And if you actually think you could care for him, or have a relationship...'

'I think that isn't a possibility now,' Emma answered. 'He barely wants to talk to me.'

'Because you told him about my ultimatum, and then you basically chose me,' Meghan answered bluntly. 'I don't blame him, Emma.'

'I can't believe after all this you're taking his side!'

'I'm not. I'm just trying to see things as a rational adult rather than a panicked older sister.' Meghan smiled wryly. 'I'm still not sure of anything.'

'What am I supposed to do, then? Go and tell him I changed my mind?' *That* wouldn't go over well. 'I'm not sure he's a good bet as a relationship anyway, Meghan. He told me he wasn't interested in one when we first saw each other again, and that he doesn't trust anyone, ever. And I believe him.'

'And no wonder, if his business partner framed him.' Meghan sighed. 'I really don't know. If you guys did decide to get together, it would be a hard road ahead. And you aren't used to that.'

'What?' Emma nearly choked on her wine. 'What do you mean, I'm not used to that?'

'I mean, you haven't been in a serious relationship, with all of its ups and downs. You've never committed to anyone or anything for the long haul. I don't think you've ever stayed in the same place for more than a year or two.'

Emma couldn't deny the truth of her sister's words but she still felt stung. 'There's a reason for all that, you know.'

'I know, because of Mom and Dad's divorce.'

'Not just their divorce,' Emma half mumbled. 'Mom leaving the way she did...not having any interest in us...'

'You made it pretty clear you weren't interested in her, Emma,' Meghan answered gently.

'And why should I, when she rejected us?' Emma demanded.

'She asked you to live with her a year later, didn't she? Out in Arizona.'

'Yes, and that was a complete failure.' Emma shook her head, not wanting to dwell on a memory that still had the power to hurt her. 'Total disaster. I left after only two months.' Meghan was silent and Emma glanced at her suspiciously. 'What?'

'Nothing,' Meghan said as she uncurled herself from the sofa. 'But it's getting late and I want to kiss Ryan goodnight.' She hesitated and then said, 'If you really do think Larenzo is innocent, Emma, and you really do care for him, you're going to have to try. That's all I'm saying.'

'And just a few days ago you practically threatened to disinherit me if I was friendly with him,' Emma couldn't keep from reminding her sourly.

'I know, I'm sorry. I panicked. But he is Ava's father, and you do seem to care for him. So…'

'So,' Emma answered with a sigh. *So what?*

Meghan's words rattled around in her head for the rest of the visit. Did she want to try with a man who had already declared he had no interest in her, couldn't trust? And yet those evenings she'd spent with Larenzo, the way they'd been as a family, had been so incredibly sweet. And she knew he was still attracted to her, just as she was to him. But was that enough?

Emma knew he'd been hurt badly by his business partner, and was perhaps irrevocably damaged by his time in prison. Did she want to try?

She was no nearer an answer to that question when she headed back to New York on the train on Saturday evening, packed with people returning to the city after a long weekend away. Ava was fractious and the train was delayed, so by the time she stumbled into the apartment at nine o'clock at night she was completely exhausted. Ava had fallen asleep in the cab on the way back from the station, and so Emma put her right to bed.

The apartment was silent and dark, and after a second's hesitation Emma went into the hall, flicking on the lights as she looked for Larenzo.

She finally found him in the study, slouched in one of the club chairs, a tumbler of whisky in his hand. His shirt was unbuttoned so she could see the bronzed column of his throat, and his hair was rumpled, his jaw shadowed with stubble. He looked sexy and dangerous and yet also almost unbearably sad as he glanced up at her with pain-filled eyes.

'So,' he said, his voice slightly slurred from the whisky. 'You came back.'

CHAPTER TWELVE

LARENZO GAZED AT Emma standing in the doorway, her hair creating a golden nimbus about her lovely face, and thought he was seeing a vision. Perhaps he'd drunk more whisky than he'd realised.

'Larenzo...' she whispered and he straightened in his chair, flinging his glass onto the table where it clattered noisily.

'I didn't think you were going to return,' he said. She shook her head as she moved into the room.

'Why would you think that?'

'Why wouldn't I? You've made no secret of how you resent me forcing you to come here. And I know I did blackmail you, Emma. I know that wasn't honourable, but...' He raked a hand through his hair, realising his tongue was a little looser than he'd thought. He shrugged and reached for his whisky again. 'Even now I have no regrets. Does that make me a bad man?'

'No,' Emma said quietly. She came to sit in the chair opposite him, the chessboard they'd played so many enjoyable games on between them. 'It doesn't make you a bad man, Larenzo.'

'Are you sure about that?' he asked and took a final swallow of whisky. It burned all the way to his gut. 'Everyone in the world still seems to think I'm guilty.'

'I don't,' Emma whispered and Larenzo turned to look at her.

'Do you mean that?' he asked, and to his shame his voice choked slightly.

'Yes. I do.' She gazed at him with her lovely golden-green eyes, everything about her steady, trusting. And yet how could he possibly deserve her trust? How could he trust *her*?

'Emma…' he began, and then, because he couldn't keep himself from it, he reached out and curled his hands around her shoulders, then up so his fingers curved around the back of her skull and he cradled her face in his hands just as he had that night so long ago. Her skin was as soft and warm as he remembered, her lips just as full as he brushed his thumb across them.

Memories rushed through him, painful in their intensity, as Emma waited, her lips parted, her eyes closed.

How could he *not* kiss her?

And yet even as he bent his head, he resisted. He didn't want a fling with Emma, didn't want to hurt her, and yet he knew he wasn't capable of anything else. Even now, with everything in him aching with desire and longing, he knew that. He had no trust, no love, to give. And so he pulled away.

Emma opened her eyes and gazed at him for a long moment. Larenzo gazed back, and in the silence of their locked gazes he thought she understood. She sat back in her chair, disappointment twisting her features for a moment before she composed herself.

'So how was your weekend?' she finally asked and he managed a rusty laugh.

'Pretty awful. Yours?'

'The same.'

He nodded, not wanting to go any deeper with this conversation, knowing he wouldn't be able to handle it. 'I was thinking, I haven't seen any photographs of Ava from when she was small. You must have some.'

'Yes, I do. Would you like to see them?'

'Yes. Please.'

Emma nodded and then slipped from the room to re-trieve them. Larenzo leaned back in his chair and let out a shuddering breath, forcing back the desire that was still rampaging through his system. Nothing was going to hap-pen with Emma. He wouldn't let it.

She returned a few minutes later, a pink baby book in her hands. 'I don't have all that many,' she admitted, 'be-cause I was so sleep-deprived.'

'I suppose that's understandable,' he said, and Emma handed him the book. She settled back into her chair as he opened it and gazed in wonder at a photograph of Ava when she was first born, red-faced and wrinkly.

'She looks like a little old man.'

'Meghan told me most newborns do.'

'She also looks like she had a set of lungs on her even then.'

'That she did. She came out screaming and waving her fists.'

Larenzo smiled and turned the page. He studied each photograph in turn, transfixed by these images of his daugh-ter: first tiny and swaddled with tufts of dark hair, and then chubby-cheeked and bald when it had fallen out, and then sitting on a rug, showing two milk teeth as she grinned.

'These are wonderful,' he said and looked up at Emma. He was disconcerted to see affection suffusing her face, and now that the whisky had cleared from his brain he re-alised how much he had revealed a few moments ago. He cleared his throat and handed back the book. 'Are you still pursuing photography? Beyond pictures of Ava, I mean?'

The question jolted her out of her moment's reverie. Watch-ing Larenzo's face as he studied the pictures of their daughter had made Emma's insides twist with longing. He'd looked so loving, so *tender*. Now he was waiting for her answer and she straightened, shaking her head.

'Not really. I just didn't have the time or emotional energy for it.'

'You should start again,' Larenzo said firmly. 'You had such a gift, Emma.'

'It's nice of you to say so.'

'You don't believe me?'

She let out an uncertain laugh. 'No, I do. I think. I just...' She shrugged. 'I've let it fall by the wayside, I suppose.'

'Why do you think you stopped?'

Emma rolled her eyes. 'Because of a certain eleven-month-old, perhaps?'

Larenzo surveyed her thoughtfully, his silvery gaze seeming to see so much. 'Do you think that's really it?'

'What do you mean?' Emma demanded, but uncomfortably she heard Meghan's voice in her head. *You've never committed to anyone or anything for the long haul.* She'd loved photography, but she'd let it slide, hadn't figured out a way to pursue it with the demands of a baby. Hadn't committed to it.

'Are you afraid to exhibit them?' Larenzo asked.

Emma stiffened. 'Afraid?'

'Of trying and failing. Most people are.'

'Then most people are smart,' Emma answered before she could help herself. Larenzo arched an eyebrow, and she flushed. 'I mean, no one wants to fail.'

'If at first you don't succeed...' Larenzo quipped. Emma managed a small smile.

'In any case,' she said, trying for a brisker tone, 'I've never really been ambitious, for photography or anything else.'

'Why not?'

She shrugged, trying to put him off. These questions were too perceptive, too revealing. 'I always wanted to travel, live life on the road. A career seemed so stuffy.'

Larenzo nodded, not saying anything, and Emma wondered what he was thinking. Did he believe her? Did she even believe herself?

'Yet you gave up travel to have Ava,' he said after a moment, and Emma tensed.

'A decision I've never regretted.'

'Yet a surprising one all the same, considering your lifestyle choices previously.'

'Maybe,' Emma allowed, 'but you never know how you're going to feel until a situation arises. When I realised I was pregnant with Ava, and that she was a part of me...' Her throat thickened as she remembered the wondrous sense that here was a person to love, who would love her.

'A family,' Larenzo said softly and, blinking rapidly, Emma nodded.

'Yes. A family. Our family.'

Larenzo's eyes gleamed and for a moment they just stared at one another, overwhelmed by this simple yet incredible truth.

'Thank you, Emma,' Larenzo finally said, and although she didn't know what he was thanking her for, she still felt how it was a withdrawal. They were a family, but not the kind she wanted to be now.

A week slipped by, a week where Emma couldn't tell what was going on with her and Larenzo. They'd seemed to have come to a silent and somewhat uncomfortable truce, eating meals together, spending time with Ava. Yet the ease and enjoyment they'd had before that wretched conversation was gone, replaced with a polite and careful civility.

It made Emma ache for what they'd had, what they could have if both of them were willing to try. But she didn't even know if she had it in her to try, and Larenzo had given no indication that he wanted to start something more.

She remembered with an ache of longing that moment in the study when he'd almost kissed her, but he *hadn't* kissed her, even though her body had been sending out rocket flares of desire. There was no way Larenzo could have missed those signals. But he'd chosen to ease back, to pretend as if they hadn't been about to start something wonderful. She had to accept that.

Didn't she?

She wrestled with the question for a few days, wondering if she dared ask Larenzo if he would consider making their relationship romantic. The thought of him rejecting such an idea made everything in her cringe. She knew what rejection felt like. She'd kept herself from it for a reason.

Needing a distraction from her endlessly circling thoughts, she got out her camera and, with Ava in the stroller, headed for Central Park.

It was early December and the leaves had fallen, leaving the trees in the park bare, their stark branches silhouetted against a bright blue sky. Emma took a few photographs: the Bethesda fountain with its basin covered in a thin, glassy film of ice; the Mall, its cobblestones glittering with frost, the park benches that lined either side all empty; a rowboat that had come loose from its moorings and now drifted, empty, in the middle of the lake, bumping against the chunks of ice.

When Ava started grizzling from the cold, Emma headed back to the apartment. To her surprise Larenzo was home even though it was only a little after five. The sun was already starting to set, sending long, golden rays across the living room floor.

Emma unbuckled Ava from her stroller and peeled off

her puffy snowsuit; her daughter immediately started toddling towards Larenzo, her arms outstretched.

'I didn't think you'd be back yet,' Emma said. 'I haven't started dinner.'

'It's fine.' Larenzo scooped Ava up into his arms and nuzzled his face against her hair. Emma watched, a tightness growing in her chest. Would she ever get used to these unguarded moments when she saw so clearly how Larenzo loved his daughter? When his tenderness made her melt inside, and long for something she didn't think Larenzo had it in him to give her?

'I came home early because I wanted to talk to you,' Larenzo said, and he sounded so serious that Emma's heart seemed to flip right over. She didn't know whether to be excited or afraid.

As Larenzo put Ava back down and swivelled to her with an intent, sombre gaze she decided to be afraid.

'Is…is everything okay?'

'What?' He looked surprised, and his expression cleared a bit. 'Yes. Fine. Everything is fine.'

'It's just you were looking so serious.'

'No, no.' He ran a hand through his hair, rumpling it as he always did, his gaze distracted now. 'No, nothing's wrong. It's only there is a party I have to go to tomorrow night, an opening gala for a research company that is pioneering a new technology. A lot of people will be there, people I need to meet.'

'Okay,' Emma said after a brief pause. 'I suppose I can manage on my own for a night.' She'd meant it as a joke but Larenzo didn't even crack a smile. He looked even more serious than before.

'The thing is,' he said, 'I wondered if you would be willing to go with me.'

Emma's jaw nearly dropped. 'Go with you?'

'I can hire a babysitter, someone who is more than competent, and we don't have to leave until Ava is asleep.'

'Why do you want me to go with you?' Emma asked, and then could have kicked herself. Was she *trying* to get him to rescind the invitation?

He hesitated and then answered, 'I think it would be better if I bring someone to events such as this one.'

'Better? How?'

He sighed and raked his hand through his hair again. 'After everything that has happened, people still wonder if I was involved in criminal activity. I'm trying to build people's confidence and trust, and I think attending an event with you, the mother of my child, would help with that.'

Emma blinked, stung more than she wanted to reveal to Larenzo, or even to admit to herself. 'Well, at least you're being honest,' she said tartly.

Larenzo stared at her, a frown furrowing his forehead. 'You're angry.'

'Why should I be angry?' Emma countered, even though she didn't actually want Larenzo to answer that question. She was angry because for a moment her hopes had sailed sky-high as she'd thought Larenzo was actually asking her out on a date. She'd believed he wanted to be with her. But no, he was just using her as a way to restore his image, just as Meghan had once suggested. The realisation was bitter.

'I don't know why you should be angry,' Larenzo answered in that toneless voice Emma knew he used to mask his annoyance. 'I'm asking you to go to a party, that's all.'

That's all. 'Thanks for clearing that up,' she retorted and Larenzo spread his hands, clearly bewildered.

'What is wrong, Emma?'

'Nothing,' she replied, and blew out a breath. She was being unreasonable, she knew, by acting offended by Larenzo's invitation. He didn't know how she felt, how she wanted him to feel. 'Nothing,' she repeated, and lifted her camera from where it had been hanging around her neck.

Larenzo noticed, his eyes narrowing. 'Were you taking photos today?'

'I thought I might as well.'

'May I see?'

She hesitated, then, shrugging, handed him the camera. He flicked it on and began to scroll through the most recent photos, frowning slightly as he studied the images. Emma rescued Ava, who had crawled under the coffee table and managed to get herself stuck. Her heart was beating a little harder; she wanted Larenzo to like the photos. She wanted him to like *her*.

'They're good,' he said at last, 'if a bit bleak.'

A bit stung by the criticism, she grabbed the camera from him, setting Ava down with her other hand. Looking at the photos again, she realised they were rather bleak. The park had been full of people, but she'd made it look deserted. Empty and unloved. 'I suppose I was in a bit of a bleak mood,' she answered, and went in the kitchen to start dinner.

CHAPTER THIRTEEN

EMMA GAZED IN the mirror in her dressing room and felt the flutters start again in her belly. She'd spent a long time deciding on a dress; Larenzo had suggested she hit the boutiques on Fifth Avenue, the sky the limit, for her gown for the gala tonight.

While he'd watched Ava, Emma had gone out with Meghan, who had taken the train into the city, to shop. It had felt surreal and wonderfully decadent to try on designer gowns, swilling champagne and parading in front of mirrors.

'So do you think something is happening between you and Larenzo?' Meghan had asked. To her credit, her sister had been civil with Larenzo when she'd come to the apartment, and he'd been just as civil back. Still, it was a tense relationship, and perhaps it always would be.

'I don't know.' Emma had sunk onto the velvet chaise in the dressing room, the ivory satin of her gown poufing out around her. 'He told me he only was asking me because it would look good for his image.'

Meghan's mouth had curved wryly. 'At least he was honest.'

'I suppose.'

She'd gestured to the gown. 'What do you think about this one?'

Emma had glanced down at the crystal-beaded ivory

satin. 'It's gorgeous, but it looks too much like a wedding dress.'

Meghan had given her a look so full of sympathy that Emma had almost felt annoyed. She hadn't wanted to be pitied. She'd wanted to find a beautiful dress and enjoy her evening with Larenzo, no matter what his reasons for inviting her out.

Now she smoothed her hands down the bodice of the emerald satin gown she'd chosen. It was deceptively simple, strapless with a ruched bodice that clung to her figure before flaring out from her knees to her ankles. She'd left her hair loose about her shoulders and used only a little eyeliner and lip gloss to emphasise her features.

She couldn't remember the last time she'd worn something so elegant or felt so beautiful. She hoped Larenzo thought she looked beautiful. She hoped he would tell her so.

He tapped on the door of her bedroom, Ava squealing happily in his arms. 'Emma? Are you almost ready? I was just about to put Ava to bed and then we should go.'

'All right.' With one last glance at her reflection, she turned and opened the door. Her breath felt sucked right out of her lungs as she stared at Larenzo. She'd never seen him in black tie before. The crisp white tuxedo shirt emphasised his perfect physique, his chiselled jaw and bronzed skin. He held Ava, dressed in her pyjamas, balanced on one hip, and Emma didn't think she would ever see a man look so sexy and yet so heart-warmingly wonderful at the same time. Tuxedo and baby. A devastating combination.

Then she saw the blaze of heat in Larenzo's eyes and it suddenly felt hard to breathe. Hard to think. She moistened her lips with the tip of her tongue.

'Do you...do you like it?'

'The dress?' Larenzo clarified huskily. 'Yes. Yes, you look...stunning, Emma. Truly beautiful.'

'Thank you.' Her heart was beating so hard she thought he might be able to see it pounding through the fabric of her dress. She reached out to take Ava. 'I can put her to bed.'

'I don't think we should risk having her slobber on you,' Larenzo answered with a small smile. 'I'll do it. I don't mind.'

While Larenzo disappeared into the nursery with Ava, Emma fetched her matching wrap and clutch and then waited nervously in the hall. A few minutes later the baby-sitter, a competent woman in her forties whom Larenzo had hired from a well-reputed service, arrived, and then Larenzo came out, a finger to his lips.

'I think she's settled.'

He shook hands with the sitter and then, with one hand on the small of her back, he led Emma out of the apart-ment and into the elevator.

The elevator was huge, and yet it felt tiny and airless as they stood there, shoulders brushing, Emma's stomach clenching hard with suppressed desire.

'You look good too,' she blurted, because how could she *not* say it?

Larenzo arched an eyebrow. 'Thank you.'

She felt like an idiot, but she didn't even care. Tonight she just wanted to enjoy this time with Larenzo. Pretend, even, that it really was a date. Tomorrow they could go back to the reality of being sort of friends. Tonight was for magic.

Larenzo gazed at Emma covertly, out of the corner of his eye. She looked so very lovely standing there, like a proud, emerald flame in her dress, standing tall and straight, her chin lifted. Her hair, usually caught in a practical ponytail, was loose about her shoulders and Larenzo's palms itched with the desire and even the need to touch it. To slide his hands along her skull as he'd done the other night, but this time he wouldn't stop. He wouldn't ease away with regret. No, instead, he'd kiss her as he'd longed to then, deeply, exploring every sensitive curve and contour of her mouth, bringing her body in exquisite contact with his...

Too late Larenzo realised what this little fantasy was doing to him. He shifted discreetly, trying to ease the persistent ache in his groin, and then the doors of the elevator thankfully pinged open. It was going to be a long, uncomfortable night.

And yet he knew, as he took Emma's arm and helped her into the waiting limo, that he was going to enjoy every moment of it, with Emma by his side.

That presumption was questioned just twenty minutes later when he entered the ballroom where the gala was being held and heard the murmurs of speculation ripple through the room. Heads turned, eyes narrowed, lips pursed. Whispers seemed to mock him from every corner of the room.

Larenzo tensed, and then glanced down at Emma, who was gazing around the ballroom, enraptured. Had she noticed? Was he being too sensitive, or even paranoid? God knew he'd learned to be suspicious about everything and everyone. *Even Emma.*

Which was why they would enjoy this one evening together, and no more.

He looked up, and met the gaze of a CEO he'd been on friendly terms with before everything had come falling down. The man nodded curtly and then looked away.

In the two months since he'd been in America, Larenzo had kept a low profile, meeting privately with investors and entrepreneurs, working hard to restore his reputation one individual at a time. He hadn't gone to any major events because he hadn't wanted a reaction like this one. Yet he'd also known he needed to get out, show his face, prove to the world he had nothing to hide.

Clearly that was going to be a harder task than he'd anticipated.

Straightening, he guided Emma towards the bar in the corner. 'Champagne?' he asked and she nodded happily.

'Definitely.'

He procured glasses for them both and handed one to Emma. Tension was tightening the muscles in his shoulder blades, and he could feel the start of a headache. No one approached them, but he saw and felt the sideways glances, and knew Emma did too. She glanced up at him, her flute of champagne held to her lips.

'I see what you mean about needing to restore your image,' she said quietly.

He shrugged as if it were no matter, keeping his face blankly indifferent. He was good at that. He'd been hiding his emotions since he was a child, when the nuns at the orphanage took delight in your fear and considered any smile smug, laughter punishable.

'Shall we go chat?' Emma suggested brightly. 'That's why you're here, isn't it?'

He nodded tersely, dread pooling like acid in his stomach, corroding even the pleasure he had in being with Emma. It had been such a mistake to bring her tonight. He'd thought it would help, but now he cringed to think of her seeing his shame, the condemnation or at least awful curiosity on everyone's faces. Everyone here was wondering if he was guilty.

'Who should we talk to?' Emma pressed. 'What about the science technology guy? Is he here?'

Larenzo almost smiled at her tenacity. 'He's over there,' he said, nodding towards the other side of the ballroom, and determinedly Emma stared forward. Larenzo did smile then, wryly, and he guided her to Stephen Blane, one man, at least, who didn't think he was guilty. Or at least was willing to do business with him, guilty or not.

'Hello.' Emma stuck out her hand, which Stephen shook bemusedly. Emma was a force to be reckoned with, Larenzo thought, gazing down at her with bemused affection. She'd intimated that all of Ava's forcefulness came from him, but he knew it came from her too. She was a strong person, even if she didn't seem to realise it.

They chatted with Stephen for a while, and eventually a few other guests joined them. The conversation came in starts and stops, and Larenzo did his best to navigate its choppy waters, and ignore the occasional innuendo or sly glance, but each one rubbed him painfully raw.

Would it never end? Would he never be free from Bertrano's treachery and his own terrible mistakes?

Emma, he saw, kept her chin up the whole evening, her voice bright as she chatted determinedly with every person in their circle. But he saw the way her eyes widened when someone made some oh-so-clever quip—*How's America, Cavelli? The food's better than what you're used to, eh?*—and her body tensed. Larenzo ignored the sly innuendoes and the way people didn't always meet his eyes. They were curious, perhaps even a little afraid. He could wait it out. The people who mattered believed him.

Like Emma.

Even so, he'd never wanted her to hear this. See this. After an hour of it he'd had enough. Taking her arm, he propelled her to the dance floor.

'Let's dance.'

Clearly startled, Emma deposited her half-full flute of champagne on a waiter's tray before following him onto the floor. 'I didn't take you for a dancer.'

He wasn't, not really. 'No, why not?' he asked as he pulled her into his arms, sliding his hands down to her hips, the satin of her dress slippery under his palms. He could feel the warmth of her skin through the fabric. She draped her arms about his shoulders, her breasts brushing his chest. It was sheer torture to sway to the music and not pull her more snugly to him.

'You've always seemed so focused on work. Even when you were at the villa, you usually had your laptop with you out on the terrace. You never really relaxed, as far as I could see, except maybe a swim, and that was for exercise.'

'I know. I regret that.'

'Do you?' She tilted her head up to gaze at him, her golden-green eyes luminous, her eyebrows raised. 'Why?'

'Because I worked so hard and for what? It was all taken away in the end.' He heard bitterness spike his voice and strove to moderate his tone. 'I wish I'd enjoyed life more.'

Her lips pursed. 'You seemed to enjoy it well enough, judging from the photos I saw of you in the tabloids with one blonde beauty or another.' She glanced at him from under her lashes, waiting for his response.

His mouth tugged upwards in a smile. 'Jealous?'

'Hardly,' she scoffed.

He wished she were jealous. He wished she felt as much for him as he felt for her, even though he knew he couldn't act on it. 'That was just a form of exercise too,' he murmured, his breath fanning her cheek. He felt her shiver in response.

'Then you're obviously very fit,' she returned tartly, and he actually laughed. Emma was the only person who had ever made him laugh.

'Actually, I'm terribly out of shape. Do you know the last time I've…exercised, Emma?'

Colour washed her cheeks and he saw how her pupils dilated. This was such a dangerous conversation to have. He was flirting with fire, and yet he couldn't stop. He felt intoxicated, giddy with desire, even though he'd only had a few sips of champagne.

'I'm not sure I want to know.'

'You,' he said huskily. 'The last time was with you.'

The colour in her cheeks deepened and she looked away. Larenzo touched the tip of his finger to her chin, turned her back to face him. 'What about you?' he asked. Suddenly it was important to know.

'Me?' She let out a shaky, little laugh. 'I think the answer to that is obvious. In the nineteen months since—well, you *know*, I've been pregnant, had a baby, and been living with my sister. What do you think?'

A mixture of joy, pride, and overwhelming desire, the emotions primal and fierce, burst within him. 'Good.'

'Good?' Emma searched his face. 'Why exactly is that good, Larenzo?' she asked quietly. 'What...what are we doing here?'

He didn't answer, couldn't answer, because he knew the only thing he could say was nothing and he didn't want to say it. And Emma must have read all of that in his face for she stopped swaying to the music and broke out of his embrace.

'Excuse me,' she said, and walked quickly off the dance floor towards the ladies' room.

What was he doing? What was *she* doing? Emma stared in the mirror, saw how flushed her face was, how dark and dilated her eyes. She looked like a woman in the throes of desire. She *was* a woman in the throes of desire, and for a few exquisite moments on the dance floor she'd thought Larenzo felt something back. He'd practically been flirting with her, for heaven's sake, and then...

Then he'd pulled back. Again. Letting out a shuddering breath, Emma turned on the tap and ran cold water onto her wrists. Anything to douse this treacherous heat inside her. Every time she thought something was going to happen with Larenzo, he backed off. She didn't need to be a rocket scientist to figure out why; he'd told her himself, after all. He didn't trust people, didn't want that kind of relationship. And neither had she, for most of her life. But being with Larenzo, seeing him with Ava, had changed her.

Too bad it hadn't changed him in the same way.

Sighing, she dried her hands and turned to go back to the ballroom. Maybe she'd tell Larenzo they should call it a night. This evening had been emotionally exhausting in too many ways.

Two women brushed past Emma as they went into the ladies', their heads bent together as they gossiped. They didn't even notice her, but Emma stilled as their hushed voices penetrated the welter of her own miserable thoughts.

'He has some nerve, showing up here,' one woman said. 'I mean, *prison*.'

'It was all a bit suspect, wasn't it, his release? He confessed, after all.'

'It stinks to high heaven,' the first woman stated firmly. 'The investigation is still going on. Who knows which evidence was planted? Raguso was his mentor, you know. Like a father to him, apparently, raised him from when he was a boy. The whole thing is appalling, really.'

The women disappeared into the stalls and Emma walked out to the ballroom on stiff, wooden legs. She hadn't realised Larenzo had been *that* close to Raguso. She'd known he was his business partner, yes, but mentor? *Father figure*, raised him from when he was a boy?

And this was the man that had betrayed him?

Now his trust issues made even more terrible sense. Her steps slowed as she considered how badly Larenzo had been hurt. Could he, *would* he ever recover from that? Did she want to help him try?

You've never committed to anyone or anything for the long haul.

Could she, for Larenzo's sake? She was already falling in love with him. If she was honest, there was no falling about it. She was already there. Could she, loving him as she did, help him to heal? To trust and love again? Love *her*?

Her heart flip-flopped inside her chest like a landed fish and she pressed one hand to it as excitement and fear raced through her. She wanted to do this. She needed to try.

'You were gone a long time.'

Emma nearly jumped as Larenzo seemed to materialise next to her. She hadn't seen him approach, thanks to her whirling thoughts. Now she blinked back all the questions and offered him a smile. 'Not a very gentlemanly comment to make,' she teased, and Larenzo looked startled for a moment by her levity before he smiled faintly.

'I apologise.'

Belatedly Emma remembered how she'd left him on the dance floor. She linked her arm with his. 'Shall we dance again?'

Larenzo gazed down at her, studying her face, trying to gauge her mood.

'Please, Larenzo,' Emma said softly, and wordlessly he took her back out onto the floor.

This time when he took her in his arms Emma didn't hold anything back. She pressed her body against his, felt him tense as she wound her arms around his neck, trying to communicate in every way that she was his, that he could trust her. She knew she could hardly convince him with one dance, but it was a beginning.

It was the beginning, she hoped, of everything.

CHAPTER FOURTEEN

THEY STAYED ON the dance floor for nearly an hour, swaying to the music, needing no words. After the first dance Larenzo's body relaxed into hers, and he bowed his head so his lips brushed her hair. Emma closed her eyes and felt almost perfectly content, even as she ached for so much more. For the first time she hoped she and Larenzo might actually move on from this, to something far sweeter and deeper.

It was after eleven o'clock before they finally broke apart. Larenzo's expression was both dazed and intent as he looked down at her.

Then without any words he took her by the hand and led her off the dance floor, and away from the hotel. The December night air was a cold slap of reality but before Emma could consider what was happening between them their limo sidled to the kerb and the driver jumped out to open the door. Emma slid inside, followed by Larenzo. Their thighs touched and their hands were still linked. Neither of them spoke.

Expectation coiled more tightly inside her with every passing moment; the air felt electric, snapping with tension. Larenzo was staring straight ahead; in the darkness Emma could not see his expression, and she doubted she'd be able to read it anyway. But she *felt* his desire. She certainly felt her own.

Ten minutes passed in exquisite tension. The limo pulled up to their building and the driver opened the door.

'Good evening, Mr Cavelli,' the doorman called, but Larenzo brushed past him with no more than a nod, his hand still holding Emma's.

The elevator felt even smaller and more airless than before as they rode in silence to the penthouse. Emma could feel the heavy thuds of her heart, and each desperate breath she took sounded loud and laboured in the confines of the elevator. Larenzo's jaw was bunched, his gaze on the floor numbers as they slid past and the elevator rose higher, higher. Another breath. Her hands clenched into fists at her sides, and her wrap slithered off her shoulders, trailing to the floor.

Only a few more seconds and they would be in the apartment, they would be alone...

The doors swooshed open and Larenzo stepped out into the hallway, swiping his key card before the door creaked open. Emma followed behind him, the blood beginning to roar in her ears. She closed the door behind her as Larenzo turned to her, and even in the dim lighting of the hall she could see the hunger on his face, and it thrilled her.

He pressed her back against the door, his breathing ragged as he curled one hand around the nape of her neck and brought his lips down hard on hers.

'Mr Cavelli?'

The sound of the babysitter's voice, and her light footsteps coming down the hall, was like a bucket of ice water thrown over them. Larenzo jerked back and then turned to face the babysitter. Emma sagged against the door, disappointment swamping her along with the still-potent desire. Her lips burned.

Distantly she heard Larenzo speak to the woman, and numbly, with a murmured thanks, Emma moved aside so she could leave. The click of the door and the distant ping of the elevator seemed to echo through the foyer; Larenzo switched on the lights, bathing them both in an electric glow. Emma blinked under the bright glare, painfully conscious now at how completely the mood had been broken.

'Well.' Larenzo hesitated, his hands in the pockets of his trousers, his face partially averted from hers. 'It's late.'

Emma swallowed. 'Yes.'

The silence stretched on, but it didn't feel expectant. It felt like disappointment. Failure.

Larenzo let out a sigh so small and sad Emma almost didn't hear it. Almost didn't see the way his shoulders slumped for a single second before he straightened and turned away from her.

'Goodnight, Emma,' he said, and she watched him walk away. The click of his bedroom door shutting was as final a sound as she'd ever heard.

She stood in the hallway for a moment, then switched off the lights and breathed in the darkness. Once again Larenzo had backed off. Once again she was alone, aching with emptiness and unfulfilled desire.

But it didn't have to be this way.

The thought alone sent anticipation as well as fear racing through her, tingling every nerve ending. Quietly Emma moved through the apartment, switching on the dishwasher, tidying up the kitchen, checking on Ava. And all the while she was thinking about what she could do. What she wanted to do.

She could go in Larenzo's room, not even knock. Slip inside quietly and...

And what? Seduce him, when her only experience was that one night with him, and he had thousands of conquests notched on his proverbial bedpost?

Holding her hands up to her face, Emma let out a shaky laugh. The truth was, she had no idea what she was doing. No experience.

But she could try. Even when it was risky. Especially when it was risky. She knew bone-deep that Larenzo would keep backing off, because of his history. She was the one who needed to make the first move, take the first step. Risk her heart.

Alone in her bedroom, she gazed out at Central Park now shrouded in darkness. Her heart was starting to beat hard again, just as it had been when they'd been waiting in the elevator. When she'd been so sure something was going to happen.

But something could happen now.

Emma closed her eyes. What was the worst that Larenzo could do? Refuse her, send her back to her bedroom? It would hurt, yes, and it would be terribly awkward tomorrow, but the alternative, of doing nothing, was far worse.

Wasn't it?

Quickly she stripped off her gown and slipped on a white silk nightie that was the sexiest thing she owned. Not exactly the outfit of a great seductress, she acknowledged wryly as she glanced in the mirror. The nightie was simple but hopefully it would make her intentions clear.

Taking a deep breath, and before she could think better of it, she slipped out of her bedroom, tiptoed across the hallway, and knocked softly on Larenzo's door.

She didn't wait for him to answer, just opened the door and slipped inside, her heart beating so hard and fast she could feel it in her throat. Larenzo's bedroom was lost in shadow, the bed no more than a dark expanse in the middle, and for a moment she couldn't see Larenzo.

Then she heard his rapidly indrawn breath and she saw him standing by the window, the studs of his tuxedo shirt unfastened so it hung open, revealing the beautiful, bronzed expanse of his chest.

Emma stared at him dumbly, amazed she'd got this far and yet not knowing how to take that last step. *I've come to seduce you* sounded laughable. She moistened her lips and then croaked a beginning.

'Larenzo...'

She didn't get a chance to say anything more. As if propelled by a greater force, Larenzo strode towards her, then pulled her into his arms as his mouth came down hard and hot on hers. Excitement exploded inside her as she returned the kiss, hungry, desperate, overwhelming. Larenzo was already skimming his hands under her nightgown, tossing it the floor.

Emma pulled back his shirt; the sleeves snagged on his arms and she let out a ragged laugh as she tugged it off, the studs scattering onto the floor. She smoothed her hands along the hot, satiny skin of his chest and shoulders and let out a deep sigh of satisfaction.

She'd wanted this so, so much. And Larenzo must have too, because he barely gave her a moment to revel in the feel of him before he was carrying her to the bed, depositing her on top of the slippery satin duvet before joining her there, stretching his long, hard body out on top of hers.

She reached for the button of his trousers and with a few tugs and kicks the trousers were off, followed by his boxer shorts. Now they were both naked.

Emma drew her breath in sharply as her hand closed around the thick shaft of his arousal. Larenzo sucked in a breath too, his eyes closed, and then he leaned down and kissed her again. And again. Their limbs tangled as they drank deeply of one another, bodies pressed hot and close together, and even so Emma felt as if she couldn't get close enough.

She arched upwards as Larenzo skimmed his hand down her body before finding the juncture of her thighs and when he touched her so tenderly and yet so knowingly, she nearly wept. She'd missed this. Missed *him*, so much.

'Do you...do you have a condom?' she whispered, not wanting to break the moment but knowing she had to.

Larenzo let out a soft huff of laughter as he rolled off her. 'Actually, yes.'

Emma propped herself on her elbows. 'So you *were* hoping to get lucky,' she dared to tease.

'I guess I was. I just didn't want to admit it, even to myself.'

Her face softened and her heart ached with love for this man. This man who was such an astounding combination of pride and humility, hard and soft, need and arrogance.

'Come here,' she whispered, and held out her arms.

And Larenzo came, folding his body around her as he slid gently inside. Emma drew a quick, sharp breath at the intensity of it and he gazed down at her in concern.

'I'm not hurting you, am I?'

'No. No.' She wrapped her legs around his hips as she brought him deeper into her body. 'No,' she told him. 'Never.' It felt like a promise.

Larenzo lay with his arms around Emma, his heart still thudding and his body tingling with the aftershocks of their lovemaking. She curled her body around his, one leg across his hip, and his heart swelled with emotion, with love for her. Love he hadn't expected to feel, hadn't thought he had it in him to feel. He'd been so empty, and yet Emma had made him full again.

Yet even now he wondered. Doubted. Could this really work? He wasn't even sure what this was.

Shifting so she was resting more comfortably against him, he decided to go for light. 'So did you come in here for a reason?'

She laughed softly as she smoothed one hand down his chest. '*This* reason.'

'Ah.'

'Yes. Ah.'

They lay there in silence for a moment, and then Emma

raised herself up one elbow so she could gaze down at him.
Her face was flushed, her hair like a golden-brown cloud,
but her eyes were serious.

'Larenzo, at the party tonight, I overheard something.'

The sleepy relaxation that had been stealing through
him vanished in an instant. 'Oh?'

'Some women in the ladies'. They said…' She nibbled
her lip, and, despite the tension that was now keeping his
body rigid, Larenzo felt another wave of lust crash through
him. He almost reached for her again, to satisfy his desire
as well as to keep her from talking. He didn't know what
she was going to say, but he felt sure he didn't want to hear
it. He didn't want to talk about how people had gossiped,
speculated, *doubted*.

'They said Bertrano Raguso was your mentor,' she said
quietly. 'Like a father to you.'

He blinked, shocked, because he'd been expecting her
to talk about crime and guilt, not about Bertrano. Not
about *feelings*.

'Was he?' she asked, her voice wavering slightly, and
Larenzo shrugged.

'I told you we were close.'

'I suppose I didn't realise you were that close.' She hesitated, and then pressed her hand to his cheek, the simple
movement nearly his undoing. 'I'm so sorry,' she whispered, and the realisation that she was sorry on his account, that she was *sad* on his account, made a lump form
in Larenzo's throat and for a moment he couldn't speak.

'There's nothing you need to be sorry for,' he said
gruffly as he gathered her back into his arms. 'It had nothing to do with you.'

'I'm sorry someone you cared about so much betrayed
you so terribly. I thought it was bad enough that he was
your business partner. But a man like a father—'

'Yes.' Larenzo stared up at the ceiling, as close to weep-ing as he'd ever been. Eventually he forced the feeling back. 'Yes, he was that.'

'How did you meet him?'

No one knew the story, and yet now, to his amazement, Larenzo realised he wanted to tell Emma. He wanted her to know.

'I was attempting to pick his pocket,' he said, and she let out a little startled laugh.

'Seriously?'

'Seriously. I was twelve. I'd been living on the streets for about a year. Surviving mainly by my wits, stealing, pickpocketing, occasionally making honest money by doing odd jobs. Sleeping rough, or sometimes in a shelter. For a few months, in winter, a couple of us clubbed together in an abandoned apartment building.'

She shivered a little in his arms. 'I can't imagine how hard that must have been.'

'It was better than the orphanage,' Larenzo answered. 'At least on the street I had control of my own destiny. In the orphanage...some of the nuns were kind. Others were needlessly cruel. They enjoyed meting out punishment, seeing our pain. I hated it.' Emma didn't answer, just put her arms more tightly around him, and absently Larenzo stroked her hand as the memories assailed him and then spilled from his lips.

'Anyway, when I was twelve, I saw Bertrano. He was in his forties then, a successful businessman. I remember his coat was the softest thing I'd ever touched. Cashmere.'

'And what happened? Did he catch you?'

'Yes, even though I must say I was a very good pick-pocket. He caught me by the scruff of my neck and shook me hard. Told me he'd take me to the police, and that I'd end up in prison if...' Larenzo broke off. He *had* ended up in prison, thanks to Bertrano. Even now it hurt.

Gently Emma stroked his cheek, brought him back from

the darkness. 'If you didn't stop?' she guessed, and he nodded.

'Yes. I ran off, didn't really think anything of it. But he found me the next day, and bought me a meal. It went on like that for a few months. I was suspicious of him, but Bertrano, I think, was lonely. He'd lost his wife and son in a car accident. He had no family.'

'And you had no family.'

'No.'

'So what happened then?' Emma asked and Larenzo forced himself to continue. The memories were harder now, tainted as they were by Bertrano's betrayal, and yet he still wanted, or at least needed, to say them.

'He offered to send me to boarding school. He wanted me to do something with myself. I didn't want to at first. I knew what institutional life was like. But then one of my friends, a boy who was only ten, died. Knifed in an alleyway, and I realised I had to get out. So I accepted, and went to a school near Rome. At first I wasn't accepted, people could tell where I came from. But I didn't care. I had warm clothes and a bed and so much food. And I actually liked the learning.'

'It must have seemed like a whole new world.'

'It did. And then I won a scholarship to university, and when I graduated Bertrano asked me to work for him.' His throat had thickened again and he stared up at the ceiling, determinedly dry-eyed. 'I joined the business, and when I was twenty-five he changed it to Raguso and Cavelli Enterprises. When I was thirty, he changed it just to Cavelli. He said he wanted to bequeath the business to me, that I'd worked hard for it, for him, and I was as good as a son.'

'He loved you,' Emma said quietly. Larenzo swallowed.

'And I loved him. Which has made it all the harder to accept how he was willing to betray me.'

They were both silent, their bodies still wrapped around

one another's, the only sound their breathing. Eventually Emma stirred a bit.

'Do you think he's regretted what he did to you?' she asked quietly.

'I don't know,' Larenzo admitted. 'Even now I want to give him the benefit of the doubt. I want to believe he was just weak and afraid. I don't think he had criminal connections the whole time. I'd left a lot of areas of the company to him, and I think he got in over his head.'

'And that's why you confessed.'

'I confessed because the proof was there. I was CEO of the company, and Bertrano had put my name all over his shady dealings. I'd put my name all over it, by giving him that leeway.'

'You still could have fought it, Larenzo,' Emma insisted. 'But you didn't because you loved him. Because you were protecting him.'

He closed his eyes against the memory, and her flawless, painful understanding. 'Yes.'

She placed one hand on his cheek, forcing him to look down at her. 'That is nothing to be ashamed of.'

'Isn't it?' he demanded rawly. 'He might have loved me as his son once, but he still treated me as his stooge. And I let him.'

'He was an old, weak, frightened man.'

'You're pardoning him?' Larenzo demanded and Emma shook her head, certainty blazing from her eyes.

'No. I'm pardoning you.'

He took her hand in his then, and pressed it to his lips. Their gazes held, the communication between them silent and pure. *You are understood. Forgiven. Loved.*

'Thank you,' he whispered and she smiled even as her eyes filled with tears.

'Do you know that's what you said after the last time we made love? You don't need to thank me, Larenzo.'

'I've never told anyone all of that before,' he said. 'I'm grateful that you listened. That you understood.'

'I'm grateful you told me,' she answered, and they didn't speak after that. They didn't need to.

CHAPTER FIFTEEN

THE NEXT MORNING Emma got up with Ava while Larenzo slept. The sleep of the just, she thought with a wry smile as she gazed down at him. He looked glorious stretched out in bed, the sheet tangled around his hips, one arm thrown over his head, the morning sunlight touching his body with gold.

Ava let out another yowl and reluctantly Emma turned away from Larenzo. Her heart was light as she changed and fed Ava; last night things had finally shifted. Larenzo's story of his childhood made her heart ache with sorrow and grief for the lonely boy he'd been, but she was also thankful, so thankful, that he'd told her. They could go on from here, Emma thought. They could build something strong and true. Last night they had laid its foundation.

She was standing by the stove, scrambling eggs, Ava sitting in her high chair banging a spoon on the tray, when Larenzo came into the kitchen. He'd changed into jeans and a T-shirt but his hair was still rumpled, his jaw dark with stubble, and he looked so sexy that Emma's insides clenched hard on a spasm of longing.

'Hey,' he said, and she just about managed to keep her voice sounding normal as she answered.

'Hey.'

'Dada!' They both looked in surprise at Ava and then at each other as she proudly said it again. 'Dada.'

'That's right, sweetheart,' Emma said, her voice a little choked, and Larenzo scooped his daughter up into his arms.

'Aren't you the clever one?'

Ava grinned and patted his cheeks and then squirmed to get down. Larenzo let her down, watching in bemusement as she cruised from chair to table leg. 'She really will be walking soon.'

'Yes, maybe by Christmas.' Which was only a few weeks away. Emma turned back to the eggs and a silence stretched between them, one that was not precisely uncomfortable, but not comfortable either. She didn't know what it was…or what was happening between them.

'Emma,' Larenzo said finally, and she braced herself against that tone.

'Don't,' she said softly, her back to him as she stared down at the mess of eggs. 'Don't try to let me down easily, Larenzo. Not after last night. Not after everything.'

She heard him sigh, a long, weary sound. 'I'm grateful for last night,' he said. 'For…for everything.'

'But?' she prompted, and heard how her voice wavered. She didn't wait for him to tell her. 'Let me guess. But you don't have anything to give because you've been too hurt. You can't trust anyone. You're not looking for a relationship. Yada-yada-yada.'

Larenzo didn't answer and Emma forced herself to turn around. She could feel the tears start in her eyes and she blinked them back, determined to be angry instead of afraid. Strong instead of weak. 'Am I right?'

'A few weeks ago,' Larenzo said slowly. 'A few days ago, even, you were right.'

The first frail thread of hope began to unspool inside her soul. 'But?' she prompted again, and this time she waited.

'But I don't want to live my life in an emotional void. Perhaps I needed that for a while, after everything. It was a way of protecting myself, I suppose. Of…healing.'

'You're a regular armadillo,' she managed to tease, and he offered the most wonderful, crooked smile.

'That's me.' He didn't say anything more and Emma drew in a deep breath.

'Larenzo, are you telling me, in your awkward, emotionally stunted way, that you actually want to try something? With me? A relationship?'

He rubbed a hand over his face. 'Yes, in my—what was it? Awkward, emotionally stunted way, I am.'

With a laugh Emma rushed into his arms. Ava, clinging to a kitchen cupboard, regarded them both curiously as Emma buried her face in Larenzo's shirt and tried not to weep. 'I'm just happy,' she said with a trembling laugh and a sniff, and Larenzo stroked her hair.

'I am too,' he said, and he sounded wondering. 'But, Emma, the other stuff still applies. I don't...I don't know how much I have in me. I still don't feel...' He paused, searching for words, and Emma waited. 'Like a whole man. As if I've truly put the past behind me.'

'You've taken steps,' Emma answered firmly. 'That's the important thing, Larenzo. You can't expect everything to fall into place all at once. But it will.' She believed that absolutely. 'It will.'

He nodded, still looking doubtful, and she continued, 'And the past will always be there. You can't forget it. You can only learn to live with it.'

'With your help,' Larenzo said, and put his arms around her. Emma couldn't remember when she'd felt so happy, so *joyful*.

'Now I know what the woman in the photo feels like,' she said and Larenzo smiled faintly before kissing her lips.

'So do I.'

They had nearly three weeks of that joy. Things went on the same in many ways; Larenzo still worked, and Emma still stayed at home with Ava. But everything felt different. Everything *was* different, because they were a family now, in every sense.

Larenzo kissed her the moment he got home from work, and Ava squealed to be picked up. They spent the evenings together, watching a DVD or playing a game or just chatting; sometimes they would sit on the sofa, Emma's feet in Larenzo's lap while he worked and she studied the photographs she'd taken that day.

Her creativity had exploded along with her joy; suddenly she saw pictures everywhere, and she spent many crisp wintry days trawling the city streets with Ava in tow, snapping photos and capturing moments. So many wonderful moments.

'You really should try to exhibit these,' Larenzo said when she showed him her latest round of photos, candids of various people around the city who had been happy to have their picture taken.

'I wouldn't even know how to begin,' Emma answered. 'But I'll think about it. I'm just happy to be feeling creative again. I felt dormant for so long, just struggling through each day.'

'I know how that feels.'

'Was that…was that how you were in prison?' she asked hesitantly. They still hadn't talked about his time in prison, and after that one night of confession they hadn't spoken about the past at all. They were, as Larenzo had said, focused on the future. Their future.

'I suppose,' he answered now. 'I felt…not just dormant, but dead inside. As if there was nothing left to live for. As if I wasn't even alive, not in the way that counted.'

'And when you realised you could walk free?' she asked softly. 'That new evidence had been found?'

'It didn't sink in for a while. I didn't believe it, at first.

And then when I actually got out...' He shook his head. 'Feelings don't go away as quickly as that. I still felt empty.'

'And now?' she whispered.

'I'm filling up,' he told her, and she laughed to see the wicked gleam enter his eyes. 'You're filling me up,' he said, and reached for her.

If the days continued on as normal, the nights were wonderfully changed, long and pleasure-filled. Emma didn't think she'd ever tire of exploring Larenzo's amazing body, or having him revere hers. She wondered how she'd lived so long without knowing the pleasure of such intimacy with another person.

Larenzo clearly wondered the same thing, for one night after they'd made love he ran his hand along her hip and asked, 'So how come you were a virgin at age what? Twenty-six?'

She wriggled around to face him. 'Is it really so odd?'

'In this day and age, I'd say so.'

She shrugged. 'I just never met the right guy, I suppose.'

'But you must have had boyfriends.'

She hesitated, uncomfortably aware at how this conversation was leading them both into the uncharted and unknown territory of her past. 'A few, but no one serious. Obviously.'

'So?'

'I didn't want to get that close to somebody,' Emma said after a moment. 'I liked being on my own.'

'Why?' Larenzo asked, frowning.

'I suppose my parents' divorce affected me badly,' Emma admitted. Larenzo had been honest with her about so much; the least she could do was be honest in return. And it was hardly as if she had some great tragedy or injustice in her past, not as he had. 'My mother left,' she continued. 'When I was twelve. She'd had enough of moving every two or three years. She wanted to return to the States, live in one place.'

'And your father didn't want to?'

'I don't know if she gave him a choice. I wasn't aware of any tension or fights, at least. Just one morning at breakfast she told us all she was leaving. Going back to America. I thought she meant for a vacation.'

'And she didn't take you?'

'No.' Emma shook her head, the memory making her eyes sting even now. 'No, she didn't even suggest it. In fact...' She trailed off, and Larenzo slid his hand in hers, a small gesture of solidarity that strengthened her to continue. 'In fact, I asked her to take me. I was closer to her than to my father, mainly because he was so wrapped up in his work. And...she said no.'

'I'm sorry, Emma,' he said quietly.

'So am I.' She sighed and rolled onto her back. 'It is a terrible feeling, to be rejected like that by your own mother.'

'Yes,' Larenzo agreed. 'It is.'

Emma stiffened. 'I'm so stupid and callous,' she exclaimed. 'I'm sorry—'

'No, don't be.' He smiled and stroked his hand back up her hip, all the way to her shoulder. 'We were talking about you. Why do you think she said no?'

'I don't know. I didn't ask. I acted kind of bratty, to be honest, and made like I wanted to be with my dad anyway. And she went off to Arizona and met someone else.' Those were the facts, and yet Emma thought Larenzo could guess at the years of confusion and pain she'd felt at the way her mother had so easily left her.

'And then what happened?' he asked.

'We lost touch over the years. She did ask me to visit, to live with her for a year, when I was in high school. I went, and it was so awkward and just...awful. She was wrapped up in this new guy and he didn't want to have anything to do with me.' She paused, remembering the tension, the arguments, the misery. 'I told her I was leaving, and she didn't even seem to care.' She remembered telling her mother she was going, willing her to insist she wanted her to stay. She hadn't. 'I suppose it felt like another kind of rejection. After that we hardly spoke or saw each other at all.'

Larenzo gathered her up in his arms. 'And that made you stay away from real relationships?'

'I guess, although I didn't connect the dots that simply. But I've always moved around a lot, and I've spent a lot of time on my own. I never felt like I needed anything or anyone else.'

'So what changed you?'

'You did,' she said simply. 'You were the first person that made me want to be different.'

'I'm glad,' Larenzo said softly. 'Because you made me want to be different too.'

And during those few weeks, their happiness was not unalloyed; the past continued to mar the perfect landscape of their joy, as Emma had known it would, as she'd warned Larenzo it would, and yet...

It was hard. Harder than she'd expected.

More than once she woke up in the middle of the night to an empty bed, and when she went in search of Larenzo she'd find him in his study, working or sometimes just staring into space.

'I've had trouble sleeping since prison,' he told her, but Emma saw the way his gaze flicked away from hers, and she felt there was more he wasn't saying.

Several times she went out with Ava and returned late, to be faced with Larenzo's sudden and inexplicable wrath.

'You should have phoned,' he stormed one night when Emma had come back after dinner.

'I tried,' she answered as calmly as she could. Ava was squirming to get out of her snowsuit. 'But the reception was bad—'

'In Manhattan?' he scoffed. 'You can get reception anywhere. Or were you not in Manhattan?'

Emma sat back on her heels and looked up, meeting his gaze steadily. 'Are you accusing me of something, Larenzo?' she asked quietly and he sagged suddenly, looking older than his thirty-five years.

'No. No, of course not,' he said, and they both dropped it, but each of those tense interactions made Emma weary. Understanding someone had trust issues and living with it were two very different things.

But even worse than Larenzo's bouts of suspicion were the dark moods that overtook him so he retreated into himself and nothing Emma did could reach him. Eventually he'd come out of it again, whether it was hours or days, and he would shoot her a look of apology that Emma accepted with a silent nod. He had hard memories; she understood that. It didn't make it any easier to deal with.

The week before Christmas she went to New Jersey with Ava to visit Meghan. She'd already told her sister she would be spending Christmas in the city with Larenzo; Meghan had been disappointed but understanding.

'You look tired,' she said when she met Emma at the train station. 'Is Ava keeping you up at night?'

'No, she's actually sleeping through for once.' Emma opened the car door and began to buckle Ava into her car seat. 'I'm fine.' She avoided her sister's gaze as she said it; the truth was, she was tired because Larenzo had been up in the night, unable to sleep, and when Emma had confronted him about it he'd become angry and stalked off. In the morning they hadn't mentioned the argument, and now Emma wondered if it would always be like this.

'Are you happy?' Meghan asked bluntly. 'With Larenzo? Because I'll be honest, Em, you don't actually look that happy.'

'I am happy,' Emma protested. 'I love him.'

'Loving someone doesn't always equal happiness.'

'It should,' Emma answered as she stared out of the window. 'It should,' she said again, and she heard the defeat in her voice.

They drove in silence for a few minutes, the muted landscape of the suburbs in winter streaming by. 'So what's going on?' Meghan asked eventually. 'Because obviously something is.'

Emma sighed. 'Nothing, really, it's just…you were right. It's hard sometimes. Larenzo has a lot of…'

'Emotional baggage?'

'Yes. But I do too,' Emma said quickly, and to her surprise Meghan nodded.

'More than you think.'

'Now what's that supposed to mean?'

'Come on, Emma. Most people whose parents divorced when they were kids manage to get over it and have healthy relationships of their own.'

Emma stiffened. 'So what are you saying exactly? That I'm some kind of freak?'

'No, of course not,' Meghan answered. 'But Mom leaving was really hard on you. Maybe because of our lifestyle growing up, all the moves, all the different cities and schools. You never had a friend for long.'

'I know.' When she'd been about eight or so she'd stopped investing so much in friendships. In the circuit of international schools, people were always on the move. And she hadn't minded; you had a friend for a while, and then someone left, and you found someone else. It had been simple—until her mother had been the one to find someone else.

'So perhaps that's why Mom leaving you affected you so much,' Meghan finished gently. Emma stared out of the window.

'I asked her to take me with her,' she said after a moment. 'I don't think you knew that.'

'No,' Meghan said quietly. 'I didn't.'

'She said no. Obviously.' Emma took a deep breath. 'So that might be the reason why I'm a little gun-shy when it comes to relationships.'

'Maybe,' Meghan allowed, and Emma could tell she wanted to say something else.

'What is it? You might as well give it to me straight. It's not like you to hold back.'

'There was...stuff Mom didn't tell you,' Meghan said slowly. 'Because you were so young.'

'Stuff?' Emma stiffened. 'What kind of stuff?'

'She was depressed,' Meghan answered after a moment. 'Really depressed. She told me about it, when I was in college. She was trying to get help, but it was hard.'

'Depressed...?'

'Did you never notice anything? How tired she was, and how...I don't know...listless sometimes?'

Distantly Emma recalled how much her mother had slept. Often when she'd come home from school, her mother would be napping. She hadn't thought much of it, perhaps because she'd had no one to compare her mother to. 'I don't know,' she said finally. 'Maybe, a bit, but...'

'When she went back to America she went into a clinic,' Meghan said. 'For depression. She was there for six months. That's why you couldn't come.'

Emma swivelled to gape at her sister. 'And she never told me? Not once, in fifteen years?'

'I think she felt ashamed,' Meghan said quietly.

Emma sank back against the seat. Just as Larenzo had felt ashamed. And yet in both cases honesty, although harder, would have been so much better. So much more healing.

'I wish I'd known,' she muttered. 'She could have told me when I came to live with her.'

'I think she just wanted to forget that part of her past, of herself.'

'And that visit was a disaster,' Emma reminded her. 'It wasn't just about the depression, Meghan.'

'I'm not saying it was. I just wanted you to understand the whole picture. As for that time in Arizona…you left pretty quickly, Emma. Maybe that felt to Mom like you were rejecting her.'

'So you're blaming me?' Emma demanded, more hurt than she wanted to admit or reveal.

'No, I'm only asking you to look at it from both sides.'

Meghan fell silent, and Emma turned back to the window. Look at it from both sides? She realised she'd been clinging to her entitlement as the wronged party for so long. Her mother had rejected her. Her mother had failed her. It was a child's view, and one she wasn't actually all that proud of.

She wanted things to be different with Larenzo. *She* wanted to be different, to be patient and understanding of the man she loved, and to trust that he would put the past to rest, stay with her and love her for ever…even if he had trouble trusting her in the same way.

'Love is complicated,' she finally said to Meghan, and her sister laughed.

'You've got that right.'

Her conversation with Meghan was still rattling around in her head when she returned to New York that evening. Meghan had helped her to deal with her past issues, and maybe she needed to help Larenzo deal with his. Not just by being patient or loving, not just by waiting, but by dealing with them once and for all.

Ava had fallen asleep on the train, and Emma hefted her over one shoulder as she wriggled her way out of the cab and then up to the apartment.

Larenzo met her at the door, taking Ava from her aching arms. He put Ava to bed and then rejoined her in the living room, looking slightly wary, as he always did after she'd returned from her sister's. As if he were still afraid she might leave him.

'Larenzo, I've realised something,' she said, and now he looked even more suspicious.

'Oh?'

'We can't go on like this.'

He stilled, his face wiped of expression. 'I see.'

'No, you don't,' she said in exasperation. 'I'm not leaving you. I want you to leave me, for a little while.' He stared at her, nonplussed, and she took a deep breath. 'I want you to go back to Sicily.'

Larenzo's eyebrows snapped together. 'No. Never.'

'I want you to see Bertrano.'

'No,' he said again, his voice as hard as she'd ever heard it. 'I have no desire to see him again, Emma. Ever.'

'Don't you think you need closure?' Emma asked softly. 'For both our sakes? Meghan was talking to me and I realised how much of my past I'd avoided. I thought I could put all my bad memories in a box and pretend they didn't exist. But it doesn't work that way.'

'It can.'

'Please, Larenzo. Just to finally learn why he did what he did. To make peace with it, if you can.'

Larenzo flicked his gaze away from hers. 'And if I can't?'

'You can, Larenzo.' Emma laid her hand on his arm. 'I know you can.'

He said nothing for a long, long moment, and she could see the emotions battling in his eyes, on his face. Then slowly, painfully, he nodded.

CHAPTER SIXTEEN

LARENZO STOOD IN the small waiting room of the high-security prison near Terni, in central Italy. Sweat prickled his scalp and his stomach did a queasy flip. Just a little over two months ago he'd been behind those locked steel doors. He'd walked out a free man, but returning to the place where he'd felt so hopeless was not a comfortable feeling.

He took a deep breath and let it out slowly. He'd been waiting for fifteen minutes for the guard to tell Bertrano he had a visitor. Larenzo hadn't asked his former mentor if he could visit; he hadn't wanted to give Bertrano the opportunity to refuse. And he hoped, now that he was actually here, Bertrano wouldn't. He'd realised, in the few days since Emma had confronted him, that she'd been right. He needed to talk to Bertrano. He needed to understand.

'Come with me,' the guard told him in Italian, and with a terse nod Larenzo followed him through the heavy steel door, past the metal detector, and then to a holding cell where he was patted down before finally emerging in the visiting room, a dour place with half a dozen non-contact phone booths. Bertrano waited in one.

Just the sight of him caused shock and something worse, something like loss, to jolt through him. Bertrano was slouched in his chair, his face haggard and lined so he looked far older than his sixty-seven years. He lifted his bleary glance to Larenzo as he sat down, then looked away again, seemingly indifferent.

Larenzo took a deep, even breath and then picked up the phone. After a moment Bertrano picked up his.

'So you came,' he said flatly.

'Yes. I came. Which is more than I can say you did for me.' He hadn't wanted to start this conversation with bitterness, yet he couldn't seem to keep himself from it. Bertrano just shrugged. 'Did you think I wouldn't?' Larenzo asked, and the old man shrugged again.

'Frankly,' he answered, 'I didn't really care.'

Larenzo blinked. He realised he'd expected Bertrano's shame, his guilt, his anger, even his defensiveness...but this indifference shocked him.

'Why?' he asked eventually.

Bertrano glanced at him, shaggy eyebrows raised. 'Why what?'

'Why did you do it?' Larenzo asked, his voice low. 'I thought about it many times. I had many hours in prison to think about why you would betray me in such a fashion.'

To his amazement Bertrano let out a hoarse, rasping laugh. 'Betray you?' he repeated. 'Even now, you can think that?'

Larenzo stared at him. 'What do you mean?'

Slowly Bertrano shook his head. 'After all this time,' he said. 'After everything I've done, you still want an explanation? Isn't it obvious, Larenzo? Or are you just being blind? *Cazzaro,*' he spat, and Larenzo recoiled at the insult.

'I am not an idiot,' he said coolly. 'I am trying to understand—'

'Understand what? It's all pretty simple to me. I used you, Larenzo. I framed you. Which part don't you understand?' He shook his head before looking away.

'I know that. What I don't understand is how you could do such a thing, after all—' he broke off, feeling a pressure building in his chest, before he continued tightly '—after all our time together. You rescued me, Bertrano.

You *saved* me, you treated me with such kindness, and then to betray—'

'Oh, enough with the hurt feelings,' Bertrano said, flapping his hand. 'Enough, enough.' He leaned forward, his eyes glittering with a malice Larenzo had never seen before. 'Why do you think I saved you, Larenzo? You, a Palermo street rat, worthless, hopeless, rough and untaught? Why would I save *you*?'

Larenzo stared at him, the pressure in his chest painful now, taking over his whole body. He stared at the man he'd once thought of as his father and could not speak.

'No answer, eh?' Bertrano nodded. 'That's because the only answer is the one you've refused to accept, even when it was staring you in the face. You were my safety net, Larenzo. My backup plan. No more than that.'

Larenzo's hand was clenched so hard around the phone his fingers ached and his knuckles were white. 'Tell me what you mean,' he demanded.

'I wanted someone I could blame,' Bertrano said simply. 'That's all you ever were. What is the English expression?' He closed his eyes briefly, his mouth curving in a cold, cruel smile. 'A stooge.'

Larenzo didn't answer, couldn't speak. The question that burned in his throat was one he was too ashamed to say. And yet somehow he found himself saying it, needed to say it. To hear the answer. 'Didn't…didn't you ever care about me?'

Bertrano gazed at him pitilessly. 'No.'

And still he resisted that awful truth. 'But so many years…my schooling, the business…' But he wasn't thinking of that. He was remembering days at the beach, and evenings playing chess, and the way he'd felt loved and accepted by Bertrano. All of it false? All of it a *ploy*? He shook his head, unable to process it. Desperate to deny it.

'I was fond of you,' Bertrano allowed, 'in a way. You

were so eager to please, after all. But the reason I sought you out, Larenzo, was so I could put the blame on you if it all went bad.' He sagged against his seat. 'Which, of course, it did.' He shook his head. 'Your lawyers were tenacious, I'll grant you that. I thought I'd destroyed any evidence that could convict me. I suppose it's my own fault.' He shrugged wearily and looked away, a man who no longer had any hope. Just as Larenzo had been. Just as he felt now, for he was starting to see how it all made terrible sense.

The questions Bertrano had first asked, about whether he had family, or if anyone would come looking for him. Anyone who would care. And then how Bertrano had encouraged Larenzo to pursue his separate business interests while he tended to the rest. Putting the business into Larenzo's name. He'd thought Bertrano was being kind, but he'd actually just been constructing an elaborate web in which to ensnare him. All of it, everything, had been false. A lie. This was so much worse than what Larenzo had thought. Grief poured through him in an unrelenting river, a grief deeper and darker than any he had known before.

Bertrano let out a weary sigh. 'Poor Larenzo,' he mocked. 'Always wanting to be loved.'

Larenzo could take no more. He slammed the phone down so hard it cracked the cradle and then walked out of the visiting room without looking back.

Outside he braced his hands against the roof of his hired car and took several deep, even breaths to calm his racing heart.

All of it a lie. All of it a ploy.

Even now, he could scarcely believe it. This was what he'd come back for? This was to help him move on? Then, with a new, cold clarity stealing over him, Larenzo realised it would. Because now he knew that nothing was real. No one could be trusted.

* * *

Emma paced the living room restlessly, trying to suppress the anxiety that had settled like a stone in her stomach, weighing her down. Larenzo had been gone three days. He was due back tomorrow, on Christmas Eve, and yet he hadn't contacted her in over forty-eight hours. The last time she'd spoken to him had been when he'd arrived in Terni, intending to visit Bertrano in the morning. He'd sounded resolute and yet also upbeat, and Emma had felt so thankful for his willingness to do this, so admiring of his courage. Now she wondered sickly just what he had found.

She tweaked an ornament on the Christmas tree she'd had the doorman bring up to the apartment. She'd bought it outside the Natural History Museum, a mammoth tree whose top touched the ceiling. Ava was enchanted by it, but it meant Emma had had to decorate only the top half of the tree so her newly walking daughter couldn't pull all the decorations off.

Still, she thought the apartment looked beautiful, decorated for Christmas. Besides the tree she'd bought a nativity scene and set it up in the hall. Boughs of evergreen and holly garlanded every doorway, and filled the rooms with their fresh, spicy scent. She glanced under the tree to where she'd put several presents: a few toys for Ava, and a photograph for Larenzo. Her chest tightened as she thought of them all spending Christmas together, a family.

Why did she feel now as if it might not happen? *Why had he not called her?*

She heard the sound of the front door opening and everything in her stilled. Larenzo wasn't due back until tomorrow and yet he was the only one with a key card. Then she heard the slow, deliberate tread, and Larenzo appeared in the doorway. He looked…he looked as he had that night so long ago now when he'd come to the villa. Haggard. Resigned. As if he was missing an elemental part of himself.

Emma pressed one hand to her hard-beating heart. 'Larenzo. I wasn't expecting you until tomorrow.'

He tossed his key card on the table and walked past her, to the drinks cabinet, just as he had before.

'I decided to come home early.'

'Why didn't you call?' Not wanting to sound accusing, Emma strove to moderate her tone. 'I was worried about you. What...what happened with Bertrano?'

Larenzo poured himself a whisky, his back to her. 'He told me the truth.'

'What do you mean—?'

'It was very enlightening,' he cut across her. He turned around, the tumbler of whisky held to his lips as he leaned against the cabinet. 'Very enlightening,' he repeated, and took a long swallow.

Emma shook her head slowly. 'Why don't you enlighten me, then?' she asked, trying to smile. 'I was worried.'

'Were you?' He sounded disbelieving and Emma's insides lurched with fear.

'Yes, I was. Please, Larenzo. Tell me what is going on.'

'Perhaps you should tell me what's going on,' Larenzo returned coolly. 'Because it occurred to me, Emma, how easily you agreed to come live with me here. For a woman who was hell-bent on keeping me from her child, you changed your tune rather quickly. Rather conveniently.' He took another sip of whisky, watching her all the while through narrowed eyes.

'I don't understand what you're implying, Larenzo,' Emma answered. She tried to keep her voice calm, although she felt like screaming. Like flying at him and slapping some sense into him, because she could see he was in self-destruct mode and she didn't know how to get him to stop. 'Larenzo, please. Let's talk about this...'

'I am talking about this. I'm talking about the fact that you were desperate to have me out of your and Ava's lives, and then all of a sudden you changed. You'd called a law-yer, after all. You were serious, Emma. And then you just caved. Why?'

'Because I realised I wanted you involved in Ava's life,' she answered steadily. 'I know what it's like to have an ab-sentee parent and I didn't want that for Ava. I didn't want that for you. You're a good father, Larenzo.' He didn't an-swer and Emma took a step towards him. 'Please tell me what happened in Italy.'

'What happened is I woke up and realised how deluded I've been about people. Everyone wants something, Emma. Everyone's looking out for the main chance. Even you. Especially you.'

She gasped, the sound one of pure pain. *'Especially* me?'

'You've got a pretty sweet deal here, haven't you? Lux-ury apartment in the city, every expense paid for.'

'I offered to pay my way—'

'Of course you would. You'd want to seem convincing.'

'Convincing? Convincing of what?'

'You wanted me to look out for you. To take care of you. Maybe you're even hoping for marriage.'

She shook her head slowly. 'What on earth has got into you, Larenzo? What did that evil man say to you?'

'Evil man? But you said he was just weak and afraid. You had quite a lot of sympathy for him, as I recall.'

'I had sympathy for you,' she corrected. 'Although it's disappearing fast.'

'Is it?' Larenzo's mouth curved in a cold smile. 'Good.'

'Good? *Good*?' Her voice rose in a scream as her hands clenched into fists. 'Are you going to throw away every-thing we've built together simply because of something Bertrano said to you?'

'Everything we've built?' Larenzo arched an eyebrow. 'It doesn't seem that much to me. A few weeks, Emma. That's all.'

Emma gaped at him, unable to believe that everything could fall apart so quickly. So utterly. 'What are you saying, Larenzo?' she demanded. 'How does Ava fit into any of this?'

'Ava is my daughter and I will have a place in her life,' Larenzo answered. 'Always. That won't change.'

'But us?' Emma forced herself to ask. 'What about us?'

For a second, no more, Larenzo looked conflicted. Tormented. Then his expression ironed out to pitiless blankness and he shook his head. 'There is no us.'

Emma couldn't keep herself from giving one small gasp of pain. 'I don't know what that man told you...' she began but Larenzo didn't say anything. She drew in a ragged breath. 'You know what? It doesn't even matter. I don't care what Bertrano Raguso told you, because nothing makes what you've said to me justifiable. You say you don't trust people,' she continued, her voice shaking. 'Well, I trusted you, Larenzo, and I shouldn't have.' A muscle flickered in his jaw, but that was all the response she got. She felt like hitting him, hurting him, and so she did the only way she knew how. 'I hate you!' she spat. 'I hate you for making me care about you, and then doing this.' And with tears spilling down her cheeks, she snatched up Ava and stormed down the hall.

Alone in her bedroom, she sagged against the door. Ava squirmed to get down and Emma let her before sinking slowly to the floor, her knees drawn up to her chest. Her head was spinning, tears still trickling down her cheeks. How had it come to this so quickly, so terribly?

She felt as she had when Larenzo had been dragged off by the police. *She felt as she had when she'd left her mother's.*

The realisation was like a lightning streak of pain. She was acting just as she had then, storming away, refusing to engage. She didn't even remember what the argument with her mother had been about, the one that had set them both off and made Emma leave. She just remembered feeling furious and hurt and unloved, and instead of staying and battling it out she'd booked a ticket back to Berlin, where her father had been living at the time.

This time, did she possess the strength and courage not to walk away, but to stay and fight? Fight for herself, fight for Larenzo, fight for their family.

Walking away had been a way to protect herself, to pretend she wasn't hurt when she'd spent years aching inside. She wasn't going to make the same mistake now. She'd learned that much, at least.

Taking a deep breath, Emma rose from the floor. She picked up Ava, settling her on her hip, and then flung open her bedroom door and marched out into the living room.

The sight of Larenzo slouched in a chair, his head in his hands, made her insides twist with sorrow.

'I'm not,' she announced, 'going to let you do this.'

Larenzo looked up, his hair ruffled, his skin nearly grey with exhaustion. 'Excuse me?'

'I'm not going to let you destroy us, Larenzo. Whatever Bertrano told you, it's not worth it. I'm not going to let you throw away the happiness we've found together simply because some selfish old man is trying to ruin it for you and for us.' She took a deep breath and then ploughed on. 'I love you, you know. I'm not giving up. Not that easily. I gave up on my mother, when I was a teenager. Meghan helped me to see my part in the failure of our relationship. I'm not giving up on you.'

He stared at her for a long moment and then looked away without speaking. So it wasn't going to be easy. She couldn't say she was surprised.

'I want to show you something,' she said, and, setting Ava down on the floor, she marched over to the Christmas tree and retrieved a present from underneath it. She thrust it towards Larenzo; he took it, resting it in his lap, making no move to open it.

'It's my Christmas present to you,' Emma stated. 'Open it.'

He glanced up at her, and then, with a tiny shrug, he opened the present. The frame was made of silver, an elaborate twisting of ivy that Emma had liked because it was a live and growing thing, just as their relationship was. Their family was.

And the picture the frame held—it was of their family. It had been taken a few weeks ago at the playground. Emma had put the camera on a tripod and timer and run over to pose with Larenzo and Ava; their faces were all smooshed together, filled with laughter. It wasn't a candid moment, but it was close, and it was a picture that was filled with love and happiness. With joy.

Larenzo stared down at it for an endless moment. Emma held her breath as he traced their three faces with his fingers. Then he closed his eyes briefly and her heart gave a painful squeeze. 'Emma.'

'Larenzo,' she said softly, waiting.

He didn't speak for a long moment. Finally he said, 'Bertrano told me that he...he never cared for me. The only reason he'd ever approached me was to use me.' He looked up then, his face so unbearably bleak. 'So if things went wrong, he could blame it all on me. It's diabolical, really, to use a child that way. But he did and it worked.'

'Oh, Larenzo.' She stared at him helplessly; she could not imagine what hearing that must have felt like. A whole new and worse kind of grief.

'The thing is, I never even guessed. I never doubted, growing up, that he cared about me. Oh, I was suspicious at first, of course I was. But the more time he spent with me, the safer I felt... I really did think he loved me, like a son.' He shook his head slowly. 'Even when he betrayed me, I thought how it must have hurt him. How it must have been a hard decision to make. What a fool I am,' he spat, his voice thick with disgust. 'What a blind fool.'

'You're a person who, despite everything, believes the best of people. That's not a bad thing, Larenzo.'

'I took the blame because I loved him,' he said starkly. 'I could have fought it. I might have even won. But I didn't because I wanted to spare him. Spare the man who felt only contempt for me.' He looked away from her. 'It makes me feel sick.'

'But Bertrano is the sick one, Larenzo. Sick and sad and cruel to treat anyone, much less a child, that way. Don't blame yourself for his evil.' She took a step towards him, longing to touch him, to hold him, but afraid even now he might pull away. 'Don't let his evil taint what we have.'

The silence stretched on as Larenzo kept his face averted. Emma had no idea what he was thinking, but she felt instinctively that their whole lives hung in the balance of this moment.

'I thought I loved you,' he said finally. 'But I'm not sure any more I know what love is.'

'I know what love is,' Emma answered. 'Love is waking up in the night with Ava. Love is the three of us laughing around the dinner table. Love is turning over in bed and seeing you sleeping with a smile on your face that I know I put there. And,' she finished, her heart starting to pound, 'love is trusting that we'll keep going no matter what happens. We'll stay together and we'll battle it out. I won't walk away and neither will you, and neither of us will let the other try to.' She felt her lips tremble and she blinked the tears back. 'Please, Larenzo.'

'Dada!' Ava squealed, jerking them out of the intensity of the moment. Emma watched, her breath held, as her daughter toddled towards Larenzo, stumbling as she reached him so he caught her in his arms and brought her up to his chest. He closed his eyes, his lips brushing Ava's hair.

'I'm sorry,' he whispered. Everything in Emma protested until Larenzo opened his eyes and gazed at her with so much hunger and need and love she nearly swayed where she stood. 'I'm sorry for putting you through so much. I'm sorry for being so…imperfect.'

'We're all imperfect.'

'I'm sorry for hurting you.' He stood up, Ava still in his arms, and walked towards her. 'I love you, Emma. And I'm so thankful you stayed and fought for me. For us.'

'Me too,' she whispered, and then he was folding her in his arms, and even better he was kissing her, as Ava patted both their cheeks.

'Dada,' she crowed. 'Mama.'

'Family,' Larenzo said, and kissed Emma again.

EPILOGUE

One year later

'CAREFUL NOW!' LARENZO called as Emma mounted the stepladder. She threw him a teasing glance over her shoulder and took another step up, the star in her hand.

It was Christmas Eve, and she was putting the star on top of their tree. Outside the city was blanketed in snow, and only that morning they'd had a birthday party for Ava, with Meghan and Ryan and his new baby sister Ella coming into the city to celebrate.

It had been a wonderful, crazy year, full of excitement and joy. So much joy. Emma had finally submitted her photographs and had had her first exhibition in SoHo. In May the investigation had finally concluded and Larenzo's innocence had been proclaimed in all the papers. The gossip had trickled away, and Larenzo's business had gone from strength to strength, as he'd built his client list and invested in innovative new technology.

They'd moved from the luxurious penthouse apartment to a Brownstone overlooking the park, with bedrooms for the children they hoped one day to have. Ava was already obsessed with babies, and Emma was looking forward to introducing her to a new brother or sister, whenever it happened.

Now she stood on her tiptoes and perched the star on top of the tree.

'Is it straight?' she asked.

'Perfectly,' Larenzo answered.

'Star!' Ava crowed and, smiling at them both, Emma came down from the ladder.

She glanced at the star and then burst out laughing. 'It's completely crooked.'

'I like it,' Larenzo answered as he pulled her towards him, Ava squirming as usual to get right between them. 'It reminds me of how you love me despite my many imperfections.'

Emma shook her head, smiling. 'You seem pretty perfect to me,' she said, and kissed him.

* * * * *

One eyebrow spiked. 'You seem so confident I'm going to hand myself to you on a silver platter. Isn't that a tad foolish?'

There was that tone again—the one that said she didn't believe him. That she thought this was some sort of twisted game on his part.

'I guess we'll find out one way or the other when the sordid details are laid out for you on Monday. All you need to concern yourself about today is picking out an engagement ring that makes the right statement.'

Eva's striking green eyes clashed with his and that lightning bolt struck again. 'And what statement would that be?' she challenged.

Zaccheo let loose the chilling half-smile that he knew made his enemies quake. 'Why, that you belong to me, of course.'

Seven Sexy Sins

The true *taste of temptation!*

From greed to gluttony, lust to envy,
these fabulous stories explore what seven sexy sins
mean in the twenty-first century!

Whether pride goes before a fall, or wrath leads to
a passion that consumes entirely, one thing is certain:
the road to true love has never been more enticing!

So you decide:

How can it be a sin when it feels so good?

Sloth—Cathy Williams

Lust—Dani Collins

Pride—Kim Lawrence

Gluttony—Maggie Cox

Greed—Sara Craven

Wrath—Maya Blake

Envy—Annie West

Seven titles by some of
Mills & Boon Modern Romance's
most treasured and exciting authors!

A MARRIAGE
FIT FOR A SINNER

BY
MAYA BLAKE

Published in Great Britain 2015
by Mills & Boon, an imprint of Harlequin (UK) Limited,
Eton House, 18-24 Paradise Road, Richmond, Surrey, TW9 1SR

© 2015 Maya Blake

ISBN: 978-0-263-25086-2

Harlequin (UK) Limited's policy is to use papers that are natural,
renewable and recyclable products and made from wood grown in
sustainable forests. The logging and manufacturing processes conform
to the legal environmental regulations of the country of origin.

Printed and bound in Spain
by CPI, Barcelona

Maya Blake's hopes of becoming a writer were born when she picked up her first romance aged thirteen. Little did she know her dream would come true! Does she still pinch herself every now and then, to make sure it's not a dream? Yes, she does!

Feel free to pinch her too, via Twitter, Facebook or Goodreads! Happy reading!

Books by Maya Blake

Mills & Boon Modern Romance

Married for the Prince's Convenience
Innocent in His Diamonds
His Ultimate Prize
Marriage Made of Secrets
The Sinful Art of Revenge
The Price of Success

The Untameable Greeks

What the Greek's Money Can't Buy
What the Greek Can't Resist
What the Greek Wants Most

The 21st Century Gentleman's Club

The Ultimate Playboy

In December 2015 look out for *Brunetti's Secret Son* featuring Romeo from *A Marriage Fit for a Sinner*

Visit the Author Profile page
at millsandboon.co.uk for more titles.

CHAPTER ONE

'ONE PLATINUM CHRONOGRAPH WATCH. A pair of diamond-studded cufflinks. Gold signet ring. Six hundred and twenty-five pounds cash, and…Obsidian Privilege Card. Right, I think that's everything, sir. Sign here to confirm return of your property.'

Zaccheo Giordano didn't react to the warden's sneer as he scrawled on the barely legible form. Nor did he react to the resentful envy in the man's eyes when his gaze drifted to where the sleek silver limousine waited beyond three sets of barbed wire.

Romeo Brunetti, Zaccheo's second-in-command and the only person he would consider draping the term *friend* upon, stood beside the car, brooding and unsmiling, totally unruffled by the armed guard at the gate or the bleak South East England surroundings.

Had Zaccheo been in an accommodating mood, he'd have cracked a smile.

But he wasn't in an accommodating mood. He hadn't been for a very long time. Fourteen months, two weeks, four days and nine hours to be exact. Zaccheo was positive he could count down to the last second if required.

No one would require it of him, of course. He'd served his time. With three and a half months knocked off his eighteen-month sentence *for good behaviour.*

The rage fused into his DNA bubbled beneath his skin. He showed no outward sign of it as he pocketed his belongings. The three-piece Savile Row suit he'd entered prison in stank of decay and misery, but Zaccheo didn't care.

He'd never been a slave to material comforts. His need for validation went far deeper. The need to elevate himself into a better place had been a soul-deep pursuit from the moment he was old enough to recognise the reality of the life he'd been born into. A life that had been a never-ending whirlpool of humiliation, violence and greed. A life that had seen his father debased and dead at thirty-five.

Memories tumbled like dominoes as he walked down the harshly lit corridor to freedom. He willed the overwhelming sense of injustice that had festered for long, harrowing months not to explode from his pores.

The doors clanged shut behind him.

Zaccheo froze, then took his first lungful of free air with fists clenched and eyes shut. He absorbed the sound of birds chirping in the late-winter morning sun, listened to the distant rumble of the motorway as he'd done many nights from his prison cell.

Opening his eyes, he headed towards the fifteen-foot gate. A minute later, he was outside.

'Zaccheo, it's good to see you again,' Romeo said gravely, his eyes narrowing as he took him in.

Zaccheo knew he looked a sight. He hadn't bothered with a razor blade or a barber's clippers in the last three months and he'd barely eaten once he'd unearthed the truth behind his incarceration. But he'd spent a lot of time in the prison gym. It'd been that or go mad with the clawing hunger for retribution.

He shrugged off his friend's concern and moved to the open door.

'Did you bring what I asked for?' he asked.

Romeo nodded. '*Sì*. All three files are on the laptop.'

Zaccheo slid onto the plush leather seat. Romeo slid in next to him and poured them two glasses of Italian-made cognac.

'*Salute,*' Romeo muttered.

Zaccheo took the drink without responding, threw back the amber liquid and allowed the scent of power and affluence—the tools he'd need for his plan to succeed—to wash over him.

As the low hum of the luxury engine whisked him away from the place he'd been forced to call home for over a year, Zaccheo reached for the laptop.

Icy rage trembled through his fingers as the Giordano Worldwide Inc. logo flickered to life. His life's work, almost decimated through another's greed and lust for power. It was only with Romeo's help that GWI hadn't gone under in the months after Zaccheo had been sent to prison for a crime he didn't commit. He drew quiet satisfaction that not only had GWI survived—thanks to Romeo—it had thrived.

But his personal reputation had not.

He was out now. Free to bring those culpable to justice. He didn't plan on resting until every last person responsible for attempting to destroy his life paid with the destruction of theirs.

Shaking out his hand to rid it of its tremble, he hit the Open key.

The information was thorough although Zaccheo knew most of its contents. For three months he'd checked and double-checked his sources, made sure every detail was nailed down tight.

He exhaled at the first picture that filled his screen.

Oscar Pennington III. Distant relative to the royal family. Etonian. Old, if spent, money. Very much part of the establishment. Greedy. Indiscriminate. His waning property portfolio had received a much-needed injection of capital exactly fourteen months and two weeks ago when he'd become sole owner of London's most talked about building—The Spire.

Zaccheo swallowed the savage growl that rumbled from his soul. Icily calm, he flicked through pages of Pennington celebrating his revived success with galas, lavish dinner parties and polo tournaments thrown about like confetti. One picture showed him laughing with one of his two children.

Sophie Pennington. Private education all the way to finishing school. Classically beautiful. Ball-breaker. She'd proven beyond a doubt that she had every intention of becoming Oscar's carbon copy.

Grimly, he closed her file and moved to the last one.

Eva Pennington.

This time the growl couldn't be contained. Nor could he stem the renewed shaking in his hand as he clicked her file.

Caramel-blonde hair tumbled down her shoulders in thick, wild waves. Dark eyebrows and lashes framed moss-green eyes, accentuated dramatically with black eyeliner. Those eyes had gripped his attention with more force than he'd been comfortable with the first time he'd looked into them. As had the full, bow-shaped lips currently curved in a smouldering smile. His screen displayed a head-and-shoulders shot, but the rest of Eva Pennington's body was imprinted indelibly on Zaccheo's mind. He didn't struggle to recall the petite, curvy shape, or that she forced herself to wear heels even though she hated them, in order to make herself taller.

He certainly didn't struggle to recall her individual atrocity. He'd lain in his prison bed condemning himself for being astounded by her singular betrayal, when the failings of both his parents and his dealings with the *establishment* should've taught him better. He'd prided himself on reading between the lines to spot schemers and gold-diggers ten miles away. Yet he'd been fooled.

The time he'd wasted on useless bitterness was the most excruciating of all; time he would gladly claw back if he could.

Firming his lips, he clicked through the pages, running through her life for the past year and a half. At the final page, he froze.

'How new is this last information?'

'I added that to the file yesterday. I thought you'd want to know,' Romeo replied.

Zaccheo stared at the newspaper clipping, shock waves rolling through him. *'Sì, grazie…'*

'Do you wish to return to the Esher estate or the penthouse?' Romeo asked.

Zaccheo read the announcement again, taking in pertinent details. Pennington Manor. Eight o'clock. Three hundred guests. Followed by an intimate family dinner on Sunday at The Spire.

The Spire…the building that should've been Zaccheo's greatest achievement.

'The estate,' he replied. It was closer.

He closed the file as Romeo instructed the driver.

Relaxing against the headrest, Zaccheo tried to let the hum of the engine soothe him. But it was no use. He was far from calm.

He'd have to alter his plan. Not that it mattered too much in the long run.

A chain is only as strong as its weakest link. While all three Penningtons had colluded in his incarceration, this new information demanded he use a different tactic, one he'd first contemplated and abandoned. Either way, Zaccheo didn't plan to rest until all of them were stripped of what they cherished most—their wealth and affluence.

He'd intended to wait a day or two to ensure he had Oscar Pennington where he wanted him before he struck. That plan was no longer viable.

Bringing down the family who'd framed him for criminal negligence couldn't wait till Monday.

His first order of business would be tackled *tonight*.

Starting with the youngest member of the family—Eva Pennington.

His ex-fiancée.

Eva Pennington stared at the dress in her sister's hand. 'Seriously? There's no way I'm wearing that. Why didn't you tell me the clothes I left behind had been given away?'

'Because you said you didn't want them when you moved out. Besides, they were old and out of fashion. I had *this* couriered from New York this morning. It's the latest couture and on loan to us for twenty-four hours,' Sophie replied.

Eva pursed her lips. 'I don't care if it was woven by ten thousand silk worms. I'm not wearing a dress that makes me look like a gold-digger *and* a slut. And considering the state of our finances, I'd have thought you'd be more careful what you splashed money on.' She couldn't stem her bewilderment as to why Sophie and her father blithely ignored the fact that money was extremely tight.

Sophie huffed. 'This is a one-of-a-kind dress, and, unless I'm mistaken, it's the kind of dress your future husband likes his women to wear. Anyway, you'll be out of it in less than four hours, once the right photographs have been taken, and the party's over.'

Eva gritted her teeth. 'Stop trying to manage me, Sophie. You're forgetting who pulled this bailout together. If I hadn't come to an agreement with Harry, we'd have been sunk come next week. As to what he likes his women to wear, if you'd bothered to speak to me first I'd have saved you the trouble of going to unnecessary expense. I dress for myself and no one else.'

'Speak to you first? When you and Father neglected to afford me the same courtesy before you hatched this plan behind my back?' Sophie griped.

Eva's heart twisted at the blatant jealousy in her sister's voice.

As if it weren't enough that the decision she'd spent the past two weeks agonising over still made her insides clench in horror. It didn't matter that the man she'd agreed to marry was her friend and she was helping him as much as he was helping her. Marriage was a step she'd rather not have taken.

It was clear, however, her sister didn't see it that way. Sophie's escalating discontentment at any relationship Eva tried to forge with their father was part of the reason Eva had moved out of Pennington Manor. Not that their father was an easy man to live with.

For as long as she could remember, Sophie had been possessive of their father's attention. While their mother had been alive, it'd been bearable and easier to accept that Sophie was their father's preferred child, while Eva was her mother's, despite wanting to be loved equally by both parents.

After their mother's death, every interaction Eva had tried to have with their father had been met with bristling confrontation from Sophie, and indifference from their father.

But, irrational as it was, it didn't stop Eva from trying to reason with the sister she'd once looked up to.

'We didn't go behind your back. You were away on a business trip—'

'Trying to use the business degree that doesn't seem to mean anything any more. Not when *you* can swoop in after three years of performing tired ballads in seedy pubs to save the day,' Sophie interjected harshly.

Eva hung on to her temper by a thread, but pain stung deep at the blithe dismissal of her passion. 'You know I resigned from Penningtons because Father only hired me so I could attract a suitable husband. And just because my dreams don't coincide with yours—'

'That's just it. You're twenty-four and still *dreaming*. The rest of us don't have that luxury. And we certainly don't land on our feet by clicking our fingers and having a millionaire solve all our problems.'

'Harry is saving *all of us*. And you really think I've *landed on my feet* by getting engaged for the second time in two years?' Eva asked.

Sophie dropped the offensive dress on Eva's bed. 'To everyone who matters, this is your first engagement. The other one barely lasted five minutes. Hardly anyone knows it happened.'

Hurt-laced anger swirled through her veins. '*I* know it happened.'

'If my opinion matters around here any more, then I suggest you don't broadcast it. It's a subject best left in the past, just like the man it involved.'

Pain stung deeper. 'I can't pretend it didn't happen because of what occurred afterwards.'

'The last thing we need right now is any hint of scandal. And I don't know why you're blaming Father for what happened when you should be thanking him for extricating you from that man before it was too late,' Sophie defended heatedly.

That man.

Zaccheo Giordano.

Eva wasn't sure whether the ache lodged beneath her ribs came from thinking about him or from the reminder of how gullible she'd been to think he was any different from every other man who'd crossed her path.

She relaxed her fists when they balled again.

This was why she preferred her life away from their family home deep in the heart of Surrey.

It was why her waitress colleagues knew her as Eva Penn, a hostess at Siren, the London nightclub where she also sang part-time, instead of Lady Eva Pennington, daughter of Lord Pennington.

Her relationship with her father had always been difficult, but she'd never thought she'd lose her sister so completely, too.

She cleared her throat. 'Sophie, this agreement with Harry wasn't supposed to undermine anything you were doing with Father to save Penningtons. There's no need to be upset or jealous. I'm not trying to take your place—'

'Jealous! Don't be ridiculous,' Sophie sneered, although the trace of panic in her voice made Eva's heart break. 'And you could never take my place. I'm Father's right hand, whereas you...you're nothing but—' She stopped herself and, after a few seconds, stuck her nose in the air. 'Our guests are arriving shortly. Please don't be late to your own engagement party.'

Eva swallowed down her sorrow. 'I've no intention of being late. But neither do I have any intention of wearing a dress that has less material than thread holding it together.'

She strode to the giant George III armoire opposite the bed, even though her earlier inspection had shown less than a fraction of the items she'd left behind when she'd moved out on her twenty-first birthday.

These days she was content with her hostess's uniform when she was working or lounging in jeans and sweaters while she wrote her music on her days off. Haute couture, spa days and primping herself beautiful in order to please anyone were part of a past she'd happily left behind.

Unfortunately this time there'd been no escaping. Not when she alone had been able to find the solution to saving her family.

She tried in vain to squash the rising memories being back at Pennington Manor threatened to resurrect.

Zaccheo was in her past, a mistake that should never have happened. A reminder that ignoring a lesson learned only led to further heartache.

She sighed in relief when her hand closed on a silk wrap. The red dress would be far too revealing, a true spectacle for the three hundred guests her father had invited to gawp at. But at least the wrap would provide a little much-needed cover.

Glancing at the dress again, she shuddered.

She'd rather be anywhere but here, participating in this sham. But then hadn't her whole life been a sham? From parents who'd been publicly hailed as the couple to envy, but who'd fought bitterly in private until tragedy had struck in the form of her mother's cancer, to the lavish parties and expensive holidays that her father had secretly been borrowing money for, the Penningtons had been one giant sham for as long as Eva could remember.

Zaccheo's entry into their lives had only escalated her father's behaviour.

No, she refused to think about Zaccheo. He belonged to a chapter of her life that was firmly sealed. Tonight was about Harry Fairfield, her family's saviour, and her soon-to-be fiancé.

It was also about her father's health.

For that reason alone, she tried again with Sophie.

'For Father's sake, I want tonight to go smoothly, so can we try to get along?'

Sophie stiffened. 'If you're talking about Father's hospitalisation two weeks ago, I haven't forgotten.'

Watching her father struggle to breathe with what the doctors had termed a cardiac event had terrified Eva. It'd been the catalyst that had forced her to accept Harry's proposition.

'He's okay today, isn't he?' Despite her bitterness at her family's treatment of her, she couldn't help her concern for her remaining parent. Nor could she erase the secret yearning that the different version of the father she'd connected with very briefly after her mother's death, the one who wasn't an excess-loving megalomaniac who treated her as if she was an irritating inconvenience, hadn't been a figment of her imagination.

'He will be, once we get rid of the creditors threatening us with bankruptcy.'

Eva exhaled. There was no backing out; no secretly hoping that some other solution would present itself and save her from the sacrifice she was making.

All avenues had been thoroughly explored—Eva had demanded to see the Pennington books herself and spent a day with the company's accountants to verify that they were indeed in dire straits. Her father's rash acquisition of The Spire had stretched the company to breaking point. Harry Fairfield was their last hope.

She unzipped the red dress, resisting the urge to crush it into a wrinkled pulp.

'Do you need help?' Sophie asked, although Eva sensed the offer wasn't altruistic.

'No, I can manage.'

The same way she'd managed after her mother's death; through her father's rejection and Sophie's increasingly unreasonable behaviour; through the heartbreak of finding out about Zaccheo's betrayal.

Sophie nodded briskly. 'I'll see you downstairs, then.'

Eva slipped on the dress, avoiding another look in the mirror when the first glimpse showed what she'd feared most. Her every curve was accentuated, with large swathes of flesh exposed. With shaky fingers she applied her lipstick and slipped her feet into matching platform heels.

Slipping the gold and red wrap around her shoulders, she finally glanced at her image.

Chin up, girl. It's show time.

Eva wished the manageress of Siren were uttering the words, as she did every time before Eva stepped onto the stage.

Unfortunately, she wasn't at Siren. She'd promised to marry a man she didn't love, for the sake of saving her precious family name.

No amount of pep talk could stem the roaring agitation flooding her veins.

CHAPTER TWO

THE EVENT PLANNERS had outdone themselves. Potted palms, decorative screens and subdued lighting had been strategically placed around the main halls of Pennington Manor to hide the peeling plaster, chipped wood panelling and torn Aubusson rugs that funds could no longer stretch to rectify.

Eva sipped the champagne she'd been nursing for the last two hours and willed time to move faster. Technically she couldn't throw any guest out, but *Eight to Midnight* was the time the costly invitations had stated the party would last. She needed something to focus on or risk sliding into madness.

Gritting her teeth, she smiled as yet another guest demanded to see her engagement ring. The monstrous pink diamond's sole purpose was to demonstrate the Fairfields' wealth. Its alien weight dragged her hand down, hammering home the irrefutable point that she'd sold herself for her pedigree.

Her father's booming voice interrupted her maudlin thoughts. Surrounded by a group of influential politicians who hung onto his every word, Oscar Pennington was in his element.

Thickset but tall enough to hide the excess weight he carried, her father cut a commanding figure despite his recent spell in hospital. His stint in the army three decades ago had lent him a ruthless edge, cleverly counteracted by his natural charm. The combination made him enigmatic enough to attract attention when he walked into a room.

But not even that charisma had saved him from economic devastation four years ago.

With that coming close on the heels of her mother's ill-

ness, their social and economic circles had dwindled to nothing almost overnight, with her father desperately scrambling
to hold things together.

End result—his association with Zaccheo Giordano.

Eva frowned, bewildered that her thoughts had circled
back to the man she'd pushed to the dark recesses of her
mind. A man she'd last seen being led away in handcuffs—

'There you are. I've been looking for you everywhere.'

Eva started, then berated herself for feeling guilty. Guilt
belonged to those who'd committed crimes, who lied about
their true motives.

Enough!

She smiled at Harry.

Her old university friend—a brilliant tech genius—
had gone off the rails when he'd achieved fame and wealth
straight out of university. Now a multimillionaire with
enough money to bail out Penningtons, he represented her
family's last hope.

'Well, you found me,' she said.

He was a few inches taller than her five feet four; she
didn't have to look up too far to meet his twinkling soft
brown eyes.

'Indeed. Are you okay?' he asked, his gaze reflecting
concern.

'I'm fine,' she responded breezily.

He looked unconvinced. Harry was one of the few people
who knew about her broken engagement to Zaccheo. He'd
seen beneath her false smiles and assurances that she could
handle a marriage of convenience and asked her point-blank
if her past with Zaccheo Giordano would be a problem. Her
swift *no* seemed to have satisfied him.

Now he looked unsure.

'Harry, don't fret. I can do this,' she insisted, despite the
hollowness in her stomach.

He studied her solemnly, then called over a waiter and exchanged his empty champagne glass for a full one. 'If you

say so, but I need advanced warning if this gets too weird for you, okay? My parents will have a fit if they read about me in the papers this side of Christmas.'

She nodded gratefully, then frowned. 'I thought you were going to take it easy tonight?' She indicated his glass.

'Gosh, you already sound like a wife.' He sniggered. 'Leave off, sweetness, the parents have already given me an earful.'

Having met his parents a week ago, Eva could imagine the exchange.

'Remember why *you're* doing this. Do you want to derail the PR campaign to clean up your image before it's even begun?'

While Harry couldn't care less about his social standing, his parents were voracious in their hunger for prestige and a pedigree to hang their name on. Only the threat to Harry's business dealings had finally forced him to address his reckless playboy image.

He took her arm and tilted his sand-coloured head affably towards hers. 'I promise to be on my best behaviour. Now that the tedious toasts have been made and we're officially engaged, it's time for the best part of the evening. The fireworks!'

Eva set her champagne glass down and stepped out of the dining-room alcove that had been her sanctuary throughout her childhood. 'Isn't that supposed to be a surprise?'

Harry winked. 'It is, but, since we've fooled everyone into thinking we're *madly* in love, faking our surprise should be easy.'

She smiled. 'I won't tell if you don't.'

Harry laid a hand across his heart. 'Thank you, my fair Lady Pennington.'

The reminder of why this whole sham engagement was happening slid like a knife between her ribs. Numbing herself to the pain, she walked out onto the terrace that overlooked the manor's multi-acre garden.

The gardens had once held large koi ponds, a giant summer house and an elaborate maze, but the prohibitive cost of the grounds' upkeep had led to the landscape being levelled and replaced with rolling carpet grass.

A smattering of applause greeted their arrival and Eva's gaze drifted over the guests to where Sophie, her father and Harry's parents stood watching them.

She caught her father's eye, and her stomach knotted.

While part of her was pleased that she'd found a solution to their family problems, she couldn't help but feel that nothing she did would ever bring her closer to her sister or father.

Her father might have accepted her help with the bailout from Harry, but his displeasure at her chosen profession was yet another bone of contention between them. One she'd made clear she wouldn't back down on.

Turning away, she fixed her smile in place and exclaimed appropriately when the first elaborate firework display burst into the sky.

'So…my parents want us to live together,' Harry whispered in her ear.

'What?'

He laughed. 'Don't worry, I convinced them you hate my bachelor pad so we need to find a place that's *ours* rather than mine.'

Relief poured through her. 'Thank you.'

He brushed a hand down her cheek. 'You're welcome. But I deserve a reward for my sacrifice,' he said with a smile. 'How about dinner on Monday?'

'As long as it's not a paparazzi-stalked spectacle of a restaurant, you're on.'

'Great. It's a date.' He kissed her knuckles, much to the delight of the guests, who thought they were witnessing a true love match.

Eva allowed herself to relax. She might find what they were doing distasteful, but she was grateful that Harry's visit to Siren three weeks ago had ended up with him bailing her out, and not a calculating stranger.

'That dress is a knockout on you, by the way.'

She grimaced. 'It wasn't my first choice, but thank you.'

The next series of firework displays should've quieted the guests, yet murmurs around her grew.

'*Omigod*, whoever it is must have a death wish!' someone exclaimed.

Harry's eyes narrowed. 'I think we may have a last-minute guest.'

Eva looked around and saw puzzled gazes fixed at a point in the sky as the faint *thwopping* sound grew louder. Another set of fireworks went off, illuminating the looming object.

She frowned. 'Is that…?'

'A helicopter heading straight for the middle of the fireworks display? Yep. I guess the organisers decided to add another surprise to the party.'

'I don't think that's part of the entertainment,' Eva shouted to be heard over the descending aircraft.

Her heart slammed into her throat as a particularly elaborate firework erupted precariously close to the black-and-red chopper.

'Hell, if this is a stunt, I take my hat off to the pilot. It takes iron balls to fly into danger like that.' Harry chuckled.

The helicopter drew closer. Mesmerised, Eva watched it settle in the middle of the garden, her attention riveted to its single occupant.

The garden lights had been turned off to showcase the fireworks to maximum effect so she couldn't see who their unexpected guest was. Nevertheless, an ominous shiver chased up her spine.

She heard urgent shouts for the pyrotechnician to halt the display, but another rocket fizzed past the rotating blades.

A hush fell over the crowd as the helicopter door opened. A figure stepped out, clad from head to toe in black. As another blaze of colour filled the sky his body was thrown into relief.

Eva tensed as if she'd been shot with a stun gun.

It couldn't be...

He was behind bars, atoning for his ruthless greed. Eva squashed the sting of guilt that accompanied the thought.

Zaccheo Giordano and men of his ilk arrogantly believed they were above the law. They didn't deserve her sympathy, or the disloyal thought that he alone had paid the price when, by association, her father should've borne some of the blame. Justice ensured they went to jail and stayed there for the duration of their term. They weren't released early.

They certainly didn't land in the middle of a firework display at a private party as if they owned the land they walked on.

The spectacle unfolding before her stated differently.

Lights flickered on. Eva tracked the figure striding imperiously across the grass and up the wide steps.

Reaching the terrace, he paused and buttoned his single-breasted tuxedo.

'Oh, God,' she whispered.

'Wait...you know this bloke?' Harry asked, his tone for once serious.

Eva wanted to deny the man who now stood, easily head and shoulders above the nearest guests, his fierce, unwavering gaze pinned on her.

She didn't know whether to attribute the crackling electricity to his appearance or the look in his eyes. Both were viscerally menacing to the point of brutality.

The Zaccheo Giordano she'd had the misfortune of briefly tangling with before his incarceration had kept his hair trimmed short and his face clean-shaven.

This man had a full beard and his hair flowed over his shoulders in an unruly sea of thick jet waves. Eva swallowed at the pronounced difference in him. The sleek, almost gaunt man she'd known was gone. In his place breathed a Neanderthal with broader shoulders, thicker arms and a denser chest moulded by his black silk shirt. Equally dark trousers hugged lean hips and sturdy thighs to fall in a precise inch above expensive handmade shoes. But nothing of his attire disguised the aura he emanated.

Uncivilised. Explosively masculine. Lethal.

Danger vibrated from him like striations on baking asphalt. It flowed over the guests, who jostled each other for a better look at the impromptu visitor.

'Eva?' Harry's puzzled query echoed through her dazed consciousness.

Zaccheo released her from his deadly stare. His eyes flicked to the arm tucked into Harry's before he turned away. The breath exploded from her lungs. Sensing Harry about to ask another question, she nodded.

'Yes. That's Zaccheo.'

Her eyes followed Zaccheo as he turned towards her family.

Oscar's look of anger was laced with a heavy dose of apprehension. Sophie looked plain stunned.

Eva watched the man she'd hoped to never see again cup his hands behind his back and stroll towards her father. Anyone would've been foolish to think that stance indicated supplication. If anything, its severe mockery made Eva want to do the unthinkable and burst out laughing.

She would've, had she not been mired in deep dread at what Zaccheo's presence meant.

'Your ex?' Harry pressed.

She nodded numbly.

'Then we should say hello.'

Harry tugged on her arm and she realised too late what he meant.

'No. Wait!' she whispered fiercely.

But he was either too drunk or genuinely oblivious to the vortex of danger he was headed for to pay attention. The tension surrounding the group swallowed Eva as they approached. Heart pounding, she watched her father's and Zaccheo's gazes lock.

'I don't know what the hell you think you're doing here, Giordano, but I suggest you get back in that monstrosity and leave before I have you arrested for trespass.'

A shock wave went through the crowd.

Zaccheo didn't bat an eyelid.

'By all means do that if you wish, but you know exactly why I'm here, Pennington. We can play coy if you prefer. You'll be made painfully aware when I tire of it.' The words were barely above a murmur, but their venom raised the hairs on Eva's arms, triggering a gasp when she saw Sophie's face.

Her usually unflappable sister was severely agitated, her face distressingly pale.

'*Ciao*, Eva,' Zaccheo drawled without turning around. That deep, resonant voice, reminiscent of a tenor in a soulful opera, washed over her, its powerfully mesmerising quality reminding her how she'd once longed to hear him speak just for the hell of it. 'It's good of you to join us.'

'This is my engagement party. It's my duty to interact with my guests, even unwelcome ones who will be asked to leave immediately.'

'Don't worry, *cara*, I won't be staying long.'

The relief that surged up her spine disappeared when his gaze finally swung her way, then dropped to her left hand. With almost cavalier laziness, he caught her wrist and raised it to the light. He examined the ring for exactly three seconds. 'How predictable.'

He released her with the same carelessness he'd captured her.

Eva clenched her fist to stop the sizzling electricity firing up her arm at the brief contact.

'What's that supposed to mean?' Harry demanded.

Zaccheo levelled steely grey eyes on him, then his parents. 'This is a private discussion. Leave us.'

Peter Fairfield's laugh held incredulity, the last inch of

champagne in his glass sloshing wildly as he raised his arm. 'I think you've got the wrong end of the stick there, mate. You're the one who needs to take a walk.'

Eva caught Harry's pained look at his father's response, but could do nothing but watch, heart in her throat, as Zaccheo faced Peter Fairfield.

Again she was struck by how much his body had changed; how the sleek, layered muscle lent a deeper sense of danger. Whereas before it'd been like walking close to the edge of a cliff, looking into his eyes now was like staring into a deep, bottomless abyss.

'Would you care to repeat that, *il mio amico*?' The almost conversational tone belied the savage tension beneath the words.

'Oscar, who *is* this?' Peter Fairfield demanded of her father, who seemed to have lost the ability to speak after Zaccheo's succinct taunt.

Eva inserted herself between the two men before the situation got out of hand. Behind her, heat from Zaccheo's body burned every exposed inch of skin. Ignoring the sensation, she cleared her throat.

'Mr and Mrs Fairfield, Harry, we'll only be a few minutes. We're just catching up with Mr Giordano.' She glanced at her father. A vein throbbed in his temple and he'd gone a worrying shade of puce. Fear climbed into her heart. 'Father?'

He roused himself and glanced around. A charming smile slid into place, but it was off by a light year. The trickle of ice that had drifted down her spine at Zaccheo's unexpected arrival turned into a steady drip.

'We'll take this in my study. Don't hesitate to let the staff know if you need anything.' He strode away, followed by a disturbingly quiet Sophie.

Zaccheo's gaze swung to Harry, who defiantly withstood the laser gaze for a few seconds before he glanced at her.

'Are you sure?' Harry asked, that touching concern again in his eyes.

Her instinct screamed a terrible foreboding, but she nodded. 'Yes.'

'Okay. Hurry back, sweetness.' Before she could move,
he dropped a kiss on her mouth.

A barely audible lethal growl charged through the air.

Eva flinched.

She wanted to face Zaccheo. Demand that he crawl back
behind the bars that should've been holding him. But that
glimpse of fear in her father's eyes stopped her. She tugged
the wrap closer around her.

Something wasn't right here. She was willing to bet the
dilapidated ancestral pile beneath her feet that something
was seriously, *dangerously* wrong—

'Move, Eva.'

The cool command spoken against her ear sent shivers
coursing through her.

She moved, only because the quicker she got to the bottom of why he was here, the quicker he would leave. But
with each step his dark gaze probed her back, making the
walk to her father's study on the other side of the manor the
longest in her life.

Zaccheo shut the door behind him. Her father turned from
where he'd been gazing into the unlit fireplace. Again Eva
spotted apprehension in his eyes before he masked it.

'Whatever grievance you think you have the right to air,
I suggest you rethink it, son. Even if this were the right time
or place—'

'I am *not* your son, Pennington.' Zaccheo's response held
lethal bite, the first sign of his fury breaking through. 'As
for why I'm here, I have five thousand three hundred and
twenty-two pieces of documentation that proves you colluded with various other individuals to pin a crime on me
that I didn't commit.'

'What?' Eva gasped, then the absurdity of the statement
made her shake her head. 'We don't believe you.'

Zaccheo's eyes remained on her father. 'You may not, but your father does.'

Oscar Pennington laughed, but the sound lacked its usual boom and zest. When sweat broke out over his forehead, fear gripped Eva's insides.

She steeled her spine. 'Our lawyers will rip whatever evidence you think you have to shreds, I'm sure. If you're here to seek some sort of closure, you picked the wrong time to do it. Perhaps we can arrange to meet you at some other time?'

Zaccheo didn't move. Didn't blink. Hands once again tucked behind his back, he simply watched her father, his body a coiled predator waiting to strike a fatal blow.

Silence stretched, throbbed with unbearable menace. Eva looked from her father to Sophie and back again, her dread escalating. 'What's going on?' she demanded.

Her father gripped the mantel until his knuckles shone white. 'You chose the wrong enemy. You're sorely mistaken if you think I'll let you blackmail me in my own home.'

Sophie stepped forward. 'Father, don't—'

'Good, you haven't lost your hubris.' Zaccheo's voice slashed across her sister's. 'I was counting on that. Here's what I'm going to do. In ten minutes I'm going to leave here with Eva, right in front of all your guests. You won't lift a finger to stop me. You'll tell them exactly who I am. Then you'll make a formal announcement that I'm the man your daughter will marry two weeks from today and that I have your blessing. I don't want to trust something so important to phone cameras and social media, although your guests will probably do a pretty good job. I noticed a few members of the press out there, so that part of your task should be easy. If the articles are written to my satisfaction, I'll be in touch on Monday to lay out how you can begin to make reparations to me. However, if by the time Eva and I wake up tomorrow morning the news of our engagement isn't in the press, then all bets are off.'

Oscar Pennington's breathing altered alarmingly. His

mouth opened but no words emerged. In the arctic silence that greeted Zaccheo's deadly words, Eva gaped at him.

'You're clearly not in touch with all of your faculties if you think those ridiculous demands are going to be met.' When silence greeted her response, she turned sharply to her father. 'Father? Why aren't you saying something?' she demanded, although the trepidation beating in her chest spelled its own doom.

'Because he can't, Eva. Because he's about to do exactly as I say.'

She rounded on him, and was once again rocked to the core by Zaccheo's visually powerful, utterly captivating transformation. So much so, she couldn't speak for several seconds. 'You're out of your mind!' she finally blurted.

Zaccheo's gaze didn't stray from its laser focus on her father. 'Believe me, *cara mia*, I haven't been saner than I am in this moment.'

CHAPTER THREE

ZACCHEO WATCHED EVA'S head swivel to her father, confusion warring with anger.

'Go on, Oscar. She's waiting for you to tell me to go to hell. Why don't you?'

Pennington staggered towards his desk, his face ashen and his breathing growing increasingly laboured.

'Father!' Eva rushed to his side—ignoring the poisonous look her sister sent her—as he collapsed into his leather armchair.

Zaccheo wanted to rip her away, let her watch her father suffer as his sins came home to roost. Instead he allowed the drama to play out. The outcome would be inevitable and would only go one way.

His way.

He wanted to look into Pennington's eyes and see the defeat and helplessness the other man had expected to see in his eyes the day Zaccheo had been sentenced.

Both sisters now fussed over their father and a swell of satisfaction rose at the fear in their eyes. Eva glanced his way and he experienced a different punch altogether. One he'd thought himself immune to, but had realised otherwise the moment he'd stepped off his helicopter and singled her out in the crowd.

That unsettling feeling, as if he were suffering from vertigo despite standing on terra firma, had intrigued and annoyed him in equal measures from the very first time he'd seen her, her voice silkily hypnotic as she crooned into a mic on a golden-lit stage, her fingers caressing the black microphone stand as if she were touching a lover.

Even knowing exactly who she was, what she represented,

he hadn't been able to walk away. In the weeks after their first meeting, he'd fooled himself into believing she was different, that she wasn't tainted with the same greed to further her pedigree by whatever means necessary; that she wasn't willing to do whatever it took to secure her family's standing, even while secretly scorning his upbringing.

Her very public denouncement of any association between them on the day of his sentencing had been the final blow. Not that Zaccheo hadn't had the scales viciously ripped from his eyes by then.

No, by that fateful day fourteen months ago, he'd known just how thoroughly he'd been suckered.

'What the hell do you think you're doing?' she muttered fiercely, her moss-green eyes firing lasers at him.

Zaccheo forced himself not to smile. The time for gloating would come later. 'Exacting the wages of sin, *dolcezza*. What else?'

'I don't know what you're talking about, but I don't think my father is in a position to have a discussion with you right now, Mr Giordano.'

Her prim and proper tones bit savagely into Zaccheo, wiping away any trace of twisted mirth. That tone said he ought to *know his place*, that he ought to stand there like a good little servant and wait to be addressed instead of upsetting the lord of the manor with his petty concerns.

Rage bubbled beneath his skin, threatening to erupt. Blunt nails bit into his wrist, but the pain wasn't enough to calm his fury. He clenched his jaw for a long moment before he trusted himself to speak.

'I gave you ten minutes, Pennington. You now have five. I suggest you practise whatever sly words you'll be using to address your guests.' Zaccheo shrugged. 'Or not. Either way, things *will* go my way.'

Eva rushed at him, her striking face and flawless skin flushed with a burst of angry colour as she stopped a few feet away.

Out on the terrace, he'd compelled himself not to stare too long at her in case he betrayed his feelings. In case his gaze devoured her as he'd wanted to do since her presence snaked like a live wire inside him.

Now, he took in that wild gypsy-like caramel-blonde hair so out of place in this polished stratosphere her family chose to inhabit. The striking contrast between her bright hair, black eyebrows and dark-rimmed eyes had always fascinated him. But no more than her cupid-bow lips, soft, dark red and sinfully sensual. Or the rest of her body.

'You assume I have no say in whatever despicable spectacle you're planning. That I intend to meekly stand by while you humiliate my family? Well, think again!'

'Eva…' her father started.

'No! I don't know what exactly is going on here, but I intend to play no part in it.'

'You'll play your part, and you'll play it well,' Zaccheo interjected, finally driving his gaze up from the mouth he wanted to feast on more than he wanted his next breath. *That'll come soon enough*, he promised himself.

'Or what? You'll carry through with your empty threats?'

His fury eased a touch and twisted amusement slid back into place. It never ceased to amaze him how the titled rich felt they were above the tenets that governed ordinary human beings. His own stepfather had been the same. He'd believed, foolishly, that his pedigree and connections would insulate him from his reckless business practices, that the Old Boys' Club would provide a safety net despite his poor judgement.

Zaccheo had taken great pleasure in watching his mother's husband squirm before him, cap in hand, when Zaccheo had bought his family business right from underneath his pompous nose. But even then, the older man had continued to treat him like a third-class citizen…

Just as Oscar Pennington had done. Just as Eva Pennington was doing now.

'You think my threats empty?' he enquired softly. 'Then do nothing. It's after all your privilege and your right.'

Something of the lethal edge that rode him must have transmitted itself to her. Apprehension chased across her face before she firmed those impossibly sumptuous lips.

'Do nothing, and watch me bury your family in the deepest, darkest, most demeaning pit you can dream of. Do nothing and watch me unleash a scandal the scale of which you can only imagine on your precious family name.' He bared his teeth in a mirthless smile and her eyes widened in stunned disbelief. 'It would be *my* privilege and pleasure to do so.'

Oscar Pennington inhaled sharply and Zaccheo's gaze zeroed in on his enemy. The older man rose from the chair. Though he looked frail, his eyes reflected icy disdain. But Zaccheo also glimpsed the fear of a cornered man weighing all the options to see how to escape the noose dangling ever closer.

Zaccheo smiled inwardly. He had no intention of letting Pennington escape. Not now, not ever.

The flames of retribution intensifying within him, he unclasped his hands. It was time to bring this meeting to an end.

'Your time's up, Pennington.'

Eva answered instead of her father. 'How do we know you're not bluffing? You say you have something over us, prove it,' she said defiantly.

He could've walked out and let them twist in the wind of uncertainty. Pennington would find out soon enough the length of Zaccheo's ruthless reach. But the thought of leaving Eva here when he departed was suddenly unthinkable. So far he'd allowed himself a brief glimpse of her body wrapped in that obscenely revealing red dress. But that one glimpse had been enough. Quite apart from the rage boiling his blood, the steady hammer of his pulse proved that he still wanted her with a fever that spiked higher with each passing second.

He would take what he'd foolishly and piously denied

himself two years ago. He would *take* and *use*, just as they'd done to him. Only when he'd achieved every goal he'd set himself would he feel avenged.

'You can't, can you?' Oscar taunted with a sly smile, bringing Zaccheo back to the room and the three aristocratic faces staring at him with varying degrees of disdain and fear.

He smiled, almost amused by the older man's growing confidence. 'Harry Fairfield is providing you with a bridging loan of fifteen million pounds because the combined running costs of the Pennington Hotels and The Spire have you stretched so thin the banks won't touch you. While you desperately drum up an adequate advertising budget to rent out all those overpriced but empty floors in The Spire, the interest owed to the Chinese consortium who own seventy-five per cent of the building is escalating. You have a meeting with them on Monday to request more time to pay the interest. In return for Fairfield's investment, you're handing him your daughter.'

Eva glared at him. 'So you've asked a few questions about Penningtons' business practices. That doesn't empower you to make demands of any of us.'

Zaccheo took a moment to admire her newfound grit. During their initial association, she'd been a little more timid, and in her father's shadow, but it looked as if the kitten had grown a few claws. He curbed the thrill at what was to come and answered.

'Yes, it does. Would you be interested to know the Chinese consortium sold their seventy-five per cent of The Spire to me three days ago? So by my calculation you're in excess of three months late on interest payments, correct?'

A rough sound, a cross between a cough and a wheeze, escaped Pennington's throat. There was no class or grace in the way he gaped at Zaccheo. He dropped back into his chair, his face a mask of hatred.

'I knew you were a worthless bet the moment I set eyes on you. I should've listened to my instincts.'

The red haze he'd been trying to hold back surged higher. 'No, what you wanted was a spineless scapegoat, a *capro espiatorio*, who would make you rich and fat and content and even give up his life without question!'

'Mr Giordano, surely we can discuss this like sensible business-minded individuals,' Sophie Pennington advanced, her hands outstretched in benign sensibility. Zaccheo looked from the hands she willed not to tremble to the veiled disdain in her eyes. Then he looked past her to Eva, who'd returned to her father's side, her face pale but her eyes shooting her displeasure at him.

Unexpectedly and very much unwelcome, a tiny hint of compassion tugged at him.

Basta!

He turned abruptly and reached for the door handle. 'You have until I ready my chopper for take-off to come to me, Eva.' He didn't need to expand on that edict. The *or else* hung in the air like the deadly poison he intended it to be.

He walked out and headed for the terrace, despite every nerve in his body straining to return to the room and forcibly drag Eva out.

True, he hadn't bargained for the visceral reaction to seeing her again. And yes, he hadn't quite been able to control his reaction to seeing another man's ring on her finger, that vulgar symbol of ownership hollowing out his stomach. The knowledge that she'd most likely shared that hapless drunk's bed, given the body he'd once believed to be his to another, ate through his blood like acid on metal. But he couldn't afford to let his emotions show.

Every strategic move in this game of deadly retribution hinged on him maintaining his control; on not letting them see how affected he was by all this.

He stepped onto the terrace and all conversation ceased. Curious faces gaped and one or two bolder guests even tried to intercept him. Zaccheo cut through the crowd, his gaze on the chopper a few dozen yards away.

She would come to him. As an outcome of his first salvo, nothing else would be acceptable.

His pulse thudded loud and insistent in his ears as he strolled down the steps towards the aircraft. The fireworks amid which he'd landed had long since gone quiet, but the scent of sulphur lingered in the air, reminding him of the volatility that lingered beneath his own skin, ready to erupt at the smallest trigger.

He wouldn't let it erupt. Not yet.

A murmur rose behind him, the fevered excitement that came with the anticipation of a spectacle. A *scandal*.

Zaccheo compelled himself to keep walking.

He ducked beneath the powerful rotors of his aircraft and reached for the door.

'Wait!'

He stopped. Turned.

Three hundred pairs of eyes watched with unabashed interest as Eva paused several feet from him.

Behind her, her father and sister stood on the steps, wearing similar expressions of dread. Zaccheo wanted them to stew for a while longer, but he found his attention drawn to the woman striding towards him. Her face reflected more defiance than dread. It also held pride and not a small measure of bruised disdain. Zaccheo vowed in that moment to make her regret that latter look, make her take back every single moment she'd thought herself above him.

Swallowing, he looked down at her body.

She held the flimsy wrap around her like armour. As if that would protect her from him. With one ruthless tug, he pulled it away. It fluttered to the ground, revealing her luscious, heart-stopping figure to his gaze. Unable to stem the frantic need crashing through him, he stepped forward and speared his fingers into the wild tumble of her hair.

Another step and she was in his arms.

Where she belonged.

* * *

The small pocket of air Eva had been able to retain in her lungs during her desperate flight after Zaccheo evaporated when he yanked her against him. Her body went from shivering in the crisp January air to furnace-hot within seconds. The fingers in her hair tightened, his other arm sliding around her waist.

Eva wanted to remain unaffected, slam her hands against his chest and remove herself from that dangerous wall of masculinity. But she couldn't move. So she fought with her words.

'You may think you've won, that you own me, but you don't,' she snapped. 'You never will!'

His eyes gleamed. 'Such fire. Such determination. You've changed, *cara mia*, I'll give you that. And yet here you are, barely one minute after I walked out of your father's study. Mere hours after you promised yourself to another man, here you are, Eva Pennington, ready to promise yourself to me. Ready to become whatever I want you to be.'

Her snigger made his eyes narrow, but she didn't care. 'Keep telling yourself that. I look forward to your shock when I prove you wrong.'

That deadly smile she'd first seen in her father's study reappeared, curling fear through her. It reeked with far too much gratification to kill that unshakeable sensation that she was standing on the edge of a precipice, and that, should she fall, there would be no saving her.

She realised the reason for the smile when he lifted her now bare fingers to his eye level. 'You've proved me right already.'

'Are you completely sure about that?' The question was a bold but empty taunt.

The lack of fuss with which Harry had taken back his ring a few minutes ago had been a relief.

She might not have an immediate solution to her family's

problems, but Eva was glad she no longer had to pretend she was half of a sham couple.

Zaccheo brought her fingers to his mouth and kissed her ring finger, stunning her back to reality. Flashes erupted as his actions were recorded, no doubt to be streamed across the fastest mediums available.

Recalling the conversation she'd just had with her father, she tried to pull away. 'This pound-of-flesh taking isn't going to last very long, so I suggest you enjoy it while it lasts. I intend to return to my life before midnight—'

Her words dried up when his face closed in a mask of icy fury, and his hands sealed her body even closer to his.

'Your first lesson is to stop speaking to me as if I'm the hired help. Refraining from doing so will put me in a much calmer frame of mind to deal with you than otherwise,' he said with unmistakeable warning.

Eva doubted that anyone had dared to speak to Zaccheo Giordano in the way she referred, but she wasn't about to debate that point with him with three hundred pairs of eyes watching. She was struggling enough to keep upright what with all the turbulent sensations firing through her at his touch. 'Why, Zaccheo, you sound as if you've a great many lessons you intend to dole out...' She tried to sound bored, but her voice emerged a little too breathless for her liking.

'Patience, *cara mia*. You'll be instructed as and when necessary.' His gaze dropped to her mouth and her breath lodged in her sternum. 'For now, I wish the talking to cease.'

He closed the final inch between them and slanted his mouth over hers. The world tilted and shook beneath her feet. Expertly sensual and demanding, he kissed her as if he owned her mouth, as if he owned her whole body. In all her adult years, Eva had never imagined the brush of a beard would infuse her with such spine-tingling sensations. Yet she shivered with fiery delight as Zaccheo's silky facial hair caressed the corners of her mouth.

She groaned at the forceful breach of his tongue. Her arms drifted over his taut biceps as she became lost in the potent magic of his kiss. At the first touch of his tongue against hers, she shuddered. He made a rough sound and his sharp inhalation vibrated against her. His fingers convulsed in her hair and his other hand drifted to her bottom, moulding her as he stepped back against the aircraft and widened his stance to bring her closer.

Eva wasn't sure how long she stood there, adrift in a swirl of sensation as he ravaged her mouth. It wasn't until her lungs screamed and her heart jackhammered against her ribs did she recall where she was…what was happening.

And still she wanted to continue.

So much so she almost moaned in protest when firm hands set her back and she found herself staring into molten eyes dark with savage hunger.

'I think we've given our audience enough to feed on. Get in.'

The calm words, spoken in direct counteraction to the frenzied look in his eyes, doused Eva with cold reality. That she'd made even more of a spectacle of herself hit home as wolf whistles ripped through the air.

'This was all for *show*?' she whispered numbly, shivering in the frigid air.

One sleek eyebrow lifted. 'Of course. Did you think I wanted to kiss you because I was so desperate for you I just couldn't help myself? You'll find that I have more self-restraint than that. Get in,' he repeated, holding the steel and glass door to the aircraft open.

Eva brushed cold hands over her arms, unable to move. She stared at him, perhaps hoping to find some humanity in the suddenly grim-faced block of stone in front of her. Or did she want a hint of the man who'd once framed her face in his hands and called her the most beautiful thing in his life?

Of course, that had been a lie. Everything about Zaccheo

had been a lie. Still she probed for some softness beneath that formidable exterior.

His implacable stare told her she was grasping at straws, as she had from the very beginning, when she'd woven stupid dreams around him.

A gust of icy wind blew across the grass, straight into her exposed back. A flash of red caught her eye and she blindly stumbled towards the terrace. She'd barely taken two steps when he seized her arm.

'What the hell do you think you're doing?' Zaccheo enquired frostily.

'I'm cold,' she replied through chattering teeth. 'My wrap...' She pointed to where the material had drifted.

'Leave it. This will keep you warm.' With one smooth move, he unbuttoned, shrugged off his tuxedo and draped it around her shoulders. The sudden infusion of warmth was overwhelming. Eva didn't want to drown in the distinctively heady scent of the man who was wrecking her world, didn't welcome her body's traitorous urge to burrow into the warm silk lining. And most of all, she didn't want to be beholden to him in any way, or accept any hint of kindness from him.

Zaccheo Giordano had demonstrated a ruthless thirst to annihilate those he deemed enemies in her father's study.

But she was no longer the naive and trusting girl she'd been a year and a half ago. Zaccheo's betrayal and her continued fraught relationship with her father and sister had hardened her heart. The pain was still there—would probably always be there—but so were the new fortifications against further hurt. She had no intention of laying her heart and soul bare to further damage from the people she'd once blithely believed would return the same love and devotion she offered freely.

She started to shrug off the jacket. 'No, thanks. I'd prefer not to be stamped as your possession.'

He stopped her by placing both hands on her arms.

Dark grey eyes pinned her to the spot, the sharper, icier

burst of wind whipping around them casting him in a deadlier, more dangerous light.

'You're already my possession. You became mine the moment you made the choice to follow me out here, Eva. You can kid yourself all you want, but this is your reality from here on in.'

CHAPTER FOUR

@Ladystclare OMG! Bragging rights=mine! Beheld fireworks w/in fireworks @P/Manor last night when LadyP eloped w/convict lover! #amazeballs

@Aristokitten Bet it was all a publicity stunt, but boy that kiss? Sign me up! #Ineedlatinlovelikethat

@Countrypile That wasn't love. That was an obscene and shameless money-grabbing gambit at its worst! #Donotencouragerancidbehaviour

EVA FLINCHED, her stomach churning at each new message that flooded her social-media stream.

The hours had passed in a haze after Zaccheo flew them from Pennington Manor. In solid command of the helicopter, he'd soared over the City of London and landed on the vertiginous rooftop of The Spire.

The stunning split-level penthouse's interior had barely registered in the early hours when Zaccheo's enigmatic aide, Romeo, had directed the butler to show her to her room.

Zaccheo had stalked away without a word, leaving her in the middle of his marble-tiled hallway, clutching his jacket.

Sleep had been non-existent in the bleak hours that had followed. At five a.m., she'd given up and taken a quick shower before putting on that skin-baring dress again.

Wishing she'd asked for a blanket to cover the acres of flesh on display, she cringed as another salacious offering popped into her inbox displayed on Zaccheo's tablet.

Like a spectator frozen on the fringes of an unfolding train wreck, she read the latest post.

@Uberwoman Hey ConvictLover, that flighty poor little rich girl is wasted on you. Real women exist. Let ME rock your world!

Eva curled her fist, refusing to entertain the image of any woman rocking Zaccheo's world. She didn't care one way or the other. If she had a choice, she would be ten thousand miles away from this place.

'If you're thinking of responding to any of that, consider yourself warned against doing so.'

She jumped at the deep voice a whisper from her ear. She'd thought she would be alone in the living room for at least another couple of hours before dealing with Zaccheo. Now she wished she'd stayed in her room.

She stood and faced him, the long black suede sofa between them no barrier to Zaccheo's towering presence.

'I've no intention of responding. And you really shouldn't sneak up on people like that,' she tagged on when the leisurely drift of those incisive eyes over her body made her feel like a specimen under a microscope.

'I don't sneak. Had you been less self-absorbed in your notoriety, you would've heard me enter the room.'

Anger welled up. 'You accuse *me* of being notorious? All this is happening because *you* insisted on gatecrashing a private event and turning it into a public spectacle.'

'And, of course, you were so eager to find out whether you're trending that you woke up at dawn to follow the news.'

She wanted to ask how he'd known what time she'd left her room, but Eva suspected she wouldn't like the answer. 'You assume I slept at all when sleep was the last thing on my mind, having been blackmailed into coming here. And, FYI, I don't read the gutter press. Not unless I want the worst kind of indigestion.'

He rounded the sofa and stopped within arm's length. She stood her ground, but she couldn't help herself ogling the breathtaking body filling her vision.

It was barely six o'clock and yet he looked as vitally masculine as if he'd been up and ready for hours. A film of sweat covered the hair-dusted arms beneath the pulled-up sleeves, and his damp white T-shirt moulded his chiselled torso. His black drawstring sweatpants did nothing to hide thick thighs and Eva struggled to avert her gaze from the virile outline of his manhood against the soft material. Dragging her gaze up, she stared in fascination at the hands and fingers wrapped in stained boxing gauze.

'Do you intend to spend the rest of the morning ogling me, Eva?' he asked mockingly.

She looked into his eyes and that potent, electric tug yanked hard at her. Reminding herself that she was immune from whatever spell he'd once cast on her, she raised her chin.

'I intend to attempt a reasonable conversation with you in the cold light of day regarding last night's events.'

'That suggests you believe our previous interactions have been unreasonable?'

'I did a quick search online. You were released yesterday morning. It stands to reason that you're still a little affected by your incarceration—'

His harsh, embittered laugh bounced like bullets around the room. Eva folded her arms, refusing to cower at the sound.

He stepped towards her, the tension in his body barely leashed. 'You think I'm a *"little affected"* by my incarceration? Tell me, *bella*,' he invited softly, 'do you know what it feels like to be locked in a six-by-ten, damp and rancid cage for over a year?'

A brief wave of torment overcame his features, and a different tug, one of sympathy, pulled at her. Then she reminded herself just who she was dealing with. 'Of course not. I just don't want you to do anything that you'll regret.'

'Your touching concern for my welfare is duly noted. But I suggest you save it for yourself. Last night was merely you and your family being herded into the eye of the storm. The real devastation is just getting started.'

As nightmarish promises went, Zaccheo's chilled her to the bone. Before she could reply, several pings blared from the tablet. She glanced down and saw more lurid posts about what *real women* wanted to do to Zaccheo.

She shut the tablet and straightened to find him slowly unwinding the gauze from his right hand, his gaze pinned on her. Silence stretched as he freed both hands and tossed the balled cloth onto the glass-topped coffee table.

'So, do I get any sort of itinerary for this impending apocalypse?' she asked when it became clear he was content to let the silence linger.

One corner of his mouth lifted. 'We'll have breakfast in half an hour. After that, we'll see whether your father has done what I demanded of him. If he has, we'll take it from there.'

Recalling her father's overly belligerent denial once Zaccheo had left the study last night, anxiety skewered her. 'And if he hasn't?'

'Then his annihilation will come sooner rather than later.'

Half an hour later, Eva struggled to swallow a mouthful of buttered toast and quickly chased it down with a sip of tea before she choked.

A few minutes ago, a brooding Romeo had entered with the butler who'd delivered a stack of broadsheets. The other man had conversed in Italian with a freshly showered and even more visually devastating Zaccheo.

Zaccheo's smile after the short exchange had incited her first panic-induced emotion. He'd said nothing after Romeo left. Instead he'd devoured a hearty plate of scrambled eggs, grilled mushrooms and smoked pancetta served on Italian bread with unsettling gusto.

But as the silence spread thick and cloying across the room she finally set her cup down and glanced to where he stood now at the end of the cherrywood dining table, his hands braced on his hips, an inscrutable expression on his face.

Again, Eva was struck by the change in him. Even now he was dressed more formally in dark grey trousers and a navy shirt with the sleeves rolled up, her eyes were drawn to the gladiator-like ruggedness of his physique.

'Eva.' Her name was a deep command. One she desperately wanted to ignore. It held a quiet triumph she didn't want to acknowledge. The implications were more than she could stomach. She wasn't one for burying her head in the sand, but if her father had done what Zaccheo had demanded, then—

'Eva,' he repeated. Sharper. Controlled but demanding.

Heart hammering, she glanced at him. 'What?'

He stared back without blinking, his body deathly still. 'Come here.'

Refusing to show how rattled she was, she stood, teetered on the heels she'd had no choice but to wear again, and strode towards him.

He tracked her with chilling precision, his eyes dropping to her hips for a charged second before he looked back up. Eva hated her body for reacting to that look, even as her breasts tingled and a blaze lit between her thighs.

Silently she cursed herself. She had no business reacting to that look, or to any man on any plane of emotion whatsoever. She had proof that path only ended in eviscerating heartache.

She stopped a few feet from him, made sure to place a dining chair between them. But the solid wood couldn't stop her senses from reacting to his scent, or her nipples from furling into tight, needy buds when her gaze fell on the golden gleam of his throat revealed by the gap in his shirt. Quickly crossing her arms, she looked down at the newspapers.

That they'd made headlines was unmistakeable. Bold black letters and exclamation marks proclaimed Zaccheo's antics. And as for *that* picture of them locked together…

'I can't believe you landed a helicopter in the middle of a fireworks display,' she threw out, simply because it was easier than acknowledging the other words written on the page binding her to Zaccheo, insinuating they were something they would never be.

He looked from her face to the front-page picture showing him landing his helicopter during a particularly violent explosion. 'Were you concerned for me?' he mocked.

'Of course not. You obviously don't care about your own safety so why should I?'

A simmering silence followed, then he stalked closer. 'I hope you intend to act a little more concerned towards my well-being once we're married.'

Any intention of avoiding looking at him fled her mind. '*Married?* Don't you think you've taken this far enough?' she snapped.

'Excuse me?'

'You wanted to humiliate my father. Congratulations, you've made headlines in every single newspaper. Don't you think it's time to drop this?'

His eyes turned into pools of ice. 'You think this is some sort of game?' he enquired silkily.

'What else can it be? If you really had the evidence you claim to have, why haven't you handed it over to the police?'

'You believe I'm bluffing?' His voice was a sharp blade slicing through the air.

'I believe you feel aggrieved.'

'Really? And what else did you *believe*?'

Eva refused to quail beneath the look that threatened to cut her into pieces. 'It's clear you want to make some sort of statement about how you were treated by my father. You've done that now. Let it go.'

'So your father did all this—' he indicated the papers '—just to stop me throwing a childish tantrum? And what about you? Did you throw yourself at my feet to buy your family time to see how long my bluff would last?'

She flung her arms out in exasperation. 'Come on, Zaccheo—'

They both stilled at her use of his name. Eva had no time to recover from the unwitting slip. Merciless fingers speared into her hair, much as they had last night, holding her captive as his thumb tilted her chin.

'How far are you willing to go to get me to be *reasonable*? Or perhaps I should guess? After all, just last night you'd dropped to an all-time low of whoring yourself to a drunken boy in order to save your family.' The thick condemnation feathered across her skin.

Rage flared in her belly, gave her the strength to remain upright. He stood close. Far too close. She stepped back, but only managed to wedge herself between the table and Zaccheo's towering body. 'As opposed to what? Whoring myself to a middle-aged criminal?'

He leaned down, crowding her further against the polished wood. 'You know exactly how old I am. In fact, I recall precisely where we both were when the clock struck midnight on my thirtieth birthday. Or perhaps you need me to refresh your memory?' His smooth, faintly accented voice trailed amused contempt.

'Don't bother—'

'I'll do it anyway, it's no hardship,' he offered, as if her sharp denial hadn't been uttered. 'We were newly engaged, and you were on your knees in front of my penthouse window, uncaring that anyone with a pair of decent binoculars would see us. All you cared about was getting your busy, greedy little hands on my belt, eager to rid me of my trousers so you could wish me a happy birthday in a way most men fantasise about.'

Her skin flushed with a wave of heat so strong, she feared spontaneous combustion. 'That wasn't my idea.'

One brow quirked. 'Was it not?'

'No, you dared me to do it.'

His mouth twitched. 'Are you saying I forced you?'

Those clever fingers were drifting along her scalp, lazily caressing, lulling her into showing her vulnerability.

Eva sucked in a deep breath. 'I'm saying I don't want to talk about the past. I prefer to stick to the present.'

She didn't want to remember how gullible she'd been back then, how stupidly eager to please, how excited she'd been that this god of a man, who could have any woman he wanted with a lazy crook of his finger, had pursued *her*, chosen *her*.

Even after learning the hard way that men in positions of power would do anything to stay in that power, that her two previous relationships had only been a means to an end for the men involved, she'd still allowed herself to believe Zaccheo wanted her for herself. Finding out that he was no better, that he only wanted her to secure a *business deal*, had delivered a blow she'd spent the better part of a year burying in a deep hole.

At first his demands had been subtle: a business dinner here, a charity event there—occasions she'd been proud and honoured to accompany him on. Until that fateful night when she'd overheard a handful of words that had had the power to sting like nothing else.

She's the means to an end. Nothing more...

The conversation that had followed remained seared into her brain. Zaccheo, impatiently shutting her down, then brazenly admitting he'd said those words. That he'd used her.

Most especially, she recalled the savage pain in knowing she had got him so wrong, had almost given herself to a man who held such careless regard for her, and only cared about her pedigree.

And yet his shock when she'd returned his ring had made her wonder whether she'd done the right thing.

His arrest days later for criminal negligence had confirmed what sort of man she'd foolishly woven her dreams around.

She met his gaze now. 'You got what you wanted—your name next to mine on the front page. The whole world knows I left with you last night, that I'm no longer engaged to Harry.'

His hand slipped to her nape, worked over tense muscles. 'And how did Fairfield take being so unceremoniously dumped?' he asked.

'Harry cares about me, so he was a complete gentleman about it. Shame I can't say the same about you.'

Dark grey eyes gleamed dangerously. 'You mean he wasn't torn up at the thought of never having access to this body again?' he mocked.

She lifted a brow. 'Never say never.'

Tension coiled his body. 'If you think I'll tolerate any further interaction between you and Fairfield, you're severely mistaken,' he warned with a dark rumble.

'Why, Zaccheo, you sound almost jealous.'

Heat scoured his cheekbones and a tiny part of her quailed at her daring. 'You'd be wise to stop testing me, *dolcezza*.'

'If you want this to stop, tell me why you're doing this.'

'I'm only going to say it one more time, so let it sink in. I don't intend to stop until your father's reputation is in the gutter and everything he took from me is returned, plus interest.'

'Can I see the proof of what you accuse my father of?'

'Would you believe even if you saw it? Or will you cling to the belief that I'm the big, bad ogre who's just throwing his weight about?' he taunted.

Eva looked down at the papers on the table, every last one containing everything Zaccheo had demanded. Would her father have done it if Zaccheo's threats were empty?

'Last night, when you said you and I…' She stopped, unable to process the reality.

'Would be married in two weeks? *Sì*, I meant that, too. And to get that ball rolling, we're going shopping for an engagement ring in exactly ten minutes, after which we have a full day ahead, so if you require further sustenance I suggest you finish your breakfast.'

He dropped his fingers from her nape and stepped back. With a last look filled with steely determination, he picked up the closest paper and walked out of the room.

CHAPTER FIVE

Their first stop was an exclusive coat boutique in Bond Street. Zaccheo told himself it was because he didn't want to waste time. The truth mocked him in the form of needing to cover Eva Pennington's body before he lost any more brain cells to the lust blazing through his bloodstream.

In the dark cover of her family terrace and the subsequent helicopter journey home, he'd found relief from the blatant temptation of her body.

In the clear light of day, the red dress seemed to cling tighter, caress her body so much more intimately that he'd had to fight the urge to lunge for her each time she took a breath.

He watched her now, seated across from him in his limo as they drove the short twenty-minute distance to Threadneedle Street where his bankers had flown in the diamond collection he'd requested from Switzerland.

Her fingers plucked at the lapel of the new white cashmere coat, then dropped to cinch the belt tighter at her tiny waist.

'You didn't need to buy me a coat,' she grumbled. 'I have a perfectly good one back at my flat.'

He reined in his fascination with her fingers. 'Your flat is on the other side of town. I have more important things to do than waste an hour and a half sitting in traffic.'

Her plump lips pursed. 'Of course, extracting your pound of flesh is an all-consuming business, isn't it?'

'I don't intend to stop at a mere pound, Eva. I intend to take the whole body.'

One eyebrow spiked. 'You seem so confident I'm going to hand myself to you on a silver platter. Isn't that a tad foolish?'

There was that tone again, the one that said she didn't believe him.

'I guess we'll find out one way or the other when the sordid details are laid out for you on Monday. All you need to concern yourself about today is picking out an engagement ring that makes the right statement.'

Her striking green eyes clashed with his and that lightning bolt struck again. 'And what statement would that be?' she challenged.

He let loose a chilling half-smile that made his enemies quake. 'Why, that you belong to me, of course.'

'I told you, I've no intention of being your possession. A ring won't change that.'

'How glibly you lie to yourself.'

She gasped and he was once again drawn to her mouth. A mouth whose sweet taste he recalled vividly, much to his annoyance. 'Excuse me?'

'We both know you'll be exactly who and what I want you to be when I demand it. Your family has too much at stake for you to risk doing otherwise.'

'Don't mistake my inclination to go along with this farce to be anything but my need to get to the bottom of why you're doing this. It's what families *do* for each other. Of course, since you don't even speak about yours, I assume you don't know what I'm talking about.'

Zaccheo called himself ten kinds of fool for letting the taunt bite deep. He'd lost respect for his father long before he'd died in shame and humiliation. And watching his mother whore herself for prestige had left a bitter taste in his mouth. As families went, he'd been dealt a bad hand, but he'd learned long ago that to wish for anything you couldn't create with your own hard-working hands was utter folly. He'd stopped making wishes by the time he hit puberty. Recalling the very last wish he'd prayed night and day for as a child, he clenched his fists. Even then he'd known fate would laugh at his wish for a brother or sister. He'd known that wish, despite his mother being pregnant, would not come true. He'd *known*.

He'd programmed himself not to care after that harrowing time in his life.

So why the hell did it grate so much for him to be reminded that he was the last Giordano?

'I don't talk about my family because I have none. But that's a situation I intend to rectify soon.'

She glanced at him warily. 'What's that supposed to mean?'

'It means I had a lot of time in prison to re-examine my life, thanks to your family.' He heard the naked emotion in his voice and hardened his tone. 'I intend to make some changes.'

'What sort of changes?'

'The type that means you'll no longer have to whore out your integrity for the sake of the great Pennington legacy. You should thank me, since you seem to be the one doing most of the heavy lifting for your family.'

Zaccheo watched her face pale.

'I'm not a whore!'

He lunged forward before he could stop himself. 'Then what the hell were you doing dressed like a tart, agreeing to marry a drunken playboy, if not for cold, hard cash for your family?' The reminder of what she wore beneath the coat blazed across his mind. His temperature hiked, along with the increased throbbing in his groin.

'I didn't do it for money!' She flushed, and bit down on her lower lip again. 'Okay, yes, that was part of the reason, but I also did it because—'

'Please spare me any declarations of *true love*.' He wasn't sure why he abhorred the idea of her mentioning the word love. Or why the idea of her mentioning Fairfield's name filled him with rage.

Zaccheo knew about her friendship with Fairfield. And while he knew their engagement had been a farce, he hadn't missed the camaraderie between them, or the pathetic infatuation in the other man's eyes.

Sì, he was jealous—Eva would be his and no one else's. But he also pitied Fairfield.

Because love, in all forms, was a false emotion. Nothing but a manipulative tool. Mothers declared their love for their children, then happily abandoned them the moment they ceased to be a convenient accessory. Fathers professed to have their children's interest at heart because of *love*, but when it came right down to it they put themselves above all else. And sometimes even forgot that their children *existed*.

As for Eva Pennington, she'd shown how faithless she was when she'd dropped him and distanced herself mere days before his arrest.

'I wasn't going to say that. Trust me, I've learned not to toss the word *love* about freely—'

'Did you know?' he sliced at her before he could stop himself.

Fine brows knitted together. 'Did I know what?'

'Did you know of your father's plans?' The question had been eating at him far more than he wanted to admit.

'His plans to do what?' she asked innocently. And yet he could see the caginess on her face. As if she didn't want him to probe deeper.

Acrid disappointment bit through him. He was a fool for thinking, perhaps *wishing*, despite all the signs saying otherwise, that she'd been oblivious to Oscar Pennington's plans to make him the ultimate scapegoat.

'We're here, sir.' His driver's voice came through the intercom.

Zaccheo watched her dive for the door. He would've laughed at her eagerness to get away from the conversation that brought back too many volatile memories, had he not felt disconcerting relief that his question had gone unanswered.

He'd been a fool to pursue it in the first place. He didn't need more lies. He had cold, hard facts proving the Penningtons' guilt. Dwelling on the whys and wherefores of Eva's actions was a fool's errand.

He stepped out into the winter sunshine and nodded at the bank director.

'Mr Giordano, welcome.' The older man's expression vacillated between obsequiousness and condescension.

'You received my further instructions?' Zaccheo took Eva's arm, ignoring her slight stiffening as he walked her through the doors of the bank.

'Yes, sir. We've adhered to your wishes.' Again he caught the man's assessing gaze.

'I'm pleased to hear it. Otherwise I'm sure there would be other banks who would welcome GWI's business.'

The banker paled. 'That won't be necessary, Mr Giordano. If you'll come with me, the jewellers have everything laid out for you.'

It should've given him great satisfaction that he'd breached the hallowed walls of the centuries-old establishment, that he'd finally succeeded where his own father had tried so hard and failed, giving his life in pursuit of recognition.

But all Zaccheo could hear, could *feel*, was Eva's presence, a reminder of why his satisfaction felt hollow. She was proof that, despite all he'd achieved, he was still regarded as the lowest of the low. A nobody. An expendable patsy who would take any treatment his betters doled out without protest.

We shall see.

They walked down several hallways. After a few minutes, Eva cleared her throat. 'What instructions did you give him?' she asked.

He stared down at her. 'I told him to remove all pink diamonds from the collection and instruct my jewellers that I do not wish to deal with diamonds of that colour in the future.'

'Really? I thought pink diamonds were all the rage these days?'

He shrugged. 'Not for me. Let's call it a personal preference.'

The penny dropped and she tried to pull away from his hold. He refused to let go. 'Are you really that petty?' she asked as they approached a heavy set of oak doors. 'Just because Harry gave me a pink diamond...' Her eyes widened when he caught her shoulders and pinned her against the wall. When she started to struggle, he stepped closer, caging her in with his body.

'You'll refrain from mentioning his name in my presence ever again. Is that understood?' Zaccheo felt his control slipping as her scent tangled with his senses and her curvy figure moved against him.

'Let me go and you'll need never hear his name again,' she snapped back.

'Not going to happen.' He released her. 'After you.'

She huffed a breath and entered the room. He followed and crossed to the window, struggling to get himself under control as the director walked in with three assistants bearing large velvet trays. They set them on the polished conference table and stepped back.

'We'll give you some privacy,' the director said before exiting with his minions.

Zaccheo walked to the first tray and pulled away the protective cloth. He stared at the display of diamonds in all cuts and sizes, wondering for a moment how his father would've reacted to this display of obscene wealth. Paolo Giordano had never managed to achieve even a fraction of his goals despite sacrificing everything, including the people he should've held dear. Would he have been proud, or would he have bowed and scraped as the bank director had a few moments ago, eager to be deemed worthy of merely touching them?

'Perhaps we should get on with choosing a stone. Or are we going to stare at them all day?' Eva asked.

Eva watched his face harden and bit her tongue. She wasn't sure why she couldn't stop goading him. Did part of her want to get under his skin as he so effortlessly got under hers?

Annoyed with herself for letting the whole absurd situation get to her, she stepped forward and stared down at the dazzling array of gems. Large. Sparkling. Flawless. Each worth more than she would earn in half her lifetime.

None of them appealed to her.

She didn't want to pick out another cold stone to replace the one she'd handed back to Harry before running after Zaccheo last night.

She didn't want to be trapped into yet another consequence of being a Pennington. She wanted to be free of the guilty resentment lurking in her heart at the thought that nothing she did would ever be enough for her family. Or the sadness that came with the insurmountable knowledge that her sister would continue to block any attempt to forge a relationship with her father.

She especially didn't want to be trapped in any way with Zaccheo Giordano. That display of his displeasure a few moments ago had reminded her she wanted nothing to do with him. And it was not about his temper but what she'd felt when her body had been thrust against his. She'd wanted to be held there…indefinitely.

Touching him.

Soothing his angry brow and those brief flashes of pain she saw in his eyes when he thought she wasn't looking.

God, even a part of her wanted to coax out that heart-stopping smile she'd glimpsed so very rarely when he was pursuing her!

What was wrong with her?

'Is that the one you wish for?'

She jumped and stared down at the stone that had somehow found its way into her palm. She blinked in shock.

The diamond was the largest on the tray and twice as obscene as the one that had graced her finger last night. No wonder Zaccheo sounded so disparaging.

'No!' She hastily dropped it back into its slot. 'I'd never wear anything so gratuitous.'

His coldly mocking gaze made her cringe. 'Really?'

Irritation skated over her skin. 'For your information, I didn't choose that ring.'

'But you accepted it in the spirit it was given—as the cost of buying your body in exchange for shares in Penningtons?'

Icy rage replaced her irritation. 'Your continuous insults make me wonder why you want to put up with my presence. Surely revenge can't be as sweet as you wish it if the object of your punishment enrages you this much?'

'Perhaps I enjoy tormenting you.'

'So I'm to be your punching bag for the foreseeable future?'

'Is this your way of trying to find out how long your sentence is to be?'

'A sentence implies I've done something wrong. I *know* I'm innocent in whatever you believe I've done.'

His smile could've turned a volcano into a polar ice cap. 'I've found that proclamations of innocence don't count for a thing, not when the right palm is greased.'

She inhaled at the fury and bitterness behind his words. 'Zaccheo...'

Whatever feeble reply she'd wanted to make died when his eyes hardened.

'Choose the diamond you prefer or I'll choose it for you.'

Eva turned blindly towards the table and pointed to the smallest stone. 'That one.'

'No.'

She gritted her teeth. 'Why not?'

'Because it's pink.'

'No, it's not...' She leaned closer, caught the faint pink glow, and frowned. 'Oh. I thought—'

A mirthless smile touched his lips. 'So did I. Perhaps I'll change bankers after all.' He lifted the cover of the second tray and Eva stared dispassionately at the endless rows of sparkling jewels. None of them spoke to her. Her heart hammered as it finally dawned on her why.

'Is there any reason why you want to buy me a new ring?'

He frowned. *'Scusi?'*

'When you proposed the first time, you gave me a different ring. I'm wondering why you're buying me a different one. Did you lose it?' Despite the circumstances surrounding his proposal and her subsequent rejection of him, she'd loved that simple but exquisite diamond and sapphire ring.

'No, I didn't lose it.' His tone was clipped to the point of brusqueness.

'Then why?'

'Because I do not wish you to have it.'

Her heart did an achy little dance as she waited for further elaboration. When she realised none would be forthcoming, she pulled her gaze from his merciless regard and back to the display.

He didn't want her to have it. Why? Because the ring held special meaning? Or because she was no longer worthy of it?

Berating herself for feeling hurt, she plucked a stone from the middle of the tray. According to the size chart it sat in mid-range, a flawless two carat, square-cut that felt light in her palm. 'This one.' She turned and found him staring at her, his gaze intense yet inscrutable.

Wordlessly, he held out his hand.

Her fingers brushed his palm as she dropped the stone and she bit back a gasp as that infernal electricity zinged up her arm.

His eyes held hers for a long moment before he turned and headed for the door. The next few minutes passed in a blur as Zaccheo issued clipped instructions about mountings, scrolls and settings to the jeweller.

Before she could catch her breath, Eva was back outside. Flashes went off as a group of paparazzi lunged towards them. Zaccheo handed her into the car before joining her. With a curt instruction to the driver, the car lurched into traffic.

'If I've achieved my publicity quota for the day, I'd like to be dropped at my flat, please.'

Zaccheo focused those incisive eyes on her. 'Why would I do that?'

'Aren't we done? I'd catch a bus home, but I left my handbag and phone at Pennington Manor—'

'Your belongings have been brought to my penthouse,' he replied.

'Okay, thanks. As soon as I collect them, I'll be out of your hair.' She needed to get out of this dress, shower and practise the six songs she would be performing at the club tonight. Saturday nights were the busiest of the week, and she couldn't be late. The music producer who'd been frequenting the club for the last few weeks might make another appearance tonight.

A little bubble of excitement built and she squashed it down as that half-smile that chilled her to the bone appeared on Zaccheo's face.

'You misunderstand. When I mentioned your belongings, I didn't mean your handbag and your phone. I meant everything you own in your bedsit has been removed. While we were picking your engagement ring, your belongings were relocated. Your rent has been paid off with interest and your landlady is busy renting the property to someone else.'

'What on earth are you talking about?' she finally asked when she'd picked up her jaw from the floor and sifted through his words. 'Of course I still live there. Mrs Hammond wouldn't just let you into my flat. And she certainly wouldn't arbitrarily end my lease without speaking to me first.'

Zaccheo just stared back at her.

'How dare you? Did you threaten her?'

'No, Eva. I used a much more effective tool.'

Her mouth twisted. 'You mean you threw so much money at her she buckled under your wishes?'

He shrugged rugged, broad shoulders. 'You of all people

should know how money sways even the most veracious hearts. Mrs Hammond was thrilled at the prospect of receiving her new hip replacement next week instead of at the end of the year. But it also helps that she's a hopeless romantic. The picture of us in the paper swayed any lingering doubts she had.'

Eva's breath shuddered out. Her landlady had lamented the long waiting list over shared cups of tea and Eva had offered a sympathetic ear. While she was happy that Mrs Hammond would receive her treatment earlier than anticipated and finally be out of pain, a huge part of her couldn't see beyond the fact that Zaccheo had ripped her safe harbour away without so much as a by your leave.

'You had absolutely no right to do that,' she blazed at him.

'Did I not?' he asked laconically.

'No, you didn't. This is nothing but a crude demonstration of your power. Well, guess what, I'm unimpressed. Go ahead and do your worst! Whatever crimes you think we've committed, maybe going to prison is a better option than this...this kidnapping!'

'Believe me, prison isn't an option you want to joke with.'

His lacerated tone made her heart lurch. She looked into his face and saw the agony. Her eyes widened, stunned that he was letting her witness that naked emotion.

'You think you know what it feels like to be robbed of your freedom for months on end? Pray you never get to find out, Eva. Because you may not survive it.'

'Zaccheo... I...' She stuttered to a halt, unsure of what to make of that raw statement.

His hand slashed through the air and his mask slid back into place. 'I wanted you relocated as swiftly as possible with a minimum of fuss,' he said.

A new wave of apprehension washed over her. 'Why? What's the rush?'

'I thought that would be obvious, Eva. I have deep-seated trust issues.'

Sadly, she'd reaped the rewards of betrayed trust, but the fierce loyalty to her family that continued to burn within her made her challenge him. 'How is that my family's fault?'

His nostrils flared. 'I trusted your father. He repaid that trust with a betrayal that sent me to prison! And you were right there next to him.'

Again she heard the ragged anguish in his voice. A hysterical part of her mind wondered whether this was the equivalent of a captor revealing his face to his prisoner. Was she doomed now that she'd caught a glimpse of what Zaccheo's imprisonment had done to him?

'So you keeping me against my will is meant to be part of *my* punishment?'

He smiled. 'You don't have to stay. You have many options available to you. You can call the police, tell them I'm holding you against your will, although that would be hard to prove since three hundred people saw you chase after me last night. Or you can insist I return your things and reinstate your lease. If you choose to walk away, no one will lift a finger to stop you.'

'But that's not quite true, is it? What real choice do I have when you're holding a threat over my father's head?'

'Leave him to flounder on his own if you truly believe you're guilt-free in all of this. You want to make a run for it? Here's your chance.'

His pointed gaze went to the door and Eva realised they'd completed the short journey from the bank to the iconic building that had brought Zaccheo into her life and turned it upside down.

She glanced up at the building *Architectural Digest* had called 'innovative beyond its years' and 'a heartbreakingly beautiful masterpiece'.

Where most modern buildings boasted elaborate glass edifices, The Spire was a study in polished, tensile steel. Thin sheets of steel had been twisted and manipulated around the towering spear-like structure, making the tallest building in

London a testament to its architect's skill and innovation. Its crowning glory was its diamond-shaped, vertiginous platform, within which was housed a Michelin-starred restaurant surrounded by a clear twenty-foot waterfall.

One floor beneath the restaurant was Zaccheo's penthouse. Her new home. Her prison.

The sound of him exiting the car drew her attention. When he held out his hand to her, she hesitated, unable to accept that this was her fate.

A muscle ticced in his jaw as he waited.

'You'd love that, wouldn't you? Me helping you bury my father?'

'He's going down either way. It's up to you whether he gets back up or not.'

Eva wanted to call his bluff. To shut the door and return everything to the way it was this time yesterday.

The memory of her father in that hospital bed, strung up to a beeping machine, stopped her. She'd already lost one parent. No matter how difficult things were between them, she couldn't bear to lose another. She would certainly have no hope of saving her relationship with her sister if she walked away.

Because one thing was certain. Zaccheo meant to have his way.

With or without her co-operation.

CHAPTER SIX

EVA BLEW HER fringe out of her eyes and glanced around her. The guest suite, a different one from the one she'd slept in last night, was almost three times the size of her former bedsit. And every surface was covered with designer gowns and accessories. Countless bottles of exclusive perfumes and luxury grooming products were spread on the dresser, and a team of six stylists each held an item of clothing, ready to pounce on her the moment she took off the dress she was currently trying on.

She tried hard to see the bright side of finally being out of the red dress. Unfortunately, any hint of brightness had vanished the moment she'd stepped out of the car and re-entered Zaccheo's penthouse.

'How many more before we're done?' She tried to keep her voice even, but she knew she'd missed amiability by a mile when two assistants exchanged wary glances.

'We've done your home and evening-wear package. We just need to do your vacation package and we'll be done with wardrobe. Then we can move on to hair and make-up,' Vivian, the chief stylist, said with a megawatt smile.

Eva tried not to groan. She needed to be done so she could find her phone and call her father. There was no way she was twiddling her thumbs until Monday to get a proper answer.

Being made into Zaccheo's revenge punchbag...his *married* revenge punchbag...wasn't a role she intended to be placed in. When she'd thought there was a glimmer of doubt as to Zaccheo's threat being real, she'd gone along with this farce. But with each hour that passed with silence from her father, Eva was forced to believe Zaccheo's threats weren't empty.

Would he go to such lengths to have her choose precious gems, remove her from her flat, and hire a team of stylists to turn her into the sort of woman he preferred to date, if this was just some sort of twisted game?

Her hand clenched as her thoughts took a different path. What exactly was Zaccheo trying to turn her into? Obviously he wasn't just satisfied with attaining her pedigree for whatever his nefarious purposes were. He wanted her to look like a well-dressed mannequin while he was at it.

'Careful with that, Mrs Giordano. That lace is delicate.'

She dropped the dress, her heart hammering far too fast for her liking. 'Don't call me that. I'm not Mrs Giordano—'

'Not yet, at least, right, *bellissima*?'

Eva heard the collective breaths of the women in the room catch. She turned as Zaccheo strode in. His eyes were fixed on her, flashing a warning that made her nape tingle. Before she could respond, he lifted her hands to kiss her knuckles, one after the other. Her breathing altered precariously as the silky hairs of his beard and the warm caress of his mouth threw her thoughts into chaos.

'It's only a few short days until we're husband and wife, *sì*?' he murmured intimately, but loud enough so every ear in the room caught the unmistakeable statement of possession.

She struggled to think, to *speak*, as sharp grey eyes locked with hers.

'No…I mean, yes…but let's not tempt fate. Who knows what could happen in a *few short days*?' She fully intended to have placed this nightmare far behind her.

His thumbs caressed the backs of her hands in false intimacy. 'I've moved mountains to make you mine, *il mio prezioso*. Nothing will stand in my way.' His accent was slightly more pronounced, his tone deep and captivating.

Envious sighs echoed around the room, but Eva shivered at the icy intent behind his words. She snatched her hands from his. Or she attempted to.

'In that case, I think you ought to stop distracting me so I can get on with making myself beautiful for you.' She hoped her smile looked as brittle as it felt. That her intention to end this was clear for him to see. 'Or was there something in particular you wanted?'

His eyes held hers for another electrifying second before he released her. 'I came to inform you that your belongings have been unpacked.' He surveyed the room, his gaze taking in the organised chaos. 'And to enquire whether you wish to have lunch with me or whether you want lunch brought to you so you can push through?' He turned back to her, his gaze mockingly stating that he knew her choice before she responded.

She lifted her chin. 'Seeing as this makeover was a complete *surprise* that I'd have to *make* time for, we'll take lunch in here, please.'

He ignored her censorious tone and nodded. 'Your wish is my command, *dolcezza*. But I insist you be done by dinnertime. I detest eating alone.'

She bit her tongue against a sharp retort. The cheek of him, making demands on her time when *he'd* been the one to call in the stylists in the first place! She satisfied herself with glaring at his back as he walked out, his tall, imposing figure owning every square inch of space he prowled.

The women left three excruciating hours later. The weak sun was setting in grey skies by the time Eva dragged her weary body across the vast hallway towards the suite she'd occupied last night. Her newly washed and styled hair bounced in silky waves down her back and her face tingled pleasantly from the facial she'd received before the barely there makeup had been applied.

The cashmere-soft, scooped-neck grey dress caressed her hips and thighs as she approached her door. She'd worn it only because Vivian had insisted. Eva hadn't had the heart to tell her she intended to leave every single item untouched. But Eva couldn't deny that the off-shoulder, floor-length dress felt elegant and wonderful and exactly what she'd have chosen to wear for dinner. Even if it was a dinner she wasn't looking forward to.

Her new four-inch heels clicked on the marble floor as she opened the double doors and stopped. Her hands flew to cover her mouth as she surveyed the room. Surprise was followed a few seconds later by a tingle of awareness that told her she was no longer alone.

Even then, she couldn't look away from the sight before her.

'Is something wrong?' Zaccheo's enquiry made her finally turn.

He was leaning against the door frame, his hands tucked into the pockets of his black tailored trousers. The white V-necked sweater caressed his muscular arms and shoulders and made his grey eyes appear lighter, almost eerily silver. His slightly damp hair gleamed a polished black against his shoulders and his beard lent him a rakish look that was absolutely riveting.

His gaze caught and held hers for several seconds before conducting a detailed appraisal over her face, hair and down her body that made the tingling increase. When his eyes returned to hers, she glimpsed a dark hunger that made her insides quake.

Swallowing against the pulse of undeniable attraction, she turned back to survey the room.

'I can't believe everything's been arranged so precisely,' she murmured.

'You would've preferred that they fling your things around without thought or care?'

'That's not what I mean and you know it. You've reproduced my room almost exactly how it was before.'

He frowned. 'I fail to see how that causes you distress.'

She strolled to the white oak antique dresser that had belonged to her mother. It'd been her mother's favourite piece of furniture and one of the few things Eva had taken when she'd left Pennington Manor.

Her fingers drifted over the hairbrush she'd used only yesterday morning. It had been placed in the little stand just as she normally did. 'I'm not distressed. I'm a little disconcerted that my things are almost exactly as I left them at my flat yesterday morning.' When he continued to stare, she pursed her lips. 'To reproduce this the movers would've needed photographic memories.'

'Or a few cameras shots as per my instructions.'

She sucked in a startled breath. 'Why would you do that?'

His lashes swept down for a moment. Then he shrugged. 'It was the most efficient course of action.'

'Oh.' Eva wasn't sure why she experienced that bolt of disappointment. Was she stupid enough to believe he'd done that because he *cared*? That he'd wanted her to be comfortable?

She silently scoffed at herself.

Lending silly daydreams to Zaccheo's actions had led to bitter disappointment once before. She wasn't about to make the same mistake again.

She spotted her handbag on the bed and dug out her phone. The battery was almost depleted, but she could make a quick call to her father before it died. She started to press dial and realised Zaccheo hadn't moved.

'Did you need something?'

The corner of his mouth quirked, but the bleakness in his eyes didn't dissipate. 'I've been in jail for over a year, *dolcezza*. I have innumerable needs.' The soft words held a note of deadly intent as his gaze moved from her to the bed. Her heart jumped to her throat and the air seemed to evaporate from the room. 'But my most immediate need is sustenance. I've ordered dinner to be brought from upstairs. It'll be here in fifteen minutes.'

She managed to reply despite the light-headedness that assailed her. 'Okay. I'll be there.'

With a curt nod, he left.

Eva sagged sideways onto the bed, her grip on the phone tightening until her bones protested. In the brief weeks she'd dated Zaccheo a year and half ago, she'd seen the way women responded to his unmistakeable animal magnetism. He only needed to walk into the room for every female eye to zero in on him. She'd also witnessed his reaction. Sometimes he responded with charm, other times with arrogant aloofness. But always with an innate sexuality that spoke of a deep appreciation for women. She'd confirmed that appreciation by a quick internet search in a weak moment, which had unearthed the long list of gorgeous women he'd had shockingly brief liaisons with in the past. A young, virile, wealthy bachelor, he'd been at the top of every woman's 'want to bed' list. And he'd had no qualms about helping himself to their amorous attentions.

To be deprived of that for almost a year and a half...

Eva shivered despite the room's ambient temperature. No, she was the last woman Zaccheo would *choose* to bed.

But then, he'd kissed her last night as if he'd wanted to devour her. And the way he'd looked at her just now?

She shook her head.

She was here purely as an instrument of his vengeance. The quicker she got to the bottom of *that*, the better.

Her call went straight to voicemail. Gritting her teeth, she left a message for her father to call her back. Sophie's phone rang for almost a minute before Eva hung up. Whether her sister was deliberately avoiding her calls or not, Eva intended to get some answers before Monday.

Resolving to try again after dinner, Eva plugged in her phone to charge and left her room. She met two waiters wheeling out a trolley as she entered the dining room. A few seconds later, the front door shut and Eva fought the momentary panic at being alone with Zaccheo.

She avoided looking at his imposing body as he lifted the silver domes from several serving platters.

'You always were impeccably punctual,' he said without turning around.

'I suppose that's a plus in my favour.'

'Hmm...' came his non-committal reply.

She reached her seat and froze at the romantic setting of the table. Expensive silverware and crystal-cut glasses gleamed beneath soft lighting. And already set out in a bed of ice was a small silver tub of caviar. A bottle of champagne chilled in an ice stand next to Zaccheo's chair.

'Do you intend to eat standing up?'

She jumped when his warm breath brushed her ear. When had he moved so close?

'Of course not. I just wasn't expecting such an elaborate meal.' She urged her feet to move to where he held out her chair, and sat down. 'One would almost be forgiven for thinking you were celebrating something.'

'Being released from prison isn't reason enough to enjoy something better than grey slop?'

Mortified, she cursed her tactlessness. 'I...of course. I'm sorry, that was... I'd forgotten...' *Oh, God, just shut up, Eva.*

'Of course you had.'

She tensed. 'What's that supposed to mean?'

'You're very good at putting things behind you, aren't you? Or have you forgotten how quickly you walked away from me the last time, too?'

She glanced down at her plate, resolutely picked up her spoon and helped herself to a bite of caviar. The unique taste exploded on her tongue, but it wasn't enough to quell the anxiety churning her stomach. 'You know why I walked away last time.'

'Do I?'

'Yes, you do!' She struggled to keep her composure. 'Can we talk about something else, please?'

'Why, because your actions make you uncomfortable? Or does it make your skin crawl to be sharing a meal with an ex-convict?'

Telling herself not to rise to the bait, she took another bite of food. 'No, because you snarl and your voice turns arctic, and also because I think we have different definitions of what really happened.'

He helped himself to a portion of his caviar before he responded. 'Really? Enlighten me, *per favore*.'

She pressed her lips together. 'We've already been through this, remember? You admitted that you proposed to me simply to get yourself into the Old Boys' Club. Are you going to bother denying it now?'

He froze for several heartbeats. Then he ate another mouthful. 'Of course not. But I believed we had an agreement. That you knew the part you had to play.'

'I'm sorry, I must have misplaced my copy of the Zaccheo Giordano Relationship Guide.' She couldn't stem the sarcasm or the bitterness that laced her voice.

'You surprise me.'

'How so?' she snapped, her poise shredding by the second.

'You're determined to deny that you know exactly how this game is played. That you aristocrats haven't practised the *something-for-something-more* tenet for generations.'

'You seem to be morbidly fascinated with the inner workings of the peer class. If we disgust you so much, why do you insist on soiling your life with our presence? Isn't it a bit convenient to hold us all responsible for every ill in your life?'

A muscle ticced in his jaw and Eva was certain she'd struck a nerve. 'You think having my freedom taken away is a subject I should treat lightly?'

The trembling in her belly spread out to engulf her whole body. 'The *evidence* led to your imprisonment, Zaccheo. Now we can change the subject or we can continue to fight to see who gives whom indigestion first.'

He remained silent for several moments, his eyes boring into hers. Eva stared back boldly, because backing down would see her swallowed whole by the deadly volcanic fury lurking in his eyes. She breathed a tiny sigh of relief when that mocking half-smile made an appearance.

'As you wish.' He resumed eating and didn't speak again until their first course was done. 'Let's play a game. We'll call it *What If*,' he said into the silence.

Tension knotted her nape, the certainty that she was toying with danger rising higher. 'I thought you didn't like games?'

'I'll make an exception this time.'

She took a deep breath. 'Okay. If you insist.'

'What if I wasn't the man you think I am? What if I happened to be a stranger who was innocent of everything he's been accused of? What if that stranger told you that every day he'd spent in prison felt like a little bit of himself was being chipped away for ever? What would you say to him?' His voice held that pain-laced edge she'd first heard in the car.

She looked at his face but his eyes were downcast, his white-knuckled hand wrapped around his wine glass.

This was no game.

The tension that gripped her vibrated from him, engulfing them in a volatile little bubble.

'I'd tell you how sorry I was that justice wasn't served properly on your behalf.' Her voice shook but she held firm. 'Then I'd ask you if there was anything I could do to help you put the past behind you.'

Arctic grey eyes met hers. 'What if I didn't want to put it behind me? What if everything I believe in tells me the only way to achieve satisfaction is to make those responsible pay?'

'I'd tell you it may seem like a good course of action, but doing that won't get back what you've lost. I'd also ask why you thought that was the only way.'

His eyes darkened, partly in anger, partly with anguish. She half expected him to snarl at her for daring to dissuade him from his path of retribution.

Instead, he rose and went to dish out their second course. 'Perhaps I don't know another recourse besides crime and punishment?' he intoned, disturbingly calm.

Sorrow seared her chest. 'How can that be?'

He returned with their plates and set down her second course—a lobster thermidor—before taking his seat. His movements were jerky, lacking his usual innate grace.

'Let's say hypothetically that I've never been exposed to much else.'

'But you know better or you wouldn't be so devastated at the hand you've been dealt. You're angry, yes, but you're also wounded by your ordeal. Believe me, yours isn't a unique story, Zaccheo.'

He frowned at the naked bitterness that leaked through her voice. 'Isn't it? Enlighten me. How have *you* been wounded?'

She cursed herself for leaving the door open, but, while she couldn't backtrack, she didn't want to provide him with more ammunition against her. 'My family...we're united where it counts, but I've always had to earn whatever regard I receive, especially from my father. And it hasn't always been easy, especially when walls are thrown up and alliances built where there should be none.'

He saw through her vagueness immediately. 'Your father and your sister against your mother and you? There's no need to deny it. It's easy to see your sister is fashioning herself in the image of her father,' he said less than gently.

Eva affected an easy shrug. 'Father started grooming her when we were young, and I didn't mind. I just didn't understand why that meant being left out in the cold, especially...' She stopped, realising just how much she was divulging.

'Especially...?' he pressed.

She gripped her fork tighter. 'After my mother died. I thought things would be different. I was wrong.'

His mouth twisted. 'Death is supposed to be a profound leveller. But it rarely changes people.'

She looked at him. 'Your parents—'

'Were the individuals who brought me into the world. They weren't good for much else. Take from that what you will. We're also straying away from the subject. *What if* this stranger can't see his way to forgive and forget?' That ruthless edge was back in his voice.

Eva's hand shook as she picked up her glass of Chianti. 'Then he needs to ask himself if he's prepared to live with the consequences of his actions.'

His eyebrows locked together in a dark frown, before his lashes swept down and he gave a brisk nod. 'Asked and answered.'

'Then there's no further point to this game, is there?'

One corner of his mouth lifted. 'On the contrary, you've shown a soft-heartedness that some would see as a flaw.'

Eva released a slow, unsteady breath. Had he always been like this? She was ashamed to admit she'd been so dazzled with Zaccheo from the moment he'd walked into Siren two years ago, right until the day he'd shown her his true colours, that she hadn't bothered to look any deeper. He'd kissed her on their third date, after which, fearing she'd disappoint him, she'd stumblingly informed him she was a virgin.

His reaction had been something of a fairy tale for her. She'd made him out as her Prince Charming, had adored the way he'd treated her like a treasured princess, showering her with small, thoughtful gifts, but, most of all, his undivided time whenever they were together. He'd made her feel precious, adored. He'd proposed on their sixth date, which had coincided with his thirtieth birthday, and told her he wanted to spend the rest of his life with her.

And it had all been a lie. The man sitting in front of her had no softness, only that ruthless edge and deadly charm.

'Don't be so sure, Zaccheo. I've learnt a few lessons since our unfortunate association.'

'Like what?'

'I'm no longer gullible. And my family may not be perfect, but I'm still fiercely protective of those I care about. Don't forget that.'

He helped himself to his wine. 'Duly noted.' His almost

bored tone didn't fool her into thinking this subject had stopped being anything but volatile.

They finished their meal in tense silence.

Eva almost wilted in relief when the doorbell rang and Zaccheo walked away to answer it.

Catching sight of the time, she jumped up from the dining table and was crossing the living room when Zaccheo's hand closed over her wrist.

'Where do you think you're going?' he demanded.

'Dinner's over. Can you let me go, please? I need to get going or I'll be late.'

His brows furrowed, giving him a look of a dark predator. 'Late for what?'

'Late for work. I've already taken two days off without pay. I don't want to be late on top of everything else.'

'You still work at Siren?' His tone held a note of disbelief.

'I have to make a living, Zaccheo.'

'You still sing?' His voice had grown deeper, his eyes darkening to a molten grey as he stared down at her. Although Zaccheo's expression could be hard to decipher most of the time, the mercurial changes in his eyes often spelled his altered mood.

This molten grey was one she was familiar with. And even though she didn't want to be reminded of it, a pulse of decadent sensation licked through her belly as she recalled the first night she'd seen him.

He'd walked into Siren an hour before closing, when she'd been halfway through a sultry, soulful ballad—a song about forbidden love, stolen nights and throwing caution to the wind. He'd paused to order a drink at the bar, then made his way to the table directly in front of the stage. He'd sipped his whisky, not once taking his eyes off her. Every lyric in the three songs that had followed had felt as if it had been written for the man in front of her and the woman she'd wanted to be for him.

She'd been beyond mesmerised when he'd helped her off

the stage after her session. She'd said yes immediately when he'd asked her out the next night.

But she'd been wrong, so very wrong to believe fate had brought Zaccheo to the club. He'd hunted her down with single-minded intent for his own selfish ends.

God, how he must have laughed when she'd fallen so easily into his arms!

She yanked her arm free. 'Yes, I still sing. And I'd be careful before you start making any threats on my professional life, too. I've indulged you with the engagement-ring picking and the makeover and the homecoming dinner. Now I intend to get back to *my* reality.'

She hurried away, determined not to look over her shoulder to see whether he was following. She made it to her room and quickly changed into her going-to-work attire of jeans, sweater, coat and a thick scarf to ward off the winter chill. Scooping up her bag, she checked her phone.

No calls.

The unease in her belly ballooned as she left her suite.

Zaccheo was seated on the sofa in the living room, examining a small black velvet box. His eyes tracked her, inducing that feeling of being helpless prey before a ruthless marauder. She opened her mouth to say something to dispel the sensation, but no words emerged. She watched, almost paralysingly daunted as he shut the box and placed it on the coffee table next to him.

'Would it be too *indulgent* to demand a kiss before you leave for work, *dolcezza*?' he enquired mockingly.

'Indulgent, no. Completely out of the question, most definitely,' she retorted. Then silently cursed her mouth's sudden tingling.

He shook his head, his magnificent mane gleaming under the chandelier. 'You wound me, Eva, but I'm willing to wait until the time when you will kiss me freely without me needing to ask.'

'Then you'll be waiting an eternity.'

CHAPTER SEVEN

ZACCHEO PACED THE living room and contemplated leaving another voicemail message.

He'd already left five, none of which Eva had bothered to answer. It was nearly two a.m. and she hadn't returned. In his gloomy mood, he'd indulged in one too many nightcaps to consider driving to the club where she worked.

His temperament had been darkening steadily for the last four hours, once he'd found out what Eva's father was up to. Pennington was scrambling—futilely of course, because Zaccheo had closed every possible avenue—to find financial backing. That was enough to anger Zaccheo, but what fuelled his rage was that Pennington, getting more desperate by the hour, was offering more and more pieces of The Spire, the building that he would no longer own come Monday, as collateral. The blatant fraud Pennington was willing to perpetrate to fund his lifestyle made Zaccheo's fists clench as he stalked to the window.

The view from The Spire captured the string of bridges from east to west London. The moment he'd brought his vision of the building to life with the help of his experienced architects had been one of the proudest moments of his life. More than the properties he owned across the world and the empire he'd built from the first run-down warehouse he'd bought and converted to luxury accommodation at the age of twenty, this had been the one he'd treasured most. The building that should've been his crowning glory.

Instead it'd become the symbol of his downfall.

Ironically, the court where he'd been sentenced was right across the street. He looked down at the courthouse, jaw clenched.

He intended it to be the same place where his name was cleared. He would not be broken and humiliated as his father had been by the time he'd died. He would not be whispered about behind his back and mocked to his face and called a parasite. Earlier this evening, Eva had demanded to know why he'd been so fascinated with her kind.

For a moment, he'd wondered whether his burning desire to prove they were not better than him was a weakness. One he should *put behind him*, as Eva had suggested, before he lost a lot more of himself than he already had.

As much as he'd tried he hadn't been able to dismiss her words. Because he'd lied. He knew how to forgive. He'd forgiven his father each time he'd remembered that Zaccheo existed and bothered to take an interest in him. He'd forgiven his mother the first few times she'd let his stepfather treat him like a piece of garbage.

What Zaccheo hadn't told Eva was that he'd eventually learned that forgiveness wasn't effective when the recipient didn't have any use for it.

A weakening emotion like forgiveness would be wasted on Oscar Pennington.

A keycard clicked and he turned as the entry code released the front door.

Sensation very close to relief gut-punched him.

'Where the hell have you been?' He didn't bother to obviate his snarl. Nor could he stop checking her over from head to toe, to ascertain for himself that she wasn't hurt or hadn't been a victim of an accident or a mugging. When he was sure she was unharmed, he snapped his gaze to her face, to be confronted with a quizzical look.

Dio, was she *smirking* at him?

He watched her slide her fingers through her heavy, silky hair and ignored the weariness in the gesture.

'Is it Groundhog Day or something? Because I could've sworn we had a conversation about where I was going earlier this evening.'

He seethed. 'You finished work an hour and a half ago. Where have you been since then?'

She tossed a glare his way before she shrugged off her coat. The sight of the jeans and sweater she'd chosen to wear instead of the roomful of clothes he'd provided further stoked his dark mood.

'How do you know when I finished work?'

'Answer the question, Eva.'

She tugged her handbag from her shoulder and dropped it on the coffee table. Then she kicked off her shoes and pushed up on the balls of her feet in a smooth, practised stretch reminiscent of a ballet dancer.

'I took the night bus. It's cheaper than a cab, but it took forty-five minutes to arrive.'

'*Mi scusi?* You took the *night bus*?' His brain crawled with scenarios that made his blood curdle. He didn't need a spell in prison to be aware of what dangerous elements lurked at night. The thought that Eva had exposed herself, *willingly*, to—

'Careful there, Zaccheo, you almost sound like one of those snobs you detest so much.'

She pushed up again, her feet arching and flattening in a graceful rise and fall.

Despite his blood boiling, he stared, mesmerised, as she completed the stretches. Then he let his gaze drift up her body, knowing he shouldn't, yet unable to stop himself. The sweater, decorated with a D-minor scale motif, hugged her slim torso, emphasising her full, heavy breasts and tiny waist before ending a half-inch above her jeans.

That half-inch of flesh taunted him, calling to mind the smooth warmth of her skin. The simmering awareness that had always existed between them, like a fuse just waiting to be lit, throbbed deep inside. He'd tried to deny it earlier this evening in the hallway, when he'd discovered she still sang at Siren.

He'd tried to erase the sound of her sultry voice, the evocative way Eva Pennington performed on stage. He'd cursed himself when his body had reacted the way it had the very first time he'd heard her sing. That part of his black mood also stemmed from being viscerally opposed to any other man experiencing the same reaction he did from hearing her captivating voice, the way he had been two years ago, was a subject he wasn't willing to acknowledge, never mind tackle.

He pulled his gaze from the alluringly feminine curve of her hips and shapely legs and focused on the question that had been burning through him all night.

'Explain to me how you have two million pounds in your bank account, but take the bus to and from work.'

Her mouth gaped for several seconds before she regained herself. 'How the hell do you know how much money I have in my bank account?' she demanded.

'With the right people with the right skills, very easily. I'm waiting for an answer.'

'You're not going to get one. What I do with my money and how I choose to travel is *my* business.'

'You're wrong, *cara*. As of last night, your welfare is very much my business. And if you think I'm willing to allow you to risk your safety at times when drunken yobs and muggers crawl out of the woodwork, you're very much mistaken.'

'*Allow* me? Next you'll be telling me I need your permission to breathe!'

He spiked his fingers through his hair, wondering if she'd ever been this difficult and he'd somehow missed it. The Eva he remembered, before his eyes had been truly opened to her character, had possessed a quiet passion, not this defiant, wild child before him.

But no, there'd never been anything *child*like about Eva. She was all woman. His libido had thrilled to it right from the first.

Understandably this acute reaction was because he'd been without a woman for over a year. Now was not the time to let it out of control. The time would arrive soon enough.

She tossed her head in irritation, and the hardening in his groin threatened to prove him wrong.

'Since I need you alive for the foreseeable future, no, you don't require my permission to breathe.'

She had the nerve to roll her eyes. 'Thank you very much!'

'From now on you'll be driven to and from work.'

'No, thanks.'

He gritted his teeth. 'You prefer to spend hours freezing at a bus stop than accept my offer?'

'Yes, because the *offer* comes at a price. I may not know what it is yet, but I've no intention of paying it.'

'Why do you insist on fighting me when we both know you don't have a choice? I'm willing to bet your father didn't return a single one of your phone calls last night.'

Wide, startled eyes met his for a second before she looked away. 'I'm sure he has his reasons.'

It spoke volumes that she didn't deny trying to reach Oscar. 'Reasons more important than answering the phone to his daughter? Do you want to know what he's been up to?'

'I'm sure you're about to apprise me whether I want to hear it or not.'

'He's been calling in every single favour he thinks he's owed. Unfortunately, a man as greedy as your father cashed in most of his favours a long time ago. He's also pleading and begging his way across the country in a bid to save himself from the hole he knows I'm about to bury him in. He didn't take your calls, but he took mine. I recorded it if you wish me to play it back to you?'

Her fists clenched. 'Go to hell, Zaccheo,' she threw at him, but he glimpsed the pain in her eyes.

He almost felt sorry for her. Then he remembered her part in all this.

'Come here, Eva,' he murmured.

She eyed him suspiciously. 'Why?'

'Because I have something for you.'

Her gaze dropped to his empty hands before snapping

back to his face. 'There's nothing you have that I could possibly want.'

'If you make me come over there, I'll take that kiss you owe me from last night.' *Dio*, why had he said that? Now it was all he could think about.

Heat flushed her cheeks. 'I don't owe you a thing. And I certainly don't owe you any kisses.'

The women he'd dated in the past would've fallen over themselves to receive any gift he chose to bestow on them, especially the one he'd tucked into his back pocket.

Slowly, he walked towards her. He made sure his intent was clear. The moment she realised, her hands shot out. 'Stop! Didn't your mother teach you about the honey versus vinegar technique?'

Bitterness drenched him. 'No. My mother was too busy climbing the social ladder after my father died to bother with me. When he was alive, she wasn't much use either.'

She sucked in a shocked breath and concern furrowed her brow. 'I'm sorry.'

Zaccheo rejected the concern and let the sound of her husky voice, scratchy from the vocal strain that came with singing, wash over him instead. He didn't want her concern. But the sex he could deal with.

The need he'd been trying to keep under tight control threatened to snap. He took another step.

'Okay! I'm coming.' She walked barefooted to him. 'I've done as you asked. Give me whatever it is you want to give me.'

'It's in my back pocket.'

She inhaled sharply. 'Is this another of your games, Zaccheo?'

'It'll only take a minute to find out. Are you brave enough, *dolcezza*?' he asked.

Her gaze dropped and he immediately tilted her chin up with one finger. 'Look at me. I want to see your face.'

She blinked, then gathered herself in that way he'd always found fascinating. Slowly, she reached an arm around him. Her fingers probed until she found the pocket opening.

They slipped inside and he suppressed a groan as her fingers caressed him through his trousers. His blood rushed faster south as she searched futilely.

'It's empty,' she stated with a suspicious glare.

'Try the other one.'

She muttered a dirty word that rumbled right through him. Her colour deepened when he lifted his eyebrow.

'Let's get this over with.' She searched his right pocket and stilled when she encountered the box.

'Take it out,' he commanded, then stifled another groan when her fingers dug into his flesh to remove the velvet box. It took all the control he could muster not to kiss her when her lips parted and he glimpsed the tip of her tongue.

During his endless months in prison, he'd wondered whether he'd overrated the chemistry that existed between Eva and him. The proof that it was as potent as ever triggered an incandescent hunger that flooded his loins.

Sì, this part of his revenge that involved Eva in his bed, being inside her and implanting her with his seed, would be easy enough and pleasurable enough to achieve.

'I cannot wait to take you on our wedding night. Despite you no longer being a virgin, I'll thoroughly enjoy making you mine in every imaginable way possible. By the time I'm done with you, you'll forget every other man that you dared to replace me with.'

Her eyelids fluttered and she shivered. But the new, assertive Eva came back with fire. 'A bold assertion. But one, sadly, we'll both see unproven since there'll be no wedding *or* wedding night. And in case I haven't mentioned it, you're the last man I'd ever welcome in my bed.'

Zaccheo chose not to point out that she still had her hand in his pocket, or that her fingers were digging more firmly into his buttock.

Instead, he slid his phone from his front pocket, activated the recording app and hit the replay button.

Despite her earlier assertion that she'd grown a thicker skin, shadows of disbelief and hurt criss-crossed her face as she listened to the short conversation summoning her father to a meeting first thing on Monday. Unlike the night before where Pennington had blustered his way through Zaccheo's accusations, he'd listened in tense silence as Zaccheo had told him he knew what he was up to.

Zaccheo had given him a taster of the contents of the documents proving his innocence and the older man had finally agreed to the meeting. Zaccheo had known he'd won when Pennington had declined to bring his lawyers to verify the documents.

Thick silence filled the room after the recording ended.

'Do you believe me now, Eva? Do you believe that your family has wronged me in the most heinous way and that I intend to exact equal retribution?'

Her nostrils flared and her mouth trembled before she wrenched back control. But despite her composure, a sheen of tears appeared in her eyes, announcing her tumultuous emotion. 'Yes.'

'Take the box out of my pocket.'

She withdrew it. His instructions on the mount and setting had been followed to the letter.

'I intended to give it to you after dinner last night. Not on bended knee, of course. I'm sure you'll agree that once was enough?'

Her eyes darkened, as if he'd hurt her somehow. But of course, that was nonsense. She'd returned his first ring and walked away from him after a brief argument he barely recalled, stating that she didn't wish to be married to *a man like him*.

At the time, Zaccheo had been reeling at his lawyers' news that he was about to be charged with criminal negligence. He hadn't been able to absorb the full impact of Eva's betrayal until weeks later, when he'd already been in prison. His trial had been swift, the result of a young, overeager judge desperate to make a name for himself.

But he'd had over a year to replay the last time he'd seen Eva. In court, sitting next to her father, her face devoid of emotion until Zaccheo's sentence had been read out.

In that moment, he'd fooled himself into thinking she'd experienced a moment of agony on his behalf. He'd murmured her name. She'd looked at him. It was then that he'd seen the contempt.

That single memory cleared his mind of any extraneous feelings. 'Open the box and put on the ring,' he said tersely.

His tone must have conveyed his capricious emotional state. She cracked open the small case and slid on the ring without complaint.

He caught her hand in his and raised it, much as he had on Friday night. But this time, the acute need to rip off the evidence of another man's ownership was replaced by a well of satisfaction. 'You're mine, Eva. Until I decide another fate for you, you'll remain mine. Be sure not to forget that.'

Turning on his heel, he walked away.

Eva woke on Monday morning with a heavy heart and a stone in her gut that announced that her life was about to change for ever. It had started to change the moment she'd heard Zaccheo's recorded conversation with her father, but she'd been too shocked afterwards to decipher what her father's guilt meant for her.

Tired and wrung out, she'd stumbled to bed and fallen into a dreamless sleep, then woken and stumbled her way back to work.

Reality had arrived when she'd exited Siren after her shift to find Zaccheo's driver waiting to bring her back to the penthouse. She'd felt it when Zaccheo had told her to be ready to attend his offices in the morning. She'd felt it when she'd walked into her suite and found every item of clothing she'd tried on Saturday neatly stacked in the floor-to-ceiling shelves in her dressing room.

She felt it now when she lifted her hand to adjust her collar and caught the flash of the diamond ring on her finger. The flawless gem she'd chosen so carelessly had been mounted on a bezel setting, with further diamonds in decreasing sizes set in a platinum ring that fitted her perfectly.

You're mine, Eva. Until I decide another fate for you, you'll remain mine.

She was marrying Zaccheo in less than a week. He'd brought forward the initial two-week deadline by a whole week. She would marry him or her father would be reported to the authorities. He'd delivered that little bombshell last night after dinner. No amount of tossing and turning had altered that reality.

When she'd agreed to marry Harry, she'd known it would be purely a business deal, with zero risk to her emotions.

The idea of attaching herself to Zaccheo, knowing the depth of his contempt for her and his hunger for revenge, was bad enough. That undeniably dangerous chemistry that hovered on the point of exploding in her face when she so much as looked at him…*that* terrified her on an unspeakable level. And not because she was afraid he'd use that against her.

What she'd spent the early hours agonising over was her own helplessness against that inescapable pull.

The only way round it was to keep reminding herself why Zaccheo was doing this. Ultimate retribution and humiliation was his goal. He didn't want anything more from her.

An hour later, she sat across from her father and sister and watched in growing horror as Zaccheo's lawyers listed her father's sins.

Oscar Pennington sat hunched over, his pallor grey and his forehead covered in light sweat. Despite having heard Zaccheo's recording last night, she couldn't believe her father would sink so low.

'How could you do this?' she finally blurted when it got

too much to bear. 'And how the hell did you think you'd get away with it?'

Her father glared at her. 'This isn't the time for histrionics, Eva.'

'And you, Sophie? Did you know about this?' Eva asked her sister.

Sophie glanced at the lawyers before she replied, 'Let's not lose focus on why we're here.'

Anger shot through Eva. 'You mean let's pretend that this isn't really happening? That we're not here because Father *bribed* the builders to take shortcuts and blamed someone else for it? And you accuse me of not living in the real world?'

Sophie's lips pursed, but not before a guilty flush rushed into her face. 'Can we not do this now, please?' Her agitated gaze darted to where Zaccheo sat in lethal silence.

Eva stared at her sister, a mixture of anger and sadness seething within her. She was beginning to think they would never get past whatever was broken between them. And maybe she needed to be more like Zaccheo, and divorce herself from her feelings.

Eva glanced at him and the oxygen leached from her lungs.

God!

On Friday night, his all-black attire had lent him an air of suave but icy deadliness reminiscent of a lead in a mafia movie. Since then his casual attires, although equally formidable in announcing his breathtaking physique, had lulled her into a lesser sense of danger.

This morning, in a dark grey pinstripe suit, teamed with a navy shirt, and precisely knotted silver and blue tie, and his hair and beard newly trimmed, Zaccheo was a magnificent vision to behold.

The bespoke clothes flowed over his sleekly honed muscles and olive skin, each movement drawing attention to his powerfully arresting figure.

It was why more than one female employee had stared in

blatant interest as they'd walked into GWI's headquarters in the City this morning. It was why she'd avoided looking at him since they'd sat down.

But she'd made the mistake of looking now. And as he started to turn his head she *knew* she wouldn't be able to look away.

His gaze locked on her and she read the ruthless, possessive statement of ownership in his eyes even before he opened his mouth to speak. 'Eva has already given me what I want—her word that she's willing to do whatever it takes to make reparations.' His gaze dropped to the ring on her finger before he faced her father. 'Now it's your turn.'

CHAPTER EIGHT

'HERE'S A LIST of businesses who withdrew their contracts because of my incarceration.' Zaccheo nodded to one of his lawyers, who passed a sheet across the desk to her father.

Eva caught a glimpse of the names on the list and flinched. While the list was only half a page, she noticed more than one global conglomerate on there.

'You'll contact the CEO of each of those companies and tell them your side of the story.'

Fear flashed across her father's face. 'What's to stop them from spilling the beans?'

Zaccheo gave that chilling half-smile. 'I have a team of lawyers who'll ensure their silence if they ever want to do business with me again.'

'You're sure they'll still want your business?' Her father's voice held a newly subdued note.

'I have it on good authority their withdrawal was merely a stance. Some to gain better leverage on certain transactions and others for appearances' sake. Once they know the truth, they'll be back on board. But even if they don't come back to GWI, the purpose of your phone call would've been achieved.'

'Is this really necessary? Your company has thrived, probably beyond your wildest dreams, even while you were locked up. And this morning's stock-market reports show your stock at an all-time high.' Eva could hear the panic in her father's voice. 'Do I really need to genuflect in front of these people to make you happy?' he added bitterly.

'Yes. You do.'

Her father's face reddened. 'Look here. Judging by that rock I see on Eva's finger, you're about to marry my daughter. We're about to be *family*. Is this really how you wish to start our familial relationship?'

Bitterness pushed aside her compassion when she realised her father was once again using her as leverage for his own ends.

'You don't think this is the least you can do, Father?' she asked.

'You're taking his side?' her father demanded.

Eva sighed. 'I'm taking the side of doing the right thing. Surely you can see that?'

Her father huffed, and Zaccheo's lips thinned into a formidable line. 'I have no interest in building a relationship with you personally. You can drop dead for all I care. Right after you carry out my instructions, of course.'

'Young man, be reasonable,' her father pleaded, realising that for once he'd come up against an immoveable object that neither his charm nor his blustering would shift.

Zaccheo stared back dispassionately. No one in the room could harbour the misguided idea that he would soften in any way.

'I don't think you have a choice in the matter, Father,' Sophie muttered into the tense silence.

Eva glanced at her sister, searching for that warmth they'd once shared. But Sophie kept her face firmly turned away.

Eva jumped as her father pushed back his chair. 'Fine, you win.'

Zaccheo brushed off imaginary lint from his sleeve. 'Excellent. And please be sure to give a convincing performance. My people will contact each CEO on that list by Friday. Make sure you get it done by then.'

Her father's barrel chest rose and fell as he tried to control his temper. 'It'll be done. Sophie, we're leaving.'

Eva started to rise, too, only to find a hand clamped on her hip. The electricity that shot through her body at the bold contact had her swaying on her feet.

'What are you doing?' she demanded.

Zaccheo ignored her, but his thumb moved lazily over her hip bone as he addressed her father. 'You and Sophie may leave. I still have things to discuss with my fiancée. My secretary will contact you with details of the wedding in the next day or two.'

Her father looked from her face to Zaccheo's. Then he stormed out of the door.

Eva turned to Zaccheo. 'What more could we possibly have to discuss? You've made everything crystal clear.'

'Not quite everything. Sit down.' He waited until she complied before he removed his hand.

Eva wasn't sure whether it was relief that burst through her chest or outrage. Relief, most definitely, she decided. Lacing her fingers, she waited as he dismissed all except one lawyer.

At Zaccheo's nod, the man produced a thick binder and placed it in front of Zaccheo, after which he also left.

She could feel Zaccheo's powerful gaze on her, but she'd already unsettled herself by looking at him once. And she was reeling from everything that had taken place here in the last hour.

When the minutes continued to tick by in silence, she raised her head. 'You want my father to help rebuild the damage he caused to your reputation, but what about your criminal record? I would've thought that would be more important to you.'

'You may marry a man with a criminal record come Saturday, but I won't remain that way for long. My lawyers are working on it.'

Her heart lurched at the reminder that in a few short days she would be his wife, but she forced herself to ask the question on her mind. 'How can they do that without implicating my father? Isn't withholding evidence a crime?'

'Nothing will be withheld. How the authorities choose to apply the rule of law is up to them.'

Recalling the state of her father's health, she tightened

her fists in anxiety. 'So you're saying Father can still go to prison? Despite letting him believe he won't?'

The kick in his stare struck deep in her soul. 'I'm the one who was wronged. I have some leeway in speaking on his behalf, should I choose to.'

The implied threat didn't escape her notice. They would either toe his line or suffer the consequences.

She swallowed. 'What did you want to discuss with me?'

He placed a single sheet of paper in front of her.

'These are the engagements we'll be attending this week. Make sure you put them in your diary.'

She pursed her lips, denying that the deep pang in her chest was hurt. 'At least you're laying your cards on the table this time round.'

'What cards would those be?'

She shrugged. 'The ones that state your desire to conquer the upper class, of course. Wasn't that your aim all along? To walk in the hallowed halls of the Old Boys' Club and show them all your contempt for them?'

His eyes narrowed, but she caught a shadow in the grey depths. 'How well you think you know me.'

She cautioned herself against probing the sleeping lion, but found herself asking anyway, 'Why, Zaccheo? Why is it so important that you bring us all down a peg or two?'

He shifted in his seat. If she hadn't known that he didn't possess an ounce of humility, she'd have thought he was uneasy. 'I don't detest the whole echelon. Just those who think they have a right to lord it over others simply because of their pedigree. And, of course, those who think they can get around the laws that ordinary people have to live by.'

'What about me? Surely you can't hate me simply because our relationship didn't work out?'

'Was that what we had—a *relationship*?' he sneered. 'I thought it was a means for you to facilitate your father's plans.'

'*What?* You think I had something to do with my father scapegoating you?'

'Perhaps you weren't privy to his whole plan like your sister was. But the timing of it all was a little too convenient, don't you think? You walked away *three days* before I was charged, with a flimsy excuse after an even flimsier row. What was it? Oh, yes, you didn't want to marry *a man like me*?'

She surged to her feet, her insides going cold. 'You think I staged the whole thing? Need I remind you that you were the one who initiated our first meeting? That you were the one to ask me out?'

'An event carefully orchestrated by your father, of course. Do you know why I was at Siren that night?'

'Will you believe me if I said no?'

'I was supposed to meet your father and two of his investors there. Except none of them showed.'

She frowned. 'That's not possible. My father hates that I sing. He hates it even more that I work in a nightclub. I don't think he even knows where Siren is.'

'And yet he suggested it. Highly recommended it, in fact.'

The idea that her father had engineered their first meeting coated her mouth with bitterness. He'd used her strong loyalty to their family to manipulate her long before she'd taken a stand and moved out of Pennington Manor. But this further evidence showed a meticulousness that made her blood run cold.

'Were you even a virgin back then?' Zaccheo sliced at her.

The question brought her back to earth. 'Excuse me?'

'Or was it a ploy to sweeten the deal?'

'I didn't know you existed until you parked yourself in front of the stage that night!'

'Maybe not. But you must've known who I was soon after. Isn't that what women do these days? A quick internet search while they're putting on their make-up to go on the first date?'

Eva couldn't stop her guilty flush because it was exactly what she'd done. But not with the reprehensible intentions he'd implied. Zaccheo's all-consuming interest in her had seemed too good to be true. She'd wanted to know more about the compelling man who'd zeroed in on her with such unnerving interest.

What she'd found was a long list of conquests ranging from supermodels to famous sports stars. She'd been so intimidated, she'd carefully kept her inexperience under wraps. It was that desperately embarrassing need to prove her sophistication that had led to her boldly accepting his dare to perform oral sex on him on his thirtieth birthday. She'd been so anxious, she'd bungled it even before she'd unfastened his belt. In the face of his wry amusement, she'd blurted her inexperience.

The inexperience he was now denouncing as a ploy.

'I don't care what you think. All I care about is that I know what I'm letting myself in for now. I know exactly the type of man you are.' One whose ruthless ambition was all he cared about.

He regarded her for several tense seconds. 'Then this won't surprise you too much.' He slid a thick burgundy folder across to her. 'It's a prenuptial agreement. On the first page you'll find a list of independent lawyers who can guide you through the legalese should you require it. The terms are non-negotiable. You have twenty-four hours to read and sign it.'

She glanced from him to the folder, her mouth dropping open in shock. 'Why would I need a prenup? I've agreed to your demands. Isn't this overkill?'

'My lawyers go spare if I don't get everything in writing. Besides, there are a few items in there we haven't discussed yet.'

Something in his voice made her skin prickle. Her belly quaked as she turned the first page of the thick document. The first few clauses were about general schedules and routines, making herself available for his engagements within reason, how many homes he owned and her duty to oversee the running of them, and his expectation of her availability to travel with him on his business trips should he require it.

'If you think I'm going to turn myself into a pet you can pick up and hop on a plane with whenever it suits you, you're in for a shock.'

He merely quirked an eyebrow at her. She bristled but carried on reading.

She paused at the sixth clause. 'We can't be apart for more than five days in the first year of marriage?'

The half-smile twitched. 'We don't want tongues wagging too soon, do we?'

'You mean after the first year I can lock myself in a nunnery for a year if I choose to?'

For the first time since Zaccheo had exploded back into her life, she glimpsed a genuine smile. It was gone before it registered fully, but the effect was no less earth-shattering. 'No nunnery would accept you once you've spent a year in my bed.'

Her face flamed and the look in his eyes made her hurriedly turn the page.

The ninth made her almost swallow her tongue. 'I don't want your money! And I certainly don't need that much money *every* month.' The sum stated was more than she earned in a year.

He shrugged. 'Then donate it to your favourite charity.'

Since she wasn't going to win that one, she moved on to the tenth and last clause.

Eva jerked to her feet, her heart pounding as she reread the words, hoping against hope that she'd got it wrong the first time. But the words remained clear and stark and *frightening*. 'You want...*children*?' she rasped through a throat gone bone dry with dread.

'*Sì,*' he replied softly. 'Two. An heir and a spare, I believe you disparagingly refer to that number in your circles. More if we're lucky—stop shaking your head, Eva.'

Eva realised that was exactly what she was doing as he rose and stalked her. She took a step back, then another, until her backside bumped the sleek black cabinet running the length of the central wall.

He stopped in front of her, leaned his tall, imposing frame over hers. 'Of all the clauses in the agreement, this is non-negotiable.'

'You said they were all non-negotiable.'

'They are, but some are more non-negotiable than others.'

A silent scream built inside her. 'If this one is the most important why did you put it last?'

'Because you would be signing directly below it. I wanted you to feel its import so there would be no doubt in your mind what you were agreeing to.'

She started to shake her head again but froze when he angled himself even closer, until their lips were an inch apart. Their breaths mingling, he stared her down. Eva's heart climbed into her throat as she struggled to sift through the emotions those words on the page had evoked.

Zaccheo was asking the impossible.

Children were the reasons why her last two relationships before him had failed before they'd even begun.

Children were the reason she'd painfully resigned herself to remaining single. To spurning any interest that came her way because she hadn't been able to bear the thought of baring her soul again only to have her emotions trampled on.

She wouldn't cry. She wouldn't break down in front of Zaccheo. Not today. *Not ever.* He'd caused her enough turmoil to last a lifetime.

But he was asking the impossible. 'I can't.'

His face hardened but he didn't move a muscle. 'You can. You *will*. Three days ago you were agreeing to marry another man. You expect me to believe the possibility of children weren't on the cards with Fairfield?'

She shook her head. 'My agreement with Harry was different. Besides, he...' She stopped, unwilling to add to the flammable tension.

'He what?' Zaccheo enquired silkily.

'He didn't *hate* me!'

He seemed almost surprised at her accusation. Surprise slowly gave way to a frown. 'I don't hate you, Eva. In fact, given time and a little work, we might even find common ground.'

She cursed her heart for leaping at his words. 'I can't—'

'You have twenty-four hours. I suggest you take the time and review your answer before saying another word.'

Her stomach clenched. 'And if my answer remains the same?'

His expression was one of pure, insufferable arrogance. 'It won't. You make feeble attempts to kick at the demands of your ancestry and title, but inevitably you choose blood over freedom. You'll do anything to save your precious family name—'

'You really think so? After the meeting we just had? Are you really that blind, or did you not see the way my sister and my father treat me? We are not a close family, Zaccheo. No matter how much I wish it...' Her voice shook, but she firmed it. 'Have you stopped to think that you pushing me this way may be the catalyst I need to completely break away from a family that's already broken?'

Her terse words made his eyes narrow. But his expression cleared almost immediately. 'No, you're loyal. You'll give me what I want.'

'No—'

'Yes,' he breathed.

He closed the gap between them slowly, as if taunting her with the knowledge that she couldn't escape the inevitability of his possession.

His mouth claimed hers—hot, demanding, powerfully erotic. Eva moaned as her emotions went into free fall. He feasted on her as if he had all the time in the world, taking turns licking his way into her mouth before sliding his tongue against hers in an expert dance that had her desperately clutching his waist.

Wild, decadent heat swirled through her body as he lifted her onto the cabinet, tugged up the hem of her dress and planted himself between her thighs. Her shoulders met the wall and she gasped as one hand gripped her thigh.

Push him away. You need to push him away!

Her hands climbed from his waist to his chest, albeit far slower and in a far more exploratory fashion than her screeching brain was comfortable with. But she made an effort once she reached his broad shoulders.

She pushed.

And found her hands captured in a firm one-handed hold above her head. His other hand found her breast and palmed it, squeezing before flicking his thumb over her hardened nipple.

Sensation pounded through her blood. Her legs curled around his thickly muscled thighs and she found herself pulled closer to the edge of the cabinet, until the powerful evidence of his erection pushed at her core.

Zaccheo gave a deep groan and freed her hands to bury his in her hair. Angling her head for a deeper invasion, he devoured her until the need for air drove them apart.

Chests heaving, they stared at each other for several seconds before Eva scrambled to untangle her legs from around him. Every skin cell on fire, she struggled to stand up. He stopped her with a hand on her belly, his eyes compelling hers so effortlessly, she couldn't look away.

The other hand moved to her cheek, then his fingers drifted over her throbbing mouth.

'As much as I'd like to take you right here on my boardroom cabinet, I have a dozen meetings to chair. It seems everyone wants a powwow with the newly emancipated CEO. We'll pick this up again at dinner. I'll be home by seven.'

She diverted enough brainpower from the erotic images it was creating to reply. 'I won't be there. I'm working tonight.'

A tic throbbed at his temple as he straightened his tie. 'I see that I need to put aligning our schedules at the top of my agenda.'

She pushed him away and stood. 'Don't strain yourself too much on my account,' she responded waspishly. She was projecting her anger at her weakness onto him, but she couldn't help herself. She tugged her dress down, painfully aware of the sensitivity between her unsteady legs as she moved away from him and picked up her handbag and the folder containing the prenup. 'I'll see you when I see you.'

He took her hand and walked her to the door. 'I guarantee you it'll be much sooner than that.' He rode the lift down with her to the ground floor, barely acknowledging the keen interest his presence provoked.

Romeo was entering the building as they exited. The two men exchanged a short conversation in Italian before Zaccheo opened the door to the limo.

When she went to slide in, he stopped her. 'Wait.'

'What is it?' she demanded.

His lips firmed and he seemed in two minds as to his response. 'For a moment during the meeting, you took my side against your father. I'll factor that favourably into our dealings from now on.'

Eva's heart lifted for a moment, then plunged back to her toes. 'You don't get it, do you?'

He frowned. 'Get what?'

'Zaccheo, for as long as I can remember, all I've wished was for there to be *no sides*. For there not to be a *them* against *us*. Maybe that makes me a fool. Or maybe I'll need to give up that dream.'

His eyes turned a shade darker with puzzlement, then he shrugged. '*Sì, bellissima*, perhaps you might have to.'

And right in front of the early lunch crowd, Zaccheo announced his ownership of her with a long, deep kiss.

* * *

Eva could barely hear herself think above the excited buzz in Siren's VIP lounge as she cued the next song.

She was sure the unusually large Monday night crowd had nothing to with Ziggy Preston, the famous record producer who'd been coming to watch her perform on and off for the past month, and everything to do with the pictures that had appeared in the early-evening paper of her kissing Zaccheo outside his office this afternoon. Avoiding the news had been difficult, seeing as that kiss and a large-scale picture of her engagement ring had made front-page news.

One picture had held the caption *'Three Ring Circus'*— with photos of her three engagement rings and a pointed question as to her motives.

It'd been a relief to leave Zaccheo's penthouse, switch off her phone and immerse herself in work. Not least because blanking her mind stopped her from thinking about the last clause in the prenup, and the reawakened agony she'd kept buried since her doctor had delivered the harrowing news six years ago. News she'd only revealed twice, with devastating consequences.

She almost wished she could blurt it out to Zaccheo and let the revelation achieve what it had in the past—a swift about-face from keen interest to cold dismissal, with one recipient informing her, in the most callous terms, that he could never accept her as a full woman.

Pain flared wider, threatening the foundations she'd built to protect herself from that stark truth. Foundations Zaccheo threatened.

She clutched the mic and forced back the black chasm that swirled with desolation. Her accompanying pianist nodded and she cleared her throat, ready to sing the ballad that ironically exhorted her to be brave.

She was halfway through the song when he walked in. As usual, the sight of him sent a tidal wave of awareness through her body and she managed to stop herself from stumbling by the skin of her teeth. Heads turned and the buzz in the room grew louder.

Zaccheo's eyes raked her from head to toe before settling on her face. A table miraculously emptied in front of the stage. Someone took his overcoat and Eva watched him release the single button to his dinner jacket before pulling out a chair and seating himself at the roped-off table before her.

The sense of déjà vu was so overwhelming, she wanted to abandon the song and flee from the stage. She finished, she smiled and accepted the applause, then made her way to where he pointedly held out a chair for her.

'What are you doing here?' she whispered fiercely.

He took his time to answer, choosing instead to pull her close and place a kiss on each cheek before drawing back to stare at her.

'You couldn't make dinner, so I brought dinner to you.'

'You really shouldn't have,' she replied, fighting the urge to rub her cheeks where his lips had been. 'Besides, I can't. My break is only twenty minutes.'

'Tonight your break is an hour, as it will be every night I choose to dine with you here instead of at our home. Now sit down and smile, *mio piccolo uccello che canta*, and pretend to our avid audience that you're ecstatically happy to see your fiancé,' he said with a tone edged in steel.

CHAPTER NINE

ZACCHEO WATCHED MYRIAD expressions chase across her face. Rebellion. Irritation. Sexual awareness. A touch of embarrassment when someone shouted their appreciation of her singing from across the room. One glance from Zaccheo silenced that inebriated guest.

But it was the shadows that lurked in her eyes that made his jaw clench. All day, through the heady challenge of getting back into the swing of business life, that look in her eyes when she'd seen his last clause in the prenuptial agreement had played on his mind. Not enough to disrupt his day, but enough for him to keep replaying the scene. Her reaction had been extreme and almost...distressed.

Yes, it bothered him that she saw making a family with him abhorrent, even though he'd known going in that, had she been given a choice, Eva would've chosen someone else, someone more *worthy* to father her children. Nevertheless, her reaction had struck hard in a place he'd thought was no longer capable of feeling hurt.

The feeling had festered, like a burr under his skin, eating away at him as the day had progressed. Until he'd abruptly ended a videoconference and walked out of his office.

He'd intended to return home and help himself to fine whisky in a toast to striking the first blow in ending Oscar Pennington's existence. Instead he'd found himself swapping his business suit for a dinner jacket and striding back out of his penthouse.

The woman who'd occupied far too much of his thoughts today swayed to her seat and sat down. The pounding in his blood that had never quite subsided after that kiss in his boardroom, and increased the moment he'd entered the

VIP room and heard her singing, accelerated when his gaze dropped to her scarlet-painted lips.

Before he'd met Eva Pennington, Zaccheo had never labelled himself a possessive guy. Although he enjoyed the thrill of the chase and inevitable capture, he'd been equally thrilled to see the back of the women he'd dated, especially when the clinginess had begun.

With Eva, he'd experienced an unprecedented and very caveman-like urge to claim her, to make sure every man within striking distance knew she belonged to him. And only him. That feeling was as unsettling as it was hard to eradicate. It wasn't helped when she toyed with her champagne glass and avoided eye contact.

'I don't appreciate you messing with my schedule behind my back, Zaccheo,' she said.

He wasn't sure why the sound of his name on her lips further spiked his libido, but he wanted to hear it again. He wanted to hear it fall from her lips in the throes of passion, as he took her to the heights of ecstasy.

Dio, he was losing it. Losing sight of his objective. Which was to make sure she understood that he intended to give no quarter in making her his.

He took a bracing sip of champagne and nodded to the hovering waiters ready to serve the meal he'd ordered.

'It was dinner here or summoning you back to the penthouse. You should be thanking me for bending like this.'

She glared. 'You really are a great loss to the Dark Ages, you know that?'

'In time you'll learn that I always get my way, Eva. *Always.*'

Her eyes met his and that intense, inexplicable connection that had throbbed between them right from the very start pulled, tightened.

'Did it even occur to you that I may have said yes if you'd asked me to have dinner with you?'

Surprise flared through him, and he found himself asking, 'Would you?'

She shrugged. 'I guess you'll never know. We need to discuss the prenup,' she said.

He knew instinctively that she was about to refuse him again. A different sort of heat bloomed in his chest. 'This isn't the time or place.'

'I don't...' She paused when the waiters arrived at the table with their first course. As if recalling where they were, she glanced round, took a deep breath, and leaned forward. 'I won't sign it.'

Won't, not *can't*, as she'd said before.

Bitterness surged through his veins. 'Because the thought of my seed growing inside you fills you with horror?'

Her fingers convulsed around her knife, but, true to her breeding, she directed it to her plate with understated elegance to cut her steak.

'Why would you want me as the mother of your children, anyway? I would've thought you'd want to spare yourself such a vivid reminder of what you've been through.'

'Perhaps I'm the one to give the Pennington name the integrity it's been so sorely lacking thus far.'

She paled, and he cursed himself for pursuing a subject that was better off discussed in private. Although he'd made sure their table was roped off and their conversation couldn't be overheard, there was still more than enough interest in them for each expression flitting across Eva's face to be captured and assessed.

'So we're your personal crusade?' she asked, a brittle smile appearing on her face as she acknowledged someone over his shoulder.

'Let's call it more of an experiment.'

Her colour rose with the passionate fury that intrigued him. 'You'd father children based on an *experiment*? After what you've been through...what we've both been through, you think that's fair to the children you intend to have to be used solely as a means for you to prove a point?' Her voice was ragged and he tensed.

'Eva—'

'No, I won't be a part of it!' Her whisper was fierce. 'My mother may have loved me in her own way, but I was still the tool she used against my father when it suited her. If my grades happened to be better than Sophie's, she would imply my father was lacking in some way. And believe me, my father didn't pull his punches when the situation was re-versed.' She swallowed and raised bruised eyes to his. 'Even if I cou—wanted to why would I knowingly subject another child to what I went through? Why would I give you a child simply to use to *prove a point*?'

'You mistake my meaning. I don't intend to fail my chil-dren or use them as pawns. I intend to be there for them through thick and thin, unlike my parents were for me.' He stopped when her eyes widened. 'Does that surprise you?'

'I… Yes.'

He shrugged, even though it occurred to him that he'd let his guard down more with her than he ever had with anyone. But she had no power to hurt him. She'd already rejected him once. This time he knew the lay of the land going in. So it didn't matter if she knew his parental ambitions for the children they'd have.

'My children will be my priority, although I'll be inter-ested to see how your family fares with being shown that things can be done differently. The *right* way.'

He watched her digest his response, watched the shadows he was beginning to detest mount in her eyes. He decided against probing further. There'd been enough turbulent emo-tions today. He suspected there would be further fireworks when she found out the new business negotiations he'd com-menced this afternoon.

That a part of him was looking forward to it made him shift in his seat.

Since when had he craved verbal conflict with a woman?

Never. And yet he couldn't seem to help himself when it came to Eva.

He was debating this turn of events as their plates were removed when a throat cleared next to them.

The man was around his age, with floppy brown hair and a cocky smile that immediately rubbed Zaccheo the wrong way.

'Can I join you for a few minutes?' he asked.

The *no* that growled up Zaccheo's chest never made it. Eva was smiling—her first genuine smile since he'd walked in—and nodding. 'Mr Preston, of course!'

'Thanks. And call me Ziggy, please. Mr Preston is my headmaster grandfather.'

'What can we do for you, *Ziggy*?' Zaccheo raised an eyebrow at the furious look Eva shot him.

The other man, who was staring at Eva with an avidness that made Zaccheo's fist clench, finally looked in his direction. 'I came to pay my compliments to your girlfriend. She has an amazing voice.'

Eva blushed at his words.

Zaccheo's eyes narrowed when he noticed she wasn't wearing her engagement ring. 'Eva's my fiancée, not my girlfriend. And I'm very much aware of her exceptional talent,' he said, the harsh edge to his voice getting through to the man, who looked from him to Eva before his smile dimmed.

'Ah, congratulations are in order, then?'

'*Grazie,*' Zaccheo replied. 'Was there something else you wanted?'

'Zaccheo!' Eva glared harder, and turned to Ziggy. 'Pardon my *fiancé*. He's feeling a little testy because—'

'I want her all to myself but find other *things* standing in my way. And because you're not wearing your engagement ring, *dolcezza.*'

She covered her bare fingers with her hand, as if that would remove the evidence of the absence of his ring. 'Oh,

I didn't want to risk losing it. I'm still getting used to it.' The glance she sent him held a mixture of defiance and entreaty.

Ziggy cleared his throat again. 'I don't want to play the *Do-you-know-who-I-am?* card, but—'

'Of course I know who you are,' Eva replied with a charming laugh.

Ziggy smiled and produced a business card. 'In that case, would you like to come to my studio next week? See if we can make music together?'

Eva's pleased gasp further darkened Zaccheo's mood. 'Of course I can—'

'Aren't you forgetting something, *luce mio*?' he asked in a quietly lethal tone.

'What?' she asked, so innocently he wanted to grab her from the chair, spread her across the table and make her see nothing, no one, but him. Make her recall that she had given her word to be his and only his.

'You won't be available next week.' He didn't care that he hadn't yet apprised her of the details. He cared that she was smiling at another man as if *he* didn't exist. 'We'll be on our honeymoon on my private island off the coast of Brazil where we'll be staying for the next two weeks.'

Her eyes rounded, but she recovered quickly and took the business card. 'I'll *make* time to see you before I go. Surely you don't want to deny me this opportunity, *darling*?' Her gaze swung to him, daring him to respond in the negative.

Despite his irritation, Zaccheo curbed a smile. 'Of course. Anything for you, *dolcezza*.'

Ziggy beamed. 'Great! I look forward to it.'

The moment he was out of earshot, she turned to Zaccheo. 'How dare you try and sabotage me like that?'

'Watching you smile at another man like that fills me with insane jealousy. It also brings out the jerk in me. My apologies,' he growled. Her mouth dropped open. 'Close your mouth, Eva.'

She shook her head as if reeling from a body blow.

Welcome to my world.

'Where's your ring?' He stared at her, his control on a knife-edge.

Perhaps sensing the dangerously shifting currents, she pulled up the gold chain that hung between her pert, full breasts. His ring dangled from it.

'Put it on. Now,' he said, struggling to keep his voice even.

Undoing the clasp, she took the ring off the chain and slid it back on her finger. 'There. Can I return to work now or are you going to harangue me about something else?'

He told himself he did it because he needed to put his rampaging emotions *somewhere*. That it was her fault for pushing him to his limit. But when he plucked her from her seat, placed her in his lap and kissed her insanely tempting mouth, Zaccheo knew it was because he couldn't help himself. She *got* to him in a way no one else did.

By the time he pulled away, they were both breathing hard. Her high colour filled him with immense satisfaction, helping him ignore his own hopeless loss of control.

'Don't take the ring off again, Eva. You underestimate the lengths I'm prepared to go to in making sure you stick to your word, but for your sake I hope you start taking me seriously.'

In contrast to the vividness of Zaccheo's presence, the rest of the night passed in a dull blur after he left. By the time Eva collapsed into bed in the early hours, her head throbbed with the need to do something severely uncharacteristic. Like scream. Beat her fists against the nearest wall. Shout her anger and confusion to the black skies above.

She did nothing of the sort. More than anything, she craved a little peace and quiet.

After that kiss in the club, even more eyes had followed her wherever she went. Hushed whispers had trailed her to the bathroom. By the time her shift had ended three hours later, she'd been ready to walk out and never return.

She wouldn't, of course. Working at Siren gave her the free time to write her songs while earning enough to live on. Despite Zaccheo's heavy-handedness, she could never see a time when she'd be dependent on anyone other than herself.

'You underestimate the lengths I'm prepared to go to...'

The forceful statement had lingered long after he'd left, anchored by the heavy presence of the prenuptial agreement in her handbag.

He'd said he wouldn't negotiate. Eva didn't see that he had a choice in this matter. Refusing to marry him might well spell the end for her father, but withholding the truth and marrying him knowing she could never fulfil her part of the bargain would be much worse.

Turning in bed, she punched her pillow, dreading the long, restless night ahead. Only to wake with sunshine streaming through the window and her clock announcing it was ten o'clock.

Rushing out of bed, she showered quickly and entered the dining room just as Romeo was exiting, having finished his own breakfast. The table was set for one and Eva cursed herself for the strange dip in her belly that felt very much like disappointment.

'Good morning. Shall I get the chef to make you a cooked breakfast?' The man whose role she was beginning to suspect went deeper than a simple second-in-command asked.

'Just some toast and tea, please, thank you.'

He nodded and started to leave.

'Is Zaccheo around or has he left for the office?'

'Neither. He left this morning for Oman. An unexpected hiccup in the construction of his building there.'

Eva was unprepared for the bereft feeling that swept through her. She should be celebrating her temporary reprieve. Finding a way to see if she could work around that impossible clause. 'When will he be back?'

'In a day or two. Latest by the end of the week to be ready in time for the wedding,' Romeo said in that deep, modulated voice of his. 'This is for you.' He handed her a folded note and left.

The bold scrawl was unmistakeably Zaccheo's.

Eva,
   Treat my absence as you wish, but never as an excuse to be complacent.
   My PA will be in touch with details of your wedding dress fitting this morning and your amended schedule for the week.
   You have my permission to miss me.
Z

Ugh! She grimaced at the arrogance oozing from the paper. Balling the note, she flung it across the table. Then quickly jumped up and retrieved it before Romeo returned. The last thing she wanted was for him to report her loss of temper to Zaccheo.

Her traitorous body had a hard enough time controlling itself when Zaccheo was around. She didn't want him to know he affected her just as badly when he was absent.

By the time breakfast was delivered, she'd regained her composure. Which was just as well, because close on the chef's heel was a tall, striking brunette dressed in a grey pencil skirt and matching jacket.

'Good morning, my name is Anyetta, Mr Giordano's PA. He said you were expecting me?'

'I was expecting a phone call, not a personal visit.'

Anyetta delivered a cool smile. 'Mr Giordano wanted his wishes attended to personally.'

Eva's appetite fled. 'I bet he did,' she muttered.

She poured herself a cup of tea as Anyetta proceeded to fill up her every spare hour between now and Saturday morning.

Eva listened until her temper began to flare, then tuned

out until she heard the word *makeover*. 'I've already had one makeover. I don't need another one.'

Anyetta's eyes drifted over Eva's hair, which she admitted was a little wild since she hadn't brushed it properly before she'd rushed out to speak to Zaccheo. 'Not even for your wedding day?'

Since there wasn't likely to be a wedding day once she told Zaccheo she had no intention of signing the agreement, she replied, 'It'll be taken care of.'

Anyetta ticked off a few more items, verified that Eva's passport was up to date, then stood as the doorbell rang. 'That'll be Margaret with your wedding dress.'

The feeling of being on a runaway train intensified as Eva trailed Anyetta out of the dining room. She drew to a stunned halt when she saw the middle-aged woman coming towards her with a single garment bag and a round veil and shoebox.

'Please tell me you don't have a team of assistants lurking outside ready to jump on me?' she asked after Anyetta left.

Margaret laughed. 'It's just me, Lady Pennington. Your fiancé was very specific about his wishes, and, meeting you now, I see why he chose this dress. He did say I was to work with you, of course. So if you don't like it, we can explore other options.'

Eva reminded herself that this situation hadn't arisen out of a normal courtship, that Zaccheo choosing her wedding dress for her shouldn't upset her so much. Besides, the likelihood of this farce ever seeing the light of day was very low so she was better off just going along with it.

But despite telling herself not to care, Eva couldn't suppress her anxiety and excitement.

She gasped as the dress was revealed.

The design itself was simple and clean, but utterly breathtaking. Eva stared at the fitted white satin gown overlaid with lace and beaded with countless tiny crystals. Delicate capped sleeves extended from the sweetheart neckline and the tiniest train flared out in a beautiful arc. At the back, more crystals had been embedded in mother-of-pearl buttons that went from nape to waist. Unable to resist, Eva reached out to touch the dress, then pulled herself back.

There was no point falling in love with a dress she'd never wear. No point getting butterflies about a marriage that would never happen once she confessed her flaw to Zaccheo. Her hands fisted and she fought the desolation threatening to break free inside her.

For six years, she'd successfully not dwelt on what she could never have—a husband who cared for her and a family of her own. She'd made music her life and had found fulfilment in it. She wasn't about to let a heartbreakingly gorgeous dress dredge up agonies she'd sealed in a box marked *strictly out of bounds*.

'Are you ready to try it on?' Margaret asked.

Eva swallowed. 'Might as well.'

If the other woman found her response curious, she didn't let on. Eva avoided her gaze in the mirror as the dress was slipped over her shoulders and the delicate chiffon and lace veil was fitted into place. She mumbled her thanks as Margaret helped her into matching-coloured heels.

'Oh, I'm pleased to see we don't need to alter it in any way, Lady Pennington. It fits perfectly. Looks like your fiancé was very accurate with your measurements. You'd be surprised how many men get it wrong…'

She kept her gaze down, frightened to look at herself, as Margaret tweaked and tugged until she was happy.

Eva dared not look up in case she began to *hope* and *wish*. She murmured appropriate responses and turned this way and that when asked and breathed a sigh of relief when the ordeal was over. The moment Margaret zipped up the bag and left, Eva escaped to her suite. Putting her headphones on, she activated the music app on her tablet and proceeded to drown out her thoughts the best way she knew how.

But this time no amount of doing what she loved best could obliterate the thoughts tumbling through her head.

At seventeen when her periods had got heavier and more painful with each passing month, she'd attributed it to life's natural cycle. But when stronger painkillers had barely alleviated the pain, she'd begun to suspect something major was wrong.

Collapsing during a university lecture had finally prompted her to seek medical intervention.

The doctor's diagnosis had left her reeling.

Even then, she'd convinced herself it wasn't the end of the world, that compared to her mother's fight against cancer, a fight she'd eventually lost a year later, Eva's problem was inconsequential. Women dealt with challenging problems like hers every day. When the time came, the man she chose to spend the rest of her life with would understand and support her.

Eva scoffed at her naiveté. Scott, the first man she'd dated in the last year of university, had visibly recoiled from her when she'd mentioned her condition. She'd been so shocked by his reaction, she'd avoided him for the rest of her time at uni.

Burnt, she'd sworn off dating until she'd met George Tremayne, her fellow business intern during her brief stint at Penningtons. Flattered by his attentiveness, she'd let down her guard and gone on a few dates before he'd begun to pressure her to take things further. Her gentle rejection and confession of her condition had resulted in a scathing volley of insults, during which she'd found out exactly why her father had been pressing her to work at Penningtons after graduation.

Oscar Pennington, already secure in his conscript of Sophie as his heir, was eager to offload his remaining daughter and had lined up a list of suitable men, George Tremayne, the son of a viscount, being on the top of that list. George's near-identical reaction to Scott's had hurt twice as much, and convinced Eva once and for all that her secret was best kept to herself.

Finding out she was yet another means to an end for Zaccheo had rocked her to the core, but she'd taken consolation in the fact the secret she'd planned on revealing to him shortly after their engagement was safe.

That secret was about to be ripped open.

As she turned up the volume of her music Eva knew disclosing it to Zaccheo would be the most difficult thing she would ever do.

CHAPTER TEN

ZACCHEO SCROLLED THROUGH the missed calls from Eva on his phone as he was driven away from the private hangar. Romeo had relayed her increasingly frantic requests to reach him. Zaccheo had deliberately forbidden his number from being given to her until this morning, once he'd confirmed his return to London.

His jaw flexed as he rolled tight shoulders. The number of fires he'd put out in Oman would've wiped out a lesser man. But Zaccheo's name and ruthless nature weren't renowned for nothing, and although it'd taken three days to get the construction schedule back on track, his business partners were in no doubt that he would bring them to their knees if they strayed so much as one millimetre from the outcome he desired.

It was the same warning he'd given Oscar Pennington when he'd called yesterday and attempted an ego-stroking exercise to get Zaccheo to relent on his threats. Zaccheo had coldly reminded him of the days he'd spent in prison and invited Pennington to ask for clemency when hell froze over.

No doubt Eva's eagerness to contact him was born of the same desire as her father's. But unlike her father, the thought of speaking to Eva sent a pleasurable kick of anticipation through his blood, despite the fact that with time and distance he'd looked back on their conversations since his release with something close to dismay.

Had he really revealed all those things about his time in prison and his childhood to her?

What was even more puzzling was her reaction. She hadn't looked down her nose at him in those moments. Had in fact exhibited nothing but empathy and compassion. Pushing the bewildering thought away, he dialled her number, gratified when she picked up on the first ring.

'*Ciao*, Eva. I understand you're experiencing pre-wedding jitters.'

'You understand wrong. This wedding isn't going to happen. Not once you hear what I have to say.'

His tension increased until the knots in his shoulders felt like immoveable rocks. He breathed through the red haze blurring his vision. 'I take it you didn't miss me, then?' he taunted.

She made a sound, a cross between a huff and a sigh. 'We really need to talk, Zaccheo.'

'Nothing you say will alter my intention to make you mine tomorrow,' he warned.

She hesitated. Then, 'Zaccheo, it's important. I won't take up too much of your time. But I need to speak to you.'

He rested his head against the seat. 'You have less than twenty-four hours left as a single woman. I won't permit anything like male strippers anywhere near you, of course, but I won't be a total bore and deny you a hen party if you wish—'

'I don't want a damn hen party! What I want is five minutes of your time.'

'Are you dying of some life-threatening disease?'

'*What?* Of course not!'

'Are you afraid I won't be a good husband?' he asked, noting the raw edge to his voice, but realising how much her answer meant to him.

'Zaccheo, this is about me, not you.'

He let her non-answer slide. 'You'll be a good wife. And despite your less than auspicious upbringing, you'll be a good mother.'

He heard her soft gasp. 'How do you know that?'

'Because you're passionate when you care. You just need to channel that passion from your undeserving family to the one we will create.'

'I can't just switch my feelings towards my family off.

Everyone deserves someone who cares about them, no matter what.'

His heart kicked hard and his grip tightened around the phone as bitterness washed through him. 'Not everyone gets it, though.'

Silence thrummed. 'I'm sorry about your parents. Is... your mother still alive?' Her voice bled the compassion he'd begun to associate with her.

It warmed a place inside him even as he answered. 'That depends on who you ask. Since she relocated to the other side of the world to get away from me, I presume she won't mind if I think her dead to me.'

'But she's alive, Zaccheo. Which means there's hope. Do you really want to waste that?' Her pain-filled voice drew him up short, reminding him that she'd lost her mother.

When had this conversation turned messy and emotional?

'You were close to your mother?' he asked.

'When she wasn't busy playing up to being a Pennington, or using me to get back at my father, she was a brilliant mother. I wish... I wish she'd been a mother to both Sophie *and* me.' She laughed without humour. 'Hell, I used to wish I'd been born into another family, that my last name wasn't Pennington—' She stopped and a tense silence reigned.

Zaccheo frowned. Things weren't adding up with Eva. He'd believed her surname was one she would do just about anything for, including help cover up fraud. But in his boardroom on Monday, she'd seemed genuinely shocked and hurt by the extent of her father's duplicity. And there was also the matter of her chosen profession and the untouched money in her bank account.

A less cynical man would believe she was the exception to the abhorrent aristocratic rule...

'At least you had one parent who cared for you. You were lucky,' he said, his mind whirling with the possibility that he could be wrong.

'But that parent is gone, and I feel as if I have no one now,' she replied quietly.

The need to tell her she had him flared through his mind. He barely managed to stay silent. After a few seconds, she cleared her throat. Her next words made him wish he'd hung up.

'I haven't signed the prenup,' she blurted out. 'I'm not going to.'

Because of the last clause.

For a brief moment, Zaccheo wanted to tell her why he wanted children. That the bleak loneliness that had dogged him through his childhood and almost drowned him in prison had nearly broken him. That he'd fallen into a pit of despair when he'd realised no one would miss him should the worst happen.

His mother had emigrated to Australia with her husband rather than stay in the same city as him once Zaccheo had fully established himself in London. That had cut deeper than any rejection he'd suffered from her in the past. And although the news of his trial and sentencing had been worldwide news, Zaccheo had never once heard from the woman who'd given him life.

He could've died in prison for all his mother cared. That thought had haunted him day and night until he'd decided to do something about it.

Until he'd vowed to alter his reality, ensure he had someone who would be proud to bear his name. Someone to whom he could pass on his legacy.

He hadn't planned for that person to be Eva Pennington until he'd read about her engagement in the file. But once he had, the decision had become iron cast.

Although this course was very much a sweeter, more lasting experience, Zaccheo couldn't help but wonder if it was all worth the ground shifting so much beneath his feet.

Eva was getting beneath his skin. And badly.

Dio mio. Why were the feelings he'd bottled up for over two decades choosing *now* to bubble up? He exhaled harshly.

Rough and ruthless was his motto. It was what had made him the man he was today. 'You'll be in your wedding dress at noon tomorrow, ready to walk down the aisle where our six hundred guests will be—'

'*Six hundred?* You've invited six *hundred* people to the wedding?' Her husky disbelief made his teeth grind.

'You thought I intended to have a hole-in-the-wall ceremony?' A fresh wave of bitterness rolled over him. 'Or did you think my PA was spouting gibberish when she informed you of all this on Tuesday?'

'Sorry, I must've tuned out because, contrary to what you think, I don't like my life arranged for me,' she retorted. 'That doesn't change anything. I *can't* do this…'

Zaccheo frowned at the naked distress in her voice.

Eva was genuinely torn up about the prospect of giving herself to him, a common man only worthy of a few kisses but nothing as substantial as the permanent state of matrimony.

Something very much like pain gripped his chest. 'Is that your final decision? Are you backing out of our agreement?'

She remained silent for so long, he thought the line was dead. 'Unless you're willing to change the last clause, yes.'

Zaccheo detested the sudden clenching of his stomach, as if the blow he'd convinced himself would never come had been landed. The voice taunting him for feeling more than a little stunned was ruthlessly smashed away.

He assured himself he had another way to claim the justice he sought. 'Very well. *Ciao.*'

He ended the phone call. And fought the urge to hurl his phone out of the window.

Eva dropped the phone onto the coffee-shop table. She'd arrived at work only to discover she'd been taken off the roster due to her impending wedding. Since she had holiday due to her anyway, Eva hadn't fought too hard at suddenly finding herself with free time.

Her session with Ziggy yesterday had gone well, despite her head being all over the place. If nothing else came of it, she could add that to her CV.

Curbing a hysterical snort, she stared at her phone.

She'd done the right thing and ended this farce before it went too far. Before the longings she'd harboured in the last three days got any more out of control.

Deep in her heart, she knew Zaccheo would react the same way to her secret as Scott and George had. He wouldn't want to marry half a woman, especially when he'd stated his expectations in black and white in a formal agreement drafted by a team of lawyers, and then confounded her with his genuine desire to become a father.

So why hadn't she just told him over the phone?

Because she was a glutton for punishment?

Because some part of her had hoped telling him face-to-face would help her gauge whether there was a chance he would accept her the way she was?

Fat chance.

It was better this way. Clean. Painless.

She jumped as her phone pinged. Heart lurching, she accessed the message, but it was only the manageress from Siren, wishing her a lovely wedding and sinfully blissful honeymoon.

Eva curled her hand around her fast-cooling mug. Once the news got out that she'd broken her third engagement in two years, her chances of marrying anyone, let alone a man who would accept her just as she was, would shrink from nil to no chance in hell.

Pain spiked again at the reminder of her condition. Exhaling, she wrenched her mind to more tangible things.

Like finding a place to live.

She weighed her options, despair clutching her insides

when, two hours later, she faced the only avenue open to her. Going back home to Pennington Manor.

Reluctantly, she picked up her phone, then nearly dropped it when it blared to life. The name of the caller made her frown.

'Sophie?'

'Eva, what's going on?' The fear in her voice shredded Eva's heart.

'What do you mean?'

'I've just had to call the doctor because Father's had another episode!'

Eva jerked to her feet, sending her coffee cup bouncing across the table. 'What?'

'We got a call from Zaccheo Giordano an hour ago to say the wedding was off. Father's been frantic. He was about to call you when he collapsed. The doctor says if he's subjected to any more stress he could have a heart attack or a stroke. Is it true? Did you call off the wedding?' The strain in her sister's voice was unmistakeable.

'Yes,' Eva replied. She grabbed her bag and hurried out of the coffee shop when she began to attract peculiar looks. Outside, she shrugged into her coat and pulled up her hoodie to avoid the light drizzle.

'Oh, God. Why?' her sister demanded.

'Zaccheo wanted me to sign a prenuptial agreement.'

'So? Everyone does that these days.'

'One of the terms…he wants *children*.'

Her sister sighed. 'So he backed out when you told him?'

'No, he doesn't know.'

'But… I'm confused,' Sophie replied.

'I tried to tell him but he wouldn't listen.'

'You tried. Isn't that enough?'

Eva ducked into a quiet alley and leaned against a wall. 'No, it's *not* enough. We've caused enough harm where he's concerned. I won't go into this based on a lie.'

'Father's terrified, Eva.'

'Can I talk to him?'

'He's sleeping now. I'll let him know you called when he wakes up.' Sophie paused. 'Eva, I've been thinking…what you said on Saturday, about you not being out to replace me… I shouldn't have bitten your head off. It's just… Father isn't an easy man to please. He was relying on me to see us through this rough patch…'

'I didn't mean to step on your toes, Sophie.'

Her sister inhaled deeply. 'I know. But everything seems so effortless for you, Eva. It always has. I envied you because Mother chose you—'

'Parents shouldn't choose which child to love and which to keep at arm's length!'

'But that was our reality. He wanted a son. And I was determined to be that son. After Mother died, I was scared Father would think I wasn't worth his attention.'

'You were. You still are.'

'Only because I've gone along with whatever he's asked of me without complaint, even when I knew I shouldn't. This thing with Zaccheo… Father's not proud of it. Nor am I. I don't know where we go from here, but once we're through this, can we get together?' Sophie asked, her voice husky with the plea.

Eva didn't realise her legs had given way until her bottom touched the cold, hard ground.

'Yes, if you want,' she murmured. Her hands shook as she hung up.

The last time she'd seen Sophie's rigid composure crumble had been in the few weeks after they'd buried their mother. For a while she'd had her sister back. They'd been united in their grief, supporting each other when their loss overwhelmed them.

As much as Eva missed *that* Sophie, she couldn't stomach having her back under similar circumstances. Nor could she bear the danger that her father faced.

She wasn't sure how long she sat there.

Cold seeped into her clothes. Into her bones. Into her heart.

Feeling numb, she dug into her bag and extracted the pre-nup and read through it one more time.

She couldn't honour Zaccheo's last clause, but that didn't mean she couldn't use it to buy herself, and her father, time until they met and she explained. Despite his own past, he wanted a family. Maybe he would understand why she was trying to salvage hers.

Slowly, she dialled. After endless rings, the line clicked through.

'Eva.' His voice was pure cold steel.

'I…' She attempted to say the words but her teeth still chattered. Squeezing her eyes shut, she tried again. 'I'll sign the agreement. I'll marry you tomorrow.'

Silence.

'Zaccheo? Are you there?'

'Where are you?'

She shivered at his impersonal tone. 'I'm…' She looked up at the street sign in the alley and told him.

'Romeo will be there in fifteen minutes. He'll witness the agreement and bring it to me. You'll return to the penthouse and resume preparations for the wedding.' He paused, as if waiting for her to disagree.

'Will I see you today?' She hated how weak her voice sounded.

'No.'

Eva exhaled. 'Okay, I'll wait for Romeo.'

'Bene.' The line went dead.

The grey mizzle outside aptly reflected Eva's mood as she sat, hands clasped in her lap, as the hairdresser finished putting up her hair. Behind her, Sophie smiled nervously.

Eva smiled back, knowing her sister's nervousness stemmed from the fear that Eva would change her mind again.

But this time there was no going back. She meant to come clean to Zaccheo at the first opportunity and open herself up to whatever consequences he sought.

Just how she would manage that was a puzzle she hadn't untangled yet, but since Zaccheo was hell-bent on this marriage, and she was giving him what he wanted, technically she was fulfilling her side of the bargain.

God, when had she resorted to seeing things in shades of grey instead of black and white, truth and lie? Was Zaccheo right? Did her Pennington blood mean she was destined to do whatever it took, even if it meant compromising her integrity, for the sake of her family and pedigree?

No. She wouldn't care if she woke up tomorrow as ordinary Eva Penn instead of Lady Pennington. And she *would* come clean to Zaccheo, no matter what.

Except that was looking less likely to happen *before* the wedding. Zaccheo hadn't returned to the penthouse last night. She hadn't deluded herself that he was observing the quaint marriage custom. If anything, he was probably making another billion, or actively sowing his last wild oats. She jerked at the jagged pain that shot through her.

Sophie stood up. 'What's wrong?'

'Nothing. How's Father?'

Sophie's face clouded. 'He insists he's well enough to walk you down the aisle.' Her sister's eyes darted to the hairdresser who had finished and was walking out to get Margaret. 'He's desperate that everything goes according to plan today.'

Eva managed to stop her smile from slipping. 'It will.'

Sophie met her gaze in the mirror. 'Do you think I should talk to Zaccheo…explain?'

Eva thought about the conversation she'd had with Zaccheo yesterday, the merciless tone, the ruthless man on a mission who'd been released from prison a mere week ago. 'Maybe not just yet.'

Sophie nodded, then flashed a smile that didn't quite make it before she left Eva alone as Margaret entered.

Any hopes of talking to Zaccheo evaporated when she found herself at the doors of the chapel an hour later.

Catching sight of him for the first time since Monday, she felt her heart slam around her chest.

Romeo stood in the best-man position and Eva wondered again at the connection between the two men. Did Zaccheo have any friends? Or had he lost all of them when her family's actions had altered his fate?

The thought flitted out of her head as her gaze returned almost magnetically to Zaccheo.

He'd eschewed a morning coat in favour of a bespoke three-piece suit in the softest dove-grey silk. Against the snowy white shirt and white tie completing the ensemble, his long hair was at once dangerously primitive and yet so utterly captivating, her mouth dried as her pulse danced with a dark, decadent delight. His beard had been trimmed considerably and a part of her mourned its loss. Perhaps it was that altered look that made his eyes so overwhelmingly electrifying, or it was the fact that his face was set in almost brutal lines, but the effect was like lightning to her system the moment her eyes connected with his.

The music in the great hall of the cathedral he'd astonishingly managed to secure on such short notice disappeared, along with the chatter of the goggle-eyed guests who did nothing to hide their avid curiosity.

All she could see was him, the man who would be her husband in less than fifteen minutes.

She stumbled, then stopped. A murmur rose in the crowd. Eva felt her father's concerned stare, but she couldn't look away from Zaccheo.

His nostrils flared, his eyes narrowing in warning as fear clutched her, freezing her feet.

'Eva?' Her father's ragged whisper caught her consciousness.

'Why did you insist on walking me down the aisle?' she asked him, wanting in some way to know that she wasn't doing all of this to save a man who had very little regard for her.

'What? Because you're my daughter,' her father replied with a puzzled frown.

'So you're not doing it just to keep up appearances?'

His face creased with a trace of the vulnerability she'd glimpsed only once before, when her mother died, and her heart lurched. 'Eva, I haven't handled things well. I know that. I was brought up to put the family name above all else, and I took that responsibility a little too far. Despite our less than perfect marriage, your mother was the one who would pull me back to my senses when I went a little too far. Without her...' His voice roughened and his hand gripped hers. 'We might lose Penningtons, but I don't want to lose you and Sophie.'

Eva's throat clogged. 'Maybe you should tell her that? She needs to know you're proud of her, Father.'

Her father looked to where her sister stood, and he nodded. 'I will. And I'm proud of you, too. You're as beautiful as your mother was on our wedding day.'

Eva blinked back her tears as murmurs rose in the crowd.

She turned to find Zaccheo staring at her. Something dark, sinister, curled through his eyes and she swallowed as his mouth flattened.

I can't marry him without him knowing! He deserves to know that I can't give him the family he wants.

'My dear, you need to move now. It's time,' her father pleaded.

Torn by the need for Zaccheo to know the truth and the need to protect her father, she shook her head, her insides churning.

Churning turned into full-blown liquefying as Zaccheo stepped from the dais, his imposing body threatening to block out the light as he headed down the aisle.

She desperately sucked in a breath, the knowledge that Zaccheo would march her up the aisle himself if need be finally scraping her feet from the floor. He stopped halfway, his gaze unswerving, until she reached him.

He grasped her hand, his hold unbreakable as he turned and walked her to the altar.

Trembling at the hard, pitiless look in his eyes, she swallowed and tried to speak. 'Zaccheo—'

'No, Eva. No more excuses,' he growled.

The priest glanced between them, his expression benign but enquiring.

Zaccheo nodded.

The organ swelled. And sealed her fate.

CHAPTER ELEVEN

'GLARING AT IT won't make it disappear, unless you have superhero laser vision.'

Eva jumped at the mocking voice and curled her fingers into her lap, hiding the exquisite diamond-studded platinum ring that had joined her engagement ring three hours ago.

'I wasn't willing it away.' On the contrary, she'd been wondering how long it would stay on her finger once Zaccheo knew the truth.

The reception following the ceremony had been brief but intense. Six hundred people clamouring for attention and the chance to gawp at the intriguing couple could take a lot out of a girl. With Zaccheo's fingers laced through hers the whole time, tightening commandingly each time she so much as moved an inch away from him, Eva had been near-blubbering-wreck status by the time their limo had left the hall.

Once she'd stopped reeling from the shock of being married to Zaccheo Giordano, she'd taken a moment to take in her surroundings. The Great Hall in the Guildhall was usually booked for years in advance. That Zaccheo had managed to secure it in a week and thrown together a stunning reception was again testament that she'd married a man with enough power and clout to smash through any resistance.

Zaccheo, despite his spell in prison, remained a formidable man, one, she suspected, who didn't need her father's intervention to restore his damaged reputation. So why was he pursuing it so relentlessly? Throughout the reception, she'd watched him charm their guests with the sheer force of his charisma. By the time her father had got round to giving the edifying toast welcoming Zaccheo to the Pennington family, the effort had seemed redundant.

She watched Zaccheo now as the car raced them to the airport, and wondered if it was a good time to broach the subject burning a hole in her chest.

'Something on your mind?' he queried without raising his gaze from his tablet.

Her heart leapt into her throat. She started to speak but noticed the partition between them and Romeo, who sat in the front passenger seat, was open. Although she was sure Romeo knew the ins and outs of the document he'd been asked to witness yesterday, Eva wasn't prepared to discuss her devastating shortcomings in his presence.

So she opted for something else plaguing her. She smoothed her hands on her wedding dress. 'Do I have your assurance that you'll speak on my father's behalf once you hand over the documents to the authorities?'

He speared her with incisive grey eyes. 'You're so eager to see him let off the hook, aren't you?'

'Wouldn't you be, if it was your father?' she asked.

Eva was unprepared for the strange look that crossed his face. The mixture of anger, sadness, and bitterness hollowed out her stomach.

'My father wasn't interested in being let off the hook for his sins. He was happy to keep himself indebted to his betters because he thought that was his destiny.'

Her breath caught. 'What? That doesn't make sense.'

'Very little of my father's actions made sense to me, not when I was a child, and not as an adult.'

The unexpected insight into his life made her probe deeper. 'When did he die?'

'When I was thirteen years old.'

'I'm sorry.' When he inclined his head and continued to stare at her, she pressed her luck. 'How did he—?'

'Zaccheo,' Romeo's deep voice interrupted them. 'Perhaps this is not a subject for your wedding day?'

A look passed between the friends.

When Zaccheo looked at her again, that cool impassivity he'd worn since they'd left the reception to thunderous applause had returned.

'Your father has done his part adequately for now. Our lawyers will meet in a few days to discuss the best way forward. When my input is needed, I'll provide it. *Your* role, on the other hand, is just beginning.'

Before she could reply, the door opened. Eva gaped at the large private jet standing mere feet away. Beside the steps, two pilots and two stewardesses waited.

Zaccheo exited and took her hand. The shocking electricity of his touch and the awareness in his eyes had her scrambling to release her fingers, but he held on, and walked her to his crew, who extended their congratulations.

Eva was grappling with their conversation when she stepped into the unspeakable luxury of the plane. To the right, a sunken entertainment area held a semicircular cream sofa and a separate set of club chairs with enough gadgets to keep even the most attention-deficient passenger happy. In a separate area a short flight of stairs away, there was a conference table with four chairs and a bar area off a top-line galley.

Zaccheo stepped behind her and her body zapped to life, thrilling to his proximity. She suppressed a shiver when he let go of her fingers and cupped her shoulders in his warm hands.

'I have several conference calls to make once we take off. And you...' He paused, traced a thumb across her cheek. The contact stunned her, as did the gentle look in his eyes. 'You look worn out.'

'Is that a kind way of saying I look like hell?' She strove for a light tone and got a husky one instead.

That half-smile appeared, and Eva experienced something close to elation that the icy look had melted from his face. 'You could never look like hell, *cara*. A prickly and challenging puzzle that I look forward to unravelling, most definitely. But never like hell.'

The unexpected response startled her into gaping for several seconds before she recovered. 'Should I be wary that you're being nice to me?'

'I can be less…monstrous when I get my way.'

The reminder that he wouldn't be getting his way and the thought of his reaction once he found out brought a spike of anxiety, rendering her silent as he led her to a seat and handed her a flute of champagne from the stewardess's tray.

'Zaccheo…' She stopped when his thumb moved over her lips. Sensation sizzled along her nerve endings, setting her pulse racing as he brushed it back and forth. The heat erupting between her thighs had her pressing her legs together to soothe the desperate ache.

She hardly felt the plane take off. All she was aware of was the mesmerising look in Zaccheo's eyes.

'I haven't told you how stunning you look.' He leaned closer and replaced his thumb with his lips at the corner of her mouth.

Delicious flames warmed her blood. 'Thank you.' Her voice shook with the desire moving through her. More than anything, she was filled with the blind need to turn her head and meet his mouth with hers.

When his lips trailed to her jaw, then to the curve between her shoulder and neck, Eva let out a helpless moan, her heart racing with sudden, debilitating hunger.

His fingers linked hers and she found herself being led to the back of the plane. Eva couldn't summon a protest. Nor could she remind herself that she needed to come clean, sooner rather than later.

The master bedroom was equally stunning. Gold leaf threaded a thick cream coverlet on a king-sized bed and plush carpeting absorbed their footsteps as he shut the door.

'I intend us to have two uninterrupted weeks on the island. In order for that to happen, I need to work with Romeo to clear my plate work-wise. Rest now. Whatever's on your mind can wait for a few more hours.' Again there was no bite to his words, leaving her lost as to this new side of the man she'd married.

She stood, almost overpowered by the strength of her emotions, as he positioned himself behind her and slowly undid her buttons. The heavy dress pooled at her feet and she stood in only her white strapless bra, panties, and the garter and sheer stocking set that had accompanied her dress.

A rough, tortured sound echoed around the room. *'Stai mozzafiato,'* Zaccheo muttered thickly. 'You're breathtaking,' he translated when she glanced at him.

A fierce blush flared up. Eyes darkening, he circled her, tracing her high colour with a barest tip of his forefinger. Her gaze dropped to the sensual line of his mouth and she bit her own lip as need drowned her.

She gasped, completely enthralled, as he dropped to his knees and reached for her garter belt, eyes locked on hers. He pulled it off and tucked it deep in his inner pocket. When he stood, the hunger on his face stopped her breath, anticipation sparking like fireworks through her veins.

He lightly brushed her lips with his.

'Our first time won't be on a plane within listening distance of my staff.' He walked to the bed and pulled back the covers. He waited until she got in and tucked her in. About to walk away, he suddenly stopped. 'We will make this marriage work, Eva.'

Her mouth parted but, with no words to counter that unexpected vow, she slowly pressed her lips together as pain ripped through her.

'Sleep well, *dolcezza*,' he murmured, then left.

Despite her turmoil, she slept through the whole flight, rousing refreshed if unsettled as to what the future held.

Dressing in a light cotton sundress and open sandals, she left her hair loose, applied a touch of lip gloss and sunscreen and exited the plane.

They transferred from jet to high-speed boat with Romeo at the wheel. The noise from the engine made conversation impossible but, for the first time, the silence between Zaccheo and Eva felt less fraught. The strange but intense feeling that had engulfed them both as he'd undressed her on the plane continued to grip them as they raced towards their final destination. When she caught her hair for the umpteenth time to keep it from flying in the wind, he captured the strands in a tight grip at the base of her neck, then used the hold to pull her closer until she curved into his side. With his other arm sprawled along the back of their seat, he appeared the most at ease Eva had ever seen him.

Perhaps being forced to wait for a while to tell him hadn't been a bad thing.

She let the tension ooze out of her.

Despite the shades covering his eyes, he must have sensed her scrutiny, because he turned and stared down at her for endless minutes. She felt the power of that look to the tips of her toes and almost fell into him when he took her mouth in a voracious kiss.

He let her up for air when her lungs threatened to burst. Burying his face in her throat, he rasped for her ears only, 'I cannot wait to make you mine.'

By the time the boat slowed and pulled into a quiet inlet, Eva was a nervous wreck.

'Welcome to Casa do Paraíso,' he said once the engine died.

Enthralled, Eva looked around. Tropical trees and lush vegetation surrounded a spectacular hacienda made of timber and glass, the mid-morning sun casting vibrant shades of green, orange and blue on the breathtaking surroundings. Wide glass windows dominated the structure and, through them, Eva saw white walls and white furniture with splashes of colourful paintings on the walls perpetuated in an endless flow of rooms.

'It's huge,' she blurted.

Zaccheo jumped onto the sugary sand and grabbed her hand.

'The previous owner built it for his first wife and their eight children. She got it in the divorce, but hated the tropical heat so never visited. It was run-down by the time I bought the island from her, so I made substantial alterations.'

The mention of children ramped up the tension crawling through her belly and, despite her trying to shrug the feeling away, it lingered as she followed him up the wide front porch into the stunning living room.

A staff of four greeted them, then hurried out to where Romeo was securing the vessel. She gazed around in stunned awe, accepting that Zaccheo commanded the best when it came to the structures he put his stamp on, whether commercial or private.

'Come here, Eva.' The order was impatient.

She turned from admiring the structure to admire the man who'd created it. Tall, proud and intensely captivating, he stood at the base of a suspended staircase, his white-hot gaze gleaming dangerously, promising complete sexual oblivion.

Desire pulsed between them, a living thing that writhed, consumed with a hunger that demanded to be met, fulfilled.

Eva knew she should make time now they were here to tell him. Lay down the truth ticking away inside her like a bomb.

After years of struggling to forge a relationship with her father and sister, she'd finally laid the foundations of one today.

How could she live with herself if she continued to keep Zaccheo in the dark about the family he hoped for himself?

Her feet slapped against the large square tiles as she hurried across the room. His mouth lifted in a half-smile of satisfaction. She'd barely reached him when he swung her into his arms and stormed up the stairs.

And then the need to disclose her secret was suddenly no longer urgent. It'd been superseded by another, more pressing demand. One that every atom in her body urged her to assuage. *Now*. Before the opportunity was taken from her. Before her confession once again found her in the brutal wasteland of rejection.

His heat singed where they touched. Unable to resist, she sank her fingers into his hair and buried her face in his neck, eager to be closer to his rough primitiveness.

Feeling bold, she nipped at his skin.

His responding growl was intoxicating. As was the feeling of being pressed against the hard, masculine planes of his body when he slowly lowered her to her feet.

'I've waited so long to be inside you. I won't wait any longer,' he vowed, the words fierce, stamped with decadent intent.

Arms clamped around her waist, he walked her backwards to the vast white-sheeted bed. In one clean move, he pulled her dress over her head and dropped it. Her bra and panties swiftly followed.

Zaccheo stopped breathing as he stared down at her exposed curves.

As he'd done on the plane, he circled her body, this time trailing more fingers over her heated skin, creating a fiery path that arrowed straight between her thighs. She was swaying under the dizzying force of her arousal by the time he faced her again.

'Beautiful. So beautiful,' he murmured against her skin, then pulled her nipple into his mouth, surrounding the aching bud with heat and want.

Eva cried out and clutched his shoulders, her whole body gripped with a fever that shook her from head to toe. He moved his attention to her twin breast while his fingers teased the other, doubling the pleasure, doubling her agony.

'Zaccheo,' she groaned.

He straightened abruptly and reefed his black T-shirt over his head, exposing hard, smooth pecs and a muscle-ridged stomach. But as intensely delectable as his torso was, it wasn't what made her belly quiver. It was the intriguing tattooed band of Celtic knots linked by three slim lines that circled his upper arm. The artwork was flawless and beautiful, flowing gracefully when he moved. Reaching out, she touched the first knot. He paused and stared down at her.

It struck her hard in that moment just how much she didn't know about the man she'd married.

'You seem almost nervous, *dolcezza*.'

Eva struggled to think of a response that wouldn't make her sound gauche. 'Don't you feel nervous, even a little, your first time with a new lover?' she replied.

He froze and his lips compressed for a fraction of a second, as if she'd said something to displease him. Then his fingers went to his belt. 'Nerves, no. Anticipation that a long-held desire is about to be fulfilled? Most definitely.' He removed his remaining clothes in one swift move.

Perfection. It was the only word she could think of.

'Even when you've experienced it more than a few dozen times?'

She gasped when his fingers gripped hers in a tight hold. When he spoke, his voice held a bite that jarred. 'Perhaps we should refrain from the subject of past lovers.'

Hard, demanding lips slanted over hers, his tongue sliding into her mouth, fracturing the last of her senses. She clung to him, her body once again aflame from the ferocious power of his.

Cool sheets met her back and Zaccheo sprawled beside her. After an eternity of kissing, he raised his head.

'There are so many ways I wish to take you I don't know where to begin.'

Heat burst beneath her skin and he laughed softly.

'You blush with the ease of an innocent.' He trailed his hand down her throat, lingering at her racing pulse, before it curved around one breast. 'It's almost enough to make me forget that you're not.' Again that bite, but less ferocious this time, his accent growing thicker as he bent his head and tongued her pulse.

She jerked against him, her fingers gliding over his warm skin of their own accord. 'On what basis do you form the opinion that I'm not?' she blurted before she lost her nerve.

He stilled, grey eyes turning that rare gunmetal shade that announced a dangerously heightened emotional state. His hand abandoned her breast and curled around her nape in an iron grip. 'What are you saying, Eva?' His voice was a hoarse rumble.

She licked nervous lips. 'That I don't want to be treated like I'm fragile…but I don't wish my first time to be without mercy either.'

He sucked in a stunned breath. 'Your *first… Madre di Dio.*' His gaze searched hers, his breathing growing increasingly erratic.

Slowly, he drew back from her, scouring her body from head to toe as if seeing her for the first time. He parted her thighs and she moved restlessly, helplessly, as his eyes lingered at her centre. Stilling her with one hand, he lowered his head and kissed her eyes, her mouth, her throat. Then lower until he reached her belly. He licked at her navel, then rained kisses on her quivering skin. Firm hands held her open, then his shoulders took over the job. Reading his intention, she raised her head from the pillow.

'Zaccheo.' She wasn't sure whether she was pleading for or rejecting what was coming.

He reared up for a second, his hands going to his hair to twist the long strands into an expert knot at the back of his head. The act was so unbelievably hot, her body threatened to melt into a useless puddle. Then he was back, broad shoulders easily holding her legs apart as he kissed his way down her inner thighs.

'I know what I crave most,' he muttered thickly. 'A taste of you.'

The first touch of his mouth at her core elicited a long, helpless groan from her. Her spine arched off the bed, her thighs shaking as fire roared through her body. He held her down and feasted on her, the varying friction from his mouth and beard adding an almost unholy pleasure that sent her soaring until a scream ripped from her throat and she fell off the edge of the universe.

She surfaced to feel his mouth on her belly, his hands trailing up her sides. That gunmetal shade of grey reflected deep possession as he rose above her and kissed her long and deep.

'Now, *il mio angelo*. Now I make you mine.'

He captured her hands above her head with one hand. The other reached between her thighs, gently massaging her core before he slid one finger inside her tight sheath. His groan echoed hers. Removing his finger, he probed her sex with his thick shaft, murmuring soft, soothing words as he pushed himself inside her.

'Easy, *dolcezza*.'

Another inch increased the burn, but the hunger rushing through her wouldn't be denied. Her fingers dug into his back, making him growl. 'Zaccheo, please.'

'*Sì*, let me please you.' He uttered a word that sounded like an apology, a plea.

Then he pushed inside her. The dart of pain engulfed her, lingered for a moment. Tears filled her eyes. Zaccheo cursed, then kissed them away, murmuring softly in Italian.

He thrust deeper, slowly filling her. Eva saw the strain etched on his face.

'Zaccheo?'

'I want this to be perfect for you.'

'It won't be unless you move, I suspect.'

That half-smile twitched, then stretched into a full, heart-stopping smile. Eva's eyes widened at the giddy dance her heart performed on seeing the wave of pleasure transform his face. Her own mouth curved in response and a feeling unfurled inside her, stealing her breath with its awesome power. Shakily, she raised her hand and touched his face, slid her fingers over his sensual mouth.

He moved. Withdrew and thrust again.

She gasped, her body caught in a maelstrom of sensation so turbulent, she feared she wouldn't emerge whole.

Slowly his smile disappeared, replaced by a wild, predatory hunger. He quickened the pace and her hands moved to his hair, slipping the knot free and burying her fingers in the thick, luxurious tresses. When her hips moved of their own accord, meeting him in an instinctive dance, he groaned deep and sucked one nipple into his mouth. Drowning in sensation, she felt her world begin to crumble. The moment he captured her twin nipple, a deep tremor started inside her. It built and built, then exploded in a shower of lights.

'*Perfetto.*'

Zaccheo sank his fingers into Eva's wild, silky hair, curbing the desire to let loose the primitive roar bubbling within him.

Mine. Finally, completely mine.

Instead he held her close until her breathing started to return to normal, then he flipped their positions and arranged her on top of him.

He was hard to the point of bursting, but he was determined to make this experience unforgettable for her. Seeing his ring on her finger, that primitive response rose again, stunning him with the strength of his desire to claim her.

His words on the plane slashed through his mind.

Sì, he *did* want this to work. Perhaps Eva had been right. Perhaps there was still time to salvage a piece of his soul…

Her eyes met his and a sensual smile curled her luscious mouth. Before he could instruct her, she moved, taking him deeper inside her before she rose. Knowing he was fast losing the ability to think, he met her second thrust. Her eyes widened, her skin flushing that alluring shade of pink as she chased the heady sensation. Within minutes, they were both panting.

Reaching down, he teased her with his thumb and watched

her erupt in bliss. Zaccheo followed her, his shout announcing the most ferocious release he'd experienced in his life.

Long after Eva had collapsed on top of him, and slipped
into an exhausted sleep, he lay awake.

Wondering why his world hadn't righted itself.

Wondering what the hell this meant for him.

CHAPTER TWELVE

Eva came awake to find herself splayed on top of Zaccheo's body.

The sun remained high in the sky so she knew she hadn't slept for more than an hour or two. Nevertheless, the thought that she'd dropped into a coma straight after sex made her cringe.

She risked a glance and found grey eyes examining her with that half-smile she was growing to like a little more than she deemed wise.

He brushed a curl from her cheek and tucked it behind her ear. The gentleness in the act fractured her breathing.

'*Ciao, dolcezza.*'

'I didn't mean to fall asleep on you,' she said, then immediately felt gauche for not knowing the right after-sex etiquette.

He quirked a brow. 'Oh? Who did you mean to fall asleep on?' he asked.

She jerked up. 'No, that's not what I meant...' she started to protest, then stopped when she saw the teasing light in his eyes.

She started to settle back down, caught a glimpse of his chiselled pecs and immediately heat built inside her. A little wary of how quickly she was growing addicted to his body, she attempted to slide off him.

He stopped her with one hand at her nape, the other on her hip. The action flexed his arm and Eva's gaze was drawn to the tattoo banding his upper arm.

'Does this have a special meaning?'

His smile grew a little stiffer. 'It's a reminder not to accept less than I'm worth or compromise on what's important to me. And a reminder that, contrary to what the privileged would have us believe, all men are born equal. It's power that is wielded unequally.'

Eva thought of the circumstances that had brought her to this place, of the failings of her own family and the sadness she'd carried for so long, but now hoped to let go of.

'You wield more than enough share of power. Men cower before you.'

A frown twitched his forehead. 'If they do, it is their weakness, not mine.'

She gave an incredulous laugh. 'Are you saying you don't know you intimidate people with just a glance?'

His frown cleared. 'You're immune to this intimidation you speak of. To my memory, you've been disagreeable more often than not.'

She traced the outline of the tattoo, revelling in the smooth warmth of his skin. 'I've never been good at heeding bellowed commands.'

The hand on her hip tightened. 'I do not bellow.'

'Maybe not. But sometimes the effect is the same.'

She found herself flipped over onto her back, Zaccheo crouched over her like a lethal bird of prey. 'Is that why you hesitated as you walked down the aisle?' he asked in a harsh whisper. The look in his eyes was one of almost…hurt.

Quickly she shook her head. 'No, it wasn't.'

'Then what was it? You thought that I wasn't good enough, perhaps?' he pressed. And again she glimpsed a hint of vulnerability in his eyes that caught at a weak place in her heart.

She opened her mouth to *finally* tell him. To lay herself bare to the scathing rejection that would surely follow her confession.

The words stuck in her throat.

What she'd experienced in Zaccheo's bed had given her a taste that was unlike anything she'd ever felt before. The need to hold on to that for just a little while longer slammed into her, knocking aside her good intentions.

Eva knew she was playing with volcanic fire, that the eventual eruption would be devastating. But for once in her life, she wanted to be selfish, to experience a few moments of unfettered abandon. She could have that.

She'd sacrificed herself for this marriage, but in doing so she'd also been handed a say in when it ended.

And it would be sooner rather than later, because she couldn't stand in the way of what he wanted...what he'd been deprived of his whole life...a proper family of his own.

She also knew Zaccheo would want nothing to do with her once he knew the truth. Sure, he wasn't as monstrous as he would have others believe, but that didn't mean he would shackle himself to a wife who couldn't give him what he wanted.

She squashed the voice that cautioned she was naively burying her head in the sand.

Was it really so wrong if she chose to do it just for a little while?

Could she not live in bliss for a few days? Gather whatever memories she could and hang on to them for when the going got tough?

'Eva?'

'I had a father-daughter moment, plus bridal nerves,' she blurted. He raised a sceptical eyebrow and she smiled. 'Every woman is entitled to have a moment. Mine was thirty seconds of hesitation.'

'You remained frozen for five *minutes*,' he countered.

'Just time enough for anyone who'd been dozing off to wake up,' she responded, wide-eyed.

The tension slowly eased out of his body and his crooked smile returned. Relief poured through her and she fell into the punishing kiss he delivered to assert his displeasure at her hesitation.

She was clinging to him by the time he pulled away, and Eva was ready to protest when he swung out of bed. Her protest died when she got her first glimpse of his impressive manhood, and the full effect of the man attached to it.

Dry-mouthed and heart racing, she stared. And curled her fingers into the sheets to keep from reaching for him.

'If you keep looking at me like that, our shower will have to be postponed. And our lunch will go cold.'

A blush stormed up her face.

He laughed and scooped her up. 'But I'm glad that my body is not displeasing to you.'

She rolled her eyes. *As if.* 'False humility isn't an attractive trait, Zaccheo,' she chided as he walked them through a wide door and onto an outdoor bamboo-floored shower. Despite the rustic effects, the amenities were of the highest quality, an extra-wide marble bath sitting opposite a multi-jet shower, with a shelf holding rows upon rows of luxury bath oils and gels.

Above their heads, a group of macaws warbled throatily, then flew from one tree to the next, their stunning colours streaking through the branches.

As tropical paradises went, Eva was already sure this couldn't be topped, and she had yet to see the rest of it.

Zaccheo set her down and grabbed a soft washcloth. 'Complete compatibility in bed isn't a common thing, despite what magazines would have you believe,' he said.

'I wouldn't know.' There was no point pretending otherwise. He had first-hand knowledge of her innocence.

His eyes flared with possession as he turned on the jets and pulled her close.

'No, you wouldn't. And if that knowledge pleases me to the point of being labelled a caveman, then so be it.'

They ate a sumptuous lunch of locally caught fish served with pine-nut sauce and avocado salad followed by a serving of fruit and cheeses.

After lunch, Zaccheo showed her the rest of the house and the three-square-kilometre island. They finished the trek on the white sandy beach where a picnic had been laid out with champagne chilling in a silver bucket.

Eva popped a piece of papaya in her mouth and sighed at the beauty of the setting sun casting orange and purple streaks across the aquamarine water. 'I don't know how you can ever bear to leave this place.'

'I learned not to grow attached to things at an early age.'

The crisp reply had her glancing over at him. His shades were back in place so she couldn't read his eyes, but his body showed no signs of the usual forbidding *do not disturb* signs so she braved the question. 'Why?'

'Because it was better that way.'

She toyed with the stem of her champagne flute. 'But it's also a lonely existence.'

Broad shoulders lifted in an easy shrug. 'I had a choice of being lonely or just…solitary. I chose the latter.'

Her heart lurched at the deliberate absence of emotion from his voice. 'Zaccheo—'

He reared up from where he'd been lounging on his elbows, his mouth set in a grim line. 'Don't waste your time feeling sorry for me, *dolcezza*,' he said, his voice a hard snap that would've intimidated her, had she allowed it.

'I wasn't,' she replied. 'I'm not naive enough to imagine everyone has a rosy childhood. I know I didn't.'

'You mean the exclusive country-club memberships, the top boarding schools, the winters in Verbier weren't enough?' Despite the lack of contempt in his voice this time round, Eva felt sad that they were back in this place again.

'Don't twist my words. Those were just *things*, Zaccheo. And before you accuse me of being privileged, yes, I was. My childhood was hard, too, but I couldn't help the family I was born into any more than you could.'

'Was that why you moved out of Pennington Manor?'

'After my mother died, yes. Two against one became unbearable.'

'And the father-daughter moment you spoke of? Did that help?' he asked, watching her with a probing look.

A tiny bit of hope blossomed. 'Time will tell, I guess. Will you try the same with your mother and stepfather?'

'No. My mother didn't think I was worth anything. My stepfather agreed.'

Her heart twisted. 'Yet you've achieved success beyond most people's wildest dreams. Surely the lessons of your childhood should make you proud of who you are now, despite hating some aspects of your upbringing?'

'I detested all of mine,' he said with harsh finality. 'I wouldn't wish it on my worst enemy.'

The savage edge of pain in his voice made her shiver. She opened her mouth to ask him, but he surged to his feet.

'I don't wish to dwell in the past.' That half-smile flashed on and off. 'Not when I have a sunset as stunning as this and a wife to rival its beauty.' He plucked the glass from her hand and pulled her up.

Tucking her head beneath his chin, he enfolded her in his arms, one around her waist and the other across her shoulders. Eva knew it was a signal to drop the subject, but she couldn't let it go. Not just yet.

She removed his shades and stared into his slate-coloured eyes. 'For what it's worth, I gave away my country-club membership to my best friend, I hated boarding school, and I couldn't ski to save my life so I didn't even try after I turned ten. I didn't care about my pedigree, or who I was seen with. Singing and a family who cared for me were the only things that mattered. One helped me get through the other. So, you see, sometimes the grass *may* look greener on the other side, but most of the time it's just a trick of the light.'

Several emotions shifted within his eyes. Surprise. Shock. A hint of confusion. Then the deep arrogance of Zaccheo Giordano slid back into place.

'The sunset, *dolcezza*,' he said gruffly. 'You're missing it.'

* * *

The feeling of his world tilting out of control was escalating. And it spun harder out of sync the more he fought it.

Zaccheo had been certain he knew what drove Eva and her family. He'd been sure it was the same greed for power and prestige that had sent his father to a vicious and premature death. It was what had made his mother abandon her homeland to seek a rich husband, turn herself inside out for a man who looked down his nose at her son and ultimately made Clara Giordano pack her bags and move to the other side of the world.

But right from the start Eva had challenged him, forced him to confront his long-held beliefs. He hadn't needed to, of course. Oscar Pennington's actions had proven him right. Eva's own willingness to marry Fairfield for the sake of her family had cemented Zaccheo's belief.

And didn't you do the same thing?

He stared unseeing at the vivid orange horizon, his thoughts in turmoil.

He couldn't deny that the discovery of her innocence in bed had thrown him for a loop. Unsettled him in a way he hadn't been for a long time.

For as long as he could remember, his goal had been a fixed, tangible certainty. To place himself in a position where he erased any hint of neediness from his life, while delivering an abject lesson to those who thought themselves entitled and therefore could treat him as if he were common. A spineless fool who would prostrate himself for scraps from the high table.

He'd proven conclusively yesterday at his wedding reception that he'd succeeded beyond his wildest dreams. He'd watched blue-blooded aristocrats fall over themselves to win his favour.

And yet he'd found himself unsatisfied. Left with a hollow, bewildering feeling inside, as if he'd finally grasped the brass ring, only to find it was made of plastic.

It had left Zaccheo with the bitter introspection of whether a different, deeper goal lay behind the burning need to prove himself above the petty grasp for power and prestige.

The loneliness he'd so offhandedly dismissed had in fact eaten away at him far more effectively than his mother's rejection and the callous disregard his father had afforded him when he was alive.

Impatiently, he dismissed his jumbled feelings. He didn't do *feelings*. He *achieved*. He *bested*. And he *triumphed*.

One miscalculation didn't mean a setback. Finding out Eva had had no previous lovers had granted him an almost primitive satisfaction he wasn't going to bother to deny.

And if something came of this union sooner rather than later... His heart kicked hard.

Sliding a hand through her silky hair, he angled her face to his. Her beauty was undeniable. But he wouldn't be risking any more heart-to-hearts. She was getting too close, sliding under his skin to a place he preferred to keep out of bounds. A place he'd only examined when the cold damp of his prison cell had eroded his guard.

He was free, both physically and in guilt. He wouldn't return to that place. And he wouldn't allow her to probe further. Satisfied with his resolution, he kissed her sexy, tempting mouth until the need to breathe forced him to stop.

The sun had disappeared. Lights strung through the trees flickered on and he nodded to the member of staff who hovered nearby, ready to pack up their picnic.

He caught the glazed, flushed look on his wife's face and came to a sudden, extremely pleasing decision.

'Tonight, *il mio angelo*, we'll have an early night.'

The first week flew by in a dizzy haze of sun, sea, exquisite food, and making love. Lots and lots of making love.

Zaccheo was a fierce and demanding lover, but he gave so much more in return. And Eva was so greedy for everything he had to give, she wondered whether she was turning into a sex addict. She'd certainly acted like one this morning, when she'd initiated sex while Zaccheo had been barely awake. That her initiative had seemed to please him had been beside the point.

She'd examined her behaviour afterwards when Zaccheo had been summoned to an urgent phone call by Romeo.

This was supposed to be a moment out of time, a brief dalliance, which would end the moment she spilled her secret to him. And yet with each surrender of her body, she slid down a steeper slope, one she suspected would be difficult to climb back up. Because it turned out that, for her, sex wasn't a simple exchange of physical pleasure. With each act, she handed over a piece of herself to him that she feared she'd never reclaim.

And that more than anything made her fear for herself when this was over.

A breeze blew through an open window and Eva clutched the thin sarong she'd thrown over her bikini. Dark clouds were forming ominously over the island. Shivering, she watched the storm gather, wondering if it was a premonition for her own situation.

Lightning flashed, and she jumped.

'Don't worry, Mrs Eva.' Zaccheo's housekeeper smiled as she entered and turned on table lamps around the living room. 'The storm passes very quickly. The sun will be back out in no time.'

Eva smiled and nodded, but she couldn't shake the feeling that *her* storm wouldn't pass so quickly.

As intense rain pounded the roof she went in search of Zaccheo. Not finding him in his study, she climbed the stairs, her pulse already racing in anticipation as she went down the hallway.

She entered their dressing room and froze.

'What are you doing?' she blurted.

'I would've thought it was obvious, *dolcezza*.' He held clippers inches from his face.

'I can see what you're doing but...*why*?' she snapped. 'You already got rid of most of it for the wedding.' Her voice was clipped, a feeling she couldn't decipher moving through her.

Zaccheo raised an eyebrow, amusement mingled with something else as he watched her. 'I take it this look works for you?'

She swallowed twice before she could speak. When she finally deciphered the feeling coursing through her, she was so shocked and so afraid he would read her feelings, she glanced over his head.

'Yes. I prefer it,' she replied.

For several seconds he didn't speak. Her skin burned at his compelling stare. Schooling her features, she glanced into his eyes.

'Then it will remain untouched.' He set the clippers down and faced her.

Neither of them moved for several minutes. The storm raged outside, beating against the windows and causing the timber to creak.

'Come here, Eva.' Softly spoken, but a command nonetheless.

'I'm beginning to think those are your three favourite words.'

'They are only when you comply.'

She rolled her eyes, but moved towards him. He swivelled in his chair and pulled her closer, parting his thighs to situate her between them.

'Was that very hard to admit?' he rasped.

Her skin grew tight, awareness that she stood on a precipice whose depths she couldn't quite fathom shivering over her. 'No.'

He laughed. 'You're a pathetic liar. But I appreciate you finding the courage to ask for what you want.'

'An insult and a compliment?' she said lightly.

'I wouldn't want you to think me soft.' He caught her hands and placed them on his shoulders. 'You realise that

I'll require a reward for keeping myself this way for your pleasure?'

The way he mouthed *pleasure* made hot need sting between her thighs. Several weeks ago, she would've fought it. But Eva was fast learning it was no use. Her body was his slave to command as and when he wished. 'You got your stylists to prod and primp me into the image you wanted. I've earned the right to do the same to you.' Her fingers curled into the hair she would've wept to see shorn.

He smiled and relaxed in the chair. 'I thought being primped and plucked to perfection was every woman's wish?'

'You thought wrong. I was happy with the way I looked before.'

That wasn't exactly true. Although she'd loved her thick and wild hair, she had to admit it was much easier to tend now the wildness had been tamed a little. And she loved that she could brush the tresses without giving herself a headache. As for the luxurious body creams she'd been provided with, she marvelled at how soft and silky her skin felt now compared to before.

But she kept all of it to herself as he untied the knot in her sarong and let it fall away. 'You were perfect before. You're perfect now. And mine,' he breathed.

Within seconds, Eva was naked and craving what only he could give her, her eventual screams as loud as the storm raging outside.

CHAPTER THIRTEEN

'COME ON, we're taking the boat out today. As much as I'd like to keep you to myself, I think we need to see something of Rio before we leave tomorrow.'

Eva stopped tweaking the chorus of the melody she'd been composing and looked up as Zaccheo entered the living room.

The perverse hope that he would grow less breathtaking with each day was hopelessly thwarted. Dressed in khaki linen trousers and a tight white T-shirt with his hair loose around his shoulders, Zaccheo was so visually captivating, she felt the punch to her system each time she stared at him.

He noticed her staring and raised an eyebrow. Blushing, she averted her gaze to her tablet.

'Where are we going?' She tried for a light tone and breathed an inward sigh of relief when she succeeded.

'To Ilha São Gabriel, three islands away. It's a tourist hotspot, but there are some interesting sights to see there.' He crouched before her, his gaze going to the tablet. Reaching out, he scrolled through her compositions, his eyes widening at the three dozen songs contained in the file.

'You wrote all these?' he asked.

She nodded, feeling self-conscious as he paused at a particularly soul-baring ballad about unrequited love and rejection. She'd written that one a week after Zaccheo had gone to prison. 'I've been composing since I was sixteen.'

His eyes narrowed on her face. 'You've had two million pounds in your bank account for over a year and a half, which I'm guessing is your shareholder dividend from your father's deal on my building?'

Warily, she nodded.

'That would've been more than enough money to pursue your music career without needing to work. So why didn't you use it?' he queried.

She tried to shrug the question away, but he caught her chin in his hand. 'Tell me,' he said.

'I suspected deep down that the deal was tainted. I hated doubting my father's integrity, but I could never bring myself to use the money. It didn't feel right.' Being proved right had brought nothing but hurt.

He watched her for a long time, a puzzled look on his face before he finally nodded. 'How was your session with Ziggy Preston?' he asked.

She saw nothing of the sour expression he'd sported that night in the club. 'Surprisingly good, considering I'd thought he'd have me on the blacklist of every music producer after your behaviour.'

An arrogant smile stretched his lips. 'They'd have had to answer to me had they chosen that unfortunate path. You're seeing him again?'

She nodded. 'When we get back.'

'Bene.' He rose and held out his hand.

She slipped her feet into one of the many stylish sandals now gracing her wardrobe and he led her outside to the jetty.

Climbing on board, he placed her in front of the wheel and stood behind her. She looked around, expecting Zaccheo's right-hand man to be travelling with them. 'Isn't Romeo coming?'

'He had business to take care of in Rio. He'll meet us there.'

The trip took twenty-five minutes, and Eva understood why the Ilha São Gabriel was so popular when she saw it. The island held a mountain, on top of which a smaller version of the Cristo Redentor in Rio had been erected. Beneath the statue, bars, restaurants, parks and churches flowed right down to the edge of a mile-long beach.

Zaccheo directed her to motor past the busy beach and round the island to a quieter quay where they moored the boat. 'We're starting our tour up there.' He pointed to a quaint little building set into the side of a hill about a quarter of a mile up a steep path.

She nodded and started to walk up when she noticed Romeo a short distance away. He nodded a greeting but didn't join them as they headed up. The other man's watchfulness made Eva frown.

'Something on your mind?' Zaccheo asked.

'I was just wondering...what's the deal with Romeo?'

'He's many things.'

'That's not really an answer.'

Zaccheo shrugged. 'We work together, but I guess he's a confidant.'

'How long have you known him?'

When Zaccheo pulled his shades from the V of his T-shirt and placed them on, she wondered whether she'd strayed into forbidden territory. But he answered, 'We met when I was thirteen years old.'

Her eyes rounded in surprise. 'In London?'

'In Palermo.'

'So he's your oldest friend?'

Zaccheo hesitated for a second. 'Our relationship is complicated. Romeo sees himself as my protector. A role I've tried to dissuade him from to no avail.'

Her heart caught. 'Protector from what?'

His mouth twitched. 'He seems to think you're a handful that he needs to keep an eye on.'

She looked over her shoulder at the quiet, brooding man.

'My father worked for his father,' he finally answered.

'In what capacity?'

'As whatever he wanted him to be. My father didn't discriminate as long as he was recognised for doing the job. He would do anything from carrying out the trash to kneecap-

ping a rival gang's members to claiming another man's bastard child so his boss didn't have to. No job was too small
or large,' he said with dry bitterness.

The blood drained from her face. 'Your father worked
for the *Mafia*?'

His jaw clenched before he jerked out a nod. 'Romeo's
father was a *don* and my father one of his minions. His role
was little more than drudge work, but he acted as if he was
serving the Pope himself.'

She glanced over her shoulder at Romeo, her stomach
dredging with intense emotions she recognised as anguish—
even without knowing what Zaccheo was about to divulge.

'That bastard child you mentioned...'

He nodded. 'Romeo. His father had an affair with one of
his many mistresses. His mother kept him until he became
too much of a burden. When he was thirteen, she dumped
him on his father. He didn't want the child, so he asked my
father to *dispose* of him. My father, eager to attain recognition at all costs, brought the child home to my mother. She
refused but my father wouldn't budge. They fought every
day for a month until she ended up in hospital. It turned out
she was pregnant. After that she became even more adamant
about having another woman's child under her roof. When
she lost her baby, she blamed my father and threatened to
leave. My father, probably for the only time in his life, decided to place someone else's needs above his ambition. He
tried to return Romeo to his father, who took grave offence.
He had my father beaten to death. And I...' his face tightened
'...I went from having a friend, a mother and father, and a
brother or sister on the way, to having nothing.'

Eva frowned. 'But your mother—'

'Had hated being the wife of a mere gofer. My father's
death bought her the fresh start she craved, but she had to
contend with a child who reminded her of a past she detested.
She moved to England a month after he died and married a

man who hated the sight of me, who judged me because of who my father was and believed my common blood was an affront to his distinguished name.' The words were snapped out in a staccato narrative, but she felt the anguished intensity behind them.

Eva swallowed hard. Stepping close, she laid her head on his chest. 'I'm so sorry, Zaccheo.'

His arms tightened around her for a heartbeat before he pulled away and carried on up the steps. 'I thought Romeo had died that night, too, until he found me six years ago.'

She glanced at Romeo and her heart twisted for the pain the unfortunate friends had gone through.

They continued up the hill in silence until they reached the building.

They entered the cool but dim interior and as her eyes adjusted to the dark she was confronted by a stunning collection of statues. Most were made of marble, but one or two were sculpted in white stone.

'Wow, these are magnificent.'

'A local artist sculpted all the patron saints and donated them to the island over fifty years ago.'

They drifted from statue to statue, each work more striking than the last. When they walked through an arch, he laced his fingers with hers. 'Come, I'll show you the most impressive one. According to the history, the artist sculpted them in one day.'

Smiling, she let him tug her forward. She gasped at the double-figured display of St Anne and St Gerard. 'Patron saints of motherhood and fertility…' She stopped reading as her heart dropped to her stomach.

Zaccheo traced a forefinger down her cheek. 'I can't wait to feel our child kick in your belly,' he murmured.

A vice gripped her heart, squeezed until it threatened to stop beating. 'Zaccheo—'

His finger stopped her. 'I meant what I said, Eva. We can make this work. And we may not have had the best of role models in parents, but we know which mistakes to avoid. That's a good basis for our children, *sì*?' he asked, his tone gentle, almost hopeful.

She opened her mouth, but no words formed. Because the truth she'd been hiding from suddenly reared up and slapped her in the face.

Zaccheo wanted children, not as a tool for revenge, but for himself. The man who'd known no love growing up wanted a family of his own.

And she'd led him on, letting him believe he could have it with her. The enormity of her actions rocked her to the core, robbing her of breath.

'Eva? What's wrong?' he asked with a frown.

She shook her head, her eyes darting frantically around the room.

'You're as pale as a ghost, *dolcezza*. Talk to me!'

Eva struggled to speak around the misery clogging her throat. 'I…I'm okay.'

His frown intensified. 'You don't look okay. Do you want to leave?'

She grasped the lifeline. 'Yes.'

'Okay, let's go.'

They emerged into bright sunlight. Eva took a deep breath, which did absolutely nothing to restore the chaos fracturing her mind.

The urge to confess *now*, spill her secret right then and there, powered through her. But it was neither the time nor the place. A group of tourist students had entered the room and the place was getting busier by the second.

Zaccheo led her down the steps. He didn't speak, but his concerned gaze probed her.

The island seemed twice as crowded by the time they descended the hill. The midday sun blazed high and sweat trickled down her neck as they navigated human traffic on the main promenade. When Zaccheo steered her to a restaurant advertising fresh seafood, Eva didn't complain.

Samba music blared from the speakers, thankfully negating the need for conversation. Sadly it didn't free her from her thoughts, not even when, after ordering their food, Zaccheo moved his chair closer, tugged her into his side and trailed his hand soothingly through her hair.

It was their last day in Rio. Possibly their last as husband and wife. Her soul mourned what she shouldn't have craved.

Unbearable agony ripped through her. She'd been living in a fool's paradise. Especially since she'd told herself it wouldn't matter how much time passed without her telling Zaccheo.

It mattered very much. She'd heard his pain when he'd recounted his bleak childhood. With each day that had passed without her telling him she couldn't help him realise his dream, she'd eroded any hope that he would understand why she'd kept her secret from him.

A moan ripped from her throat and she swayed in her seat. Zaccheo tilted her face to his and she read the worry in his eyes.

'Do you feel better?'

'Yes, much better.'

'*Bene*, then perhaps you'd like to tell me what's going on?' he asked.

She jerked away, her heart hammering. 'I got a little lightheaded, that's all.'

His frown returned and Eva held her breath. She was saved when Romeo entered. 'Everything all right?' he asked.

Romeo's glance darted to her. The knowledge in his eyes froze her insides, but he said nothing, directing his gaze back to his friend.

Zaccheo nodded. '*Sì*. We'll see you back at Paraíso.'

The moment he left, Zaccheo lowered his head and kissed her, not the hungry devouring that tended to overtake them whenever they were this close, but a gentle, reverent kiss.

In that moment, Eva knew she'd fallen in love with him.

And that she would lose the will to live the moment she walked away from him.

Their food arrived and they ate. She refused coffee and the slice of *chocotorta* the waiter temptingly offered. Zaccheo ordered an espresso, shooting her another concerned glance. Praying he wouldn't press her to reveal what was wrong just yet, she laid her head on his shoulder and buried her face in his throat, selfishly relishing the moment. She would never get a moment like this once they returned to Casa do Paraíso. He placed a gentle kiss on her forehead and agony moved through her like a living entity.

You brought this on yourself. No use crying now.

She started as the group they'd met on their exit from the museum entered the restaurant. Within minutes, someone had started the karaoke machine. The first attempt, sung atrociously to loud jeers, finished as the waiter returned with Zaccheo's espresso.

Eva straightened in her seat, watching the group absently as each member refused to take the mic. The leader cast his eyes around the room, met Eva's gaze and made a beeline for her.

'No.' She shook her head when he reached her and offered the mic.

He clasped his hands together. *'Por favor,'* he pleaded.

She opened her mouth to refuse, then found herself swallowing her rebuttal. She glanced at Zaccheo. He regarded her steadily, his face impassive. And yet she sensed something behind his eyes, as if he didn't know what to make of her mood.

She searched his face harder, wanting him to say something, *anything*, that would give her even the tiniest hope that what she had to tell him wouldn't break the magic they'd found on his island. Wouldn't break *her*.

In a way it was worse when he offered her that half-smile. Recently his half-smiles had grown genuine, were often a precursor to the blinding smiles that stole her breath…made her heart swell to bursting.

The thought that they would soon become a thing of the past had her surging to her feet, blindly striding for the stage to a round of applause she didn't want.

All Eva wanted in that moment was to drown in the oblivion of music.

She searched through the selection until she found a song she knew by heart, one that had spoken to her the moment she'd heard it on the radio.

She sang the first verse with her eyes shut, yearning for the impossible. She opened her eyes for the second verse. She could never tell Zaccheo how she felt about him, but she could sing it to him. Her eyes found his as she sang the last line.

His gaze grew hot. Intense. Her pulse hammered as she sang the third verse, offering her heart, her life to him, all the while knowing he would reject it once he knew.

She stifled a sob as the machine clicked to an end. She started to step off the stage, but the group begged for another song.

Zaccheo rose and moved towards her. They stared at each other as the clamouring grew louder. Her breath caught when the emotion in his eyes altered, morphing into that darker hue that held a deeper meaning.

He wasn't angry. Or ruthlessly commanding her to bend to his will. Or even bitter and hurt, as he'd been on the hill.

There was none of that in his expression. This ferocity was different, one that made her world stop.

Until she shook herself back to reality. She was grasping at straws, stalling with excuses and foolish, reckless hope. She might have fallen in love with Zaccheo, but nothing he'd said or done had indicated he returned even an iota of what she felt. Their relationship had changed from what it'd been in the beginning, but she couldn't lose sight of *why* it'd begun in the first place. Or why she couldn't let it continue.

Heavy-hearted, she turned back to the machine. She'd seen the song earlier and bypassed it, because she hadn't been ready to say goodbye.

But it was time to end this. Time to accept that there was no hope.

Something was wrong. It'd been since they'd walked down the hill.

But for once in his life, he was afraid to confront a problem head-on because he was terrified the results would be unwelcome. So he played worst-case scenarios in his head.

Had he said or done something to incite this troubled look on Eva's face? Had his confession on the hill reminded her that he wasn't the man she would've chosen for herself? A wave of something close to desolation rushed over him. He clenched his jaw against the feeling. Would it really be the end of the world if Eva decided she didn't want him? The affirmative answer echoing through him made him swallow hard.

He discarded that line of thought and chose another, dissecting each moment he'd spent with her this afternoon.

He'd laid himself bare, something he'd never done until recently. She hadn't shown pity or disgust for the debasing crimes his father had committed, or for the desperately lonely child he'd been. Yet again she'd only showed compassion. Pain for the toll his jagged upbringing had taken on him.

And the songs…what had they meant, especially the second one, the one about saying *goodbye*? He'd witnessed the agony in her eyes while she'd sung that one. As if her heart was broken—

A knock came at his study door, where he'd retreated to pace after they'd returned and Eva had expressed the need for a shower. Alone.

'Zaccheo?'

He steeled himself to turn around, hoping against hope that the look on her face would be different. That she would smile and everything would return to how it was before they'd gone on that blasted trip.

But it wasn't. And her next words ripped through him with the lethal effect of a vicious blade.

'Zaccheo, we need to talk.'

CHAPTER FOURTEEN

EVERY WORD SHE'D practised in the shower fled her head as Eva faced him. Of course, her muffled sobs had taken up a greater part of the shower so maybe she hadn't got as much practice in as she'd thought.

'I...' Her heart sank into her stomach when a forbidding look tightened his face. 'I can't stay married to you.'

For a moment he looked as if she'd punched him hard in the solar plexus, then ripped his heart out while he struggled to breathe. Gradually his face lost every trace of pain and distress. Hands shoved deep in his pockets, he strolled to where she stood, frozen inside the doorway.

'Was this your plan all along?' he bit out, his eyes arctic. 'To wait until I'd spoken on your father's behalf and he was safe from prosecution before you asked for a divorce?'

She gasped. 'You did that? When?' she asked, but his eyes poured scorn on her question.

'Is being married to me that abhorrent to you, Eva? So much so you couldn't even wait until we were back in London?'

'No! Believe me, Zaccheo, that's not it.'

'*Believe* you? Why should I? When you're not even prepared to give us a chance?' He veered sharply away from her and strode across the room, his fingers spiking through his hair before he reversed course and stopped in front of her once more. 'What I don't understand is why. Did I do something? Say something to make you think I wouldn't want this relationship to work?'

The confirmation that this marriage meant more to him was almost too hard to bear.

'Zaccheo, please listen to me. It's not you, it's—'

His harsh laughter echoed around the room. 'Are you *seriously* giving me that line?'

Her fists balled. 'For once in your life, just shut up and listen! I can't have children,' she blurted.

'You've already used that one, *dolcezza*, but you signed along the dotted line agreeing to my clause, remember? So try again.'

Misery quivered through her stomach. 'It's true I signed the agreement, but I lied to you. I *can't* have children, Zaccheo. I'm infertile.'

He sucked in a hoarse breath and reeled backwards on his heels. 'Excuse me?'

'I tried to tell you when I first saw the clause, but you wouldn't listen. You'd made up your mind that I'd use any excuse not to marry you because I didn't want you.'

The stunned look morphed into censure. 'Then you should've put me straight.'

'How? Would you have believed me if I'd told you about my condition? Without evidence to back it up? Or perhaps I should've told Romeo or your PA since they had more access to you than I did in the week before the wedding?'

He looked at her coldly. 'If your conscience stung you so deeply the first time round, why did you change your mind?'

Her emotions were raw enough for her to instinctively want to protect herself. But what did she have to lose? Zaccheo would condemn her actions regardless of whether she kept her innermost feelings to herself or not. And really, how much worse could this situation get? Her heart was already in shreds.

She met his gaze head on. 'You know I lost my mother to cancer when I was eighteen. She was diagnosed when I was sixteen. For two years we waited, hoping for the best, fearing the worst through each round of chemo. With each treatment that didn't work we knew her time was growing shorter. Knowing it was coming didn't make it any easier. Her death ripped me apart.' She stopped and gathered her courage. 'My father has been suffering stress attacks in the last couple of months.' She risked a glance and saw his brows clamped in a forbidding frown. 'He collapsed on Friday after you called to tell him the wedding was off.'

Zaccheo's mouth compressed, but a trace of compassion flashed through his eyes. 'And you blame me? Is that what this is all about?'

'No, I don't. We both know that the blame for our current circumstances lies firmly with my father.' She stopped and licked her lips. 'He may have brought this on himself, but the stress was killing him, Zaccheo. I've watched one parent die, helpless to do anything but watch them fade away. Condemn me all you want, but I wasn't going to stand by and let my father worry himself to death over what he'd done. And I didn't do it for my family name or my blasted *pedigree*. I did it because that's what you do for the people you love.'

'Even when they don't love you back?' he sneered, his voice indicating hers was a foolish feeling. 'Even when they treat you like an afterthought for most of your life?'

Sadness engulfed her. 'You can't help who you love. Or choose who will love you back.'

His eyes met hers for a charged second, before his nostrils flared. 'But you can choose to tell the truth no matter how tough the telling of it is. You can choose *not* to start a marriage based on lies.'

Regret crawled across her skin. 'Yes. And I'm sorry—'

His hand slashed through air, killing off her apology. Walking around her, he slammed the door shut and jerked his chin towards the sofa. He waited until she'd sat down, then prowled in front of her.

'Tell me of this condition you have.'

Eva stared at her clasped hands because watching his face had grown unbearable. 'It's called endometriosis.' She gave him the bare facts, unwilling to linger on the subject and prolong her heartache. 'It started just before I went to university, but, with everything going on with my mother, I didn't pay enough attention to it. I thought it was just something that would right itself eventually. But the pain got worse. One day I collapsed and was rushed to hospital. The diagnosis was made.' She stopped, then made herself go on. 'The doctor said the…scarring was too extensive…that I would never conceive naturally.'

She raised her head and saw that he'd stopped prowling and taken a seat opposite her with his elbows on his knees. 'Go on,' he bit out.

Eva shrugged. 'What else is there to add?' She gave a hollow laugh. 'I never thought I'd be in a position where the one thing I couldn't give would be the difference between having the future I want and the one I'd have to settle for. You accused me of starting this marriage based on lies, but I didn't know you wanted a real marriage. You did all this to get back at my father, remember?'

'So you never sought a second opinion?' he asked stonily, as if she hadn't mentioned the shifted parameters of their marriage.

'Why would I? I'd known something was wrong. Having the doctor confirm it merely affirmed what I already suspected. What was the point of putting myself through further grief?'

Zaccheo jerked to his feet and began prowling again. The set of his shoulders told her he was holding himself on a tight leash.

Minutes ticked by and he said nothing. The tension increased until she couldn't stand it any more. 'You can do whatever you want with me, but I want your word that you won't go after my family because of what I've done.'

He froze, his eyes narrowing to thin shards of ice. 'You think I want you to martyr yourself on some noble pyre for my sick satisfaction?'

She jumped to her feet. 'I don't know! You're normally so quick to lay down your demands. Or throw out orders and expect them to be followed. So tell me what you want.'

That chilling half-smile returned with a vengeance. 'What I want is to leave this place. There's really no point staying, is there, since the honeymoon is well and truly over?'

The flight back was markedly different from the outbound journey. The moment Zaccheo immersed himself in his work, she grabbed her tablet and locked herself in the bedroom.

She threw herself on the bed and sobbed long and hard into the pillow. By the time the plane landed in London, she was completely wrung out. Exhaustion seeped into her very bones and all she wanted was to curl into a foetal position and wish the world away.

She sank further into grey gloom when she descended the steps of the aircraft to find Zaccheo's limo waiting on the tarmac, along with a black SUV.

Zaccheo, wearing a black and navy pinstriped suit, stopped next to her, his expression remote and unfriendly.

'I'm heading to the office. Romeo will drive you to the penthouse.'

He strode to the SUV and drove off.

Eva realised then that throughout their conversation on the island, she'd made the same mistake as when she'd foolishly disclosed her condition before. She'd allowed herself to *hope* that the condition fate had bestowed on her wouldn't matter to that one *special person*. That somehow *love* would find a way.

A sob bubbled up her chest and she angrily swallowed it down.

Grow up, Eva. You're letting the lyrics of your songs cloud your judgement.

'Eva?' Romeo waited with the car door open.

She hastily averted her gaze from the censure in his eyes and slid in.

The penthouse hadn't changed, and yet Eva felt as if she'd lived a lifetime since she was last here.

After unpacking and showering, she trailed from room to room, feeling as if some tether she hadn't known she was tied to had been severed. When she rushed to the door for the third time, imagining she'd heard the keycard activate, she grabbed her tablet and forced herself to work on her compositions.

But her heart wasn't in it. Her mood grew bleaker when Romeo found her curled on the sofa and announced that Zaccheo wouldn't be home for dinner either tonight or the next two weeks, because he'd returned to Oman.

The days bled together in a dull grey jumble. Determined not to mope—because after all she'd been here before—Eva returned to work.

She took every spare shift available and offered herself for overtime without pay.

But she refused to sing.

Music had ceased to be the balm she'd come to rely on. Her heart only yearned for one thing. Or *one man*. And he'd made it abundantly clear that he didn't want her.

Because two weeks stretched to four, then six with no word from Zaccheo, and no answer to her phone calls.

At her lowest times, Eva hated herself for her lethargy, for not moving out of the penthouse. For sitting around, wishing for a miracle that would never materialise.

But the thought of flat-hunting, or, worse, moving back to Pennington Manor, filled her with a desperate heartache that nothing seemed to ease.

Romeo had brought her coffee this morning at the breakfast table. The pitying look he'd cast her had been the final straw.

'If you have something to say, just say it, Romeo.'

'You're not a weak woman. One of you has to take the situation in hand sooner or later,' he'd replied.

'Fine, but he won't return my calls so give him a message from me, will you?'

He'd nodded in that solemn way of his. 'Of course.'

'Tell him I'm fast reaching my tolerance level for his stupid silence. He can stay in Oman for the rest of his life for all I care. But he shouldn't expect to find me here when he deigns to return.'

That outburst had been strangely cathartic. She'd called her ex-landlady and discovered her flat was still unlet. After receiving a hefty payday from Zaccheo, the old woman hadn't been in a hurry to interview new tenants. She'd invited Eva to move back whenever she wanted.

Curiously, that announcement hadn't made her feel better—

'You've been cleaning that same spot for the last five minutes.'

Eva started and glanced down. 'Oh.'

Sybil, Siren's unflappable manageress, eyed her. 'Time for a break.'

'I don't need a—'

'Sorry, love,' Sybil said firmly. 'Orders from above. The new owner was very insistent. You take a break now or I get docked a week's wages.'

Eva frowned. 'Are you serious? Do we know who this new owner is?'

Sybil's eyes widened. 'You don't know?' When she shook her head, the manageress shrugged. 'Well, I'm not one to spread gossip. Shoo! Go put your feet up for a bit. I'll finish up here.'

Eva reluctantly handed over the cleaning supplies. She turned and stopped as the doors swung open and Ziggy Preston walked in.

The smile she tried for failed miserably. 'Ziggy, hello.'

He smiled. 'I heard you were back in town.'

She couldn't summon the curiosity to ask how he knew. 'Oh?'

'You were supposed to call when you got back. I hope that doesn't mean you've signed up with someone else? Because that'd devastate me,' he joked.

Eva tried for another smile. Failed again. 'I didn't sign with anyone, and I don't think I will.'

His face fell. 'Why not?'

She had a thousand and one reasons. But only one that mattered. And she wasn't about to divulge it to another soul. 'I've decided to give the music thing a break for a while.' Or for ever, depending on whether she felt anything but numb again.

Ziggy shoved his hands into his coat pocket, his features pensive.

'Listen, I was supposed to do a session with one of my artists tomorrow afternoon, but they cancelled. Come to the studio, hang out for a while. You don't have to sing if you don't want to. But come anyway.'

She started to shake her head, then stopped. It was her day off tomorrow. The extra shift she'd hoped to cover had suddenly been filled. She could either occupy herself at Ziggy's studio or wander Zaccheo's penthouse like a lost wraith, pining for what she could never have. 'Okay.'

'Great!' He handed her another business card, this one with his private number scribbled on the back, and left.

A couple of months ago, being pursued by a top music producer would've been a dream come true. And yet, Eva could barely summon the enthusiasm to dress the next day, especially when Romeo confirmed he'd given Zaccheo her message but had no reply for her.

Jaw clenched, she pulled on her jeans and sweater, determined not to succumb to the unending bouts of anguish that had made her throw up this morning after her conversation with Romeo.

She wasn't a pearl-clutching Victorian maiden, for heaven's sake!

Her life might *feel* as if it were over, but she'd been through the wringer more than once in her life. She'd survived her diagnosis. She'd survived her mother's death. Despite the odds, she'd mended fences with her father and sister.

Surely she could survive decimating her heart on a love that had been doomed from the start?

Deliberately putting a spring in her step, she arrived at Ziggy's studio in a different frame of mind. Looking around, she repeated to herself that *this* was a tangible dream. Something she could hang on to once Zaccheo returned and she permanently severed the ties that had so very briefly bound them.

Eva was sure she was failing in her pep talk to herself when Ziggy gave up after a third attempt to get her to sample an upbeat pop tune.

'Okay, shall we try one of yours?' he suggested with a wry smile.

Half-heartedly, she sifted through her list, then paused, her heart picking up its sluggish beat as she stared at the lyrics to the song she'd composed that last morning on the island.

'This one,' she murmured.

At Ziggy's nod, she sang the first line.

His eyes widened. 'Wow.' Nodding to the sound booth, he said, 'I'd love to hear the whole thing if you're up to it?'

Eva thought of the raw lyrics, how they offered love, pleaded for for ever and accepted any risks necessary, and breathed deeply.

If this was what it took to start healing herself, then so be it. 'Sure.'

She was singing the final notes when an electrifying wave of awareness swept over her. Her gaze snapped up to the viewing gallery above the booth, where she knew music moguls sometimes listened in on artists. Although the mirrored glass prevented her from seeing who occupied it, she swore she could smell Zaccheo's unique scent.

'Are you okay?' Ziggy asked.

She nodded absently, her gaze still on the gallery window.

'Can you sing the last two lines again?'

'Umm...yes,' she mumbled.

She really was losing it. If she couldn't sing a song she'd written with Zaccheo in mind without imagining she could feel him, smell him, she was in deep trouble. Because as she worked through the other songs Ziggy encouraged her to record, Eva realised all her songs were somehow to do with the man who'd taken her heart prisoner.

She left the studio in a daze and got into the waiting limo. Physically and emotionally drained, she couldn't connect two thoughts together. When she finally accepted what she needed to do, she turned to Romeo.

'Can you take me to Zaccheo's office, please?'

He looked up from the laptop he'd been working on. After a few probing seconds, he nodded.

A wave of dizziness hit her as they waited for the lift at GWI. She ignored the curious glances, and concentrated on staying upright, putting one foot in front of the other as she made her way down the plushly decorated corridor to Zaccheo's office.

Anyetta's coolly professional demeanour visibly altered when she saw Eva, then turned to shock as her gaze travelled from her head to her toes.

Eva wanted to laugh, but she couldn't be sure she wouldn't dissolve into hysteria. When Anyetta stood, Eva waved her away.

'I know he's not in. I was hoping *you* would email him for me.'

'But—'

'It won't take long, I promise.'

The tall brunette looked briefly bewildered, but her features settled back into serene composure and she sat down.

'Mark it *urgent*. Presumably, you can tell when he opens emails from you?' Eva asked.

Warily, Zaccheo's PA nodded.

'Good.' Eva approached, pushing back the errant curls obscuring her vision. She folded her arms around her middle and prayed for just a few more minutes of strength.

Anyetta's elegant fingers settled on the keyboard.
Eva cleared her throat.

Zaccheo.
Since you refuse to engage with me, I can only conclude that I'm free of my obligations to you. To that end, I'd be grateful if you would take the appropriate steps to end this marriage forthwith. My family lawyers will be on standby when you're ready, but I'd be obliged if you didn't leave it too late. I refuse to put my life on hold for you, so take action or I will. For the record, I won't be accepting any of the monetary compensation offered, nor will I be seeking anything from you, except my freedom. If you choose to pursue my family, then you'll do so without my involvement, because I've done my duty to my family and I'm moving on. I won't let you use me as a pawn in your vendetta against my father. You're aware of the state of my father's health, so I hope you'll choose mercy over retribution.
Regardless of your decision, I'll be moving out of the penthouse tomorrow.
Please don't contact me.
Eva.

'Send it, please,' she said.
Anyetta clicked the button, then looked up. 'He just opened it.'
Eva nodded jerkily. 'Thank you.'
She walked out with scalding tears filling her eyes. A solid presence registered beside her and when Romeo took her arm, Eva didn't protest.
At the penthouse, she dropped her bag in the hallway, tugged off her boots and coat as her vision greyed. She made it into bed as her legs gave way and she curled, fully clothed, into a tight ball. Her last thought before blessed oblivion claimed her was that she'd done it.

She'd survived her first hour with a heart broken into a million tiny pieces. If there was any justice, she might just make it through the rest of her life with a shredded heart.

CHAPTER FIFTEEN

IN THE SPLIT SECOND before wakefulness hit, Eva buried her nose in the pillow that smelled so much like Zaccheo she groaned with pure, incandescent happiness.

Reality arrived with searing pain so acute, she cried out.

'Eva.'

She jolted upright at the sound of her name. Jagged thoughts pierced her foggy brain like shards of bright light through glass.

She was no longer in her own suite, but in Zaccheo's.

Her clothes were gone, and she was stripped down to her bra and panties.

Zaccheo was sitting in an armchair next to the bed, his eyes trained on her.

And he was clean-shaven.

His thick stubble was gone, his hair trimmed into a short, neat style that left his nape bare.

Despite his altered appearance, his living, breathing presence was far too much to bear. She jerked her head away, stared down at the covers she clutched like a lifeline.

'What are you doing here?' she asked.

'You summoned me. So here I am,' he stated.

She shook her head. 'Please. Don't make it sound as if I have any power over your actions. If I did you would've answered my numerous phone calls like a normal person. And that email wasn't a summons. It was a statement of intent, hardly demanding your presence.'

'Nevertheless, since you went to so much trouble to make sure it reached me, I thought it only polite to answer it in person.'

'Well, you needn't have bothered,' she threw back hotly,

'especially since we both know you don't have a polite bone in your body. Things like *consideration* and *courtesy* are alien concepts to you.'

He looked perturbed by her outburst. Which made her want to laugh. And cry. And scream. 'Are you going to sit there with that insulting look that implies I'm out of my mind?'

'You must forgive me if that's what my expression implies. I meant to wear a look that says I was hoping for a civilised conversation.'

She threw out her hands. 'You have a damned nerve, do you know that? I...' She stopped, her eyes widening in alarm as an unpleasant scent hit her nostrils. Swivelling, she saw the breakfast tray containing scrambled eggs, smoked pancetta, coffee, and the buttered brioche she loved.

Correction. She'd *once* loved.

Shoving the covers aside, she lunged for the bathroom, uncaring that she was half-naked and looked like a bedraggled freak. All she cared about was making it to the porcelain bowl in time.

She vomited until she collapsed against the shower stall, desperately catching her breath. When Zaccheo crouched at her side, she shut her eyes. 'Please, Zaccheo. Go away.'

He pressed a cool towel to her forehead, her eyelids, her cheeks. 'A lesser man might be decimated at the thought that his presence makes you physically ill,' he murmured gravely.

Her snort grated her throat. 'But you're not a lesser man, of course.'

He shrugged. 'I'm saved by Romeo's report that you've been feeling under the weather recently.'

Eva opened her eyes, looked at him, then immediately wished she hadn't. She'd thought his beard and long mane made him gloriously beautiful, but the sight of his chiselled jaw, the cut of his cheekbones, and the fully displayed sensual lips was almost blinding.

'I can't do this.' She tried to stand and collapsed back against the stall.

With a muttered oath, he scooped her up in his arms and strode to the vanity. Setting her down, he handed her a toothbrush and watched as she cleaned her teeth.

Eva told herself the peculiar look turning his eyes that gunmetal shade meant nothing. Zaccheo had probably come to ensure she vacated his penthouse before succumbing to whatever was ailing her.

Steeling her spine, she rinsed her mouth. He reached for her as she moved away from the vanity, but she sidestepped him, her heart banging against her ribs. 'I can walk on my own two feet.'

Zaccheo watched her go, her hips swaying in that impertinent, yet utterly sexy way that struck pure fire to his libido.

He slowly followed, paused in the doorway and watched her pace the bedroom.

Although he'd primed himself for her appearance, he hadn't been quite prepared for when he'd finally returned to the penthouse last night and found her asleep in her suite. All the excuses he'd given himself for staying away had crumbled to dust.

As he'd stood over her, his racing heart had only been able to acknowledge one thing—that he'd missed her more than his brain could accurately fathom. He'd thought the daily reports on her movements would be enough. He'd thought buying Siren and ensuring she didn't overwork herself, or silently watching her from the gallery at Preston's studio yesterday, listening to her incredible voice, would be enough.

It wasn't until he'd received her email that his world had stopped, and he'd forced himself to face the truth.

He was nothing without her.

For the last six weeks he'd woken to a tormenting existence each morning. Each time, something had broken inside him. Something that would probably slot neatly under

the banner of heartache. It had nothing to do with the loneliness that had plagued his childhood and led him to believe
he needed a family to soothe the ache. It had nothing to do
with the retribution he was no longer interested in exacting
from Oscar Pennington.

It had everything to do with Eva. Flashes of her had struck
him at the most inappropriate times—like the brightness of
her smile when he was involved in tense negotiation. The
feeling of being deep inside her when he was teetering on the
edge of a platform three hundred metres above ground, with
no net to catch him should he fall. And everywhere he'd gone,
he'd imagined the faintest trace of her perfume in the air.

Nothing had stopped him from reaching out for her in
the dead of the night, when his guard was at its lowest and
all he could feel was *need*. Ferocious, all-consuming need.

Even the air of sadness that hung around her now wasn't
enough to make him *not* yearn for her.

His heart kicked into his stomach, knowing it was his
fault she wore that look.

Her throat worked to find the words she needed. He forced
himself to remain still, to erect a force field against anything
she might say.

'Let's end this now, Zaccheo. Divorce me. Surely you'd
prefer that to this mockery of a marriage?'

He'd expected it. Hell, her email had left him in no doubt
as to her state of mind.

Yet the words punched him in the gut...*hard*. Zaccheo
uttered an imprecation that wasn't fit for polite company.

*Give her what she wants. Stop this endless misery and
be done with it.*

It was the selfless thing to do. And if he needed to have
learned anything from the stunning, brave woman in front of
him, it was selflessness. She'd sacrificed herself for her family and turned over her innermost secrets when she could've
just kept quiet and reaped untold wealth. She'd continued to

stay under his roof, continued to seek him out, when fear had sent *him* running.

He *needed* to be selfless for her.

But he couldn't. He walked stiffly to the side table and poured a coffee he didn't want.

'There will be no divorce.'

She glared at him. 'You do realise that I don't need your permission?'

He knew that. He'd lived with that fear ever since she'd announced back in Rio that she didn't want to be married to him any more.

'*Sì,*' he replied gruffly. 'You can do whatever you want. The same way I can choose to tie you up in endless red tape for the next twenty years.'

Her mouth dropped open, then she shut her beautiful, pain-filled eyes. 'Why would you do that, Zaccheo?'

'Why indeed?'

She shook her head, and her hair fluttered over her shoulders. 'Surely you can't want this? You deserve a family.'

There it was again. That selflessness that cut him to the core, that forced him to let go, to be a better man. *Dio mio,* but he wanted her to be selfish for once. To claim what she wanted. To claim him!

'How very noble of you to think of me. But I don't need a family.'

Shock widened her eyes. 'What did you say?'

'I don't need a family, *il mio cuore.* I don't need anything, or anyone, if I have you.' *She* was all he wanted. He'd prostrate himself at her feet if that was what it took.

She stared at him for so long, Zaccheo felt as if he'd turned to stone. He knew that any movement would see him shatter into useless pieces.

But he had to take the leap. The same leap she'd taken on the island, when she'd shared something deeply private and heartbreaking with him.

'If you have *me*?'

He risked taking a breath. 'Yes. I love you, Eva. I've been racking my brain for weeks, trying to find a way to make you stay, convince you to stay my wife—'

'You didn't think to just *ask* me?'

'After walking away from you like a coward?' He shook his head. 'You've no idea how many times I picked up the phone, how many times I summoned my pilot to bring me back to you. But I couldn't face the possibility of you saying no.' He gave a hollow laugh. 'Believe it or not, I convinced myself I'd rather spend the rest of my life living in another country but still married to you, than face the prospect of never having even the tiniest piece of you.'

Her face crumbled and he nearly roared in pain. 'That's no life at all, Zaccheo.'

'It was a reason for me to *breathe*. A selfish but *necessary* reason for me to keep functioning, knowing I had a piece of you even if it was your name next to mine on a marriage certificate.'

'Oh, God!' Tears filled her eyes and he cursed. He wanted to take her in his arms. But he had no right. He'd lost all rights when he'd forced her into marriage and then condemned her for trying to protect herself from his monstrous actions.

He clenched his fists against the agony ripping through him. 'But that's no life for you. If you wish for a divorce, then I'll grant you one.'

'What?' Her face lost all colour. She started to reach for him, but faltered. 'Zaccheo...'

A different sort of fear scythed through him as she started to crumple.

'Eva!'

By the time he caught her she was unconscious.

Muted voices pulled her back to consciousness. The blinds in the strange room were drawn but there was enough light to work out that she was no longer in Zaccheo's penthouse. The drip in her right arm confirmed her worst fears.

'What...happened?' she croaked.

Shadowy figures turned, and Sophie rushed to her side.

'You fainted. Zaccheo brought you to the hospital,' Sophie said.

'Zaccheo...' Memory rushed back. Zaccheo telling her he loved her. Then telling her he would divorce her...

No!

She tried to sit up.

The nurse stopped her. 'The doctors are running tests. We should have the results back shortly. In the meantime, you're on a rehydrating drip.'

Eva touched her throbbing head, wishing she'd stop talking for a moment so she could—

She stared at her bare fingers in horror. 'Where are my rings?' she cried.

The nurse frowned. 'I don't know.'

'No...please. I need...' She couldn't catch her breath. Or take her eyes off her bare fingers. Had Zaccheo done it so quickly? While she'd been unconscious?

But he'd said he loved her. Did he not love her enough? Tears brimmed her eyes and fell down her cheeks.

'It's okay, I'll go and find out.' The nurse hurried out.

Sophie approached. Eva forced her pain back and looked at her.

'I hope you don't mind me being here? You didn't call when you got back so I assume you don't want to speak to me, but when Zaccheo called—'

Eva shook her head, her thoughts racing, her insides shredding all over again. 'You're my family, Sophie. It may take a while to get back to where we were before, but I don't hate you. I've just been a little...preoccupied.' Her gaze went to the empty doorway. 'Is...Zaccheo still here?'

Sophie smiled wryly. 'He was enraged that you didn't have a team of doctors monitoring your every breath. He went to find the head of the trauma unit.'

Zaccheo walked into the room at that moment, and Sophie

hastily excused herself. The gunmetal shade of his eyes and the self-loathing on his face made Eva's heart thud slowly as she waited for the death blow.

He walked forward like a man facing his worst nightmare.

Just before she'd fainted, she'd told herself she would fight for him, as she'd fought for her sister and father. Seeing the look on his face, she accepted that nothing she did would change things. Her bare fingers spoke their own truth.

'Zaccheo, I know you said…you loved me, but if it's not enough for you—'

Astonishment transformed his face. 'Not enough for *me*?'

'You agreed to divorce me…'

Anguish twisted his face. 'Only because it was what *you* wanted.'

She sucked in a breath when he perched on the edge of the bed. His fingers lightly brushed the back of her hand, over and over, as if he couldn't help himself.

'You know what I did last night before I came home?'

She shook her head.

'I went to see your father. I had no idea where I was headed until I landed on the lawn at Pennington Manor. Somewhere along the line, I entertained the idea that I would sway your feelings if I smoothed my relationship with your father. Instead I asked him for your hand in marriage.'

'You did what?'

He grimaced. 'Our wedding was a pompous exhibition from start to finish. I wanted to show everyone who'd dared to look down on me how high I'd risen.'

Her heart lurched. 'Because of what your mother and stepfather did?'

He sighed. 'I hated my mother for choosing her aristocrat husband over me. Like you, I didn't understand why it had to be an either-or choice. Why couldn't she love me *and* her husband? Then I began to hate everything he stood for. The need to understand why consumed me. My stepfather was easy to break. Your father was a little more cunning.

He used you. From the moment we met, I couldn't see be-yond you. He saw that. I don't know if I'll ever be able to forgive that, but he brought us together.' He breathed deep and shoved a hand through his short hair. 'Possessing you blinded me to what he was doing. And I blamed you for it, right along with him when the blame lay with me and my obsession to get back at you when I should've directed my anger elsewhere.'

'You were trying to understand why you'd been rejected. I tried for years to understand why my father couldn't be satisfied with what he had. Why he pushed his family ob-session onto his children. He fought with my mother over it, and it ripped us apart. Everything stopped when she got sick. Perversely, I hoped her illness would change things for the better. For a while it did. But after she died, he reverted to type, and I couldn't take it any more.' She glanced at him. 'Hearing you tell that newspaper tycoon that I was merely a means to an end brought everything back to me.'

Zaccheo shut his eyes in regret. He lifted her hand and pressed it against his cheek. 'He was drunk, prying into my feelings towards you. I was grappling with them myself and said the first idiotic thing that popped into my head. I don't deny that it was probably what I'd been telling myself.'

'But afterwards, when I asked you...'

'I'd just found out about the charges. I knew your father was behind it. You were right there, his flesh and blood, a target for my wrath. I regretted it the moment I said it, but you were gone before I got the chance to take it back.' He brought her hand to his mouth and kissed it, then her palm be-fore laying it over his heart. *'Mi dispiace molto, il mio cuore.'*

His heart beat steady beneath her hand. But her fingers were bare.

'Zaccheo, what you said before I fainted...'

Pain ravaged his face before he nodded solemnly. 'I meant it. I'll let you go if that's what you want. Your happiness means everything to me. Even if it's without me.'

She shook her head. 'No, not that. What you said before.'

He looked deep into her eyes, his gaze steady and true. 'I love you, Eva. More than my life, more than everything I've ever dared to dream of. You helped me redeem my soul when I thought it was lost.'

'You touched mine, made me love deeper, purer. You taught me to take a risk again instead of living in fear of rejection.'

He took a sharp breath. 'Eva, what are you saying?'

'That I love you too. And it tears me apart that I won't be able to give you children—'

His kiss stopped her words. 'Prison was hell, I won't deny it. In my lowest times, I thought having children would be the answer. But you're the only family I need, *amore mio.*'

Zaccheo was rocking her, crooning softly to comfort her when the doctor walked in.

'Right, Mrs Giordano. You'll be happy to hear we've got to the bottom of your fainting spell. There's nothing to worry about besides—'

'Dehydration and the need to eat better?' she asked with a sniff.

'Well, yes, there's that.'

'Okay, I promise I will.'

'I'll make sure she keeps to it,' Zaccheo added with a mock frown. He settled her back in the bed and stood. 'I'll go get the car.'

The doctor shook his head. 'No, I'm afraid you can't leave yet. You need to rest for at least twenty-four hours while we monitor you and make sure everything's fine.'

Zaccheo tensed and caught her hand in his. 'What do you mean? Didn't you say you'd got to the bottom of what ails her?' His eyes met hers, and Eva read the anxiety there.

'Zaccheo…'

'Mr Giordano, no need to panic. The only thing that should ail your wife is a short bout of morning sickness and perhaps a little bed rest towards the end.'

Zaccheo paled and visibly trembled. 'The *end*?'

Eva's heart stopped. 'Doctor, what are you saying?' she whispered.

'I'm saying you're pregnant. With twins.'

EPILOGUE

ZACCHEO EMERGED FROM the bedroom where he'd gone to change his shirt—the second of the day due to his eldest son throwing up on him—to find Eva cross-legged on the floor before the coffee table, their children cradled in her arms as she crooned Italian nursery rhymes she'd insisted he teach her.

On the screen via a video channel, Romeo leaned in closer to get a better look at the babies.

Zaccheo skirted the sofa and sat behind his wife, cradling her and their children in his arms.

'Do you think you'll make it for Christmas?' she asked Romeo. Zaccheo didn't need to lean over to see that his wife was giving his friend her best puppy-dog look.

'*Sì*, I'll do my best to be there tomorrow.'

Eva shook her head. 'That's not good enough, Romeo. I know Brunetti International is a huge company, and you're a super busy tycoon, but it's your godsons' first Christmas. They picked out your present all by themselves. The least you can do is turn up and open it.'

Zaccheo laughed silently and watched his friend squirm until he realised denying his wife anything her heart desired was a futile exercise.

'If that's what you wish, *principessa*, then I'll be there.'

Eva beamed. Zaccheo spread his fingers through her hair, resisting the urge to smother her cheek and mouth in kisses because she thought it made Romeo uncomfortable.

The moment Romeo signed off, Zaccheo claimed his kiss, not lifting his head until he was marginally satisfied.

'What was that for?' she murmured in that dazed voice that was like a drug to his blood.

'Because you're my heart, *dolcezza*. I cannot go long without it. Without you.'

Eva's heart melted as Zaccheo relieved her of their youngest son, Rafa, and tucked his tiny body against his shoulder. Then he held out his hand and helped her up with Carlo, their eldest by four minutes.

Zaccheo pulled them close until they stood in a loose circle, his arms around her. Then, as he'd taken to doing, he started swaying to the soft Christmas carols playing in the background.

Eva closed her eyes to stem the happy tears forming. She'd said a prayer every day of her pregnancy as they'd faced hurdles because of her endometriosis. When the doctors had prescribed bed rest at five months, Zaccheo had immediately stepped back from GWI and handed over the day-to-day running of the company to his new second-in-command.

Their sons had still arrived two weeks early but had both been completely healthy, much to the joy and relief of their parents. Relations were still a little strained with her father and sister, but Oscar doted on his grandsons, and Sophie had fallen in love with her nephews at first sight. But no one loved their gorgeous boys more than Zaccheo. The love and adoration in his eyes when he cradled his sons often made her cry.

And knowing that love ran just as deep for her filled her heart with so much happiness, she feared she would burst from it.

'You've stopped dancing,' he murmured.

She began to sway again, her free hand rising to his chest. She caught sight of her new rings—the engagement ring belonging to his grandmother, which he'd kept but not given her because the circumstances hadn't been right, and the new wedding band he'd let her pick out for their second, family-only wedding—and her thoughts turned pensive. 'I was thinking about your mother.'

Zaccheo tensed slightly. She caressed her hand over his heart until the tension eased out of him. 'What were you thinking?' he asked grudgingly.

'I sent her pictures of the boys yesterday.'

A noise rumbled from Zaccheo's chest. 'She's been asking for one since the day they were born.'

She leaned back and looked into her husband's eyes. 'I know. I also know you've agreed to see her at Easter after my first album comes out.'

Tension remained between mother and son, but when his mother had reached out, Zaccheo hadn't turned her away.

Standing on tiptoe, Eva caressed the stubble she insisted he grow again, and kissed him. 'I'm very proud of you.'

'No, Eva. Everything good in my life is because of *you.*' He sealed her lips with another kiss. A deeper, more demanding kiss.

By mutual agreement, they pulled away and headed for the nursery. After bestowing kisses on their sleeping sons, Zaccheo took her hand and led her to the bedroom.

Their lovemaking was slow, worshipful, with loving words blanketing them as they reached fulfilment and fell asleep in each other's arms.

When midnight and Christmas rolled around, Zaccheo woke her and made love to her all over again. Afterwards, sated and happy, he spread his fingers through her hair and brought her face to his.

'Buon Natale, amore mio,' he said. 'You're the only thing I want under my Christmas tree, from now until eternity.'

'Merry Christmas, Zaccheo. You make my heart sing every day and my soul soar every night. You're everything I ever wished for.'

He touched his forehead to hers and breathed deep. *'Ti amero per sempre, dolcezza mia.'*

* * * * *

Don't miss Romeo's story in
BRUNETTI'S SECRET SON
available December 2015.

MILLS & BOON®

MODERN™

POWER, PASSION AND IRRESISTIBLE TEMPTATION